Praise for Lynn Kerstan

"Ms. Kerstan is just a pure delight."
—*Bell, Book and Candle*

"A new star in the tradition of Mary Balogh. . . . Kerstan exhibits an unusual ability to combine an emotionally intense love story with lighter moments in a seamless story."   —The Romance Reader

"Lynn Kerstan is one of the best."
—*Old Book Barn Gazette*

"A delightful new voice."   —*Literary Times*

"Wry and wonderful. Lynn Kerstan deserves praise. . . . My question is why isn't Ms. Kerstan's name up there with other contemporary luminaries? An extraordinary storyteller."
—Romance Communications

"Lynn Kerstan steals your heart." —*Romantic Times*

continued . . .

THE GOLDEN LEOPARD

Lynn Kerstan

AN ONYX BOOK

ONYX
Published by New American Library, a division of
Penguin Putnam Inc., 375 Hudson Street,
New York, New York 10014, U.S.A.
Penguin Books Ltd, 80 Strand,
London WC2R 0RL, England
Penguin Books Australia Ltd, Ringwood,
Victoria, Australia
Penguin Books Canada Ltd, 10 Alcorn Avenue,
Toronto, Ontario, Canada M4V 3B2
Penguin Books (N.Z.) Ltd, 182–190 Wairau Road,
Auckland 10, New Zealand

Penguin Books Ltd, Registered Offices:
Harmondsworth, Middlesex, England

First published by Onyx, an imprint of New American Library,
a division of Penguin Putnam Inc.

First Printing, October 2002
10 9 8 7 6 5 4 3 2 1

In memory of Dorothy, Lady Dunnett (1923–2001),
and for the readers who love and admire
her extraordinary books.

She made the whole world to hang in the air.

Prologue

India, 1821

There was nothing like the prospect of dying half a world away to make an Englishman long for home.

Hugo, Lord Duran, had been given several months to reflect on his homeland, the one where he'd spent a grand total of eleven weeks of his life, before they came for him—two bearded, turbaned, cold-eyed men forced to bend double when they entered his cramped cell. They dragged him into the narrow passageway and hauled him to his feet.

While a third fellow clamped shackles around his ankles and wrists, Duran focused his attention on the harrowing wail that resonated along the corridor. It had persisted day and night, muffled by the thick walls of his cell, as if the ghosts of the damned stalked the prison. Now he understood what he had been hearing. It was the sound of men gone mad.

Had he howled as well? He didn't like to think so, but he might have done. Except for marking each day by scratching a line on the moldy stone wall, he had wrenched his thoughts to the past and kept them there, reliving what little was worth recalling of his aimless, dissolute existence.

Nearly always, he found solace, and even a bit of amusement, remembering Jessie.

The first time she floated into his cell, more imperious and seductive than ever, she had startled him. After all this time, why the devil would Lady Jessica Carville come back to haunt him? Theirs had been an insignificant little dalliance, one of . . . well, he'd long since lost count of his dalliances. He should have forgotten her by now.

A sharp pain at his wrists. He looked down and saw blood. In this humidity, everything made of metal rusted practically overnight, and the nizam's flunkies were having trouble securing his manacles.

Better to keep thinking about Jessie. That hurt as well, to be sure, but in a different way. He wasn't sorry to have her with him again. Never mind the trouble he'd taken to exorcize her after returning to India, or the bothersome way she kept popping into his thoughts just when he became certain he was finally shed of her. It had required a year—very well, two or three years— but eventually she'd left him alone.

Until he needed her. Until there was nothing for him but hunger and darkness and regret. From the other side of the world she came to him, all but alive and scrunched up next to him when he was awake, not touching him, but there. When he slept, he dreamed about her.

She had been beside him when he heard voices in the passageway and pressed his ear to the door, trying to ferret out the reason he'd been snatched from his horse and tossed into a small black hole. At the time no one had seen fit to explain, and when he'd made a fuss about it, they'd beaten him senseless. But it was important that he find out. India could swallow you up if you weren't careful, and besides, it wasn't in his nature to give up without a fight.

Eventually he learned his fate from two guards who paused outside his cell to discuss its occupant. It seemed that the foreign devil, at a time being calculated by the court astrologers, was to be executed. And so far as he could tell, it was for the unpardonable crime of being an Englishman.

A few other snippets of information had come his way, none of any discernible consequence. But he had committed everything he heard to memory and spent all his rational hours playing with the words and phrases, arranging and rearranging them like the pieces of a puzzle. Information, he knew from a lifetime of living on his wits, was the gambler's edge.

He had been in tight spots before. Always there came a moment when enterprise and intuition made all the difference, and when that moment came, he meant to be ready.

The shackles were finally locked into place. A rough hand shoved at his back, nearly knocking him over. He caught his balance and put one bare foot in front of the other, swearing under his breath with each wobbly step. How long since he'd eaten? Two days? Three? Damn. This was no time to collapse in a heap.

Dizziness washed over him as the little procession came to a heavy iron door. One of the guards unlocked it and pushed it open, and the sudden blast of sunlight and summer heat nearly sent Duran to his knees. Someone grabbed his arm and shoved him through the door.

He stumbled into a bleak courtyard filled with silent men who had come, he supposed, to watch the execution. Sunbaked bricks scorched the soles of his bare feet. He became aware of the tattered, sweat-stiff shirt open halfway down his chest and the loose trousers hanging low on his hips. They had stripped him of everything else soon after his capture.

It was a long walk to wherever they were going. The guards led him onto a wide street lined with dhoti-clad men, past large buildings he hadn't sufficient interest to look at, toward a flamboyant palace glittering with mirrored tiles.

He couldn't help but notice a score of women perched like butterflies on the fretted balconies, staring down at him from behind fluttering veils. He only wished he made a better appearance. Sticky, overlong hair reached past his frayed collar. A ragged growth of beard and mustache itched on his face. What would they think if his precariously suspended trousers dropped to his ankles?

He raised his manacled hands and waved at them, grinning when they gasped in chorus and fled into the zenana.

There was no time to enjoy the moment. Quickening their pace, the guards steered him up a long flight of marble stairs. More people, better-dressed people, lined the wide entrance hall. Like the others, they went silent as he drew closer and whispered to one another when he'd gone past.

He wondered when the fear would strike him. So far he felt mostly bemused, separated from what was transpiring as if it were happening to a man he did not know. But this, surely, was his last day of life. These, the last few minutes he would draw breath. He ought to be paying attention.

At the least, he could make a good show of it. He assembled in his mind the snatches of information he had gleaned from the guards. The nizam of this backwater principality had once admired the English and gone out of his way to attract them to Alanabad for tiger hunts and excessive displays of hospitality. But not long ago, one of the guests had eaten of his salt, sampled his concubines, and repaid him by making off with something of great value.

The reverent voices outside Duran's cell had used many honorifics to describe it. The Star of the Firmament. The Heart of Alanabad. The Key to the Throne. Or perhaps they were referring to the ruler himself. In any case, whatever the stolen item might be, the nizam wanted it back. Meantime he was taking revenge on any Englishman unlucky enough to get caught in his web, and right now, that Englishman was Hugo Duran.

They had come to the end of the public reception hall. Two carved doors swung open, and Duran was thrust into a massive room with high ceilings and pink marble walls. Smoke, sweet and heady, curled from strips of sandalwood hung over the copper braziers that lined the aisle. Solemn-faced men were a dozen deep on both sides of him. Soft female voices murmured from behind silk-embroidered screens.

Directly ahead, the local potentate lolled on a gilt throne shaped like the open mouth of a large cat. Ivory fangs descended from the backrest to curve above his narrow shoulders, and the armrests were supported by what looked like sharp, elongated teeth.

Beside the throne, between two tall, unlit candles, stood a marble pedestal encrusted with bright jewels. Nothing lay atop it but a crumpled cloth of gold.

Odd, that.

As a guard propelled him forward, Duran focused his attention on the nizam. The little man was wrinkled and thin, except for a prominent belly left bare to expose a diamond set in his navel. A great beak of a nose arched down to meet an upturned chin, and between them, his narrow lips were set in a rigid line. His black-eyed gaze was directed at a bowl of fruit offered him by a servant.

Duran's sunken stomach rumbled at the sight of ripe peaches, purple grapes, and fuzzy apricots. One especially plump mango seemed to whisper his name.

They had reached the stairs leading to the carpeted stage where the nizam was enthroned in full durbar, his courtiers and attendants scattered about him like ornamental statues. One of the guards grabbed Duran's shoulders and drove him to his knees. Another pressed his head to the floor and planted a sandaled foot on his neck.

The tiled floor felt cool against his cheek. He heard the nizam speak to someone who replied in a quiet voice, but his thoughts kept drifting to the mango. He imagined peeling back its skin, slowly and seductively, the way he would remove the clothes from a woman's body. He would lick it all over before biting in and letting the sweet juices and soft flesh surge into his mouth. For that mango, and for the time to savor it, he would go to his death with a song on his lips.

The guards levered him upright again, grasping his arms when his knees buckled. He cast around for Jessie, for some awareness of her, but the witch had deserted him. Feminine pique, he supposed, and singularly poor timing. She would have enjoyed watching her treacherous lover brought low.

Licking his cracked lips, he managed a teetering bow to the nizam. "Lofty Eminence," he said, his dry throat producing a froglike croak. "I am Lord Duran, honored to be your faithful servant and confused at the manner of my welcome."

The nizam turned to the straight-backed, slender man standing beside him.

Duran, who had pretended from the moment of his capture to speak no other language but English, listened with interest as the translator rendered his words into Hindi and added several of his own. "Star of the Firmament," he said, bowing to the nizam with uncommon grace. "Heart of Alanabad."

Politely, Duran kept his attention focused on the nizam, who appeared unimpressed with the proceedings. He spoke briefly, impatience clipping his words.

After a moment the translator took a step forward. "I am Shivaji," he said in a level voice. "The Powerful One has pronounced you a spy, a thief, and a cur."

Duran remembered to put a humble expression on his face. "I am sorry to hear it. Dare I suggest that the Powerful One has been misinformed by his enemies?"

Shivaji, one brow lifted, glanced across the dais to a harsh-featured man who separated himself from a group of courtiers robed, as was he, in severest black. Unlike the others, his fingers were studded with rings. His coned turban, starched and tightly wound, was embellished above his forehead with two entwined silver serpents.

One hand over his heart, he bowed to the nizam, who beckoned him closer. But when he spoke, it was directly to Shivaji. "It is known from Bombay to Calcutta that English devils may not cross the borders of Alanabad. How does he account for his presence here?"

While Shivaji translated, Duran, mordantly amused, cast about for a credible tale. For once in his life he was innocent as a babe, but no one here would believe the truth. What he required was a great thumping lie, a story that could not be verified. And at its heart must be the promise of something the nizam wanted even more than the pleasure of killing an Englishman.

"You see!" The black-clad man jabbed a finger in his direction. "He cannot reply. Lies burn in his throat, but he dare not release them. It is well. Send him to his fate, Excellency. He already stands condemned."

Duran gave him a bright, befuddled smile and turned to Shivaji for a translation, his mind working furiously. The empty pedestal. He was willing to bet that whatever the Englishman—the one who started all this trouble—had stolen, it had used to be enshrined on that pedestal, and that its value was not confined to rupees. But what the blazes had it been?

"Condemned?" he inquired of the nizam when Shivaji had finished. "For what crime, Magnificence? It was not my will that brought me here. Indeed, knowing of your prohibition, I tried again and again to escape my destiny. But every road, by twist and turn, led me to where I would not go." Lifting his head, he willed confidence into his faltering voice. "I am but a humble instrument of the gods. They have put me like an oiled blade into your hands. How you use me is in your wisdom to decide."

Shivaji waited, saying nothing.

Duran, feeling the translator's sharp gaze probe him, concentrated on the nizam's unreadable face. "I have been sent, O Heart of Alanabad, to serve you. I am charged to return that which has been foully taken from you by one of my miserable countrymen."

Shivaji paused for a breathless few moments before rendering Duran's exact words into Hindi.

The nizam, looking bored, reached for a handful of grapes and popped one into his mouth. "Does he think me a fool?" he said, chewing noisily. "This insect has come in search of more plunder. I shall have him flayed alive and fed to the crocodiles."

Shivaji's translation was solemn and inaccurate, omitting the threat in favor of a question. "How were you told of your mission?"

A diplomat, this cool-eyed man with the expressionless face and calm voice, and perhaps the brains behind the little fellow who huddled like a toad on his absurdly carved throne. How the bearded chap fit into the equation remained unclear. The nizam paid him no attention, but neither did he order him back to his place.

Duran, sensing rivalries and concealed agendas all around him, was having difficulty focusing on his own thready scheme. "This unworthy one cannot say precisely who it is who sent me, Your Loftiness. The message was given me in a dream."

Shivaji translated. The nizam made a guttural noise. The black-robed man, his nose scarlet, opened his mouth to speak.

"Naturally, I paid it no heed," Duran continued in a rush. "A man of traditional European education, I place no credit in signs and visions. And yet, as I made my way on the road from Poona to Mysore, the dream returned each night for seven nights, carried . . ."

Pausing, he wiped his damp forehead with his sleeve and took a deep, shuddering breath. It was time, past time, for a desperate gamble. He looked at the nizam, pinned on his throne between two rows of powerful teeth, and tossed the dice. "The dream was carried," he said forcefully, "in the mouth of a great jungle cat."

Shivaji, translating simultaneously now, raised a hand when the black-clad man tried to interrupt.

Duran, who'd have been glad of time to scratch up his next load of moonshine, would rather Shivaji had not interfered. But they were all looking expectantly at him, so he blundered ahead. "I know not how, O Star of the Firmament, I was able to stumble upon a place I had never been before. Alanabad is a far distance, I believe, from the road I had been on. So I must ask myself this question. How else could I have found you, had I not been sent?"

Shivaji's tone sharpened when he completed the translation and turned again to Duran. "What has been stolen, Englishman?" The question was his own, because the nizam had not spoken. "And where is it to be found?"

An old hand at lying, Duran knew his bluff was being called.

Chains rattling, he lifted one arm in the direction of the marble pedestal. The nizam and all the courtiers followed his gesture, their gazes focused on the gauzy golden cloth.

So far so good, but time was running out. Big cat. What kind? Images sprang to his mind. Tiger. Cheetah. Leopard. Lion. A one-in-four chance. Closing his eyes, Duran tossed the dice for his life.

"The leopard," he said in a transcendent voice. "I have been sent for the leopard."

Without translating this declaration for the onlookers, Shivaji crouched beside the throne and conversed softly with the nizam.

Duran had run out of guesses and theatrical gestures. Muzzy-headed and wildly hungry, he lowered his aching arm and let his gaze wander around the durbar hall.

This one was not so very different from other courts where he had spent more pleasurable time. Two attendants flicked fly whisks made of yaks' tails to drive away evil spirits, while others fluttered peacock-feather fans for the same purpose. A brawny fellow stood like a monolith, holding the princeling's golden mace and silver stick, the emblems of his power. Two boys sat cross-legged on the floor, pulling the ropes that waved a damask punkah over the throne.

Incense and silks and spices and the languor of a hot India afternoon swept over him. Black spots danced before his eyes. Fragments of the muttered conversation drifted to his ears, but he could scarcely attend them.

"He lies. Who does not know of the leopard?"

". . . all else has failed."

". . . draw out his nails and sever parts of his body one by one . . ."

"The people have lost faith . . . insurrection."

". . . secure . . . centuries."

". . . put him into my hands."

More blather. Duran grew weary of it. Clearly the nizam rated his tale a crock, which it most certainly was, but Shivaji continued to press his cause. Why the devil would he set himself to spare an obscure aristocrat's hide? Duran hoped that he'd succeed, but he wasn't counting on it.

He wanted to go home, though. God but he wanted it. He had unfinished business in England. Unfinished business with Jessie, who would not be at all pleased to see him again. It would be her bad luck if this gamble paid off.

One of the guards pushed him to his knees again. He raised his clouded gaze to the nizam, who was regarding him from a pair of wily brown eyes.

"Where is the leopard?"

Duran barely remembered to wait for the translation before replying. "It is in England, Powerful One."

"Why not in France or Portugal or Egypt?" the nizam shot back.

"In such a case, a Frenchman or a Portuguese or an Egyptian would be kneeling before you now. I know only that I must seek the leopard in my own country and return it to yours." He put his hands together in the traditional gesture of respect. "Can a dream reveal the truth, Eminence? Was I sent to you?"

There was a soft rustling from the crowd behind him as Shivaji translated his speech. When the nizam's eyes narrowed with displeasure, Duran felt a moment's triumph. His Rotund Majesty's plan to make a public spectacle of the Englishman's death had come unraveled. A challenge had been laid at his feet.

The nizam stood, and all the courtiers dropped to their knees. "Hear your fate, wretch."

Shivaji's translation followed swiftly.

"You will be put to the Trial of a Thousand Screams. If indeed the gods have chosen you, they will grant you the strength to endure it. No man has done so before."

Duran wished he had kept his mouth shut and settled for a straightforward execution.

The nizam pointed a long-nailed forefinger in his direction. "The will of the gods is ever disclosing itself in unfathomable ways. I accept the possibility that you have been sent to do their bidding."

His voice hardened, although Shivaji's translation rippled like a clear stream.

"As did my forefathers who ruled Alanabad before me, I have the gift to read the hearts of men. You are a creature of lies and false promises, Englishman. I do not trust you. But should you survive the Trial of a Thousand Screams, I shall grant you one year to find the Golden Leopard."

Chapter 1

On what was supposed to be her night of triumph, Jessica Carville moodily paced the Turkey carpet in Mr. Christie's office, feeling very much alone.

A dull pain throbbed at her temples, but she recognized it as a safe pain, low and unthreatening. The headache would not interfere with what she had to do. It must be the oncoming storm that had set her on edge. The London air crackled with the heat of late summer, and when she brushed her hand over a brass lion couchant on a side table, sparks shot from her fingertips.

The rumble of distant thunder sent her to a window, where she made an opening in the curtains to look outside. The new gas lamps lining Pall Mall shimmered in the humid air. On the street below, carriages were lined up as far as she could see.

Dear heavens. She'd never dared to hope for such a crowd. Parliament had dissolved weeks earlier, and most of the beau monde had already fled to the country. But it seemed that everyone of note still in the city had decided to attend the exhibition, if only to see what Lady Jessica had got up to now.

They had come here for gossip, of course, but they

would be disappointed. Her unsuitable profession had long since been dissected to the bone, and tonight's reception, while something out of the ordinary, was not at all the stuff of scandal.

Nonetheless, disaster hovered in the muggy air. She sensed it, the way she felt the lightning pulsing in the heavy clouds. For a few minutes she watched servants push through the crowd of onlookers to open lacquered carriage doors and let down the steps. Gentlemen in sleek evening dress descended, offering their arms to the elegant ladies who followed them. Liveried footmen bearing flambeaux led them across the pavement to the doors of Christie's auction house.

Jessica recognized most of the guests, but Christie's had also sent invitations to customers who did not move in her circle. And to her profound displeasure, an advertisement had appeared that very morning in the *Times*. She had agreed to it when the contract was signed, trusting that Mr. Christie would think better of such vulgar publicity. But he had not, and now any commoner was free to wander through the viewing rooms, rubbing shoulders with aristocrats, wolfing down her lobster patties, and guzzling her expensive champagne.

As voices floated up the staircase to the first floor, she resumed her pacing. It was the infernal waiting that gnawed at her. She could never bear being closed in.

A soft knock sounded at the door and Mr. Herbert, Christie's chief appraiser, stepped inside, a look of concern in his hazel eyes. "Nervous, my dear?"

"Not in the least," she said, and it was quite true. "But I should very much like to get on with it."

"Certainly." He went to the chair where she had draped her silver-shot gauze shawl. "The Duke of Devonshire has claimed the honor of escorting you downstairs. By your own arrangement, I shouldn't wonder."

She smiled at her mentor as he threaded the shawl around her bare arms. "I mustn't appear to be engaging in trade, you know, and there is nothing like a duke for lending one a bit of cachet."

Devonshire, waiting at the head of the stairs, greeted her with a bow and their traditional joke. "Tsk tsk, Lady Jessica. An ape leader still! I swear, there is no accounting for it."

She put her gloved hand on his sleeve. "Such a notorious pair we are—the Bachelor Duke and the Dedicated Spinster. But I am sworn to wed the day after you do, Hart, if only to confound those who have wagered in the clubs that we shall never relent. You *will* let me know if you take a sudden whim to marry?"

"To be sure. But when afflicted with a whim of that sort, I invariably scurry to my bed and have myself a nap until it passes." He led her slowly down the stairs. "You are in exceptionally fine looks tonight, Jessica. The crimson is perhaps a trifle startling at first glance, but it suits you."

"I mean to be noticed," she said, pleased at the compliment. Years ago the duke had advised her to dress herself in purest jewel tones—sapphire blues and ruby reds and emerald greens. The vibrant colors went well with her dark hair, and the simple lines of the gowns he had helped her choose flattered her tall, slender figure. She was more self-assured now, thanks to his kindness.

For the next half hour she needed every bit of confidence that a few yards of scarlet silk could provide. The duke stayed by her side while she moved around the exhibition hall, answering questions about the items to be auctioned the following day. But the moment His Grace's attention was diverted, a formidable woman accosted her and practically towed her to a glass case on the other side of the room.

"Two hundred pounds for a supper plate?" Lady Fitzmorris queried in a shrill voice, one intended to be overheard. "Highway robbery, if you ask me!"

A number of people gathered around, scenting an *incident*.

Jessica gave them a smile of welcome before turning to the dish, and voices stilled as everyone waited for her to speak. She let the silence draw out to the last possible moment.

"Do you think so, Lady Fitzmorris?" she asked gently. "That is the minimum bid we shall accept, but I expect it to fetch a great deal more. It is difficult, though, to place a value on a silver platter, even one that graced the table of Queen Elizabeth. Some would care nothing for that, as you do not, but others will consider it a fragment of history worth preserving in a collection."

"They might," Lady Fitzmorris fired back, "were there proof of what you say. But how can you possibly know who owned it centuries ago? Have you an acquaintance who actually saw it on the queen's table?"

A few people laughed, but most waited for Lady Jessica's response to the uncivil attack.

"I'm afraid not," she said, smiling as if Lady Fitzmorris had made a joke. "Before I recommend an item for purchase, I naturally consult with experts. A dinner service in this pattern is recorded in Her Majesty's household inventory, and Sir Thomas Revenon assures me that the provenance for this particular dish is indisputable."

She tilted her head, considering the plate. "I can say only that I stake my reputation on every piece in the exhibit. Should anyone buy an item and later discover it to have been misrepresented, I shall immediately refund the price in full."

"But how are we to be sure of that?" Lady Fitzmorris objected. "Have you ever made such restitution?"

"It has never been necessary. But as you have so wisely reminded us, evaluating art and historical objects is a prodigiously difficult business. I claim only a love for beautiful things and an instinct for matching people with what they will most cherish. Do you see the porcelain lady just there, on the pedestal nearest the door? Her eyes are an unusual and magnificent shade of blue." She lifted her gaze. "Precisely the color of your eyes, Lady Fitzmorris."

"Are they indeed? But what is that to the point? I have never been partial to gaudy knickknacks." Lady Fitzmorris swept through the tangle of onlookers with a disdainful sniff.

Jessica, glad to see the back of her, was reasonably certain that she would eventually meander over to that figurine, imagine a resemblance, and decide to bid on it.

"Well done," said an unwelcome voice at her ear. "The vanquished harpy flees, leaving the redoubtable Amazon in possession of the field."

The stink of gin and stale cologne made her stomach lurch. Jessica turned and greeted her brother-in-law with a curt nod. "Good evening, Gerald. How astonishing to see you here."

"Oh, but I adore these summer parties." His thin lips curled. "And I am positively agog that your little pastime is developing into a profitable enterprise. It *is* profitable, I trust? What's the use of family connections, I have always said, if they fail to put money in one's purse?"

"And what is the use of gaming, if one consistently fails to win?"

He stiffened. "I game no more than any other gentleman. But let us not pluck that crow again. M'wife has more than enough to say on the subject."

Jessica's hand itched to slap his handsome, dissipated face. Her sister *never* complained, more the pity. "You must excuse me, Gerald. I have guests to attend to."

"Then I shall trail along. It happens I've been dabbling a bit in the art trade—the odd piece here and there—and being seen in company with the dashing Lady Jessica is certain to enhance my reputation."

Aware that people were watching them, Jessica responded with a delicate shrug. "Link your name with mine," she said past a false smile, "and I shall grind you to powder."

"Not likely, sister-in-law." He seized a glass of champagne from a passing servant. "For Mariah's sake you will pretend to be in charity with me, as you have always done. But to preserve goodwill between us, I'll wander about a few minutes longer and then take a quiet leave. Cooperation, Jessica. That's the key."

He sauntered off, sipping at his drink and nodding to acquaintances, most of whom turned away. Sir Gerald Talbot was bad *ton,* a minor baronet who had married into a good family and spent most of his time gambling and evading his creditors. But he was clever, too, and ruthless. Jessica loathed him.

She closed her eyes for a moment. Could anything more go wrong? The storm had hit full force, resonating through her body like a strike of lightning. Rain pounded against the windows, and a blast of thunder rocked her on her heels. *Mingle,* she instructed herself. *Be charming. This is what you have worked for these last many years.* She forced her eyes open.

And saw him.

Time melted away. Of a sudden she was one-and-twenty again, recklessly besotted with a handsome scoundrel.

He was standing between the open doors of the exhibit hall, regarding her lazily from a pair of copper-colored eyes. She felt the heat blazing behind those eyes and sensed it coiling around her as his lips curved in a familiar, knowing smile. His mocking gaze efficiently stripped the clothes from her body.

Nothing had changed.

He had not, except that a strong sun had darkened his skin and streaked his tawny hair with pale gold. Otherwise he was just as she had tried not to remember him—tall, lean, exotic, and self-assured.

Hugo Duran. Invitation to sin.

No. Not *everything* was the same. Jessica Carville was all grown up now. A patented woman of the world. She would be accepting no more invitations from heartless men.

Soon Duran would approach. They would exchange civilized pleasantries while she made her indifference to him quite clear. Then, with exquisite politesse, she would turn her attention to her guests and deliberately ignore him. She looked forward to the pleasure of ignoring him.

But he only gave her a slight bow before entering the room, not moving in her direction at all. He wandered instead to the exhibits along the opposite wall, pausing occasionally to examine a painting or a snuffbox or a jade dragon, never looking at where she continued to stand like a fence post.

How *dare* he?

Cheeks hot with mortification, she recalled that it was precisely the sort of thing he *would* do. Duran invariably made it clear that he was in control, whatever the circumstances. It was why she feared him.

No. Feared her response to him. The way he made

her feel. The man himself was perfectly harmless, if dealt with in the proper way. He had surprised her, that was all, and she would be firmly in control of herself after a few moments to catch her breath. She ordered her feet to carry her to a safe place.

Devonshire smiled warmly when she appeared at his side. "Tomorrow's auction will be a splendid success," he assured her. "Everyone I have spoken with has promised to be here, and Stevesbury is saying that he will have the Florentine chest no matter the cost. I mean to bid against him until he pays three times its worth."

"That is most kind of you, Hart. Do raise the price if you can. The owner is in need of the money, and I ought not have tied her good fortune to my own shaky venture at Christie's."

"Ah, but you have always gambled against the odds. It is what I most admire about you." He tilted his head, examining her more closely. "You are remarkably pale, Jessica. I saw you speaking with Lady Fitzmorris. Was she horrid?"

"No more than usual. But it has been a long day," she said with a return of spirit, "and I've always loathed the dreg ends of parties. Better I go now, while the guests are still enjoying themselves."

"Have you an escort?"

"Of course I do. Let me slip out unnoticed, Your Very Proper Grace, before I begin to give the appearance of a street seller flogging her wares."

Devonshire was frowning as she moved away. She took her time about it, pausing to exchange greetings with people she knew, searching the room for Duran.

He had vanished.

And good riddance, she was telling herself when Lord Philpot planted himself in front of her and began to drone on about an Etruscan necklace he had almost bought for his wife thirty years earlier.

As if it mattered now, for pity's sake. But she had trained herself to appear interested, as a woman of business must do when dealing with potential clients. Her profession was all she had, the only thing that she cared about, and her unruly temper was never permitted to get in the way of a sale.

"Would you buy the necklace if it were offered you tonight?" she asked when there was a brief pause in his monologue.

"Indeed I would! My sweet Clarissa longed for it, but I was so very certain that it was a fake. And what if it was? She rarely asked anything for herself. I ought to have leaped at the opportunity to give her the pleasure of it." He released a small sigh. "Now it is too late, you see. Her mind is gone, or near to. She recognizes me only one day in seven of a week, and then for the briefest moment. But I would drape that golden chain around her neck in a heartbeat, aware she'd not know it from a hemp string, if a miracle put it into my hands again."

She looked more closely at his florid cheeks and doughy jowls. At the glowing eyes, welling with tears, and the tension in his shoulders. Lord Philpot had come to Christie's hoping to discover that long-lost necklace in one of the exhibit cases.

Jessica nearly forgot the urgency of escaping before Duran pounced on her. It was no coincidence, his presence here tonight. He did nothing without calculation and some devious purpose of his own. But at this moment, Lord Philpot's quest seemed vastly more important than evading a confrontation with Duran.

Envy clouded her gaze. This pudgy little man, for all his eccentric hair and pillowy face and tiresome conversation, had known a great and abiding love. His wife might not remember him, but he would remain steadfast to the end, searching for ways to make her happy.

"I'm afraid that the necklace you seek is unlikely to be found," she said gently. "Would not another, one of a similar style, do as well?"

"No, no." He shook his head, dislodging the few gingery strands of hair combed over his bald pate from both sides. Sticky with pomade, they lifted up and perversely remained aloft, creating something like a Roman arch over his shiny scalp. "It must be the real necklace."

For his pride's sake, Jessica wished she could smooth down those raised hairs. But of course she could not. Everyone would remark on it. "Will you come with me to Mr. Christie's office?" she asked, striking out in that direction and trusting him to follow her.

Still grumbling, he joined her in front of the large mantelpiece mirror where she was waiting for him. "I wish you to draw a picture of the necklace," she said. "Try to remember how it looked and send the picture to me."

"Bless you," he mumbled, his gaze fixed on the carpet. "I wish above all things to put a light into Clarissa's eyes. Sometimes she tells me stories about our life together as if I were a stranger listening to them. She recalls the old days, when I courted her, far better than I do. I mostly remember the times when I let her down. It is the regret that eats away at us, Lady Jessica. The things not done that torment us in the night."

The things done *torment us as well,* she thought. *Especially when they come back in person.*

She gave Lord Philpot a card with her direction

inscribed on it. "Do not count on me finding the necklace you seek, sir. Resign yourself to a substitute. It will be Etruscan and of similar design, if such is to be had, but that is the best I can do. It will be up to you to make Lady Philpot believe it is the one she desired. She'll want to believe that, you may be sure."

"But I cannot pretend such a thing," he objected. "It would be a lie."

"Only a very little lie, sir. A kind one. But you must do as your conscience tells you."

"I—" He cleared his throat, glancing around the room with obvious discomfort. "Yes, yes, but undertake no special search. None at all. Notify me if you come upon . . . That is, sorry to disturb you." He made a vague gesture. "You'll want to return to the exhibit hall."

She couldn't help herself. Lifting her arms, she combed her fingers through his sparse hairs and smoothed them back into place. "Do pardon me, sir, but the electricity in this stormy air has set your locks aflying. My own as well, I expect, but since I am about to take my leave, I shall cover them with my bonnet."

Not looking at him, knowing he wouldn't want her to, she went to the peg where her cloak had been hung. "You must sample the prime beef at the buffet supper, which is laid out in the room adjoining the exhibit. But before you join your friends, sir, will you be so kind as to inform Mr. Herbert that I require my carriage?"

It was what he needed after the embarrassment of her rearranging his hair—a place to go and a task. He gave her a courtly bow. "My pleasure, Lady Jessica. And I do thank you, on every count."

When he had left the room, she removed her shawl, folded it into a neat square, and laid it on the desk while she donned her satin cloak. She had always meant to take an early departure, after all. And if she was leaving a trifle earlier than she'd planned, without so much as a word to Mr. Christie or Mr. Herbert, it was only because of the storm and her headache. Nothing whatever to do with Duran.

She returned to the mirror, bonnet in hand, and gazed at her reflection. The only person she had ever lied to with any success was herself. Given time and persistence, she could make herself believe almost anything. She had lied herself into confidence, talked herself into independence, and stampeded herself into a profession wholly unsuitable for the daughter of an earl. And always she wondered when the fraud would catch up with her, as it was bound to do. Sooner or later everything would collapse around her, and she would be altogether alone.

She brushed back the tendrils of hair that had pulled loose at her temples and placed the bonnet on her head. Really, the evening had gone exceptionally well. She ought to be elated. She would muster the right amount of enthusiasm on her way back to Sothingdon House, where her secretary was waiting up to hear a report.

There was a click as the door latch lifted and a creak from unoiled hinges. She watched in the mirror as Duran entered the room with his usual indolent grace, closed the door behind him, and leaned his shoulders against it. She knew that pose all too well— one leg crossed over the other below the knees and arms folded at his chest.

Well, she had expected this, or something much like it. And better the scene play out here, in private. She was no longer so careless of her reputation as she once had been.

Deliberately, she took her time tying the ribbons of her bonnet.

"Hullo, Jessie." His voice was smooth and dark. "You are even more beautiful than I remembered."

"Lord Duran." She turned, making no hurry of it, and favored him with the polite, disinterested smile she reserved for clients who were unlikely to buy anything. "So it *was* you I glimpsed in the exhibition room. I had imagined so, but what with the crush, I could not be sure of it. You were certainly the last person I was expecting to see."

"Glimpsed?" He chuckled. "Confess it, princess. You stared as if I'd begun to sprout two horns and a tail."

"Did I? How rude of me." She moved a few steps closer so that he would not imagine she feared to approach him. "My mind must have been elsewhere at the time, but I do apologize for not making you welcome. It is always delightful to come upon a former acquaintance, especially in the summer. London is so thin of company this time of year. Remind me, will you? How long has it been since last we met?"

"Precisely six years, two months, eighteen days, twenty-three hours and—" he drew out his pocket watch and flicked it open—"seven minutes."

"Rubbish!" She had a misbegotten urge to laugh. "You are making that up."

"Probably. It felt much longer than that. But I do remember most explicitly the time we spent together. I remember, in splendid detail, what we *did* together."

"Then your memory is far more vivid than mine, sir." She was pleased to have said that with commendable nonchalance, given the mental images he had conjured with a few simple words.

What we did.

"Cat got your tongue, princess? Or have you decided to pretend that we were never lovers?"

Ice gathered at her spine. A blessing. It held her

erect and kept her cold. "Lovers? Well, I suppose so, although I have always thought that to be a ridiculous euphemism. But I have never been one to refine upon the past, and I certainly do not mean to revisit it. Were you hoping otherwise?"

He lifted his hands in a gesture of mock protest. "Not I. Hope is for those who will not seize what they want. Should I still desire you, Jessie, I would do whatever it required to have you."

"Short of force, I trust?"

For the first time, one of her arrows struck home. His eyes narrowed, and his arms dropped to his sides. "That would be out of the question. As you very well know."

"Yes." What she most hated about Duran was the ease with which he could wring honesty from her. "I'm sorry. It was a mean-spirited thing to say."

"Indeed. But you have every right to wish me to the devil. I expect you are doing so at this very moment." He cast her a benevolent smile. "It may console you to learn that your wish will be granted within a year. As a matter of fact, I could peg out at any time."

Had he picked up some deadly sickness in India? The very thought of it sent her heart plummeting. He might be a vast nuisance at close range, but a world without Duran somewhere in it would be oddly colorless.

He looked healthy enough. If anything, he was more tautly muscled than the man who used to sweep her up in his arms. But she sensed a different sort of strength in him now, as if he'd been tempered on an anvil.

"If you are ill," she said with studied calm, "I am sorry to hear it. Is that why you have returned to England?"

"You are concerned for my health? How very kind. But I'm perfectly well, save that my life is no longer my own." He made a sharp gesture as if dismissing the subject and slouched back against the door. "For the time being, my intentions are entirely honorable. The only proposition I have for you at the moment concerns a matter of business."

Business? Unaccountably insulted, she twisted the strings of her reticule between her fingers. "I already have more clients than I can possibly manage. But I'm sure that if you explain your requirements to Mr. Christie, he will refer you to someone who can be of assistance."

"I have, and he did. That's why I followed you upstairs. Christie has informed me that you are acquainted with every important collector of antiquities in England. By his account, you are the only one who can provide me the information I require."

"Mr. Christie said that?" A thrill of pride tingled at her fingers and toes. For the briefest moment, she let herself enjoy it.

"He added that I should expect no more from you than a list of names. In his opinion, you know everyone in society and nothing whatever about the profession you aspire to enter. More to the point, you are a female and therefore not to be taken seriously. He only indulges your hobby because of your connections."

Trust Hugo Duran to slam her back to earth without mercy.

At the least, he was consistent. The goodwill of others, he had always said, should never be taken into account when making important decisions. But at the time, she had thought he was referring to himself, warning her not to rely on him.

She had since learned to rely only on herself, and

credited him with teaching her to survive even the most crushing disappointments. In another thirty or forty years, she might be grateful for the lesson. Meantime, the ice at her spine had begun to melt. Her confidence was seeping away. He was still so beautiful, damn him, and she was still so weak.

"I can certainly provide you a list," she said, pleased to hear an assured voice emerge from her clogged throat. "Put in writing a description of what you are looking for and post it to my secretary. Mr. Herbert will provide you her name and direction."

"I shall call on you tomorrow," he said, as if she hadn't spoken. "Perhaps in time for breakfast. Do you remember how it used to be, Jessie? We could never have breakfast together."

"But that, I believe, is commonplace when engaging in a clandestine affair. And you needn't bother dropping by, for I shall not be at home."

He closed the space between them, moving so near that she felt his breath against her forehead when he spoke. "Don't run away, Jessie. I promise you'll not succeed."

When she tried to dodge around him, his hand grasped her forearm with just enough pressure to keep her in place. She looked down at the long, white-gloved fingers curled just below her elbow, shocked that he was touching her and astonished at what she saw.

His black coat sleeve had pulled back from his cuff, exposing a heavy gold bracelet coiled around his wrist. Not quite meeting at the center, the bracelet thickened on each side to form two knobs, each crowned with a large cabochon gem. An emerald and a ruby. Her gaze lifted to meet his eyes.

He looked amused. "Do you like it?"

"A charming bauble," she replied, withdrawing her

arm. He did not try to hold her. "But a most peculiar affectation, Duran, even for you. Unless you *wish* to be laughed at?"

"Oh, I think no one will laugh at me, princess. Certainly not to my face. And I cannot remove it, you know. Not even when I bathe."

A flash of memory. Steam rising from the water. His lean body lounging in the copper tub while she rubbed lemony soap over his chest . . .

She shook her head, willing the vision gone. "I wish to leave now, Duran. Please step out of my way."

He bowed and moved aside. "Don't forget what I said, Jessie. When I call on you tomorrow, be there. Hear me out. And when you agree to help me, you may name your reward."

Chapter 2

"You're very good at this," Duran said as the nimble fingers unbuttoned his waistcoat and slipped it off his shoulders.

"Yes." The soft voice was without expression. "I have some experience in these matters."

"I'll see to the rest." Duran tore off the stiff, high-pointed collar that had been stabbing at his neck all evening and let it drop to the threadbare carpet. Then he stood for a moment looking down at it, wondering why it kept moving about.

The whole room was moving. Shifting. Dividing itself.

A hand wrapped around his arm and led him to a pair of wingback chairs that miraculously became one chair while he was considering which of them he preferred. He let himself be turned, felt behind him for the seat cushion, and lowered himself gingerly. When it wasn't spinning, his head was splitting like a log at the sharp end of an ax.

The wages of virtuous living, he reflected sourly. Having fallen out of the habit of vice, he was having considerable difficulty falling into it again.

"If you wish, Duran-Sahib, I shall provide a remedy for the consequences of your godless immoderation."

Duran focused his bleary eyes on the slender man

who was standing in the invisible envelope of stillness that always surrounded him. Arms relaxed at his sides, Shivaji wore loose white cotton trousers and a knee-length overtunic belted with a pewter-colored sash. His straight black hair, gray streaked and parted in the middle, reached below his shoulders. He left off his turban when they were in private, and his shoes as well, but he never removed from his left earlobe the inch-long emblem of his profession.

A eunuch at the nizam's court had told Duran what it signified. "The Iron Dagger," he had whispered in a reverent tone. "The Sign of the Assassin."

There were more subtle signs as well, Duran had soon begun to notice. The hard calluses along the soles of Shivaji's narrow feet. The power in his slender hands. The controlled, assured grace with which he moved.

"The draught will ease the pain in your head," Shivaji said. "Shall I prepare it for you?"

Duran nodded assent and let his eyes drift shut. It had been a long night, the first he'd been permitted to spend outside the dingy rooms they had taken in Little Russell Street, and he had set himself to make the most of his unaccustomed freedom. Shivaji could not follow him into Christie's, nor into White's Club, where he'd gone after leaving the auction house.

The manager, remembering him, had advanced him a handful of markers on credit, and the few gamesters who had braved the thunderstorm were ripe for the plucking. He had come away with several hundred pounds that had to be hidden before Shivaji took them from him.

But where could he conceal a stash of banknotes in this sparsely furnished room? He wrenched open his eyes and looked around. There was a lumpy bed several inches shorter than his height, the shabby chair he was sitting on, a stand of drawers, a commode with a basin and shaving mirror, and not much else.

Shivaji slept on a pallet in the dressing room, where he kept the battered portmanteau and large wooden cabinet that seemed to be his only possessions. Once, when he was left alone for a few minutes, Duran had rifled through the cabinet, discovering scores of bottles and vials, packets of herbs and powders, mortar and pestle, and metal implements suitable for drawing teeth, lancing boils, and performing most any form of primitive surgery.

There were poisons, too, he had no doubt. A man under sentence of death could not help but notice potential means of dispatching him.

Escape was the ticket. Gathering and hoarding money. Making contact with people who might help him. Not many candidates for the position, once he ruled out anyone who had known him in India. His reputation there, not quite all of it earned, placed him square on the border between rakehell and traitor to his countrymen. He was, he supposed, a little of both.

There were two or three men he recalled from his previous visit to England, but the last time he'd seen them, he was collecting the gaming debts they owed. They were unlikely to remember him with any great fondness.

That left John Pageter, a decent, straitlaced military fellow who had boarded the *Bombay Caravan* in Capetown. Pageter had been reasonably good company on the voyage, despite his refusal to gamble or procure for his shipmate the occasional bottle of brandy. But any man could be corrupted. Duran had only to find Pageter's weakness and exploit it.

His thumbs pricking, he looked up to see that Shivaji had returned with a half-filled glass, which Duran accepted with a shaky hand.

"What the blazes *is* this?" He lifted the glass to the light and examined the black globules swirling in a thick, fir-green liquid. It smelled like a rotting carcass.

"Some things are better left unknown. But if you have the mettle to swallow it, your head will be clear before morning."

Remembering that he was to pay an early call on Jessica, Duran gulped the vile-tasting brew and sagged against the chair with his head thrown back, trying to keep himself from expelling it again.

Shivaji lowered himself cross-legged to the floor. "Did you conclude your business with the proprietor of the auction house?"

The pretense that any of it mattered was wearying, but Duran recognized an inquisition coming on. "I made his acquaintance, yes, but he was preoccupied with the exhibition. Not that it signified. I've a new plan now, much better than the first."

"Indeed?" It didn't sound like a question. "If the plan requires your presence in the gentlemen's club where you spent so many hours, then you must abandon it. In future, no such distractions will be permitted."

Disappointing, but not unexpected. "If you say so. But all the best contacts are to be found in the clubs. I made the acquaintance of one tonight, a chap named Sir Gerald Talbot who dabbles in the buying and selling of antiquities. He could be useful. But never mind. I quite understand that you don't like me wandering out of your sight."

"My concern is for the misuse of time, that is all. You are unfailingly under scrutiny."

"Ah, yes, the *Others*. But I've concluded you are making them up. A gaggle of Hindus could hardly skulk around London unnoticed, and I've been watching out for them."

"Were you to observe them, they would have failed in their duty."

"Which would be . . . ?"

"When first you asked if I alone was set to guard you, I replied simply that there were others. Their title is difficult to translate. 'The ones who serve unto the end' comes near to the meaning. Their leader is my eldest son."

Duran felt his mouth drop open. On the ship, whenever Shivaji expressed a wish to practice his English, they had discussed history and philosophy. But those occasions had been rare, and Duran's attempts to winkle information from his captor were always smoothly deflected. Never once had a personal word passed between them.

"That surprises you?" A smile ghosted over Shivaji's lips. "I have eight sons. When they come of age, all will take up the profession of their ancestors."

"Eight little assassins-in-training." Sometimes, even when sober, Duran felt as if he were slogging through a grotesque dream. "And what exactly must they do to earn the right to wear one of those charming earbobs? If you keep reproducing ambitious sons at such a rate, the streets will be littered with corpses."

In the silence following that pronouncement, Duran wished he had conducted himself with the humble, disarming manner he kept meaning to adopt.

When the chief assassin spoke again, his voice was unperturbed. "Only the head of the family wears the iron dagger, Duran-Sahib. It is a responsibility conferred in trust and accepted with an oath inscribed in blood. My family has served the rulers of Alanabad for seventeen generations, and I am bound in honor to obey the nizam's commands. When Arjuna takes my place, he will do the same. And like me, he will seek every means to make a killing unnecessary. We take no pleasure in it."

"Well, that's comforting, to be sure. I'd hate to think of you gloating when I'm laid out at your feet. When will that be, by the way?"

"When the time allotted you by the nizam has run out. Or before then, if you pursue your own interests instead of the duty laid upon you by the gods."

"Has there ever lived a man who did not pursue his own interests?" Duran sat forward on his chair, elbows propped on his knees and chin cupped in his hands. "The dance grows tiresome, Shivaji. Shall we, just this once, speak directly to the point? You know the leopard cannot be found. Certainly not by me. So why are you playing along with this charade? Hell, you practically instigated it. The nizam wasn't buying my story, not for a minute, but you kept working at him until he came around."

Shivaji's calm gaze never altered. "I have not the power to—how did you say it?—work him around. I merely suggested that he make use of you. You were lying, yes, but there flowed a truth beneath your words. In this mission, there are blessings to be had. It is even possible that some of those blessings will fall upon you."

"But I don't believe in your gods, Shivaji. And I can't say that I've any of my own. None who have ever given me the time of day, at any rate. I *am* sure that no self-respecting deity would send the likes of me on a quest, even a piddling one like this. Bloody hell, man. We're talking about a statue of a *cat!*"

"And what is a banner but a scrap of cloth? Yet men follow it into battle, do they not? A symbol can unite a nation. It inspires courage and endurance. Alanabad is threatened from every side by neighboring princes and foreign merchants. Within its borders, a traitor gathers followers and prepares to strike. My country relies on tradition to lend it strength. Without the Golden Leopard, which has stood guard over its fate for centuries, Alanabad will fall."

"But you have a perfectly good substitute in hand. Why not take the replica back and pass it off as the real thing? You don't need the original leopard, and you sure as hell don't need me."

"I do not expect you to give credit to my convictions. You are a man without faith. But I do expect you to follow my instructions, however foolish they may appear to you."

"Fine." Duran waved a careless hand. "I'll look for your precious leopard. I won't find it, you'll kill me, and that will be that. But while the search is on, I intend to go about it my way."

"You will take an oath not to attempt an escape?"

Duran rubbed his eyes. Dammit, even a gazetted reprobate sometimes kept a particle or two of honor salted away, if only to prove to himself that he could. His took the form of giving his word only when he meant to keep it, which was why he took care never to give it. Almost never. The last time he'd been talked into an oath was six years ago, and he'd never ceased to regret it.

"Put a gun to my head and I'll say whatever you like," he admitted with a grin. "But I'll be lying."

"Then I must see to it your efforts fail." Rising, Shivaji took the empty glass from the table. "Sleep now. In the morning you may explain your new plan."

"Wake me early," Duran advised. "I have an appointment with a lady."

From the entrance to the dressing room, Shivaji cast him a somber look before disappearing inside.

Duran waited until the door had closed before pulling himself upright and tottering over to the bed. He still had to find a place to hide his money. Under the pillow for the night, he decided when no better location presented itself. Tomorrow he would return the folded banknotes to the pair of narrow inner pockets concealed near the flap of his trousers. He had sewn them there himself, using needle, thread, and a patch of fabric filched from his tailor. Although Shivaji skimped on the accommodations, he had agreed that his prisoner required a fashionable wardrobe to move about in Society.

Chuckling, Duran began to unbutton his trousers. Perhaps Jessica could be persuaded to take custody of his funds. And if he had his way about it, she would retrieve them from their provocative hiding places with her own hands.

Except that—

He patted the two spots where his money was stored. Had been stored.

With increasing alarm he stripped off the trousers and checked the pockets again. Empty.

He examined the floor, in case the money had fallen out. His linen drawers, in case the money had slipped inside them.

But the money was gone. All seven hundred pounds of it gone, taken while he was being stripped down to shirt and trousers by his murderous valet.

And he hadn't felt a thing. Not a bloody thing.

Chapter 3

The late-summer twilight was deepening to a velvety purple when Jessica arrived at High Tor, the Sothingdon family estate set like a grassy island among the bogs and granite outcroppings of Dartmoor.

Voices and laughter rumbled from the direction of the dining room as she stepped into the entrance hall. "Welcome home, Lady Jessica," said the butler, taking her small valise. A family retainer since before she was born, he would sooner be hung than betray surprise at her unexpected appearance. "Shall I inform his lordship of your arrival?"

"I suppose that you must, Geeson. But I don't wish to make a bother of myself while he is entertaining guests. Tell him I am tired from my journey and will speak with him in the morning."

"Very good, madam. If you will wait in the green saloon, I shall see your bedchamber prepared and your luggage carried upstairs." He led her to the first floor, pausing outside a set of double doors. "Would you care for a supper tray?"

"A bath would be most welcome, if there are servants free to prepare it. And perhaps a pot of tea and some biscuits."

Bowing, he opened the doors and stepped aside to

let her enter. "Lady Mariah will be pleased to see you."

Geeson had always enjoyed creating his own little surprises. She had not expected to find her sister in residence and wished she could put off speaking with her until she had recovered from her last encounter with someone she had not expected to see. At about this same time, only twenty-four hours ago.

What a spectacularly *trying* day it had been.

"Jessica?" Mariah's embroidery hoop dropped to the floor when she stood, her wide blue eyes magnified by her gold-rimmed spectacles. "Good heavens. Papa failed to tell me that you were to be here as well."

"That's because he had no idea I was coming." Jessica removed her bonnet and tossed it onto a sideboard. "I took a sudden impulse to breathe fresh air. Why have you been left to sit alone in this hideous parlor?"

"Oh, one hideous parlor is much like another. And I am generally alone in my own house, you know. When Papa wrote, asking me to play hostess at his shooting party, I could think of no reason to stay in Dorset. But I should have done, I suppose, because I am perfectly useless here. My sole duty is to wait in the parlor until the gentlemen have drunk their port, at which time I pour coffee and tea for them. Then I make my escape and keep well out of their way until the next evening. Mind you, it is not at all unpleasant with only five guests in residence. But the house will be overflowing before the week is out."

"Oh dear. The Glorious Twelfth." Jessica stripped off her gloves and slapped them against her skirts. "Drat. I must be off again as soon as possible."

"What's this? What's this?" The earl bustled into the parlor, his belly preceding the rest of him, his nose flushed with drink. "I'll hear nothing of the kind. You will not be off, young lady. You've only just arrived."

"And at a lamentably bad time, I'm afraid." Supposing that she ought to make a gesture of some sort, Jessica dipped into a respectful curtsy. "I cannot imagine how I forgot the first day of grouse season."

"Too long in the city, that's why. Most important day of the year. I always said it was a pity you never took to shooting. You've got the single-mindedness. You'd have been a fine shot. Demned fine."

Startled, Jessica could only attribute that compliment—a high one indeed from the hunt-mad Earl of Sothingdon—to an evening of tippling with his cronies. It was always Aubrey he had pressed to join him, acutely disappointed when his only son took no interest in slaughtering rabbits and birds. "As if you would have included a mere female in one of your shooting parties," she responded with a grin.

"Well, I don't expect I would have. But I'd have liked to see you at it, and that's a fact." To her astonishment, he came directly up to her and clasped her in a stiff embrace. "It's good to see you, Jessica," he mumbled into the side of her neck. "Demned if it's not."

It was the first time he'd taken her in his arms that she could remember. The sensation was both agreeable and uncomfortable. Not certain what to do, she patted him on his broad back as he continued to hold her, his breath reeking of tobacco and wine.

"Do return to your guests, Father," she said, carefully withdrawing herself and resisting an urge to put distance between them. "Let's have a long talk in the morning, shall we?"

"Yes. Yes, indeed." He cleared his throat, fumbled with the knot on his cravat, and made his way indi-

rectly to the door. One hand propped on the casement, he looked over at Mariah. "Never you mind the
coffee and such. Go help your sister get settled, that's
a good girl."

Jessica watched him leave, still trying to order her
thoughts after her father's decidedly unusual conduct.
He generally steered a wide berth from the disobedient daughter, the rebel child who had cut up what
little peace was to be found at High Tor.

Mariah appeared at her side, wraithlike in her plain
gown of unflattering gray, her brown hair sleeked back
and twisted into a tight chignon. Her skin was abnor-
mally pale, even in the golden candlelight, and dark
shadows made little quarter moons under her eyes.
"Shall we go upstairs now?" she asked, her voice tentative. "Or wait for your maid to unpack your things?"

"By all means, let us go." Jessica heard the impatience in her tone and was sorry for it, but Mariah's
shy deference never failed to put her out of temper.
She led the way to the second floor and down the
passageway to the farthest end of the west wing.

When old enough to leave the nursery, she had chosen for herself the most remote room in the house,
the one where she had discovered the priest hole. It
was connected to a steep, narrow staircase that ran
alongside the chimney all the way to the cellars. From
there it opened to a tunnel that wound its way to a
trapdoor concealed in a copse of oak a quarter mile
from the house. She had often used the tunnel to escape the house unseen and explore the wildest places
on the moor.

When she arrived at the bedroom door, two footmen were lowering a copper bathtub onto a tarp they
had spread over the carpet near the fireplace. Her
luggage was stacked in one corner, and a large tray

holding a teapot, cups and saucers, and several dishes filled with biscuits, tarts, and small sandwiches lay on the side table.

Geeson bowed when she entered the room. "I have been unable to locate your maid, Lady Jessica."

He had been waiting to express his disapproval, the old fuddy-duddy. "That's because Dorothy is still in London, I would imagine. And yes, I traveled all this way without a silly young girl to lend me a semblance of propriety. She is to accompany my secretary, who will join me within a day or two. Meanwhile I am perfectly capable of fending for myself."

"Very good, madam." He eased past her to the door, a smile tugging at the corners of his mouth. "You will advise me if you require assistance."

When he was gone, Jessica turned to her frowning sister. "It's a game we play. He means no insult."

Mariah shivered. "He terrifies me. But almost everyone does. I can never think how to explain myself when I do something wrong."

"But then, you never do anything wrong. You are nearly as proper as Aubrey, who hasn't set a foot off the thorny path to heaven since first he levered himself upright. How is he, by the way?"

"About to become a father again. Harriet is due sometime in October. Didn't you know?"

Jessica shrugged. "We do not communicate. I expect four children keep him too busy to write, and I have been preoccupied with my business."

"Yes." Mariah went to the sideboard, her back to Jessica as she strained tea into the cups. "I saw the announcement of your reception and exhibit in the *Times*. It arrives days late, of course, but I always enjoy reading news of you. And this time, an entire quarter page! What was it the headline said? 'An Exclusive and Unparalleled Collection Personally Selected by Lady Jessica Carville.' My own sister, singled out in such a way by the newspapers. But what with the delay, I sometimes become confused about dates." She glanced over at Jessica. "Am I mistaken, or was not your auction on for today?"

Jessica, amazed by such naiveté, decided not to explain about the costly advertisement. "It wouldn't do for me to hover about Christie's like a shopkeeper, you know. I never intended being there for the actual sale."

"But don't you want to know what happened? I cannot imagine why you chose to leave at such a time."

"It wasn't planned," Jessica said, glad for the chance to speak three honest words. With deliberate nonchalance, she joined Mariah at the tea tray and plucked an almond biscuit from a saucer. "Last night after the exhibition I felt uncommonly energetic. Sleep was out of the question, but I couldn't bear to do *nothing,* and there was nothing for me to do. Helena was to attend the auction and supervise the details, so I took it in my head to set out for High Tor and await the outcome here."

She nibbled at the biscuit, wishing Mariah would look at her. Or say something. But she went on chipping sugar from the block with fierce concentration, and Jessica found herself rushing to fill the silence. "I'd a case of nerves, I suppose. The heat was truly oppressive. But the storm had let up—did I mention the storm?—and if I left right away, I could avoid the morning traffic. Then, once on the road, I could not help but travel straight through. You know how I am."

"Did something unpleasant happen at the exhibition?" Mariah asked with surprising perception.

The image of Duran swam in and out of her vision. Jessica turned, resting her hips on the sideboard, and watched the servants carry in kettles of hot water. A maid followed, her arms filled with plush towels.

They appeared to float, silent images from a dream. A low sound, like the wings of insects, buzzed in her ears. Steam billowed over the copper tub in cloudy puffs that rose to the high ceiling, fogging the room and sifting through her in warm, damp waves.

She had fled Duran. She had run from him without dignity, or pride, or even a reason she could bear to acknowledge. Duran was in London, so she must be elsewhere, at a place he would not dare to come.

"Let me help you undress," someone said.

Jessica realized that she was standing by the bed, gazing blankly at the counterpane. She looked up, startled to find the servants gone. The fog that had enveloped her was no more than a soft haze hovering over the steaming bathwater.

Mariah, standing behind her, began to unclasp the hooks and tapes on her carriage dress. "Are you feeling ill? A few minutes ago I asked you a question, and you wandered away as if you hadn't heard me."

Jessica stepped out of her skirt and fumbled at the buttons on her high-necked bodice. "I'm perfectly fine, although I believe I could fall asleep standing up. Perhaps I'll do without the bath and go directly to bed."

"That would be best, I expect. You might nod off in the tub and drown. Shall I inform the staff that you are not to be disturbed?"

"Yes, please." Jessica was not so weary that she failed to hear the tension in her sister's voice. "What is it, Mariah? You are aching to tell me something."

"It can wait until tomorrow." Mariah came around her and pushed Jessica's limp fingers from the buttons.

"Oh dear. Something unpleasant. Well, do get it over with, or I'll not sleep a wink."

"I saw the list, you see. Papa asked me to assign

rooms to the guests, as if I'd any notion where to put them. Already I've gone wrong, placing Lord Inglewood on the second floor because I didn't know about his arthritis. He has since been moved, of course, and so has Sir Ridgely, who wanted a view of Devil's Tor."

Jessica bit back a snappish demand that Mariah come to the point. On the rare occasions her sister spoke at all, she circled the topic like a fish flirting with a baited hook.

"The thing is," Mariah said, undoing the last button and stepping away, "Colonel Lord Pageter is to be here."

After so great a buildup, Jessica was both relieved and annoyed to hear such an inconsequential bit of news. "Indeed? I wasn't aware he had returned to England. Where has he been all this time? Oh yes. Capetown. I remember now. We went to Portsmouth to see him off. You said that he had no family to wave good-bye, so you dragged me along with you to do the honors, and we arrived an hour after the ship had sailed."

Red spots blazed on Mariah's white cheeks. "We should have been there. You were all but betrothed to him."

"I was nothing of the sort. Mother did everything in her power to promote the match, but there was never the slightest chance I would marry him. As he very well knew, poor fellow, although he was far too polite to object when we were practically thrown at each other. The weeks he spent at High Tor must have been excruciating for him. Wherever he turned, there I was. Mother seated me next to him at table every single night and went so far as to put him in the bedchamber next to this one, hoping that lust would propel him through the adjoining door and between my legs."

"Good heavens, Jessica." Mariah spun her around and attacked the laces of her corset. "You mustn't say such things!"

"Whyever not? You should understand, better than anyone, how ruthless Mother could be. Fortunately Pageter had no more interest in me than I in him, and he was too honorable to sell himself in exchange for a substantial marriage settlement. I always wondered why he continued to visit after I had refused him." She stifled a yawn. "It was for the hunting, I suppose. He was a dedicated sportsman."

"Papa liked him for it," Mariah said, her voice muted.

"Oh, indeed. He had finally got a proper son-in-law in his sights, one who'd cheerfully tramp the moorlands with him, and I turned the chap away. If he'd known I would descend on High Tor this week, I would suspect him of making another try at arranging a match. Although surely Pageter is married by now. He struck me as the sort to want a cozy fireside and a nestful of children."

Mariah tugged the corset away, folded it neatly, and crossed to a stand of drawers. "Have you never wanted that for yourself?"

"Not enough to relinquish my freedom." Jessica sat on the edge of the bed to remove her stockings. "I don't think of it, really. One cannot hope for everything. I prefer to set goals that can be achieved without relying on someone else. Males are notoriously undependable, you know. To subject myself to one of them in marriage would be intolerable."

"Each case is different," Mariah protested. "You cannot say that Mama was ever subjected to Papa."

"Hardly." Jessica wished that Mariah would go away and let her collapse into bed, but she could not bring herself to be as nasty as she felt at the moment.

She *did* care for her sister, although the two of them had never been close. They were so very different in nature. When they were children, High Tor had been an armed camp—Jessica at war with her mother while the rest of the family did Lady Sothingdon's bidding. Eventually Mariah had made an unhappy marriage because she was too weak to stand up for herself.

Jessica had no intention of being sucked back into the family quagmire. Escaping had been hard enough. They all had to pay for the choices they had made, didn't they? And she had troubles enough of her own.

She heard the door open and looked up in time to see Mariah vanish into the passageway. Another quietly desperate retreat, like all the others she had made. The door closed gently, the latch falling into place with scarcely a sound.

Rather sure she had just failed her sister in some unnameable way, Jessica crawled up the bed until her head reached the pillow and let herself drop like a stone.

Chapter 4

Three days passed before Jessica received news of the auction.

She had just returned from a morning walk when she saw the letter, several pages thick, on a salver in the entrance hall. Snatching it up, she rushed to her bedchamber—the only place in the house where she could be assured of privacy—and broke the seal with trembling fingers.

For a moment she could not bear to look. Putting aside Helena's letter, she spread the other sheets of paper side by side on her writing table and drew up a chair. Her secretary, in neat, precise handwriting, had dutifully recorded each item on offer, the price paid, the buyer, and a breakdown of the commissions due to Christie's and to Lady Jessica.

Taking a deep breath, she began to read.

By the time she had reached the last page, she was making small sounds of excitement. And when she saw the amounts bid for Lady Erskine's Elizabethan platter and Florentine chest, she let out a whoop of glee.

Every single item had been purchased, and at a price considerably higher than she had anticipated. Higher even than she had allowed herself to hope for. Jumping to her feet, she scooped up the gray cat that had wandered in through the door she'd forgot to close and danced the startled creature around the room. "I'm a success, Oscar! A roaring great goddess of a success!"

The cat clung to her shoulder with extended claws, ears flattened and tail swishing in protest.

She came to a stop and lowered him onto the bed. "Sorry, old lad. It's just that I have no one else to celebrate with."

No one to tell, either, not anyone who would understand what it meant to her. It was a lonely triumph, to be shared only with a cat that had little affection for her. Oscar had simply decided that her room was the safest place to hide out. Two score of men were now in residence at High Tor, and there were few places a cat could go without being stepped on by a careless booted foot.

She wandered back to the writing table and picked up her secretary's letter. It began with an apology. Helena had caught a summer cold and would not join her until it had passed. Jessica was sorry to hear it. She had counted on leaving High Tor as soon as Helena arrived with the bank drafts, intending to deliver at least one of them in person. Lady Erskine was in need of the money, and Jessica had planned to evaluate the contents of her home and help her choose what she could bear to part with for a future sale. The remote Northumberland estate would be an excellent place to reside for a few weeks. Like Oscar, she required a safe place to go to ground.

The thought of it filled her with self-loathing. Above all things she hated weakness, most especially in herself. She feared it, too. People who thought they knew her would be amazed to discover how constantly, how profoundly, she lived in fear of what she might do. Of what she had done. Of what she might become.

She stomped her feet, one after the other—her way of exorcizing her demons. One, two. One, two. One, two! Oscar rumbled a growl and dove under the bed.

No one—not even a cat—could bear her company for very long.

She drew a few steadying breaths and returned to Helena's letter. The auction was described with just the sort of particulars her secretary knew she would relish. She read the long middle section twice, imagining Lord Stevesbury's inflated sense of self-importance as he beat out the Duke of Devonshire for not one but *four* valuable pieces. They were not nearly so valuable as the price he paid for them, but he would boast of his success for a good long time. She must remember to praise him for his excellent taste when next they met.

Lady Fitzmorris had bought the blue-eyed figurine, bringing along her son-in-law to do the bidding for her. Jessica checked the list to see what she had paid. Oh my. It more than made up for the trouble the woman had tried to create at the reception.

By Helena's report, Mr. Christie was delighted with the results of the sale, although he was taking great pains to claim all the credit for Jessica's ideas. He very well *ought* to be pleased, considering the money he had made and the attention she had brought to his auction house. Most of the guests had never thought of setting foot there until Lady Jessica made Christie's a fashionable place to be.

She skimmed several anecdotes, knowing that Helena, with her acerbic wit, would tell the stories far better in person. Then she came to a long postscript at the end of the letter.

"A gentleman, Lord Duran, was inquiring for you at the auction. I gathered that he had applied first at

Sothingdon House, which was confirmed by Phillips when I returned home. Naturally we did not provide Lord Duran with your direction, as you had told us it was to be kept private. But the gentleman, who is newly returned from India, claims to have made your acquaintance several years ago and appears most anxious to speak with you on a matter of some urgency. Should you wish to make an exception for him, please let me know by return post. He has called twice this very day, and I must tell you, Jessica, that he is a difficult man to fend off."

Didn't she know it!

Jessica spent the next three hours writing letters, one to Helena with strict instructions to have Duran turned away whenever he called, and the others to clients who would wish to know the price their merchandise had fetched. She'd have taken pleasure dispatching so much excellent news, had not Duran felt all but present in the room. She had put distance between them, but she could not stop thinking about him.

She dropped hot wax onto each of her letters and stamped it with her seal, using exceptional vigor. Take *that*! she thought. And *that*! Every one of those letters declared her independence. She had worked exceptionally hard for nearly six years to build her reputation, endured criticism and sometimes downright ostracism from the high sticklers, and finally made a glorious success.

Never mind what she had given up in the process. She had made her choices, and it was too late to second-guess them now.

Oscar had emerged from beneath the bed to twine about her ankles, which he only did if he was hungry. When she tried to pet him, wanting to touch some-

thing warm and alive, he jerked away, the fur along
his spine standing straight up in an unmistakable sign
of rejection.

"Come along, wretch," she said, gathering her letters and heading for the passageway. "When I've got
Father to frank these, we'll go to the kitchen and find
you something to eat."

Oscar trotted alongside her, tail high with anticipation, until she came to a halt at the top of the main
staircase that curved down to the entrance hall. Male
voices, several of them, echoed from the high walls
and domed ceiling.

She nearly turned back, but what was the use?
There would be no escaping them so long as she remained at High Tor. She still wore her plain brown
walking dress and half boots, and her hair was coming
loose from its pins, but none of her father's grouse-
hunting friends cared anything for that. The men invited to Sothingdon's famous shooting parties came
precisely because there would be no females demanding their attention and requiring them to be on
good behavior. She often thought that she could arrive
at the dinner table wearing only her chemise without
attracting the slightest notice.

Oscar padded ahead of her, turning once to make
sure she was following. As her feet hit the steps—one,
two, one, two—she shaped her lips into an aloof,
don't-talk-to-me smile. But halfway down the stairs,
where they began the sweeping curve to the entrance
hall, she caught sight of her father shaking hands with
a man she recognized.

John Pageter. She paused for a moment, wondering
if this encounter ought to be postponed. She was far
from looking her best, and it would be less awkward
for the both of them if they met without her father
looking on.

She studied his face, brown from the South African sun, his well-formed nose and square chin combining to produce an effect that was both strong and sweetly pleasant. She remembered him as kind and a trifle shy with women. He had certainly been shy in *her* company.

With the awareness of a soldier who had come under scrutiny, he glanced up the staircase and caught her gaze. Immediately his lips widened into a smile, a friendly smile, no trace of a hidden purpose in it.

More at ease now, she continued down the stairs and moved to her father's side. Near the front door Geeson was accepting hat and gloves from another guest, but with Pageter blocking her view, she could see nothing but a set of wide shoulders.

Pageter's brown eyes were warm as he bowed to her. "Lord Sothingdon has been kind enough to welcome an additional guest," he said, "a friend I quite improperly invited to accompany me to High Tor. In my defense, he has a slight connection with the family. I believe, Lady Jessica, that you are acquainted with him."

Her breath caught in her throat. Pageter continued speaking as he moved aside and beckoned to the other gentleman, but she knew already who he must be. Cold with dread, she raised her head and gave Duran a haughty look as he made his bow to her father, and then to her.

She had expected a look of triumph, or at least the familiar mocking amusement in his eyes. But he only greeted her pleasantly—a polite murmur of her name, no more—before returning his attention to the earl.

Pageter made the introductions, praising Duran's skill with a gun as if that were sufficient justification for his intrusion into a party where he'd not been invited. She longed to slap the both of them.

Duran silenced Pageter with a wave of his hand. "It is unpardonable of me to descend on you without an invitation, Lord Sothingdon. I seem to have left my manners in India. There was good hunting there, of course, but I missed the pleasures of tramping the English countryside in pursuit of partridge and grouse. When Pageter told me that he was off for several weeks to do precisely that, the temptation to impose on him—and on you—was overwhelming."

Jessica could practically feel her father dissolving under Duran's flattery. He always played the right notes, the ones that appealed to his victim's pride or favorite hobbyhorse. That tribute to English shooting parties had won the earl's heart in an instant.

"Well, well, I'm glad to have you here," he said gruffly. "A good time for it, what? Pageter has told me that you know my daughter."

Duran spared her a polite glance. "Only very slightly, I'm afraid. We met a number of years ago at one of those overcrowded London parties. I expect the charming Lady Jessica has no recollection of me at all."

"My lamentable memory," she said coolly, wondering if she imagined a flash of humor in his eyes.

"Lord Sothingdon," he said, turning back to his host, "I hope you will do me the honor of accepting a token of my gratitude for your hospitality. While I was purchasing a gun—several of them, I must confess—at Joseph Manton's establishment, I asked him to select one that you might approve for yourself."

Duran made a gesture, and two men approached from the shadows.

Jessica, who had failed to notice them, was as astonished as the earl when they stepped forward and bowed. Both were dark-skinned and quietly exotic, clad in white tunics belted with wide gray sashes over loose white trousers. They wore turbans, which were knotted just above their right ears, and the younger man was holding a large, flat mahogany case. The older one undid the clasp and raised the lid.

Sothingdon gasped.

Jessica could not imagine what her father found so wonderful about the contents. The leather-lined case held a long-barreled rifle with a shiny wooden stock, along with the usual implements for loading and cleaning. But what of it? He was an extravagant collector of guns and already owned several score of them.

Nonetheless, he was undeniably impressed. When the gun was lifted from the case and put into his hands, he caressed it with the affection he might have given to a new grandchild. "Splendid workmanship," he said, sounding a bit dazed. "Splendid."

"I had thought you would be interested in the new percussion ignition," said Duran, "but Manton was sure you'd prefer the traditional flintlock."

"Oh, yes. Yes indeed. I don't hold with these modern experiments. Apt to blow up in your hands, what?"

"I certainly hope not," Duran replied. "I bought two of them for myself."

"Then you must explain your reasons. Come along to my study and we'll have a whisky while the servants see to your rooms. Jessica, make certain the gentlemen are settled, will you?"

And thus, she thought, glaring at Duran's straight back, did the serpent slither into the garden.

Chapter 5

Men were never so provoking as when they failed to do what was expected of them.

Jessica's expectations had been suitably modest—a diligent pursuit by Duran and disdainful evasion by her. But for three days—not that she was counting—he had brazenly ignored her. If they chanced to encounter each other, he bowed and smiled, but before she could give him the cut direct, he continued by without a word.

Only last evening she had joined the gentlemen at dinner, accompanied by a reluctant Mariah, only to find that Duran had abandoned his usual seat near her father for a place clear the other end of the table. Was that a coincidence, or had he learned that she'd arranged to be seated across from him?

He appeared to be enjoying himself. Most of the laughter at the table came from the group surrounding him, while she was stuck between her tongue-tied sister and the gout-ridden Lord Marley, who was too busy forking in collops of veal to converse.

Once, as she lifted her glass of wine for a sip, she glanced up to see Duran gazing directly at her. For a few tense moments voices faded and all the air left the room. They seemed to be attached to opposite ends of a magnetized wire. Until he grinned, and she realized she was spilling wine down the bodice of her dress.

Luckily she was wearing red, to match the wine. She covered her humiliation with an observation about the weather to Lord Marley, who grunted a reply, and waited a decent interval before suggesting to Mariah that they withdraw. Her sister, who had toyed with a slice of roast duck for the entire meal, practically bolted from the room, leaving Jessica to make a solitary, dignified exit. Had Duran been paying attention, he would have been impressed.

If his strategy of ignoring her was designed to intrigue, and she expected that it was, he was going to be disappointed. She had no intention whatever of approaching him. Never mind that she sometimes found herself circling him like a shark. It was no more than he deserved for paddling into her territory.

Besides, how else was she to deduce what he was up to? If Duran had come to High Tor merely for the shooting, she would eat an unplucked partridge.

He did shoot, though, every day. At first she watched from a distance, perched on a flat rock atop one of the high tors that gave the estate its name, but she felt uneasy there on her own. Exposed, as if other watchers had secreted themselves on the tor, spying on her the way she was spying on Duran.

Once she was nearly certain she had spotted a dun-colored figure crouched behind an outcropping of stone. But when she rose to take a better look, there was only a clump of bracken. The next morning she saw a flash, and then another, like sunlight reflecting off glass, from a hill the other side of where the gentlemen were gathered. For a long time she focused her gaze on that hill, but no more flashes caught her eye.

Duran had got on her nerves, she decided. That would explain it. But the sensation of being observed grew stronger, and on the third morning she abandoned the desolate tors and joined a snoozing Lord Marley at the crest of a grassy hill overlooking the target range. There, in the shade provided by a pair of oaks, were three high-backed benches mounded with cushions and a low table laid out with apples and pears.

Spying in comfort, thought Jessica, settling down with a pear to the accompaniment of Lord Marley's snores. Below, perhaps fifty yards away, the sportsmen clustered in groups, drinking mugs of brandy-laced coffee and placing wagers.

The serious business of bagging partridges and gray grouse would not begin until tomorrow, she knew. Sothingdon shooting parties followed a predictable schedule. Yesterday the men had gone after the elusive Dartmoor hares, and today would be devoted to pigeon-trap shooting.

There was no mistaking Duran, the midmorning sunlight gilding his hair as he prowled among the drabber beasts of the field. Waiting quietly to one side, laden with powder flask, shot belt, and a pair of rifles, was his loader, the young Hindu who had accompanied him to High Tor.

The other Hindu stood alone on the same bare hillock where Jessica had seen him each day, as still as a pillar of salt in his long white tunic and snowy turban. Lord Duran's valet, according to the servants, all of whom were in awe of the man. He never ate meat, they said, and he had healed Bridget's runny eyes with drops and soothed the turn boy's burned hands with an ointment he taught the boy's mother to make, and he spoke the King's English like Quality except for some words he didn't know. He asked polite enough, though, and smiled when the words weren't the sort you could say in front of the vicar. He put them in mind of a vicar, come to think of it, heathen though he be.

She'd wanted to learn more about Duran's odd attendants, but even under her father's benign rule, gossiping with the servants was frowned upon. Mostly by the servants themselves, she had realized when the talkative footman she'd been plying for information was shushed by the parlor maid.

Duran, looking relaxed, was conversing with John Pageter and two other gentlemen while servants unloaded three large wooden boxes from a wagon and carried them to a spot about thirty yards beyond where the men were standing. Not long after, the first pigeon was loosed and promptly brought down by her father's bullet. In turn, each of the gentlemen took a shot, with Duran among the few who missed.

He missed his second shot as well, laughing when Sir Gareth offered the use of his spectacles. He made a show of assuming the proper stance on his third try. This time the pigeon fell. With a theatrical gesture of relief, he bowed to an enthusiastic round of applause.

"Well, then," said Lord Marley, who had awakened at the first shot. "I have won two hundred guineas and lost half of it back. The young man appears to be finding his range."

"You were betting on Lord Duran?"

"Against him. Nearly all the wagering is focused on Duran, him being a stranger and an erratic shot. He don't mind losing, though, I'll give him that much."

"Has he lost a great deal?"

"To be precise, he's missing, not losing. Says he foreswore gaming, but doesn't object if others use him for their own wagers. It's young Pageter who's playing deep. Owes me twelve hundred already, and the stakes will triple once the real shooting begins. There's gaming in the evenings as well, although I wouldn't bet against Duran at the whist table. Pageter's winning a little there, but not enough to cover his other losses."

She could hardly believe what she was hearing. John Pageter was the most serious-minded, upright man she had ever known. Of course he gambled—all gentlemen did—but never to excess. Not John. Something was wrong here.

Suddenly unable to watch any longer, she took leave of Lord Marley and set out for the house, hoping that Helena would arrive today with the bank drafts for her clients. That would provide the excuse she needed to leave High Tor and its most annoying resident.

The post had arrived, she saw by the orderly chaos in the entrance hall. Geeson was sorting the contents of the leather bag into neat piles and laying them out on a sideboard while footmen with chased-silver trays moved up and down the staircase, delivering letters to the guest rooms and quickly returning for another stack.

Smiling when she came up to him, Geeson handed her three letters, two from clients and one from her secretary, which she opened and read immediately. Helena's cold had worsened, but she expected to be well enough to travel before the end of the week. Lord Duran had stopped calling at the town house.

No surprise there. Jessica was scanning the last of Helena's message when Mariah, an open letter in her hand, slipped from the drawing room and walked unsteadily toward the staircase. Her face was pale as milk.

Jessica moved to intercept her. "What is it? Have you received bad news?"

Mariah gazed at her kidskin slippers. "No. Not really. But I shall have to leave for Dorset." The letter fluttered in her hand. "Do you suppose it would be acceptable for me to wait until morning? But there's no reason—is there?—since it won't be dark for hours and hours yet."

The foyer was no place to extract the reason for her distress. "Come with me," Jessica said, gripping her arm and towing her toward the rear passageway.

By the time they arrived at the one place in the house that was certain to be deserted, Mariah had begun to weep. "Why are we here?" she whimpered.

"Because I hate it here." Jessica unlatched the door and tugged her sister into the conservatory. And stopped as if she had slammed into an invisible wall. "God in heaven, Mariah. Did you do this?"

Brilliant sunlight streamed through clear glass panes, all of them intact. Directly ahead, the tiled floor gave way to gravel paths, a pair of them, each winding through a patchwork of lush green plants and bright flowers. Stunned, she released Mariah's arm to examine an herb garden filled with rosemary, feverfew, St. John's wort, and lavender.

Who could have done this? Not her father, who wouldn't know a turnip from his elbow.

Mariah was still standing by the door, her expression confused and miserable. "I didn't think you'd ever set foot in here, Jessica. Perhaps I should have told you. I had nothing to do with it, of course."

The accustomed, unwelcome impatience itched at Jessica's skin. "Never mind the conservatory," she said briskly. "What is in that letter?"

Mariah glanced down at her fisted hand and the paper crunched inside it. "A disappointment. Gerald wishes me to return to Dorset immediately. He doesn't say when he expects to arrive, but I am to be there when he does. So you see, I must set out this afternoon, in case he has already . . ." Her voice, faltering toward the end, faded altogether.

"Rubbish. Why must you scamper home because he has snapped his fingers? And I should be very much surprised if he has the least intention of joining you there. Not until matters are settled between us."

"Us? You and Gerald?"

"A question of business, that is all. I intend to put an end to his scheming. For now, simply write him back and say that it is not convenient for you to leave High Tor."   •

When there was no response, Jessica returned to the door where Mariah stood with tears streaming down her too-thin face. She made a helpless gesture, her eyes clouded with resignation. Jessica had seen that look before, in the eyes of a lamb caught in the boggy moorlands and slowly sinking to its death. Unable to reach it, she had watched until the ground closed over the lamb's small head. She had watched a horse die in the same fashion, and a dozen years ago, three escaped prisoners of war had been gulped up only a mile from the house. If you didn't know where to put your feet, Dartmoor could be lethal.

"It will be all right," Jessica managed to say, not at all sure how one went about giving comfort. After a moment, she wrapped an arm around her sister's waist and led her to a small bench. They sank on it together, their skirts billowing.

Long minutes passed. Jessica's arm grew numb. Then, abruptly, Mariah slid to the edge of the bench and dug into her pocket for a handkerchief. "G-Gerald doesn't like to be crossed," she said. "And I did promise, you know, to obey him."

"What of it?" Jessica waited until Mariah blew her nose. "A promise to the devil need not be kept. *Should* not be kept. Has he struck you?"

"Matters between a husband and wife," Mariah said after a pause, "must not be discussed with others."

"Yes, then. He beats you. He has, I know, spent all your dowry and sold everything of value, including your riding horse. Ginger. I remember her. You loved her. Do you love him?"

"What does it matter now?" Mariah clambered to her feet. "I am married to him. And truly, it is always best to do as he says."

Jessica swallowed her first several responses and carefully disciplined her tone. "You have received no letter. It won't arrive for several days, if at all. So you see, there is no reason to go home."

"You would have me *lie* to him? Oh, I could never do that. I am a terrible liar."

"Then leave it to me. We'll speak of this later, when I've had time to make plans. Promise you won't do anything foolish."

Mariah produced a watery laugh. "Do you know, Jessica, I believe I am more afraid of you than of Gerald."

She hadn't meant that to hurt, Jessica knew, but surprisingly, it did. Still, she would play the ogre if an ogre was required. She rose, wandered to a patch of lavender, and plucked a spike of blossoms. They were silvery with moisture. "You have not explained how the conservatory came to be restored. Come, walk with me."

"Oh, dear," said Mariah, catching her up near a table strewn with potted violets. "I dislike being the one to tell you. This is all the work of Mrs. Bellwood, a widow who lives near Ridington when she is not in residence here. For the past three years, she has been Papa's mistress."

The lavender snapped in Jessica's hand. "Oh, my. Have you met her?"

"Several times. I quite like her. Without raising the slightest fuss, she has brought order to the household.

The servants are sworn to secrecy about her existence, of course. You're not . . . that is, you don't object?"

"I think it's marvelous. But why isn't she here now?"

"That wouldn't be proper. Whenever Papa has guests, she returns to her cottage."

"Then you must take me there and introduce us. Perhaps tomorrow, when your eyes are not red and swollen. Why don't you place cucumber slices over the lids and have a nap before dinner? I can potter about here on my own."

Mariah, openly relieved to escape, sped to the door.

Jessica went slowly in the other direction, pausing to enjoy the small, neat plots of flowering plants marked out with smooth white stones. Deeper into the conservatory she discovered grapes and pineapples, artichokes, flats for winter cauliflowers, and rows of potted lemon and orange trees, shiny leaved and heavy with fruit.

When last she entered the conservatory, it had been all to rack and ruin. Her mother, after insisting it be expanded from a small orangery, had quickly lost interest in the project. Jessica remembered broken panes of glass, dead stumps where miniature trees had bloomed, and flourishing weeds crawling with insects. The open garden at the far end had become a pool of mud.

Now, looking ahead of her, she saw a graystone wall set with a wide door. It stood open, and she went through to an enclosed garden with a square marble pool at its center. Fish, golden and brindled and dove white, glided among the lily pads. There was an openworked pergola threaded with vines, and roses climbed the white trellises behind a pair of wrought-iron benches.

She sat on the lip of the fountain, which was no

more than a foot high, and dipped her hand into the cool water. The fish, side fins and tails whisking frantically, fled to the other side of the pool and huddled together in the shadows. Something new and strange had come into their world, bringing chaos. They didn't want her there.

No one wanted her, not really, and she didn't care. Not any longer. She had grown up a wild child in a rigid family that still considered her an embarrassment, and since taking residence in London, there had been no opportunity to develop friendships. Only with her capable secretary, Helena, and the sweet-natured Duke of Devonshire could she let down her guard. Perhaps that would change now that her business had staggered onto firmer ground.

In all likelihood, though, she would remain isolated. The ladies of her class viewed her with suspicion and the gentlemen, wedded or otherwise, regarded her as an opportunity waiting to be seized. Her every word and action was marked down, parsed, and pronounced upon by a bored and pitiless society. She felt, sometimes, as if she were closed up in an hourglass, her life sifting slowly away under the critical regard of strangers.

On occasion, and quite seriously, she had given thought to marrying for freedom. By the simple expedient of becoming a wife, she would acquire the gloss of respectability only a husband could provide, along with a degree of liberty that no single woman was permitted to enjoy. But in exchange for those privileges—

And that was where the imagined bargain always collapsed. She had only herself to barter, and could never decide which bits and pieces of Jessica Carville to put on offer.

Only a thin slice of her intelligence, to be sure.

Nearly every man she'd ever met was off-put by indications of a working mind inside her pretty little head.

Not a jot of her temper. They would flee like startled grouse.

They wouldn't like her humor, either, but these days it generally kept itself well concealed, even from herself. Duran used to—

She slapped her palm against the water, sending a spray over her skirts.

What had she been thinking of before he intruded? Oh, yes. Wedding a man willing to provide what she needed while demanding nothing in return. A man who would be satisfied to look upon her without touching. Perhaps a cit with social aspirations. Being the daughter of an earl ought to be of some use, should it not? And she required a man who would permit her to carry on her business and keep the money she earned for herself.

Really, she did not require a husband. Not for very long. She would do much better as a widow.

She stared into the pool, looking beyond her reflection to the fishes cowering among the ornamental grasses. Any one of them had more love in its little heart than she did. Six years ago, she had thrown all of hers into the wind.

Well, that was nothing to the point, was it? Her troubles were hers alone. And now, Mariah's troubles were hers as well. Some way must be found to separate the poor goose from her husband. Tonight, immediately after dinner, she would recruit her father's help. He'd always had a soft spot for Mariah, the obedient daughter who never ruffled the household waters.

Unlike his rebellious child, who was now wearing some of the household waters on her bodice and skirts. Across the pond, four carp eyed her morosely.

From the far end of the conservatory came the sound of a door opening and closing, followed by the crunch of leather on gravel as someone approached the garden. Her skin began to tingle. Moments later a tall, loose-limbed figure, altogether at ease, arrived at the entrance to the garden.

"I very much wish you had brought *me* a gun," she said.

Chuckling, Duran stepped into the courtyard and gave her an overly deferential bow. "Could you have hit me?"

"Oh, eventually. I would have kept trying until I did."

"Yes, well, if you have it in mind to kill me, I'm afraid you'll have to go to the end of the queue and wait your turn." His smile became diffident. "Are you angry with me for invading your home? You should have expected it. I warned you not to run away."

"Did you? I must not have been listening. And did you really expect me to salute and obey?"

After a startled look, he broke out laughing.

"I'm quite serious, Duran. You have no right—"

"I know, I know. And you're far too serious, my sweet, which is not at all how I remember you."

"Life is a serious matter, sir, although you do not appear to have noticed. It seems you have taken a vow of perpetual boyhood, with nothing more consequential to do with yourself than drink, game, and carouse with undiscriminating women."

"A boy could do worse. What would you say if I told you that I have been, for longer than I care to recall, chaste as a monk, peaceful as a Quaker, and sober as the Archbishop of Canterbury? Well, nearly so. And for all I know, the current archbishop tipples like an East India Company clerk. But you take my point."

"And don't believe a word of it. What is more," she said, pleased to hear the stern chord in her voice, "I care nothing for how you choose to behave, so long as your frivolities don't include me."

"Ah." Head tilted, eyes a trifle narrowed, he regarded her from top to toe. "I have been mistaken. What with the advertisement in the news rags and your presence at the auction house, I had assumed you to be precisely what I am looking for—an expert in the business of art and antiquities. But now, and I am sorry for it, I see that you are instead the headmistress of the Academy for Young Women with Pokers Up Their Backsides."

Astonished and hurt, she nearly toppled into the fishpond. At the same time, she wanted to launch herself at him with fingernails extended. Except that they were clipped short, and what he had said was appallingly close to the truth.

He had meant to pry her off her moral high horse, and by God, he had succeeded. Jessica Carville, spouting moralistic platitudes. Whom had she imagined she was fooling? Not Duran, who knew all too well her rebellious spirit and restless, passion-hungry flesh. What secrets could she withhold from him now? Tears burned at the corners of her eyes.

A boot, lightly dusted after a morning in the fields, appeared next to her hip. She regarded it for a few moments, willing the tears to evaporate.

"Ought I to grovel for your pardon?" he asked, not sounding in the least like a man on the verge of groveling.

"No. I was insufferable. I deserved a blistering set-down."

He leaned forward, arm on knee, until his head was nearly even with hers. "Jessie, if I hadn't spoken as I did, we would have continued crossing swords to no purpose save the exercise of our wits. I need your help. And because you have set yourself to resist me, I fired a broadside. It was, I believe, a necessary tactic."

"Oh, good heavens, Duran. Have done with the military metaphors." The man would tie her in knots if ever she let him get hold of her at both ends. "Everything you do is calculated for effect. Even your insults come bearing plots. How have you suborned poor John Pageter, I wonder? How do you even *know* him?"

"When the ship reprovisioned at Capetown, the colonel was among the new passengers who came aboard." The lines at his temples crinkled with amusement. "As I understand it, he narrowly escaped being leg-shackled to you. The poor frightened fellow ran all the way to Africa."

"Only so far as Africa? I must be losing my touch." She produced a chilly smile. "*You* ran all the way to India."

"And even there I could not escape you," he said after a moment. "But I was joking about Pageter. He told me your mother had been promoting a match that neither of you wished, although he much admired you. I believe he was in love with someone else at the time, but the lady was not in a position to return his affections. He left to avoid causing her pain."

"A common excuse, I believe, when a man does not wish to marry a woman he has dallied with."

"Ah. Now you are talking about me, Jessie. About us. Are you certain that you wish to?"

"What I wish, of course, is to be rid of you." It was true. Her pulse raced. Her throat was dry. All the familiar, unwanted symptoms of exposure to Hugo Duran. "You have made use of a perfectly nice man to insinuate yourself into this house, where you bribed my father to make you welcome. Your purpose cannot be honorable."

"That is not a word, I agree, generally linked to my name. But perhaps you should reserve judgment until you have heard what my purpose is." He hadn't moved, that she'd noticed, nor had she, but he seemed a great deal closer. "Is it so much to ask, a few minutes of your time and a chance to explain?"

She studied the ground. With Duran, nothing was that simple. To give him the slightest opening was to invite an invasion. She had made herself vulnerable to him once, and he had hurt her. But she took responsibility for that. She had not meant to care for him, or even known that she did, until he left her. It had been a devastating surprise.

And in all fairness, how could he have known her feelings, if she did not?

"Humility does not suit you," she said finally. "You do not ask, however soft your voice. You *demand*. And if that fails, you deceive. But pray get on with it, sir, so that I may decline to do whatever it is you want of me."

"Well, I would," he said in a friendly voice, "but your father expects me to join him for a trial of his new gun. Shall we speak after supper? And in the meantime, my dear, see if you can do something about that grudge you are carrying."

Pride stiffened her back. "I have no idea what you mean."

"No?" He looked sorrowful. "You never used to lie."

"I had a good teacher."

"Then I have more to regret than I had thought." He stepped away and bowed. "Tonight, Jessica. Do not fail me."

Chapter 6

The day was already turning hot. Duran, on his way to the shooting ground, longed to strip off his jacket, but Sothingdon observed strictest propriety in matters of sport. Rigid formality would surround even this late-morning exercise.

He had been told that only the younger men—those on the morning side of sixty, he supposed—would take part in the target shooting. By his standards, that made what he intended to do a trifle less reprehensible.

John Pageter, waving a greeting, fell in step with him not far from the house.

"Prepare yourself," Duran said. "I feel a bout of exceptional accuracy coming on."

"This would be the time for it," Pageter agreed, his freckled face serene under the wide-brimmed hat he wore. "I shall try not to appear smug when I rake in your winnings. Will you lose most of it back tonight at the whist table?"

"I won't be there. Which reminds me. When I vanish after dinner, devise some excuse for me."

A lifted brow was Pageter's only response.

Duran regarded him for a moment before returning his gaze to the path. A man of few questions, Colonel Lord Pageter, and even fewer answers. After several months on ship in his company, Duran had decided that behind all that stalwart British calm lay a deep reservoir of more stalwart British calm. All of it grounded, marrow deep, in traditional British honor, the sort most men proclaimed and neglected to practice.

Pageter was the genuine article, a solid, pleasant-faced gentleman you'd want at your back in a fight, which made his complicity in these money-raising ploys something of a mystery. Duran, an expert on the subject, had yet to detect a trace of larceny in the fellow's character. Unfortunate, that. He'd prefer to be making use of a less virtuous man.

Not that Pageter failed to know the score. Duran had told him as much about the nizam and the leopard as he was likely to believe, and with his usual composure, Pageter had accepted it straightaway.

"Odd chaps, some of these native rulers," he'd said, going on to offer whatever assistance Duran required, so long as he wasn't expected to commit an actual crime or help do away with Shivaji and his associates.

Now, his schemes smoothly in play, Duran found himself pricked by needles of conscience. "I will pay you back," he said into the companionable silence.

"I've no doubt of it. The hope of repayment is what inspires me to see that you escape."

And if I don't? The unspoken question hung in the air, deliberately ignored by them both.

"It will take time," Duran advised him. "Years, probably."

"I don't mind. There is little I want, and where I spent the past few years, there was even less to buy. I can well afford to advance you a stake. And if your gaming fails to scrape up the funds you require, I shall procure passage for you to . . . Where is it you plan to scarper?"

"Brazil, I think. Or Peru."

They had paused, as if by common agreement, in the shelter of a copse not far from their destination. For the most part they kept distance between them, to avoid suspicion of complicity in precisely the sort of scam they were running. Being compelled to share a suite of rooms had been a setback, but none of the other guests appeared to have noticed.

In the shadows, a lone bird chirping overhead, Duran seized the chance to ask a question he would not, in the usual course of things, even think of asking. "Why are you doing this, John?"

Smiling, Pageter looked directly into his eyes. "There is someone I care about. When first I met her, she was beset with difficulties, but I could do nothing for her. Nor can I now, these many years later, although her troubles have multiplied."

"Jessica?"

"Jessica as well, I suppose, in her way. But I was speaking of another woman. And that is all I will say of her, because truly, I cannot be of service to her now. Which is why I offer to you what help I can. One must keep the waters stirred, you see."

Duran had the feeling he ought to know what Pageter was talking about. He knew damned well he should let it go. But of late, he hadn't always been feeling and acting like himself. Something was chipping away at who he had always been, as if trying to carve a decent man from a scoundrel. "Which waters would those be?"

"What?" Pageter must have been lost in his own private thoughts. "Oh, I was referring to the pool at Bethesda. In the Bible, one of the Gospels, I think. People with ailments gathered there, hoping for a miracle. And sure enough, now and again an angel would come down and stir the waters. The first person to dive in was cured. Something of the sort. I ought to spend more time with the scriptures."

His freckles, bronze on flushed skin, grew darker with his obvious embarrassment. "The thing is, I cannot be of help to the one I would give my life for. She is unable to make her way into the healing waters. But best as I can, I mean to keep them stirred for others to take advantage of. In this case you, and after you, someone else."

If possible, Duran was even more embarrassed than the man standing opposite him. He understood what Pageter was saying, though. No one could live thirty-four years in India without becoming conscious of endless circles whirling about one's ears. What passes one on the right side invariably comes about again on the left. Like, yes, stirred waters.

"I don't imagine," he ventured, "that *I* could do something for your . . . friend?"

There was a brief hesitation before Pageter spoke. "No," he said. "Nothing."

Duran knew it for a lie. "Well, if you think of something, let me know. Unlike some, I've no objection to the occasional high crime or misdemeanor."

As if regretting the confidence he'd shared, Pageter resumed walking. "In that case," he said just as they were emerging from the copse, "I wonder that you have not eliminated your troublesome valet."

"Believe me," Duran said, spotting Shivaji standing in his usual place overlooking the shooting field, "I think of little else."

When Duran returned, considerably wealthier after a remarkable demonstration of target shooting, Shivaji was waiting for him in the bedchamber.

"We shall return to London in the morning," he

said, his dark eyes uncommonly stern. "You will inform your host of our departure."

Duran, at the bootjack, smothered his initial reaction and took his time removing the second boot. "I haven't finished here," he said. "It may not appear the case, but I *am* making progress."

"I have seen none."

"If you required a daily report, you should have said so. For one thing, I have asked Sir Fenster Barber how to trace the relations of a gentleman who died last year in India, a friend who supposedly gave me letters and parcels to deliver. That would be our thief, or course. Sir Fenster has written to his solicitors, instructing them to conduct an investigation."

"To what purpose? We are not certain of his true name. And do you imagine the thief dispatched the leopard to his family by common post?"

"Well, we've no idea what he'd been up to, given that he was dead when you found him. It's *your* bloody theory the leopard made its way to England."

"But not to this estate, where you take holiday."

"On the contrary. I'm laboring like bloody Hercules. Winning the cooperation of a stubborn female is all twelve tasks rolled into one."

"I do not believe the lady looks kindly upon you. What will induce her to assist us?"

"My charm? No, she's got herself immune to that. But her curiosity will snare her in the end. It would be easier if I knew of something she wanted in return, but nothing has disclosed itself."

"It is apparent to me, Duran-Sahib, that she wishes for you to take yourself away."

Grinning, Duran peeled off his shooting jacket and tossed it on a chair. "I made a rather abrupt departure several years ago, and she hasn't quite forgiven me the manner of it. The last thing I want is to repeat that mistake, which—may I point out?—is precisely what you have in mind for me to do. This is a delicate matter. I need more time."

"You have tonight," came the uncompromising reply.

"In that case, you should apply to your gods for a miracle. The lady has agreed to meet me after dinner, but I cannot simply pounce upon her with my request. Jessica is a creature of flight. One does not snatch a falcon from the sky, dear fellow. One offers the lure and hopes she will deign to accept it."

Chapter 7

It had required a surprising degree of courage for Jessica to request a meeting with her father. In the Sothingdon household, personal matters—save for births, marriages, and deaths, which could hardly be overlooked—were never discussed. And until now, having no desire to enmesh herself in the affairs of her family, she had been a willing participant in the conspiracy of silence.

She was reluctant still, but since Mariah would do nothing to help herself, someone had to take up the spear. As his debts mounted, Gerald was becoming ever more erratic and brutal. He had been rescued ten years ago from determined creditors by the wedding settlement Mariah brought him, and in his current situation, Jessica wouldn't put it past him to consider a similar ploy. The first stage would be to eliminate his now-inconvenient wife.

Gerald was of only moderate intelligence, but he had always been cunning and resourceful. She did not underestimate the difficulties that lay ahead.

She had been pacing in the study nearly an hour before her father, his round cheeks flushed after several glasses of port, entered with unconcealed distaste and took his seat behind the heavy oak desk.

"Come, my dear," he said, regarding her with the

expression of a hare pinned in the sights of a rifle. "Tell me quickly what is on your mind. I do not mean to put you off, but the whist game cannot get underway without me."

When confronted with an unpleasant situation, men invariably provided themselves with an escape route. Forcing a smile, Jessica dropped onto a chair across from him. "Then let us come directly to the target. I wish you to help Mariah secure a legal separation from Sir Gerald."

Sothingdon slammed his palms on the desk. "A separation? Have you run mad?"

"It should not be difficult, so long as Mariah is supported by her family and receives the backing of your influential friends."

"But she has said nothing of this. Whatever put such an idea into your head?"

"She requires protection. Gerald beats her."

"Does he, by God?" Sothingdon lapsed back onto his chair. "For what reason?"

"Reason?" She took a long, calming breath. "What reason could there possibly be? Mariah is meek as a lamb. She would never provoke him. He needs to punish someone for his own failures, I expect. And he has a frightful temper. One day he'll lose all control."

Looking stunned, the earl pulled out his handkerchief and used it to blot his face. Briefly, his eyes were concealed from her. But when he removed the damp square of linen, she saw the blank expression she recognized from her childhood. In a matter of seconds, he had detached himself from the web of unpleasantness and responsibility.

But what had she expected? She met his eyes, saying nothing, until his gaze slid away.

"I shall speak to Gerald," he murmured, "if you

think it will do any good. Beyond that, I cannot interfere. Nor, I am sure, will the courts meddle with the legal right of a husband to discipline his wife. Unless there are other grounds on which a separation might be obtained?"

"There might be. I don't know. We require legal advice."

"No, Jessica. No wretched lawyers poking about and asking impertinent questions of the servants and neighbors. I would return the same answer to Mariah, were she here to speak for herself. But Mariah knows better than to embroil the family in a scandal. Only *you* would consider dragging us through the courts and exposing us to scurrilous reports in the newspapers. And all to no purpose, I must add. Sir Gerald would surely prevail."

"Gerald is a rotter. Everyone in London knows it. If the Carvilles stood against him, he wouldn't have a chance. How can you think of abandoning her, Father? She's your firstborn child. Don't you care what happens to her?"

There was a silence.

"Of course I care," he said at last, unconvincingly. "But I must also weigh the consequences of taking action. Not those that would fall upon me, I assure you, for I am too old to be concerned about my own reputation. And you have long since abandoned any care for yours." His face was the color of ripe plums. "A Carville, a daughter of the Earl of Sothingdon, in *trade*! But have I tried to stop you, Jessica? Have I?"

He had diverted the subject. She had to steer it back on course.

But hell was descending. She rubbed her left hand against the arm of the chair, barely able to feel her fingers. The candles on the desk were brighter than before. Their flames, haloed with orange and green, danced like maenads in the hot, airless room.

"Indeed," her father was saying, "I have given you everything you asked. A London Season after the year of mourning for your mother. An allowance. A *generous* allowance, and a carriage and horses, and I pay for their stabling as well. You have the use of my town house, and did I not lend you three thousand pounds not so long ago?"

"S-several years ago, Father, and it has been repaid with interest." This had to end quickly, before she disgraced herself. And she had accomplished nothing. Nothing. "You have been generous, yes. If you believe me indebted to you, by all means send an accounting. If you want me out of the town house, I'll find other lodgings. But this conversation, Father, is not about me. Mariah must not suffer for my failings."

He had begun to wring his damp handkerchief between his hands. They were callused fingers, long and thick, on a sportsman's hands. Hands that trembled. "You must consider how a scandal would affect Aubrey," he said. "As the fourteenth Earl of Sothingdon, I am custodian of an honorable name. It must be passed unblemished to my heir, and to his. That is what he expects. It is his right."

"Rubbish. Aubrey has an inflated sense of his own importance. He was born with"—Duran's words sprang to her tongue—"with a poker up his backside."

"Jessica!"

"Well, he was. And I fail to see why Mariah must be sacrificed on the altar of Aubrey's scrupulous sensibilities."

"There are his children to consider as well, and his wife. You may have evaded responsibility for anyone but yourself, but others cannot so easily ignore what

is due to one's name and family. I am certain Mariah
does not. Marriage is a lifelong commitment. It cannot
be revoked simply because she now finds the circumstances unsatisfactory. One makes promises before
God and the law, accepts one's responsibilities, and
endures. There is no other honorable choice."

He was speaking now of his own marriage, she realized with a stab of sympathy. How could she have
imagined he would help? Year after year he had compromised, and accepted, and endured. His imagination
did not encompass an alternative.

Yellow and blue-green, the light condensed into a
zigzag pattern. She could scarcely see him now. It
would come and go by its own timetable, she knew,
but closing her eyes, she willed the vision to fade.
Above all things, her father must not know what
was happening.

"If Gerald comes for her," she said, "will you at
least try to keep Mariah here, under your protection?"

"Certainly." The earl sounded relieved to have
something positive to offer. "I'll tell him she is acting
as my hostess and that I require her to remain for
several weeks. But I cannot overrule him. As Mariah's
husband, it is his right to determine where she
resides."

"I know." In her voice she heard the anger she was
trying to repress. It had been a mistake to approach
her father. He was the last man who would exert himself to rescue a daughter embroiled in an unhappy
marriage. "You'll wish to join your friends," she said
more calmly. "Please go on without me."

He all but kicked over his chair in his haste to depart. She winced. Even slight sounds would pain her
now, and bright lights. Words were increasingly hard
to form. It was coming on quickly.

Opening her eyes, she saw only a dark tunnel coruscated with green light. She dared not navigate the crowded passageway, nor take the chance of meeting Duran. She could not speak with him tonight.

The servants' stairs, then. If she could find the entrance door.

Wreathed in cigar smoke, Duran sipped at a glass of excellent port, parried jokes with automatic good humor, and tried not to look at the mantelpiece clock. Unlike his host, he was finding it difficult to escape the dinner table.

Sothingdon, after receiving a message from a servant, had departed as soon as the covers were removed, leaving his guests to their analysis of Lord Duran's mystifying accuracy on the target range that afternoon.

"Not so astonishing, I assure you," he said when Marley demanded an accounting of his transformation. "I was finally allowed to shoot at something that didn't move."

"I'll wager your luck won't hold when the partridges are flushed," Benneton put in, his nose ruddy with sunburn.

"I profoundly hope you're wrong," Duran said, coming to his feet. "Luck is all I have to rely upon. Anyone for coffee?"

But Jessica, to his disappointment, was not waiting for him in the parlor. He had expected to find her in company with her sister. Accepting a cup of coffee from Lady Mariah, he carried it with him on a search of the public rooms on the first floor, rejecting invitations to make a fourth at whist or take a stick at the billiard table and wondering where the devil Jessica had got off to.

After a while he made his way downstairs, passing a florid-faced Sothingdon going in the opposite direction. The earl, his eyes fixed on the marble stairs, didn't appear to notice him.

He was considering this uncharacteristic behavior as he made his way toward the back of the house and the conservatory, where he had found Jessica that morning. Perhaps she was waiting for him there. He was just passing the library and the earl's study when, a little distance down the passageway, a swirl of sapphire blue disappeared into the wall.

The illusion was explained when, drawing closer, he saw the outline of a servants' door. But servants didn't wear expensive taffeta or scent themselves with lilac water. Not wanting it to seem he had been following her, he returned to the main staircase and hurried to the third floor, arriving in time to see Jessica emerge from the wall and move slowly toward her room at the far end of the wing.

She was walking as though putting the slightest weight on the floor would crush it. Once she paused with one hand pressed against the wall for support. He started to approach her, but halted when she slowly continued to her room and went inside.

Moments later a maid, shaking her head, came out and, with a curtsy to Duran, went on about her business.

Something was wrong, although he couldn't begin to guess what it was. Not for a minute did he imagine that Jessica, having agreed to meet with him, had changed her mind. Were that the case, she would have told him so with a flourish. Stepping into the shadows of an alcove, he waited several minutes, considering his alternatives.

They narrowed into one. And it wasn't, he thought, striding purposefully down the passageway, as if she expected him to have any manners.

A gentleman would have knocked. No, a gentleman

would not be seeking admittance to her bedchamber at all.

Duran, being a gentleman only when it suited him, raised the old-fashioned brass latch handle and, pleased to find she had not secured the lock, stealthily opened the door.

Chapter 8

One candle, set on a dressing table, cast a small circle of light on the far side of the bedchamber. Beyond it, silhouetted against the windows, Jessica was slowly closing the curtains.

Duran cushioned the latch bar with his thumb so that it dropped soundlessly into place.

She must have sensed his presence. Letting go the curtain, she turned.

Even from across the room, he saw the strained look at her lips and around her eyes. The effort it required to hold herself straight. "My manners are inexcusable," he said into the taut silence. "But we had an appointment, Jessie, and you would not have broken it without reason. I'll not leave here until you tell me why."

Although he was speaking quietly, she had flinched at his first word. He watched her draw two deep breaths, and another.

"I cannot meet with you tonight," she murmured. "Tomorrow, perhaps. Please go."

He moved closer, stopping when she lifted a hand. "You didn't answer my question."

"It's nothing. A headache. But sound makes it worse, and light. After a night's sleep I shall be perfectly fine."

He wasn't sure he believed her, but only a cad would make a point of it. "As you wish, princess. I'll send Lady Mariah to—"

"Don't. Please. No one must know."

"Your maid, then, or whomever else you name. I will not leave you here alone, so make a choice."

She lowered her head, squeezing out the words one by one. "You, I suppose. Just long enough to help me with my gown."

Remembering how she used to command him, urgently, to disrobe her, he crossed to where she stood and began slipping the pearl-shaped buttons at her nape from their loops. His fingertips felt numb.

Head bowed, she stood perfectly still when he reached inside her bodice to unloose the tapes attaching it to her waistband. In a whisper of satin, the skirt pooled at her feet.

Next he removed the bodice, carefully tugging the puffy sleeves down her arms. Once, when his hand brushed her bare shoulder, she made a tiny sound of pain.

His heart was pounding like the feet of elephants on a dry Deccan riverbed. The simplest touch hurt her. More than once, more than a score of times in the aftermath of battle, he had held a dying comrade in his arms. He had schooled himself to feel nothing. To feel was to lose control of himself, and what good was he then?

Closing his mind to what he was doing, he stripped her with practiced efficiency. When an underslip of soft muslin had joined her skirt on the carpet, he untied the bow on her corset and unwrapped the laces from their hooks. She hadn't used to wear a corset. The Jessica he remembered could never bear to be confined.

She hadn't played by the rules, either. Not so many

years ago, defying every convention, she had leaped into an affair with a man far beneath her in birth, breeding, and fortune. He still wondered why.

Obviously she had come to regret it. And rightly so.

A short time later, clad only in stockings and a filmy shift, she placed her hand on his for support and stepped away from the mound of fabric ringing her ankles.

His hand burned where she touched him, all too briefly, before she let go and moved slowly toward the bed. He felt the effort it cost her, that silent pilgrimage, and knew better than to offer assistance. The single candle carved her out in ivory against the long black shadow she cast on the wall.

Helplessly, he watched her lower herself on the edge of the tall bed and begin to remove her stockings. That much intimacy, he understood, was forbidden him.

So be it. But if she thought he'd walk away from her now, she was about to learn otherwise. Approaching her from the opposite side of the bed, he spoke in the softest tone he could produce. "I'm going to draw down the bedcovers and arrange the pillows for you. Then I'll leave, but only for a short time."

She looked over her shoulder at him in alarm.

"If you lock the door while I'm gone, I'll direct your father to send for a physician. Probably I should do so in any case. But I mean to try something else first, and it will not require me to betray your secret." That was a lie, but only a small one. "Is there anything I can bring you when I return?"

For a time he thought she wasn't going to answer. The bed readied and the pillows fluffed, he was on his way out when he heard a sound—one word—coming from the bed. She had accepted his intention to return.

"Yes," he said. "I'll bring ice."

Next door, in the small parlor that linked the two bedchambers assigned to Lords Pageter and Duran, Arjuna was cleaning and oiling their guns. Duran gestured him to continue and proceeded quickly to the dressing room where Shivaji sat cross-legged on the floor, eyes closed and hands resting, palms upturned, on his knees.

Only his lips moved when he spoke. "The lady has agreed to assist us?"

Duran required a few seconds to decipher the question. "I—no. We hadn't a chance to discuss it. She is ill with a headache."

"A common excuse, I believe, when a female does not wish to cooperate." Shivaji rose in a single, fluid motion. "We shall walk no farther on this false trail. You will prepare to depart in the early morning."

"Aren't you listening?" Duran seized a handful of Shivaji's tunic. "She's *ill*. Everything hurts her. Sound. Light. She can't bear to be touched. Look, there must be something in your demon's closet to help her. Laudanum?"

Shivaji studied him for several moments, as if seeking something in his face. "Is the pain concentrated on one side of her head?"

Duran tried to remember how she had looked. What she had said. "I don't know," he admitted, releasing his grip and taking a step back. "Is that significant?"

"It is usually the case. I suspect she suffers from a type of severe, recurring headache that generally afflicts women, although I have an uncle who experiences them regularly." Shivaji went to the wooden cabinet, which was set on a small table in the corner of the dressing room, and began removing vials and packets from the drawers. "There is no remedy. In safe amounts laudanum is ineffective, and it can create a harmful dependency. Will the Lady Jessica permit me to examine her?"

"She doesn't want anyone to know. I insisted on keeping watch. She asked for ice."

"Very well. I shall prepare a draught of lavender tea infused with cloves and feverfew, and brew a tea with ginger root that should be given her if she is nauseated. Since you are to sit with her, perhaps you will wish to change your clothing. Do so while I send Arjuna to procure what is required. Then I shall tell you what to expect and how to deal with it."

Half an hour later, a cyclone of instructions whirling in his head, Duran reentered Jessica's darkened bedchamber with a large tray carefully balanced between two shaking hands. On it were a pair of teapots, a glass and a cup, a small silver bucket filled with ice, another brimming with hot water, a pile of linen napkins and towels, and three basins stacked one on top of the other. Arjuna would be sent at intervals to replenish the supplies.

"Sleep is best," Shivaji had advised several times. "Never disturb her when she sleeps, and do not be so busy trying to help that you keep her awake."

She wasn't sleeping now. Duran set the tray on a table near the door, moved the lone candle to a spot on the mantelpiece where its light did not reach the bed, and approached her on stockinged feet. "Can you swallow some lukewarm tea? It's made with herbs that may dull the pain a bit. I have ice, if you prefer. But I'm told it's best to wrap the ice in towels and—"

When she winced he clamped his lips together, mentally kicking himself.

At the corners, her mouth curved. "Tea," she said on a puff of air.

Relief made him clumsy, but he managed to fill the

cup and carry it to the bed without spilling more than half the contents. She had struggled upright. He put one hand at her back to hold her while she drank, a fragrance of lavender and cloves wafting from the cup and mingling with the delicate lilac scent she favored.

Her hair was pinned in coils. When she had emptied the cup he set it aside and, still holding her, began gently to remove the pins with his other hand. She leaned forward to make it easier. While he dealt with the side closest to him she experienced no difficulty, but when he touched the right side of her head, a cry escaped her.

Instantly he stopped, his hand hovering above her.

"It will feel better," she whispered, "when the pins are out."

Removing them was agonizing for her, he could tell, but she made no sound as one by one they slid free and her long, heavy hair spread around her shoulders. He banked pillows behind her—Shivaji had suggested that—and gave her a second cup of the tea. She drank most of it before turning her head away.

Dismissing him. He sensed her withdrawing into herself and understood that she was now to be left alone.

He withdrew as well, to finish closing the curtains. Then he slumped onto a hard-backed chair and sat with his elbows propped on his knees and his face buried in his hands. He couldn't bear seeing her like this. Not Jessica, who had always charted her own course and commanded the elements like a goddess. At least that was the impression she had given him during the short time they spent together.

Had he left the party a few minutes earlier, they would never have met at all. It was supposed to have been his last night in London, and he'd stopped by Lady Somebody's ball on a hunt for several gentlemen who owed him money. Meandering from room to room, he neatly cornered his prey and accepted whatever they were carrying—banknotes, rings, pocket watches—to cover their gaming debts. Naturally he couldn't let it be known that he was departing on an India trader the very next morning. They'd never have paid up.

His voyage to England, a dream he was unaware he'd had until the opportunity presented itself, had come to nothing in the end. His expectations had been too high, perhaps, and the reality too bloody realistic.

His very distant cousin Bertram, eleventh Baron Duran, turned out to have been a successful drunkard and a dismal gambler before tripping over one of his wife's lapdogs and tumbling down a flight of stairs. He left behind him a mountain of debts, a bad-tempered wife, two ill-favored daughters, and a besmirched title that, in the absence of any closer male relation, had devolved upon an astonished Hugo Duran. The agent who finally located him in Calcutta had conveyed the news without mentioning the debts and the daughters.

Down on his luck at the time, Duran had quite fancied the notion of assuming his new position. Within a week he'd sold his small house and his string of excellent horses and set out for his ancestral home.

Six months later, gazing on the derelict house and weedy gardens, he bade farewell to that most treacherous of whores—hope.

The property was not entailed, and the owner of a nearby estate, eager to expand his holdings, paid a decent price for Duran's inheritance. He ought to have pocketed the money and hared straightaway back to India, where he might have lived in style for several years. But for reasons that still eluded him, he had paid his cousin's debts and made generous provisions for the two unlovely daughters, who thanked him by demanding he provide them husbands as well. That meant extravagant dowries, and there went the last of his money.

Or nearly the last, because he had set aside the fare to India and a few hundred pounds for a London holiday. The Season was in full swing, the viscount to whom he'd sold his property had offered to sponsor him, and for several weeks he cut a dash at all the best places.

England suited him. He even liked the climate. But far too soon he was attending his last party and making a final circuit of the ballroom when he saw, gazing at him from a pair of wide, curious eyes, a stunningly beautiful young woman.

There was no accounting for his dizzying suspicion that his life had just unalterably changed.

As it turned out, only the next three weeks were affected. He'd paid a substantial penalty to secure passage on a later sailing and spent his days gambling for funds to keep himself afloat in the meantime. His nights had been spent with Lady Jessica Carville.

A small sound cut into his reflections, and the bedchamber door opened to admit Shivaji with a trayful of fresh supplies. He set it on the table and stood for a considerable time looking down at the still, pale figure on the bed. Then he beckoned Duran into the passageway.

"The pain increases," he said. "She grows restless. Soon she will awaken, and then you may wrap cloths dipped in warm water around her wrists and ankles to draw the blood from her head. The packets of crushed ice should be placed on her forehead, temples, or at the back of her neck—but only if she wishes. The pain, as I expect you have realized, is on the right side. If she allows it, you should massage these points." Shivaji lifted his hands and applied pressure to Duran's temples, a point between his eyes, and various places on his scalp. "Let her guide you," he cautioned. "And remain near her with a basin. She will be sick."

His chest aching as if something inside were straining to get out, Duran returned to the chair at Jessica's bedside and resumed his vigil.

Not long after, she began to choke.

He was there in a heartbeat, supporting her with one hand and holding a basin with the other while she retched uncontrollably. When the spasms calmed he fed her cool ginger tea with a spoon, dabbed her chin with a soft napkin, and watched her sag back onto the pillows with a hushed moan.

He had scarcely put the soiled basin aside and taken hold of a clean one when the cycle began again. For what felt like a month in purgatory, he struggled to discern what she needed and to provide it. Nearly always he was guessing what to do, sure he'd muddle it up, wondering if he ought to bring in Shivaji to help. Jessica deserved better than a fumbling, flustered amateur.

But at other times, he felt a strange communion with her. Without direction he somehow knew to rub her temple just so, or where to place the cloth-wrapped ice, or when to do nothing at all.

In the heat, he had stripped down to his shirtsleeves. Sweat plastered the cambric against his skin and glued his hair to his scalp. Dropping onto the chair after a particularly rough bout with Jessie's nausea, he watched until she began to relax against the sheets.

Sleep, he whispered. It was a prayer.

After a time, when her breathing was soft and even, he dragged his gaze from her face and looked toward the only source of light in the room. On the mantel-piece, the lone candle burned steadily, a beacon in the dark.

A lantern against a black sky. He blinked, but the apparition—the memory—failed to dissolve.

A cold shiver passed through his body. Once before, on another harrowing night, he had watched a single light emerge from the darkness, bringing with it, he had been sure, his salvation.

He'd been a prisoner then, as he was now. But the *Bombay Caravan* had been a floating cage, and at sea, escape was out of the question. He had all but re-signed himself to six months of incarceration when a storm drove the ship perilously close to the Madagas-car coast. After a night's battle the seamen fought free and the ship, heading south, was near to rounding the island when the driving rain sputtered and then ceased altogether. Within an hour the swells had smoothed, the clouds had blown clear, and like a snuffed candle, the wind abruptly died.

For nearly a week the becalmed ship lay anchored within sight of the coast, the shrouds hanging limp from the yardarms. Seamen and passengers passed the time with eyes uplifted, watching for a breeze to stir the canvas.

All but Hugo Duran, who prowled the decks with the scent of land curling in his nostrils. Now and again he leaned against the rail, his gaze arrowed on the shoreline, a featureless green smear suspended be-tween the indigo sea and the hazy blue sky. At this latitude humidity blurred everything—destination, dis-tance, and above all, reason.

Only a mile away, he kept thinking. An easy target for a strong swimmer. He need only reach the water undetected.

Easier said than done, with Shivaji never far away.

But even his relentless jailer slept on occasion, and their neighbors in the aft section of the trader, a hard-drinking lot of former Company soldiers, usually made enough noise to cover a surreptitious exit from the tiny cabin. He often stole out late at night to stand, half naked in the cooling breeze, staring up at the winking stars. Shivaji was used to him going. He wouldn't suspect a thing.

Although the return of the wind would scotch his chances, Duran cautiously bided his time until the eighth night. In part he was waiting for the new moon, but that proved unnecessary when high, rainless clouds congealed overhead, obscuring even the stars. Well after midnight, when the bored watch had gathered at the poop for a light meal of cold roasted potatoes and tea, he made his way to the foredeck, climbed over the rail, handed himself along one of the taut anchor chains, and slipped into the bath-warm water. Ducking, he swam steadily beneath the surface, lifting his head only to steal an occasional gulp of air until he was well beyond the canopy of light cast by the ship's lanterns. Then he struck out full speed for shore.

At first navigation was simple. So long as the ship was at his back, the coast had to be straight ahead. Occasionally he looked over his shoulder, checking his position, puzzled because the ship appeared to be drifting sideways.

When he had been in the water about twenty minutes, he paused to take stock of his situation. By this time he ought to be well out of sight of the ship. Instead, like a dandelion puff against black velvet, the golden light of the ship's lanterns were still visible. Only now, instead of being behind him, they shone almost directly to his right.

Panic seized him. Fighting it off, he made himself vertical and let himself sink. If he was close to shore, and he bloody well ought to be, the land would be sloping upward.

But it was a long time—a very long time—before his feet touched ground.

There at sea bottom, he realized what had gone wrong. For the brief moments his toes were in contact, he felt them scraping along sand-scoured rock. A current, damn it, and a strong one. All this time, inexorably, it had been carrying him parallel to the shoreline.

Disoriented, he hung limp as seaweed in the soothing seawater, yielding to its dark seduction. He had cast the dice, as he had done at the nizam's court, gambling for his life on a single throw. This time, it appeared he had lost.

But what did it matter? He had no family, his friends were widely scattered, and his reputation was shot to hell. Who would miss him?

Well, *he* would. However brutal his life, however lonely, he wanted more of it. Half a century at least, if only to drink good cognac and watch the sun go down.

Kicking hard against the stony ledge, he shot upward like a flare and reached the surface with just enough strength to suck in a lungful of air.

Going down had been a mistake, but coming up did not noticeably improve his situation. The fuzzy ball of light that marked the position of the ship was his only point of reference, but it was significantly dimmer now. Treading water, he watched the ship float slowly away.

It wasn't moving, of course. Lifting his hand, he reaffirmed there was not the slightest breath of wind. Only air, he thought, air pressing down on him, laden with moisture and nearly as heavy as the water beneath.

The current had him firmly in its grip, sweeping him

alongside the island and away from the ship. Swimming at a right angle to it, as he had been doing, ought to have broken him free. But something, perhaps the contours of the land beneath him, perhaps a confluence of warm and cool water in this particular place, had created a lethal trick of nature.

Madagascar was out of his reach.

There was only one chance now. Turning, putting the glimmer of ship's lights to his left, he swam with determined strokes for the open sea. Some currents were narrow, he knew, and weaker at one side. If he managed to get loose without exhausting himself, he could make his way, chastened and resigned, back to his prison.

But his energy was waning far sooner than he would have guessed. The long months of imprisonment in Alanabad must have weakened him. The warm water leached his strength like a lover.

He forced himself to concentrate. Without a landmark for positioning, not even a star in sight, he couldn't tell if he was making progress. And even if he broke free of the current, what then? Cut off from the shore, the ship perhaps miles to his left, the open ocean ahead of him, and to his right—well, if he'd wanted to go in that direction, he might as well have traveled along with the current. It was getting wherever it was going faster than he could swim.

For a few moments he rested, bobbing like a cork, morbidly amused by the irony of it all. He had succeeded in escaping his own personal assassin, only to meet an unsatisfactory and impersonal death in the middle of nowhere. A few passing fish would be pleased, he supposed, to dine on his corpse.

He'd no idea which direction he was facing now. He made a small circle in the water, looking carefully, but the ship had vanished. Stopping had been a mistake. With nothing to position by, he had no idea which way to go.

And then, not twenty yards away, a lantern snapped open, casting a small golden arc over the prow of a dinghy. Standing there, his hand wrapped around the lantern pole, was Shivaji, his face a mask carved out in shadows. Behind him, hunched on the benches, two figures held their oars straight out and still.

Not sure he had been seen, Duran raised an arm and waved it back and forth. There was no response. He called out, or tried to, but the scratchy noise from his swollen throat barely reached his own ears.

The boat remained motionless on the glassy water. They couldn't see him, then. He had to move closer, splashing to draw their attention. But his arms would scarcely lift. He could manage only a dog paddle, his aching legs trailing behind him like strands of kelp. But that was all right. He hadn't far to go. Soon enough, Shivaji would spot him.

He beat directly ahead for what seemed a long time, but the light never altered. He should be nearer, dammit. The light should be brighter. He lifted his head trying to gauge the distance. It looked the same. How could that be?

Redoubling his efforts, he was certain he had covered at least twenty yards before he paused, breathlessly treading water, to search again for the light. His eyes, glazed with saltwater, felt on fire. But yes. He was sure of it. The lantern was closer than it had been.

Certain now that they could see him, he waved again and forced his leaden arms and legs to propel him through the turgid sea. Fifteen yards. Ten. His body burned with the effort. Five yards. The folds of Shivaji's robe streamed like honey from his wide belt, where a curved blade hung in a jeweled leather case. His eyes glowed like coals.

Duran reached up, his hand inches from the prow.

No hand descended to help him. His fingertips brushed the rough wood and hit water again. Shivaji stared down at him.

To Duran's horror, the boat began moving away from him. He looked beyond the lantern, past Shivaji, to the oarsmen.

They were rowing backwater.

He nearly laughed. Shivaji had not come to save him.

He had come to watch him die.

A pleasure he would be denied, damn his eyes. In an explosion of pride and rage, Duran sucked in a long breath, twisted around and down like an otter, and drove himself away from the boat until his lungs were near to bursting. Forced at last to the surface, he lifted only chin and mouth to seize another breath before dropping.

Long before his breath ran out again, his leg muscles had cramped up beyond recall. There were only his arms now, pulling him by inches through the water, in which direction he had no idea. The way his luck had been running, he would no doubt rise up to find himself directly alongside Shivaji's sightseeing boat.

But it wasn't there, not that he could tell, when he surfaced for the last time. He smiled before sinking back into the warm sea that was to be his tomb. On his own terms, though. He could take futile pride in that. When nothing mattered but the manner of his dying, he had chosen to do it a free man.

It occurred to him belatedly that a prayer might be in order, just in case God was in an especially merciful mood. But before the thought completed itself, consciousness was slipping beyond his reach. He must have tried to breathe. He hadn't meant to, but water flooded his mouth, seared down his throat, choked his lungs. Black on black, his mind collapsed in on itself.

A noise—the spit of a guttering candle—exploded in his ears. Blinded by sweat, Duran lurched from his chair in Jessica's room and shook himself like a dog. The nightmare, whether dreaming or waking, never failed to reduce him to rags.

He hadn't drowned, of course. He'd awakened in the dinghy, facedown in bilge water and vomit, with someone pounding on his back. Later he'd awakened again in the ship's brig, manacles clamped around his wrists and ankles, where he was kept for several weeks on half rations. When Shivaji finally permitted him to leave the dark prison, no word of what had happened passed between them. None was necessary.

Now, alone with a sleeping Jessica, he felt death hovering again at his shoulder. He padded to the bed and studied the outline of her head against the pillowcase. He could see little else. Behind him, the solitary candle hoarded its frail light.

Leaning closer, he detected a line between her brows. Her hands were fisted at her sides. But her breathing remained steady, and as he watched, her shoulders appeared to relax. Pain, then, but not bad enough to waken her.

The light ought to be replenished before it went out altogether. He stole back to the mantelpiece, took an unlit candle, and held its wick to the dying flame. The transfer of fire came just in time. As the old candle reduced itself to a puddle of wax, light sprang from the new one, brassy as a Calcutta nautch girl.

He placed the candle in a silver-gilt holder on the other side of the mantelpiece, arrested by the dancing flame. It seemed to take life from a stream of air, but the windows were clear the other side of the room, closed and draped with heavy damask curtains.

The air must be coming down the chimney shaft. That would explain it. Taking the candle, he set it on the flagstone hearth. After a moment, the flame went still. Puzzled, he moved the candle from place to place on hearth and mantel, but the distinctive fluttering only recurred when he put it on the left side of the mantel. Experimenting further, he detected movement when he held the candle against the carved oak wainscoting to the left of the fireplace.

What the devil? Air was seeping into the room from behind the wall, that was certain, but he couldn't tell from where.

A tiny click drew his attention to the door, which opened to admit a shaft of pale light from the passageway. Arjuna's face appeared, along with a beckoning hand.

After a last pause by the bed, where he saw no change in Jessie's appearance, Duran unwillingly obeyed the summons to his own room.

Shivaji was waiting for him. "You must leave the lady to her servants now. To be discovered in her room would create difficulties for you both."

Duran opened his mouth to object and closed it again. She would not be glad to awaken to a scandal. His own head had begun to throb, but he could put that down to sleeplessness and tension. A pinprick compared to what she had suffered. Was suffering even now.

He glanced back at the door, wanting to rush through it and to her bedside again. He had seen her through the night. He wanted to watch her open her eyes, smiling because the pain was gone. He needed to make sure it was over.

Shivaji was speaking again. ". . . depart at ten o'clock. You will wish to bid farewell to your host."

"Not that again!" Duran's hand ached to plant itself on Shivaji's chin. "I leave when I'm sure Lady Jessica is well and after I have secured her help. Not before. Not one bloody minute before."

By the end he was shouting, or near to, and Shivaji has grappled him by the shoulders.

"Control yourself," came the smooth, unruffled voice. "Information passes quickly among servants. We have been as discreet as possible, but your presence in the lady's bedchamber may already be known. I cannot permit our mission to be compromised by a dispute with her family."

"Then you ought to have recruited a eunuch."

"If you do not lower your tone," Shivaji advised him coolly, "I shall be forced to silence you."

"You're queasy about noise? Very well, then. We'll take it to the moors." Duran spun on his heel and wrenched open the door. "Follow me or put a knife in me."

Chapter 9

When Duran came to a halt at woodland's edge, the sky had begun to lighten. He stood there for several minutes, breathing heavily, watching strands of mist weave through the oak branches and scatter in the freshening breeze.

What had he been thinking, to charge out of the house and demand that Shivaji *follow* him, for God's sake. Not bloody likely. Each morning, his slender fingers curled around the razor he was holding to Duran's lathered throat, the assassin-valet put him forcibly in mind of his own place in the order of things. There was no mistaking a show of power when it scraped past one's jugular vein.

Or glowed from a jeweled bracelet on his wrist.

The bauble had attracted a good deal of attention from his fellow guests, and he'd provided a dozen explanations, each more nonsensical than the last, for wearing it. But none of his stories were so preposterous as the truth.

The Nizam of Alanabad liked to mark his possessions with emblems of his wealth and power. He wrapped diamond-crusted collars around the necks of his hunting leopards, shackled prisoners of stature in chains of silver, and had selected for his captured English nobleman an intricately carved casing of gold twisted around a core of Toledo steel. The bangle could only be removed by applying a pair of tiny probes to a concealed lock, and Shivaji held the keys.

There were, he was told, other mechanisms secreted on the underside of the bracelet. They masked needles coated with poison.

He had been given a telling demonstration of what would occur if he tampered with the bracelet. The craftsman, with evident pride, had clamped a model around the belly of a rat and instructed Duran to touch the carved surface with the tip of a knife. Nothing happened the first eight times, but his ninth effort triggered one of the needles. Within a minute, the hapless animal lay dead. Then Duran was blindfolded and the golden bracelet applied to his wrist.

"What if something—a dinner fork, perhaps—accidentally hits the wrong spot on this thing?" he asked as the shackle clicked into place.

"Ah," said the craftsman mournfully. "That would be most unfortunate."

Since then Duran had learned that the bracelet could take considerable banging about without damage to itself or to him, and only a deliberate effort to pry out the jewels, scrape off the gold, or unlock the clamp would set loose one of those deadly needles. Even so, the poison-studded bangle was a constant reminder of his powerlessness. He despised it.

A soft whistle floated from a rise of hills to his left. The sound reminded him of a bird—he didn't know the name of it—reputedly favored by Shiva the Destroyer.

Shivaji, his own personal destroyer, must have emerged from the servants' door behind the house and passed him by when he wasn't looking. Leaving *him* to follow, which was, he supposed, as it should be. At least the delay gave him a little time to reel in his straying wits and put together a plan.

He struck out across the sheep-manicured lawn, his feet imprinting the dew-damp grass, his eyes searching the rocky hills for a sign of his quarry. Between the landscaped gardens and the hills stretched a long tract of moorland that all the guests had been warned to avoid. There was no sure footing there.

The pearl-gray sky cupped the black tor like an oyster shell. He picked his way over the hissing ground, not committing his full weight until the mud stopped short of his ankles. He'd charged out without putting on his boots or availing himself of the privy room, which he was now beginning to regret. Covering the last hundred yards in a dash, he ducked behind an outcropping of granite stones to relieve himself

Shortly after, the summoning whistle sounded again, echoing off the hills and seeming to come from everywhere at once. He emerged from the sheltering stones and began his climb to the top of Devil's Tor.

Concentration eluded him. His thoughts kept sliding back to the room where Jessie was sleeping. He hoped to God she was sleeping. That he would be permitted to see her again. In the next few minutes he had to convince Shivaji to let him remain at High Tor, but he'd already used every argument he could think of to get himself here in the first place

The path into the steep hills curled and dipped, winding around boulders and skirting treacherous bogs. At times, one wrong step would have sent him off a high escarpment. He was fairly out of breath when the path made a sharp turn and opened onto an odd sort of clearing. Standing stones, taller than he by a foot or more, circled a flat space perhaps twenty yards in diameter.

Poised dead center, unyielding as a slab of granite, was Shivaji.

Aware of cold sweat streaming between his shoulder blades, Duran sauntered to the nearest of the stones and slouched against it with his arms folded. "How neglectful of me," he said. "I forgot to bring a gun."

"It would have been taken from you along the way."

"Oh, quite. By the Others."

"Believe what you will." A hint of impatience edged Shivaji's soft words. "You wish to speak with me, I believe, on the subject of our departure."

Duran had thrown himself against the assassin's iron will often enough to know the futility of argument. This time, curious to see if it would make a difference, he meant to tack in the direction Shivaji wanted him to go. "In fact, I've no particular objection to leaving," he said with a shrug. "Shooting at birds is an overrated pastime, and since you allow me no money for wagering at cards, the evenings are tedious. There's only one female of interest on the premises, and she wishes me to the devil. By all means, let us be off."

There was the slightest hesitation before Shivaji spoke. "A short time ago you felt otherwise."

"Not at all. Given a choice, I'd always take London over this backwater. But did you not wish me to track down the nizam's toy?"

As always, baiting Shivaji was a staggering waste of time. "So I do," he said in his tranquil voice. "You are accomplishing nothing here. In London you will contrive to examine the passenger records of ships departing Madras following the theft of the leopard."

"And will the thief have inscribed 'accompanied by a purloined icon' beside his name, do you suppose?

Because if he didn't, I cannot imagine how we'll distinguish him from the other passengers."

"Then," Shivaji continued mildly, "you will employ our replica to draw the attention of collectors. Should one of them bear a name that appears on the passenger list—"

"Yes, yes, I know that part of the plan. It's *my* plan. But the timing is all wrong. There's no use flogging our fake icon in London while everyone of consequence is in the country. And there's also the small matter of persuading the East India Company to give me access to the shipping records. I am not precisely in their good graces."

"Then you must convince them of your good intentions."

"If it comes to that." Easy enough to concede the impossible. They were more likely to haul him into a storeroom and beat the stuffing out of him. "But we still need Lady Jessica, who can put us directly in touch with the collectors. And what have we to lose? Should nothing come of my new proposal, we can revert to the original plan in the spring."

"The spring will be too late, Duran-Sahib. Only a little time remains to you."

The air deadened.

"What do you mean?" But already he knew the answer. He had been tricked. "The nizam gave me a *year*."

"You have misunderstood. The time commenced at the moment he issued his ruling."

"B-but that's absurd," Duran said, disaster beating like wings in his throat. "The journey alone has eaten up the better part of a year."

"It required eighteen weeks to create the replica. We were nearly seven months on ship, and we have passed sixteen days in England. By my calculations, twenty-five days remain to you. I would advise that you make good use of them."

Twenty-five days? Duran sagged against the stone at his back. It was the only thing keeping him upright, that stone and, perhaps, a thin tracery of pride. Dear God. Willy-nilly, his year had shrunk to less than a month. No time to raise money. To plot an escape. No time to spend with Jessica.

Profoundly shaken, he produced a harsh laugh. "Good use? We both know this leopard hunt is a sham. There's one chance in a million it made it to England, or anywhere else, in one piece. By now any thief with a grain of sense would have pried out the gems, melted the gold, and sold the lot. The nizam must have known that. So far as I can tell, I'm as superfluous to his schemes as drawers on a whore. Why didn't you slit my throat in a Madras alley and have done with it?"

"To preserve the illusion of the search," Shivaji replied after a rare hesitation. "We were certain to be followed to Madras. It was necessary to take ship."

"And were we followed here as well?"

"That is unlikely. As you have realized, the nizam never intended you to arrive in England. But his people must believe in your quest, for while they await your promised return with the leopard, they will not permit the noble prince's enemies to remove him from the throne."

"Then he miscalculated. He should have given me a *decade* to find it."

Shivaji's lashes flickered. "As ever, his judgment of the people's tolerance was precise. There is turmoil throughout the countryside. Crops fail and sickness afflicts the children. Foreigners seize the best land and wrest commerce from our hands. Even so, Alanabad would endure the times of trouble as it has always done, if not for Malik Rao. He leads the worshipers of Nagas, and his influence has grown so great that the nizam was compelled to admit him to the Inner Council. At your trial, it was Rao who called for your execution."

"I remember him." A rough-featured man dressed all in black. Blunt fingers mollusked with rings. A cone-shaped turban sporting a pair of silver snakes. In a land speckled with odd fellows, he had been odder than most. "Who is Nagas?"

"The Nagas are serpent deities. Their worshipers were an insignificant cult until Rao chose them to advance his own ambitions. Our people are superstitious, and the leopard's disappearance has made them fearful. Rao astounds them with displays of simple magic and preaches that the Nagas have power to save Alanabad. Already his followers number in the thousands. Only the return of the leopard will discredit him and restore the people's faith in themselves."

For all Duran cared, Alanabad could go to the snakes. It was his own future—all thirty-three days of it—that concerned him now. Escape. And Jessica. Like an underground river she flowed quietly through his every thought. Echoes of her pain thrummed at his nerve ends.

Let her be sleeping.

He pulled himself away from the standing stone and began to circle the clearing. "The common folk may be superstitious, but you are an educated man. Why are you here, waiting like a midwife for me to whelp a leopard? Surely you see how ridiculous this is."

"The gods—"

"Are you their puppet? The nizam's? You could take ship for India tomorrow with the replica and leave me here to go about my business. Who would know or care?"

For a time he thought Shivaji did not mean to answer. The assassin's gaze had lifted to the bluing sky. The first rays of the sun limned his turban with gold.

"It was my duty to guard the leopard," he said at length. "I must make amends by returning it to Alanabad. The true leopard, Duran-Sahib."

Guilt! An emotion that Duran had explored to its depths. Jubilant, he wished he could break off the conversation until he'd figured some way to exploit Shivaji's unexpected vulnerability. But he was locked in an immediate battle he had to win.

"What's the difference?" he asked. "You said it was an exact copy. A mama leopard couldn't tell the two of them apart."

"The replica will satisfy the people, yes, and preserve the nizam's throne. But only for a short time. The gods who placed Alanabad under the protection of the Golden Leopard will not be mocked."

"That's one way of looking at it, I suppose." Duran was feeling a little better now. The leopard had been stolen on Shivaji's watch, and he wanted it back. Under all that silky calm lay a healthy bedrock of frustration and pride. Under different circumstances, Duran could imagine liking the fellow.

"It is not important that you understand," Shivaji said. "Like my own, your fate has been inscribed. We are bound together, wheel and axle, on this journey."

"The question being, who will drive? Little has been accomplished, I know, but I thought I had more time." *Twenty-five days.* If he kept gnawing on that, it would paralyze him. "We need Lady Jessica. Give me another chance to recruit her."

"That would be unwise. Your interest in the lady is not confined to our search."

Duran turned with a start. "Because I played nursemaid to her headache? It was a damn lucky turn of events, her being ill and me on the spot to take advantage of it. Mind you, I'm not cut out to mop brows and catch vomit in a basin." He gave a delicate shudder. "But I acted my part to the hilt, don't you think?"

"It did not appear that you were feigning concern."

"Good. Then I may have fooled her as well. An insignificant incident between us several years ago caused a breach of trust, but perhaps she will now think better of me."

Shivaji raised a noncommittal eyebrow.

"In any case," Duran continued while he held the advantage, "I want one thing to be clear. Tell the Others. Under no circumstance is she to be harmed."

He looked up to see Shivaji directly in front of him, the Iron Dagger gleaming at his earlobe. "Very well, Duran-Sahib. We wish no harm to come to those who assist us. But I am sworn to see that you do not escape the nizam's judgment."

"Unless I find the leopard, of course."

"Even when you do." Shivaji's long fingers curled lightly over the slave bracelet. "My instructions make no allowance for success. In twenty-five days, or before then if I so choose, you will die. That is your destiny."

Plain enough. But nothing had changed. Finding the leopard had never been in the cards. "I don't believe in destiny," he said, "except the one I create for myself."

"Few are given the privilege to choose their own fates. If you wish to protect the lady, you must swear she will not be drawn into any scheme designed to escape your responsibility. Or to escape me."

Duran pulled free his hand and resumed his prowling. Another bond settled around his throat. Responsibility. Jessica. An oath.

Would he break his word to save his life? Was there any other way out of this deadlock?

"I could swear to do whatever it is you want," he said at length, "but it would be the word of a scoundrel. Ask anyone who ever knew me what my honor is worth."

"I have done so. Before we departed from India, I made a study of you."

"I trust you were appropriately shocked."

Shivaji made a dismissive gesture. "Mercenaries are not an unknown species in my country."

"Even those who train the soldiers of his own country's enemies?"

"The East India Company is not your country, and its enemies are often capriciously selected. You were angry."

God yes. Burning rage, and on its heels, cold retribution. But he was careful not to react to what Shivaji had learned of him. The assassin was probing for his weaknesses, and no one was allowed to come close to this one.

Easier, he decided, to swear the oath and get it over with. It meant surrendering any last-ditch effort to enlist Jessie's help, but that was just as well. When he grew desperate, and he expected to, his oath would be her only protection.

"So, what do I do? Go on one knee? Place my hand on somebody's holy writings?"

"Your word will suffice. Do you give it?"

He turned to face Shivaji. "Lady Jessica will not be told of any escape plans I make," he said in a flat tone, "nor will she be permitted, even by indirection, to assist me in any way. I swear it."

"Very well. In return I shall grant you a little time, perhaps two days, to secure her cooperation."

"Make it three," Duran said, trying not to show his relief. "She's ill. And you understand that I shall be required to tell her the truth. Most of it, at any rate."

"It would be better otherwise. Should indiscretion lead to difficulties for me or my subordinates, your present incarnation will be terminated."

"Oh, now *there's* a charming euphemism. I'm excessively fond of my current incarnation, thank you very much. And your elastic moral sensibilities astonish me. All this to-do about preserving your insignificant little kingdom on a foundation of truth, but nary a qualm about cutting me down like a weed."

"To kill you is my duty," Shivaji said. "My dharma. It is written that one shall not absolve oneself from an obligation consequent on one's birth, even if it involves evil. For all undertakings are surrounded by evil as fire is surrounded by smoke."

"Oh, well, then. If it's *written*." Shaking his head, Duran made his way to the footpath. "But really, my good fellow, you ought to find something less crackbrained to read."

Chapter 10

Duran slogged through the rest of the day in a weary haze, Jessica never far from his thoughts. Someone was tending to her, he knew, but he couldn't ask how she was, nor, quite naturally, did the servants volunteer the information. Short of barging into her bedchamber to see for himself, there was nothing he could do.

The same could be said, he supposed, about the year that had suddenly compressed itself into twenty-five days. About the death sentence he had never quite believed in until Shivaji made it clear what he was facing. And about the choices open to him—actively seek the leopard and die in a few weeks, or abandon the hunt and die now.

Escape had seemed a simple enough matter with an entire year to play in, covertly hoarding money and laying his plans. Even the Others, however many they were and however conscientious, could not have tracked his every move for so long a time. But they could keep him well boxed in for the short time he had left.

While tramping across the moorlands, Arjuna at his side and the sounds of gunfire all around him, he evaluated his options with the detachment of an experienced campaigner on the eve of battle. Above all, he knew, there must be no predictable routine for the Others to exploit. He required to be constantly on the move, carrying his opponents into unfamiliar territory. Jessica's help was the linchpin. In her company, he could undertake a tour of potential leopard holders, the targets selected by an expert. Shivaji could hardly object to that.

Meantime he had to secure passage on a ship bound for South America, one scheduled to sail no later than his deadline. And he must see to it that his Grand Tour wound up within reach of the harbor, in case he had not managed to elude his captors before then.

What else? *What else?*

Now and again, confronted with a black grouse, he accepted a loaded rifle from Arjuna and took his shot, paying little attention to the results even though Pageter would be laying wagers on his tally for the day. Considering his distracted state of mind, he hoped that Pageter was betting him to lose.

He walked. He thought. He shot. He wanted, more than anything else, to know that Jessica was no longer in pain. In a fair universe, he would be the one laid low with a brutal headache.

Shortly after noon, summoned by a whistle, the scattered sportsmen gathered alongside a narrow late-summer river where a luncheon had been spread out under a silk pavilion. There, separated at last from his gun bearer, Duran was able to steal a few words in private with John Pageter, who took the news of the abbreviated deadline with a shrug.

"Then we must get on with it," he said, adding a chicken leg to his plate. "Under the circumstances you can't be choosy about where you wind up, so I think you should have passage booked out of several ports.

Liverpool and Plymouth at the very least, although
the shipping schedules will decide for us in the end.
You may safely leave the business to me."

"With pleasure." Duran accepted slices of roast
beef from a servant, although the prospect of eating
turned his stomach. "And with gratitude, although I'm
sure you don't want to hear it. But Shivaji will be
watching for trouble. Assuming I manage to lead him
on a wild goose chase across England, how am I to
stay in touch with you?"

"Perhaps Lady Jessica will agree to serve as intermediary. Or do you still mean to engage her in your
schemes?"

"Some of them. But she cannot be involved with
my escape, even inadvertently. On that point, I'm
afraid, there is no room for compromise."

"Ah." With no change of expression, Pageter
turned to speak with Sir Clyde Wilcombe, allowing
Duran to move past him in the queue.

Glancing around, Duran spotted the reason for Pageter's evasive action. Arjuna had taken a position
under a nearby tree, his dark-eyed gaze focused attentively on the privileged gentlemen lined up at the buffet table. The young man—not yet in his twenties,
Duran would guess—was an inch or two shorter than
his father, broader in the shoulders, and not so lean.
There was a sweetness about his lips and unabashed
curiosity in his eyes as he looked upon the aristocrats
of a culture so unlike his own.

Despite Arjuna's youth, Duran recognized in him
all of Shivaji's ruthless dedication to duty. No weak
link there, unfortunately. And while Arjuna addressed
him only in Hindi, he was fairly sure the boy spoke
English reasonably well. He had concealed his own
facility with languages often enough to recognize the
tactic. No doubt Arjuna reported to his father every-

thing he overheard of Duran's conversation, along with what he guessed from a little surreptitious lip-reading.

If it came down to it, the assassin-in-training would readily put a dagger between the *sahib*'s ribs.

For the rest of the long afternoon, burning under Arjuna's scrutiny, he was careful to keep distance between himself and Pageter. It was a disgruntled Lord Marley, sitting in a Bath chair on the lawn when Duran made his sleepy way back to the house, who informed him that he had brought down a record number of birds that afternoon. And that Pageter had been betting on him to win.

A glimmer of optimism creaked past his defenses. By the grace of some benevolent fate, he had drawn a surprisingly crafty friend to his corner. If he could lure Jessica there as well, he might just have a chance.

Not for the first time, he pushed aside his qualms about embroiling two decent people in his troubles. Pageter knew the score, and soon Jessica would know nearly all of it. Both were free to walk away at any time.

In the dressing room, Shivaji awaited him with hot water, clean linens, a folded sheet of paper, and the ghost of a frown. After reading the brief message, which his valet had doubtless read before him, Duran made a request that led to a dispute, which rather to his surprise, he won.

All at once nervous, exultant, and resolute, he permitted a tight-lipped Shivaji to help him dress for dinner, selecting a gold brocade waistcoat with a small inside pocket to hold Jessica's note and its directions to their meeting place.

Soon. Soon. In two hours, give or take a bit, he would lure her into his web.

If she listened.

If she believed him.
If she gave a damn.

At precisely five minutes before the appointed time, Duran set out for his appointment.

The room to which Jessica had directed him was in the east wing and on the second floor, a position similar to that occupied by her own chambers at the opposite end of the house. Not far down the passageway, a velvet rope suspended between two waist-high brass pillars marked the point beyond which guests were excluded. He ducked to the other side and proceeded along the corridor toward the shadowy outline of a door.

The hand wrapped around the grip of the heavy case he carried had begun to perspire. So had his other hand, he realized when he raised it to knock. He paused to regather his savoir faire before rapping lightly.

After a heart-stopping silence, Jessica's voice gave him permission to enter. The delay had been just long enough to remind him that she had reluctantly granted this favor and was capable of snatching it away in an instant. With amused respect, he opened the door and stepped inside.

Like the passageway, the rectangular room was badly lit. To his left a bed draped with burgundy velvet sprawled atop a three-stepped pedestal, with plump cupids aiming gilt arrows from the nibs of the bedposts. Across the way, a half-open door appeared to lead to a dressing room.

To his right, separated from the sleeping area by a lush expanse of carpet, a sitting room of sorts was stocked with a sofa, several chairs, a secretaire, what looked to be a game table, and a small dining table set with china and silver. Everything was meticulously arranged and spotlessly clean, as if the resident expected to return momentarily.

"I call it the shrine," Jessica said, rising from a wingback chair and moving around it to face him. "Only the servants ever come here. We'll not be disturbed."

Realizing he was still holding the case, Duran set it down and was about to approach her when she picked up a candle brace and crossed to a spot in the middle of the room. He drank her in, slim and elegant in a simple moss-green gown, her hair caught up in a loose knot. A surge of pure lust shot through him.

It was sublimely inappropriate, but he couldn't help himself. Adversary or ally, Jessie was the most splendid female he had ever met. Even with shadows under her eyes. As he drew closer, he saw the fine-grained skin tightly drawn over her cheekbones and the small single line that marred the smoothness of her forehead.

"This was my mother's chamber," she said in a dispassionate tone that reminded him of Shivaji. "The last few years of her life she rarely left it. And this is her portrait." Turning, she lifted the candle brace toward a life-size painting suspended between two narrow mirrors. "As you see, we look very much alike."

At first glance, he would not have agreed. The woman in the picture, full bosomed and somewhat plump, appeared to be in her forties. Exotic in purple satin with explosions of silver lace at her neck and wrists, she was seated on a thronelike chair with her lavishly ringed fingers folded in her lap. Dark eyes gazed imperiously from a face too round for beauty, and thick mahogany hair flowed from a center part in the style of a young, unmarried girl.

Hair very like Jessie's, he realized, as were the near-black eyes and the brows slightly winged at the tips. The straight posture was hers as well, and the forthright gaze.

"Don't you agree?" she asked, a breath of urgency in her voice.

Ghosts prowled this room. Coming up beside her, he felt their malevolence as he examined Lady Sothingdon's face. "The coloring is somewhat similar," he said thoughtfully. "But otherwise, no, I shouldn't think the resemblance particularly noteworthy."

"We are more alike in character than appearance," she said. "Mother despised the picture, although it flatters her. When she sat for it, she looked considerably older and weighed several stone more. She had always been overfond of sweets and cordials. In any case, she refused to pay the artist, but Papa secretly settled the account. It was the only time I know of that he ever defied her wishes. Not long after her death, he had the painting brought down from the attic and mounted here. I cannot think why."

"Perhaps to annoy her?"

Jessica's lips curved in a faint smile. "I hope that was the reason. The servants are convinced her spirit inhabits this room, and no one who worked at High Tor when she was alive can be persuaded to enter. Those who sleep in the rooms above claim to hear her shrieking in pain, the way she was used to do when—"

He took the candle brace from her trembling hand. "When—?"

She looked neither at the portrait nor at him. "Soon after Mariah was born, Mother began to experience headaches. She ascribed them to the horrors of childbirth and barred Papa from her bed. With concessions and bribes he won his way back there, pleading the need for an heir to the title, but to general disappointment, I popped out next. It was several years before she yielded again to Papa's advances. Aubrey's birth was a relief to us all."

The personal revelation astonished him. Duran kept a politely interested expression on his face, wondering why Jessica had suddenly chosen to expose the family's soiled laundry.

She was studying the portrait again. "Mother, though, was left with a problem. Having delivered an heir, thereby surrendering her most powerful weapon, she required another means of controlling the household. So the migraines returned, more intense than before, and any strain on her nerves—or so she insisted—sent her into agony. Everyone took care never to cross her will."

Having watched Jessica endure a single night of agony, he could understand why Lady Sothingdon's family strove to protect her. But Jessica seemed remarkably unsympathetic.

"Come," she said, striking out for the other end of the chamber. "I wish to show you something else."

He trailed behind her, perplexed by her mood and the odd confidences she had chosen to share with him. It made him realize how little he really knew about her. His own errand, so compelling when he came into the room, seemed less important than taking this strange journey with her.

She paused by an innocuous stretch of wall. "As you might imagine, I was always the worst offender in the household—disobedient, insubordinate, obstinate, and as my mother swore to all who would listen, her unkindest tormenter. Also cruel and unnatural, because I paid no heed to the consequences of my actions. And she was quite right. This is why."

Where cherrywood wainscoting met burgundy silk wall covering, a line of plaster animal faces ran the length of the room. Jessica paused by an openmouthed lion with an elaborate mane and poked her little finger into one of its eyes. "When I was very young I used to hover outside her door and weep, certain that I had caused the pain that made her scream. Now, of course, I know that making a loud noise is the last thing a migraine sufferer is likely to do."

She withdrew her finger and gestured him to have a look. Stepping forward, he put his eye against the lion's and saw through it to a room on the other side of the wall. A closet, he would guess, identifying a row of shelves. A colza lamp on one of them cast sparse light over stacks of folded linens.

"What confused me," Jessica said as he glanced over at her, "were the sounds I heard between Mother's cries. She appeared to be speaking in a perfectly natural voice to her companion, a vicious, batlike woman who enforced Mother's will on the household. But of course, I am somewhat prejudiced. It was Clothilde who caned me when I misbehaved."

Duran's hands curled into fists. At the school for the children of East India Company functionaries, he had been regularly caned until it occurred to him to stop showing up for lessons. For him the indignity had been more wounding than the pain, and he suspected Jessica had felt the same. But for a young girl, there would have been no way to escape.

He studied her face as she spoke, her tone reflective, her gaze unfocused. "They rarely left this room, but I watched for my chance, and when it came, I filched the housekeeper's keys, let myself inside, and dug out this hole. It opens to the linen closet next door, as you saw, and for several months, I hid in that closet and spied on this room through the lion's eye. During that time, Mother experienced none of the headaches she was pretending to endure. I saw her sitting with Clothilde at the game table, drinking wine and playing cards, now and gain remembering to emit a terrible cry. From then on, there was no controlling me. I did exactly as I liked and despised those who allowed her to manipulate them."

"Did you tell anyone what you had seen?"

"To be sure. Tact has never been my long suit. I marched directly to Papa and made my case, even offering to take him to my spy hole so he could see for himself. But he had developed the habit of yielding to her, you see. To admit she had gulled him for so long would make him look a fool. I was not wise enough to understand that for him, knowing the truth would be more painful than continuing to live the lie. He forbade me to set foot in this wing of the house, and I was never again to speak of my misguided fantasies to anyone. You will have noticed that I am disobeying him."

"I'm surprised he didn't close up your spy hole."

"So was I, when I came here after her death." Her lips curved. "I often wonder if he used it. In any case, it makes no difference now."

But it did, he could tell. In the candlelight, shadows carved hollows of worry in her cheeks and under her eyes.

Old ghosts, restless and unhappy, reaching out from the past. When he was not vigilant, they broke through his own defenses as well.

"Have I embarrassed you?" she asked, looking at him directly for the first time since he entered the room. "How tedious of me. You came on a mission of your own, and here I am spewing family secrets like a volcano."

"I don't mind," he said. "But I admit that I'm puzzled. Why did you wish me to know this?"

"Not very subtle, was I? You may take that as a

mark of desperation. I was trying to explain why I would not permit you to summon help last night. Must I spell it out by the letter?"

"Only if you expect me to understand," he said with a rueful smile.

"I wish only to silence you. I am, you see, very much like my mother. I have inherited the color of her hair and eyes, her temper, her drive to be in control of every situation, and of course, the migraines. I do not wish anyone at High Tor to know about them."

"Because . . . ?"

"What is it to you?" she snapped, spinning on her heel and striding quickly to the other side of the long room. "I have said all I can. Too much. And all wasted."

He was right behind her, close enough to put a hand on her shoulder. At the touch she stopped immediately, stiff as a gravestone. "Not wasted, Jessie. Unnecessary. You had only to ask."

"Last night you threatened to tell my father. Send for a doctor."

"That's because you scared the devil out of me. I may have been as useless as feathers on a fish, but at least I was there to fill a cup with lavender tea and hold out a basin. If necessary, I could have summoned help. Dear God, how do you survive an attack like that on your own?"

"I don't," she replied after a moment. "In London, my servants are well prepared to assist me. When I travel I am generally accompanied by my secretary, who is nearly as solicitous as you. The point is, I am almost never at High Tor, and only my family needs to be spared. They dislike me for a number of reasons, which I no doubt provide in abundance. But I prefer to be judged for what I am, not for my likeness to my mother."

"Which may be," he said carefully, "in your own mind. You refine too much on a superficial resemblance."

"Perhaps. But the consequences remain. Lady Sothingdon, never mind she'd been dead these last seven years, continues to rule this house and family with an iron will."

"Except for you."

"Oh, me most of all," she said, moving toward the chair she had been occupying when he entered. "I expect you'll find cognac in the sideboard cabinet. And then you must explain precisely why you are here and what it is you wish me to do."

The melancholy was gone from her voice, and the hesitation as well. What she had confided had been difficult to say, especially to him, and he understood that the subject was never again to be addressed. After locating the cognac, he poured a large helping for himself and looked a question at her.

"Thank you, no," she said. "I have a feeling that in the next few minutes, I shall require to have all my wits about me."

Now that the opportunity he had sought was upon him, he found it oddly difficult to proceed. Truth. Slippery, disorderly truth. A well-devised lie was much easier to tell and far more likely to be believed. He rested his hips against the sideboard and crossed his ankles, testing the position for comfort.

"I have been sent to England," he said with a dry mouth. "On a mission, so to speak. That is, I am delegated to find a . . . well, an object, on which the fate of a small principality may depend."

There. That was straightforward enough.

Jessica appeared unimpressed. "Was it stolen?"

"As a matter of fact, yes. But the Englishman who made off with it was subsequently found dead in lodgings near the Madras docks. It was a fever, we think. In any event, the object was no longer with him, and we deduced that he had passed it on to someone who had shipped home to England."

"Or perhaps it never left India at all," she said. "You have come a long way, it seems, on what could well be a futile errand. Or have you scratched up a clue to its location?"

"None whatsoever." He smiled. "I require your help to track it down. And there is something more. A deadline. Unless I find the object within the next four weeks, the consequences will be—shall we say?—unpleasant."

Her gaze, water clear, met his. "Unless I am very much mistaken, India is a considerable distance from England. How can anyone there possibly know if you have succeeded or failed?"

Nothing escaped her. He took another drink, the cognac burning down his throat. "It's becoming apparent you'll not be satisfied with the abridged version of this tale. But I fear the alternative is a very long story indeed, most of it privileged information."

"Oh, I'm perfectly willing to keep your secrets," she said. "And since I slept most of the day away, I wouldn't mind a bit of evening entertainment." She drew up her legs on the chair, propped her elbow on the armrest, and rested her chin on her hand. "Will you mind sitting over here, where I can see your face?"

He did mind. But taking the decanter with him, he went to the chair across from her, noticing the marks on the carpet where it had been dragged from its previous location. She had arranged everything to her liking, and almost certainly provided the cognac as well. It had always been his favorite drink.

Her steady gaze was disconcerting. Settling on the

chair, he leaned back with his head against the bolster and pretended to look at the ceiling, acutely aware of her scent and the slight rustle of her gown as she breathed.

Everything depended on the next few minutes. Unless she agreed to cooperate, he would have no excuse—none that Shivaji would accept—to remain in her company. He would be swept back to London and ordered to examine shipping records, for all the good that would do.

On the whole, his prospects were decidedly grim. Unless the leopard strolled out of a hedgerow and jumped into his arms, it was never going to be found. Not in four weeks. Not in a lifetime.

Which were, in his case, one and the same.

"Duran?" Jessica's voice was tinged with amusement. "Cat got your tongue?"

Chapter 11

During the long silence Jessica diverted her thoughts from a mild pain at her temples, the echo of last night's headache, and focused instead on Duran's long, tapered fingers twisting the stem of his cognac snifter. He was mentally rehearsing his speech, she supposed. Putting his lies in order.

He needn't have troubled. She had already decided to pretend to believe him.

"A little more than a year ago," he said at last, "I was traveling alone from Poona to Mysore when my horse lost a shoe. I went looking for a blacksmith, but at every village I came to, I was directed to yet another village. The locals were deliberately steering me into the remote principality of Alanabad, sending word by pigeon that I was on my way. When I finally arrived at a fairly good-size town, an armed patrol was waiting to clap me in irons."

He looked up from his contemplation of the glass. "Do stop me if the narrative gets muddled. Before now, I've never told anyone this story."

She had no doubt of that. "I am following you well enough, thank you."

"Very well, then. They took me to the capital, where I was imprisoned for several months. The nizam—that's the ruler—had it in for Englishmen because one of them stole a valuable icon, and he was making a grand show of my trial to impress his people."

He frowned at her over the glass. "It's about to get complicated. A cult of fanatics was using the theft of the national idol to turn the people against the nizam. Their leader, an ambitious politician who claims to be the reincarnation of some deity or other, demanded that an example be made of the foreign devil. Matters were getting out of hand until I came up with a proposal."

"Let me guess. You volunteered to find this missing idol. What *is* it, by the way?"

"So much for impressing you with my ingenuity," he said, sounding disgruntled. "It is a statue of a leopard supposedly presented by Krishna to one of the nizam's ancestors as a symbol of the family's divine right to rule. Or some such nonsense."

Nonsense being the relevant word, she thought, preserving the expression of mild interest on her face. "So the nizam told you to run along and find his statue and bring it back. Why would he trust the likes of you with such an errand?"

"He didn't. An unexpected ally spoke on my behalf. But I'll get to him later. Malik Rao, the cult leader, was calling for my blood, so the nizam, who turned out to be a clever chap, figured a way to give everyone a bit of satisfaction. If I could prove the gods had sent me to recover the leopard, I would be granted the opportunity to do so. All I had to do was survive the Trial of a Thousand Screams."

"Good heavens." She scrutinized what little she could see of his flesh. "You appear to have come through it relatively intact. Or are you missing a few vital bits of your anatomy?"

"Any particular piece of me you would be sorry to forfeit?"

Heat rose to her cheeks. "I'd as soon all of you went missing."

He turned on her the intense regard she remembered far too well. And deplorably, its effect on her had not diminished over the years. Passion like a windstorm, leaving her empty of caution and good sense, had once driven her into his arms. She longed to feel again that rush of desire for a man, for this particular man. She ached to feel like a woman who is desired.

But no. To feel was to lose herself.

"I'm not sure," he said quietly, "that we shall ever escape our past, any more than we can disregard what exists between us now. If you tell me you don't sense it, I won't believe you. It is practically visible whenever we are together. But I'll say no more on the subject, if that is your wish."

It was. She had feared precisely this, a confrontation that forced her to acknowledge what she could not bear to face. Past reason, beyond hope, she still wanted him. And that was why she had met with him here, under the scornful gaze of her mother. Her very own guardian devil. In this room, she could not be seduced into folly.

Room? In truth, it was a battlefield. Beneath their civilized exchange of words raged a war for ascendancy and control. His weapons were the customary ones—charm, lies, and the potent male beauty that always rendered her breathless. But she was wiser now. Her defenses were strong. She did not mean to lose.

"Go on with your story," she said with a precise blend of courtesy and indifference.

The gleam in his eyes confirmed that the battle was joined. "Very well, Boadicea. After the nizam made his ruling, I was taken to a room at the top of a round tower. A good-size audience gathered in the courtyard to enjoy the festivities, which began with the official torturer circling the balcony and whetting his blades to enthusiastic cheers. The citizens of Alanabad are partial to public executions. They made rather a fuss when told the actual paring of flesh would occur indoors, so the court musicians were brought out to entertain them. Peddlers sold refreshments in the courtyard, and there were jugglers and acrobats. Meantime, I had come up with yet another grand idea. You won't guess this one."

"I wouldn't presume to try."

"Well, it pleased the nizam, though rather better than I intended. But I'm getting ahead of myself. My role in the Trial of a Thousand Screams was, of course, to scream, which I did quite effectively until my voice gave out and a flunkey took over. Now and again pots of blood were poured down the tower wall to show what a fine job the torturer was doing. Chicken blood, I think. Three hours later, to mingled disappointment and rejoicing, the nizam announced that I was, miraculously, still alive. Should Krishna grant me a complete recovery, which was likely to require several months, a ceremony would be held to celebrate."

"Months? Since you were the object of a miraculous cure, why not a swift one?"

"That might smack of trickery. The people had to believe I'd really been chopped up, you see. They wanted me to suffer."

"That," she said, "I can well understand."

He chuckled. "Rao's gang of bullies had been going about spreading rumors and making trouble, so the nizam was being especially cautious. But primarily, the delay was needed to create what I am about to show you."

He rose with feline grace and retrieved the leather case he'd left by the door.

She took her time about it, but curiosity finally sent her to the game table where he was removing a soft leather bag from his coat pocket. There were three keys inside, and one by one he fitted them into holes neatly concealed by the tooling. Then he raised the lid.

Inside was a shallow tray divided into small, felt-lined sections, each containing a vial or bottle. Rather like an apothecary's chest, she was thinking, until he lifted out the shelf. Beneath it, nestled in a bedding of thick black velvet, lay an object wrapped in oilcloth. He removed the bundle and placed it at the center of the table.

Pausing, he glanced over at her. "You'll better appreciate this, I expect, with more light."

While she brought two lamps from the mantelpiece, he began to strip away the oilcloth. Beneath it was a wrapping of leather, and under that, a sheath of muslin layered in thin bands like a mummy's casing. He located a loose end and began to unwind the gauze.

Jessica moved closer, drawn in spite of herself by a flutter of anticipation. As he peeled away the last of the binding, she glimpsed flashes of color—red and blue and green and crystal white—against a background of rich, gleaming gold.

When the entire figure had been revealed, she saw a leopard about the size of a house cat, its spots picked out in gemstones as large as her thumbnail. It was seated on its haunches, tail curled around its front paws, the expression on its carved face aloof, regal, and smug. But the eyes, two cabochons of a deep yellow-orange stone she had never before encountered, were alert and wary. "I am not to be trifled with," they seemed to warn.

She looked over at Duran, who was attentively observing her reactions. "May I?"

He nodded, his smug expression rather like the leopard's.

She moved slowly around the table, examining the figure from all angles. It was splendidly formed, defining the sleek grace, the taut musculature, the serene confidence and lethal strength of a magnificent animal.

With both hands she lifted the statue, astonished at its weight. Then, holding a lamp a bare two inches away, she examined the gems. Sapphires, rubies, emeralds, and diamonds captured the light and scattered it across the ceiling and walls.

"As you see, the leopard is solid gold," Duran said. "Just enough alloy mixed in to give it the proper strength. And the stones are genuine."

"Perhaps. I am not an expert appraiser. I do know that paste gems, if produced by a talented artisan, can stand up to all but the closest scrutiny. The figure itself may be of some base metal coated with gold. Have you had it examined?"

Scowling, he leaned over to study the carving. "In fact, this is the first time I've seen it. But I am assured it is an exact replica of the original."

"But how could the artist have made a perfect copy without the original to serve as a model?"

"How the devil would *I* know? Perhaps that's why it took so long. In any case, the idea—*my* idea—was to draw out the possessor of the authentic idol by claiming to have it myself, or something along that line. This is, not to put too fine a point on it, prodigiously expensive bait."

"And you wanted me to spread word of it, using my influence to lend you credibility. But how did you know I had begun to trade in art and antiquities?"

"I read it in the *Times*," he said. "On the morning of your exhibition. An amazing stroke of luck, don't you think? Before seeing the notice, I had planned to advertise the statue for sale or commission Richard Christie to put it up for auction. But there is a degree of risk to making our intentions public. We may have been followed."

"Good heavens. All the way from India?"

"Rao's thugs attacked us on the road to Madras and again shortly before we took ship. It's possible they took passage on a later sailing, especially if Rao somehow learned about the replica. I had one devil of a time convincing Shivaji to let you see it."

"Shivaji? Your *valet*?"

"He is acting that part here. In Alanabad he is one of the nizam's chief advisors, but his primary duties relate to . . . security."

He had been going to say something else, Jessica thought. Perhaps he'd realized the story was already so elaborately ludicrous that another exaggeration would topple the whole edifice.

"What's the matter?" he demanded. "Your mouth is all twisted. Have you another headache?"

She was clinging to the back of a chair for balance. "N-no," she said. "I'm trying, really I am, to keep from laughing. But I don't think I can."

"Good God, Jessica!" Turning on his heel, he stalked to the other side of the room and back again, speaking all the while. "Listen to me. I know it sounds absurd, but everything I told you is the absolute truth. The nizam. Rao. The trial. How I came by this replica. The attack on the road. The whole lot of it. Well, I admit you haven't heard the entire story, but the parts I've given you are on the mark."

"But withholding selected pieces of the truth is just another way of telling an outright lie. What little details have you omitted?"

He stopped directly in front of her, lips taut and fists balled. "Have it your way. I only concealed this to protect your female sensibilities, but here it is. If I fail to trace the leopard before the deadline set by the nizam, which happens to be twenty-five"—his gaze went to the clock—"no, twenty-four days from now, Shivaji is under orders to execute me."

For an instant, anger nearly overtook her amusement. Did he think her a complete hen-wit? But it was only her vanity taking offense, and he mustn't detect even that small chink in her armor. "Oh dear," she said cheerfully. "When not polishing boots and pressing cravats, your valet is an executioner. But surely you have noticed he is older than you, and not so tall, and of slighter build as well. I should think you could take him down if you tried."

"And I assure you, madam, that Shivaji is more than capable of dispatching me by several means, none of which require the use of a weapon. If ever I doubted that, what I saw when we were under attack by Rao's followers convinced me utterly."

Did he truly expect her to believe this nonsense? After one last look at the leopard, she made her way back to the chair and erupted into laughter. Incorrigible man. The Trial of a Thousand Screams, of all things. Nizams and fanatics and stolen icons. He ought to be writing Gothick novels.

"I'm delighted to have amused you," he said, taking up a position across from her with one arm resting on the mantelpiece and the other folded behind his back. "But by God, I had six months on ship to concoct a fable. If I were out to gull you, surely I'd have come up with a more plausible story."

"Perhaps. Or you could be relying on the my-story-is-so-outrageous-that-it-must-be-true ploy. It won't wash, Duran. And when I cease being amazed at your powers of invention, I'm rather certain I shall take offense. Do you take me for a featherbrain?"

"Of course not. For all my sins, Jessie, I've never underestimated you. The story sounds ridiculous, I know. I could hear that even as I was speaking it. But I'd got used to it, you see. I *lived* every last one of the events I described to you. Look. Ask Shivaji. He'll back me up."

"I have no doubt."

"Because you think he's my paid servant."

"Or a fellow conspirator. He's not the usual sort of valet, certainly." Memories unfurled in her mind. A slender figure leaning over her. A soft, accented voice speaking from what seemed a great distance. "Did he come into my bedchamber last night?"

"You weren't meant to see him. I apologize for breaking your confidence, but I needed his help. Shivaji was the one brewed up the teas and advised me how to care for you."

"Ah. When he's not out killing people, he's busy healing them."

A smile tugged at his wide, mobile lips. "That's the devil of it. He's both sides of a coin. All sides of a polyhedron. Were you to speak with him, I have no idea what he'd tell you."

"Oh, that I should do whatever you wish, no doubt. What exactly do you expect of me?"

"I'm not altogether sure. Identify collectors of exotic antiquities, perhaps. Then we'll pay them a call, display the replica, and see what happens. I haven't worked out the details."

"But I do business only with the best families. Why would they admit you into their homes? Allow you to examine their collections?"

"An introduction from you would turn the trick,"

he said, brightening. "Or you could make the journey with us. That would be best."

Her amusement fled, trailing fury in its wake. And sadness, although she could not have said why it came to be there.

"You've no idea, have you, what you are asking," she said at length. "Let me be clear. It has required six years of study, of cultivating the favor of people I'd as soon avoid, of putting aside everything most women value, to achieve even the mild success I am beginning to enjoy. Within a year or two I hope to have paid off the last of my debts. That may seem a small thing to you, but it will mark, at last, the beginning of what I have always sought. True independence. The ability to live my life on my own terms, however circumscribed. And now that I am within reach of my goal, do you imagine I will permit you to interfere?"

He ran his fingers through already rumpled hair. "But I've no intention of harming you. How could I?"

"By exploiting my good name to sell stolen property. It's what I presume you are about, although your scheme may not be so straightforward as that. It doesn't matter. Under any circumstances, to associate with you would be disastrous."

He exhaled slowly. "There was a time you didn't feel that way."

"I know." Her pulse beat erratically. "I was foolish then, and indiscreet. Had anyone caught us out, I would have been ruined. Not that I minded greatly at the time, it's true, but now the stakes are greatly increased. Now I have more to lose than a chance of marrying well."

"But I thought you had resolved never to marry. You told me so at regular intervals, in case I harbored ambitions above my station." His voice softened. "Or were you taking care not to break my heart?"

She threw him an annoyed glance. "I'm sure there was no danger of *that*. And as you have reminded me several times since your return, there is nothing to be gained by dwelling on the past. Happily, no harm came of it. But my circumstances have changed, and the slightest breath of scandal would undo everything I have worked for."

"Have I suggested more than a business transaction? I am looking for a statue, Jessie. The only difference between this transaction and the others you engage in is that I cannot pay you."

"You aren't listening! There are a number of people, some of them malicious, who disapprove of me and are eager to prove themselves right. I am a freak of nature, sir. An unmarried woman engaged in trade. Oh, elegant trade, to be sure, but it is a short step from the shop to the streets. Even impeccable behavior cannot shield me from criticism. To be seen in company with a"—she faltered momentarily—"with a bachelor of dubious background and uncertain respectability would compromise me altogether."

"I see." His voice was tinged with self-derision. "You must pardon me. I had not understood what you would be risking."

Nor cared, she thought, a cramp gripping her stomach. He was standing quietly, his eyes focused somewhere beyond her, his brow wrinkled with thought. He'd not given up, she was sure. He was merely calculating how to leap this temporary obstacle and bend her to his will.

But she had learned prudence in a hard school, with Hugo Duran as master tutor. Rising, she brushed down her skirts and, without looking at him again, crossed to the door. "I believe there is no more to be said," she interrupted when he began to speak her name. "Put out the lights, if you will, before leaving. And don't forget to pack up your leopard."

She had just reached the velvet rope and slipped under it when he caught up with her.

"Wait, please," he said. *"Please."*

Ahead of her, the passageway was silent and empty. It was late, but there might be guests still awake behind the bedchamber doors. She turned, a finger held to her lips.

"Is there nothing," he said, obediently softening his voice, "that I can offer in exchange for your help?"

Light from the flickering wall sconces danced over his face, obscuring his eyes and his intentions. "You'll not seduce me into compliance, Duran."

His hand closed around the rope. "I wish you would permit me to try. But that possibility hadn't occurred to me. I thought there might be something else, though."

"I cannot imagine what," she said, distracted by an unwelcome notion that had sprung into her head.

Gerald. Her demonic brother-in-law. Perhaps Duran would . . . But no. That would be trading one devil for another. There wasn't a hair's difference between them, really, except that she couldn't imagine Duran brutalizing a woman.

"What if," he said, "you could help me track the leopard without putting your reputation in question? Your good taste, perhaps, but not your virtue. What if, in return for a few weeks of your time, I could secure for you a degree of latitude you have never before enjoyed? What if I gave my word to disappear within, say, three weeks or so, and never return to trouble you again? Interested?"

Preoccupied with visions of setting Duran on her brother-in-law and hoping they'd tear each other apart, she had scarcely heard what he was saying until the last few words. Never trouble her again? Was that truly what she wanted?

Of course it was. When he was near her, she longed for all the things she could never have.

"I have been advising you to leave ever since you arrived," she pointed out, studying his face. From down the passageway, a longcase clock chimed the hour. Midnight. Only that? She'd have sworn they had been together in her mother's room for much, much longer. Half a lifetime.

"You are armed with a sword of fire," he said quietly, "and have set dragons to guard your gates. It is wise to take care, princess, and to protect yourself, but not if it means closing out the world. I can give you something you want. Not without risk, I'm afraid. But if you weigh the advantages against the hazards, you may find it a good bargain."

"That begs the important question, doesn't it? How can I trust you to keep your word?"

"And how am I to persuade you that I will? All the high cards are yours, you know. My need is greater than you can imagine. I will agree to any conditions you impose. But in the end, you must put aside your fear and trust me. You must close your eyes and jump."

He had taken leave of his senses. No, he expected her to do that. To take another headlong plunge into disaster because she could not resist him.

But he had miscalculated. She was no longer an irresponsible young rebel with uncontrollable passions. "Good night, Duran," she said, smiling to show she bore him no ill will for being an arrogant nitwit.

He was over the velvet rope and at her side before she'd gone more than a few steps. With one hand on her shoulder and the other gentle on her bare forearm, he turned her to face him.

They were standing in the shadows, torchlight at his back, a chandelier illuminating the stairs some distance behind her. The bracelet on his wrist felt hot against her skin. His eyes, the color of the leopard's jeweled eyes, glowed with an inner light.

"Marry me, Jessica," he said. "Marry me."

Chapter 12

She hadn't said no.

It had been the logical, the necessary reply to Duran's astonishing proposal. The word had sprung to her throat. Done pirouettes on her tongue.

But she had only stared at him, bewildered by the softness in his eyes, and the urgency. And then she'd scampered to the stairs and down them, pausing once to glance back at the tall figure, limned with torchlight, motionless where she'd left him in the passageway.

The moment when she might have spoken had dissolved in her fear, and the remains of the long night passed in a torment of confusion and desire. Pacing her bedchamber, she had wondered what he was thinking, just there on the opposite side of the wall.

More than likely, the wretched man had been sleeping the peaceable sleep of the unjust. And never mind that she kept remembering how it had felt to be curled against his lean body, his arms wrapped around her, his soft breath teasing her hair. For all the years that had passed since they were lovers, he remained imprinted on her, flesh against flesh, their murmurs of desire and cries of pleasure echoing in her ears.

It didn't matter. Those times were gone, should never have been, would never come again.

Watching the apricot dawn of a new day, she realized that the events of the old one had taken on the insubstantiality of a dream. Stolen icons and murderous valets. Really! And that absurd offer of marriage? Another of his lies, a honeyed trap for an unwary and desperate spinster, which she was not. With her morning chocolate, she swallowed the last crumbs of temptation and prepared herself to deliver, with a flourish, the only possible answer.

No, and *no,* and *never.*

But like all her plans just lately, this one ran swiftly aground. When she went in search of her soon-to-be-rejected suitor, he had already departed for a day of shooting on the moorlands, leaving her without a target for her stored-up, vehement *no*'s. Finally, after picking at a breakfast of bacon and melon slices, she set off from the house on a mission that had nothing to do with importunate males.

Well, almost nothing. She had decided to pay a call on her father's mistress, the widowed Mrs. Bellwood, at her cottage not far from Ridington. Mariah had offered to show her the way, but being in no mood for company, she had declined. Besides, it was about Mariah that she wished to speak with Mrs. Bellwood.

With the morning sun latticing through her straw bonnet, she strode purposefully along the path of the narrow Dart, brown and sluggish in late summer, her direction carrying her away from the distant crack of gunfire. She imagined Duran swinging his rifle up, his finger tightening, a bird falling from the sky. She imagined herself in his sights, flapping her wings, straining to break free.

Pride, like a living creature, stretched and scratched in her belly. Years ago Lady Jessica Carville had publicly declared she would never marry, in part to rid herself of the ambitious admirers who dogged her heels, but mostly to keep herself from wavering. The unhappiest people she knew were married, and they were unhappy *because* they were married. If loneliness was to be her fate, she would endure it without being dictated to by a controlling husband.

And she couldn't very well change her mind now. In all the clubs, betting books were inscribed with wagers about when the finicky Lady Jessica would yield, and to whom. Gentlemen had far too much time on their hands, and she had no intention of putting money in the pockets of those who doubted her word. It would make her a laughingstock.

As for the other reasons, the true ones, those would remain right where they were, buried so deeply she need never look at them again.

The shallow, wooded valley threaded its way around the rocky Dartmoor hills and skirted patches of bog-land, transforming a journey of a few miles to a walk of several hours. She didn't mind. It was cool alongside the river. Dragonflies danced over the water, and pipits gossiped in the oak branches.

She was rounding an especially tight curve when she saw, nearly concealed by an overhanging willow, a white-clad figure hunkered near the ground. A small cry caught in her throat.

She had recognized him immediately. Realized that she was alone. Wondered if anything she had been told of him was true.

Stiff with alarm, she watched the figure uncurl itself and rise, turning to face her.

Duran's accomplice. The assassin. He held something in his hands, but she couldn't make out what it was.

Why was he here? Not waiting for her, surely. And yet, he didn't look surprised to see her.

Well, there was nothing for it but to face him down. She was miles from help, and if she tried to escape, he could chase her down in a matter of seconds. Her back stiff with apprehension, she directed her feet to a spot a few yards from where he waited. When she came to a stop, he bowed.

One of them ought to say something, she supposed. Unable to meet his gaze, she turned her attention to the object cradled between his palms. It appeared to be a basket of some sort, elongated and pointed at each end.

"A boat?"

"A prayer." He lifted it for her inspection. "And, yes, a boat."

Puzzled, she drew closer. Woven of wide-bladed, deep-green grass, the boat was about ten inches long. "How is it a prayer?"

"It will carry an offering. If I may . . . ?"

Nodding, she watched him sink onto his heels and set the boat on a flat rock. Beside it was a small leather pouch with several compartments. He opened it and withdrew a handful of rice, which he sprinkled in the boat. Atop the rice, he laid out an intricate pattern made of almonds, golden raisins, and peppercorns.

"It's lovely," she said. "I'm afraid I don't know much about your religion. Is it true that you worship many gods?"

After a moment's silence, he directed her to a place beside him, and at his gesture, she dropped to her knees. "Look down," he instructed, "and tell me what you see."

Where the river pooled behind a fallen tree trunk, the water lay smooth as a mirror. She studied the face suspended there and the eyes that gazed back at her. "I see myself, of course."

"Only a reflection of yourself, *memsahib*. It is you, and not you." His forefinger stirred the water, scattering her image. "Another manifestation of you, and yet, not you. Please to frown."

Beginning to understand, she produced a fierce scowl. "The image of a way I can be, but I'm not always that way. And of course, it's me, but not me."

"There are many paths," he said, rising, "but all of them lead to the One. Or so I believe. Shall I make for you a prayer?"

Glancing up, she saw something flash in his hand. A knife.

He moved to a patch of rush grass and sheared off a handful of sharp-edged blades.

As her thudding heart began to resume its normal rhythm, she watched him plait the grass with nimble fingers. The knife had vanished as quickly as it appeared, in an undetectable motion that almost persuaded her that he might well be, as Duran had told her, a professional killer.

But an assassin wouldn't teach catechism beside a river, would he? Or make prayer boats in a dapple-shaded glen? "You're an odd sort of valet," she said, wishing a second too late that she could call back the words.

"Are you acquainted with many valets, *memsahib*?"

"Only my father's," she admitted after some thought. "And he's generally foxed. It must be somewhat difficult for you here in England. Do you intend to remain?"

"It is my intention to return home before the year ends, but what man can predict his fate? And are we to converse only in questions?"

The glint of humor in his dark eyes surprised her. "Why not?" she asked, taking up the challenge. "I have a great many of them. Did you expect to meet me here this morning?"

"How could I?" He tied off the prow of her boat

and began to shape the stern. "But then, does any encounter occur by accident?"

"Oh, very well," she said, standing and brushing off her skirts. "I give up. No more questions. You were referring, I presume, to fate. Of course, now I can no longer ask if you believe that we lack free will, and that our actions are predestined."

"In that case, I cannot reply. But when you appeared, I was put in mind of a story. Would you like to hear it?"

She wasn't at all sure. He made her feel the way she always did in company with Duran, torn between fascination and a healthy instinct to flee. But it would be ill-mannered to leave now, before her boat was finished. She wondered where he had concealed that gleaming knife.

"I love stories," she said with unconvincing cheerfulness. "I hope this one is not to be a sermon in disguise."

"As to that, I cannot say. It is an old legend, and carries a different truth each time it is told and for each one who hears it."

He stood motionless, except for the hands weaving the blades of rush grass, and spoke in a quiet voice. "In the old times there was a princess, beautiful and brave, who fell in love with a gallant prince. He was rich, heir to a kingdom and the lodestar of his people, but in his thirtieth year, he fell ill of a mysterious sickness. The physicians tried every remedy, but nothing availed. Only a year of life remained to him, said the astrologers, mourning.

"Not wishing others to witness his decline, the prince took himself into the forest where no one could find him, although everyone searched until, despairing, the king his father called them home.

"But the princess refused to accept that he must

die. Journeying from her own country, venturing deep
into the forest, all alone she searched in vain. At last,
shortly before the day foretold by the astrologers, the
day of her beloved's doom, she came to a precipice.
At its rim, or perhaps a little beyond it, stood Yama,
the Lord of Death.

" 'Spare him,' begged the princess, dropping to her
knees. As her tears fell, they gathered at cliff's edge
and became a waterfall, which one can see to this day
if one knows where to look. 'Take me instead. Let me
die in his place.'

"Sorrowful, Yama shook his head. 'I am not called
for you, my lady. You will sleep now, and when you
waken, he will have stepped upon the moon. It will
ask *Who art thou?* And if he knows to answer *I am
thou,* he will be reborn. Perhaps in future you will
meet, and recognize each other, and love again.'

"The princess tried to stay awake, reaching out her
arms in supplication, but her eyelids closed like the
fall of night. When they opened, a year had passed,
and another went by before she found her way out
of the forest. It is not known what became of her
after that."

Jessica found herself breathing heavily, her hands
clenched in her skirts. "That's a horrible story," she
said. "It has no point to it. Well, except that everyone,
except maybe the prince, tried to do something to
change what happened. But they all failed. What's the
use of a story where people do their best, all for nothing? And why did Yama refuse to spare the prince's
life?"

"Because he is the Lord of Death. It is his nature
to kill, and his duty. He must fulfill his dharma, as
must we all."

"I don't know what dharma is. Not mercy, I take
it."

"The word encompasses many meanings. Duty, Constancy. Brightness. The order of the universe. It was only a story, *memsahib*. And after all, it is no great thing to die. The shedding of a skin, like the serpent does without a thought. Nothing more than that."

"But after molting, the snake wriggles away, quite alive."

The Hindu's lips curved in a barely perceptible smile. "So he does, I bow to your wisdom. And your boat is finished. What offering will you place in it?"

All the things he had told her, even his final evasion, were laced with messages she was helpless to interpret. And the idea of a prayer boat was suddenly repellent to her. "I brought nothing with me," she said, wanting to leave and not at all certain he would permit her to go. The river seemed to be made up of fallen tears.

"Look around you," he said gently. "Choose."

She did, wanting to weep and wondering why. She had forsworn tears a long, long time ago. Eyes blurred, she broke an umbrella of pink blossoms from the flowering rush plant he had used to create the boat. What had been severed, she decided, laying the offering in the vessel, could be put together again.

He placed her boat in her hands, took up his own, and they walked a few steps beyond the calm pool to where the water resumed its summer pavane.

The birds had gone silent. No breeze stirred. Only the river, its course determined when the hills and valleys were formed, drove its way to the sea. They set their boats on the water at the same instant, and for a time, the woven vessels with their offerings of rice and almonds, raisins and peppercorns and flowers, navigated side by side on the current. Then the river curved again, and they were lost from sight.

Her prayer, when she remembered to produce one,

was the first thing that came to her mind. And as it did, she knew it was the thing she most wanted. "Let Mariah be safe," she whispered. "Oh, and put some happiness in her hands. She'll never go after it on her own."

Looking over at the silent, enigmatic man standing beside her, the man who carried a knife and wove grass into prayers, she could not imagine what kind of request he had made of his own deity.

"You should not, I think, be walking so far without an escort," he said. "Will you return with me to the house?"

It felt as if she had been with him in this enchanted place for hours. But when she looked up through the canopy of oak, the sun stood directly overhead. Only noon, then. Plenty of time to complete her errand and return before anyone missed her. Not that anyone would. "Thank you," she said, "but I've been walking these trails nearly all my life. I'll be perfectly safe."

There was a brief silence. "Yes," he said, bowing. "You will be safe. Good day, *memsahib*."

She had gone only a little way when she looked back to see him in the same place, the breeze stirring the loose ties of his turban and the fringed ends of his gray sash. "Your name is Shivaji, I believe," she said, reluctant to go without having deciphered the puzzle of this man. "Has it a meaning?"

"I was named for Shiva," he said after a beat. "The Destroyer."

She didn't wait to hear any more.

Chapter 13

Most other days she had watched him shoot, but not today. With Arjuna at his side, Duran slogged through the August heat, dutifully swinging his rifle in the direction of any bird driven by the beaters into his vicinity. All his attention was drawn to the lookout spots where Jessica might appear. She never did.

He settled under a tree while the others gathered for lunch, pretending to doze, reflecting on Jessica's bewildered expression when he asked her to marry him. Except for the astonishment, he was unable to decipher the other emotions, a rainbow of them, that had prismed across her face.

She hadn't expected the proposal. But hell, neither had he. And she would refuse him, he was certain, as well she should. It was what, in his better moments, he wanted her to do.

Unfortunately, in a lifetime of moments, few of his could be described as "better."

What he ought to do was cut her free of all this and take himself off. He knew that, rationally.

And then, against every noble inclination he'd managed to scratch up, he reached out for her the way a drowning man grasps for a lifeline. The way he'd done off the coast of Madagascar, stretching his hand to

Shivaji, and look how that had turned out. He'd been rescued, all right, just so he could be killed later.

The fact is, a man had only himself to rely on. Enemies, lovers, gutless exploiters of the innocent—they were all the same. Someone always got hurt. Someone always did the hurting.

He should be stronger. He kept resolving to be stronger. Then he thought about not seeing her again and found it unendurable. Who would have thought he had so much feeling left in him? He'd assumed it had been burned out of him years ago.

She would, he supposed, find that amusing. Hugo Duran, gazetted rogue, lovelorn and tormented by his own conscience. He'd laugh, too, one of these days. If he survived long enough.

It was early afternoon and he'd just brought down a black grouse—by accident, considering his lack of concentration—when a liveried footman arrived from High Tor and put a folded message in his hand. Scanning it, he swallowed a bitter laugh.

"Is there a problem?" John Pageter asked, coming up beside him.

"You could say that. I'd call it a disaster."

The footman, a second message in his hand, had crossed to Arjuna. After reading it, Arjuna cast Duran a meaningful look and began assembling the rifles and appurtenances.

Duran turned back to Pageter. "I may be required to leave this afternoon. For London, I expect, but my recent guesses haven't been paying off. If I can, I'll send word where you can reach me."

"And in the meantime . . . ?"

"Forget you know me, if you're a man of good sense. I rather hope you are not."

"On that you may safely rely. But unless you have plans to the contrary, I'd prefer to remain at High Tor for the time being. Most of what I'm able to do for you can be accomplished from here."

"Yes." Duran glanced around. Arjuna was already gone, assuming he would follow, and the Others were lurking somewhere about to make sure that he did. "Keep an eye on Jess . . . Lady Jessica, will you?"

"Of course."

Pageter put out his hand and Duran took it, feeling something hard pressed against his palm before Pageter let go and turned away. Duran's fingers closed over the gift, a ring, he could tell by the shape of it, something for him to sell in an emergency. On the way back to the house, while passing under a thick overhang of oak branches, he opened his hand and looked down at an engraved gold band set with a large, square-cut emerald.

A family heirloom, damn it all. He couldn't pawn a bloody heirloom. and he'd have to figure a way to get it back to Pageter before Shivaji discovered it.

The gesture of friendship, though, he would always remember. "Always" being, in his case, not so taxing a commitment. In any case, he could not afford to indulge in sentimentality. Very shortly, he'd be face-to-face with a man who was emphatically not his friend.

Aubrey Carville, Lord Buckfast, heir to the Earl of Sothingdon and consummate prig, was waiting with folded arms and a constipated expression in the entrance hall, flanked by a pair of broad-shouldered footmen. Duran wondered if they were there to protect the Sothingdon scion or toss the Duran devil into the nearest bog. Because it would annoy Aubrey, he produced an elaborate bow.

Predictably, the scion colored to the roots of his receding hairline. He had changed little since their only prior encounter, which took place in the private room at White's Club where Duran had dragged the boy before he made a public and irrevocable mistake. Aubrey had been eighteen or nineteen then, already round as a watchtower and nearly as solid, his brown eyes blazing with conviction and rage. They were afire now as well, and his small white hands were fisted.

Still given to creating scenes, the scion, and Jessica might be in the house. "In the library," Duran said, tossing his hat and gloves to the startled footmen. "Only the two of us . . . unless you're afraid I mean to thrash you."

That would do it, Duran thought, correctly. He heard Aubrey dismiss his bodyguards, although they'd probably been told to remain close to hand, and settled his hips on a mahogany desk to await developments.

Aubrey—Duran could never think of him as Buckfast—erupted into the library like a one-man cavalry charge. "Y-you," he sputtered, "will leave here immediately. Your servants have packed. I've arranged for a coach. It's in the back, as befits tradesmen and reprobates. How dare you come here? Does your word mean nothing to you?"

"Do I go, or do I answer?" Duran smiled at him. "And if I answer, with which question shall I begin?"

Aubrey had matured, to a degree. With visible effort, he stilled his hands and planted his feet on the parquet floor. "The last one. You swore to leave England without speaking again to my sister. But here you are, under the same roof."

"To be precise, I agreed not to speak again to Lady Jessica before taking ship for India, or writing to her after I'd gone. There were no restrictions placed on what might happen if I came back."

"That's quibbling. You knew what I meant for you to do!"

"Yes. And I should never have consented to any of it. A snot-nosed boy, calling me out in front of twenty witnesses. If I hadn't clapped a hand over your mouth before it went too far, neither of us could have honorably backed down. And that, my child, would have been the last of you."

"Perhaps. But it was my duty to fight you. I should have done. If you'd killed me in a duel, you wouldn't be here now."

"Superb reasoning, as always. Do you mean to challenge me again? You may be sure that this time I won't decline. And as your father can testify, I'm a roaring good shot."

To Aubrey's credit, he didn't flinch. "I only challenge gentlemen," he said. "Blackguards I expel from my house."

"*Your* house? The present earl is, I believe, in excellent health. And partial to my company, by the way. I doubt he'll evict me."

"But he'll thank me for doing so, when he learns that you have defiled his daughter. And when you are gone, we shall deal with her as she deserves."

In a heartbeat, Duran was off the desk and halfway across the room. "*Deal* with her? Meaning what?"

"That is none of your concern. She has shamed the family. Now the family will contain the damage as best it can."

"Trust me on this," Duran said softly, gripping Aubrey's neckcloth. "Say one insulting word to your father or anyone else about the Lady Jessica and I'll put a bullet between your eyes."

When Aubrey lowered his gaze, nodding, Duran let him go. It was a mistake.

"I wonder that you express an interest," Aubrey said, adjusting his neckcloth. "A man of your stamp rarely cares what becomes of the women he whores."

The next sound was Duran's fist against Aubrey's jaw, followed by the thud of Aubrey's head against the wall. He hung there for a moment, slack-jawed, a thin line of blood trickling down his chin. Then his eyes turned up in his head, his knees buckled, and he slid slowly to the floor, leaving a trail of red on the green brocade wallpaper.

Duran, longing to hit him again, took two circuits of the room to cool his temper. A quick, clean exit seemed the best of the unsavory options on the menu. He bound Aubrey hand and foot with twine from the desk drawer, stuffed his handkerchief in the open mouth, secured it with twine, and tugged the limp body behind the desk. After some thought he wrapped a pair of warming rugs around Aubrey's arms and legs to keep him from thumping against anything loudly enough to draw attention.

The scion's heartbeat was strong and his breathing steady. All too soon, he'd be making trouble again.

Duran's hand was on the latch before he remembered the footmen. Damn. He grabbed a book from the nearest shelf, opened the door, and made a polite remark to the supposedly conscious Aubrey before closing it behind him.

A passing chambermaid gave him another chance to fend off an immediate investigation. "Lord Buckfast wishes a refreshment tray brought to the library in half an hour," he told her loudly. "For two. Lady Jessica will be joining him."

"But Lady Jessica is not at home, milord."

Damn again. No opportunity to speak with her before he left. "She is due back shortly, or so Lord Buckfast has said. Perhaps you should check with him at, say, three o'clock. He is dealing with matters of business and will not wish to be disturbed before then."

After a curtsy, the girl returned to her dusting while Duran went to the stairs and mounted them in a hurry.

When he arrived at his bedchamber, the last of the luggage was being carried out. Shivaji was nowhere in sight, thank God. He crossed immediately to the writing desk and began composing a message to Jessica.

Not long after, soundless as smoke, Shivaji materialized beside him. "What has become of the young man?"

Having considerable trouble wording his note, Duran looked up in annoyance. "I put him out of the way for the time being. He will probably recover."

"To bring charges? You forget yourself. Our mission cannot prosper under the attention of the authorities."

"That's the least of my concerns." After some thought, Duran wrote the direction of the rooms they had occupied in Little Russell Street, on the chance they'd be returning to them now. Asking Shivaji didn't seem like a good idea. He added that at his first opportunity, he would dispatch a longer letter explaining the abrupt departure. Should he apologize?

"Where is he now?"

"Who?" Duran rubbed his forehead. "Oh. In the library, behind the desk, bound and gagged."

"I will see to him," Shivaji said, a touch of resignation in his tone. "Go to the coach."

"In a minute. This is important."

"Sign it and go, or you will be carried there."

I'm sorry, he scribbled as Shivaji left the room. *Find a little faith in your heart for me, Jessie. Give me a chance to tell you what happened.*

He nearly signed his first name, thinking it would

sound more personal. More sincere. But she had never used that name with him, not even when they made love. If he trotted it out now, she was bound to be suspicious. *Duran,* he wrote, chilled. Once lost, sincerity—like virginity—could never be reclaimed.

After slipping the folded, sealed note under Jessica's door, he used the servants' stairs to the ground floor and arrived in the courtyard to find Shivaji already there, Arjuna at his side. All too quickly the coach was on its way to London, leaving Jessica and all his hopes behind.

Chapter 14

When Aubrey awoke, he was sprawled facedown on a familiar carpet . . . the one on the floor of his bedchamber. Something heavy lay across the back of his head, which throbbed like the devil, and there was broken glass strewn as far as he could see. That was only a short way, until he gingerly raised the burden and slid out from under it. Then, groaning, he sat up and examined his surroundings.

What had brought him down, or was meant to look as if it had, was the large, gilt-framed mirror that had formerly hung over the mantelpiece. The wire that held it had snapped, or been snipped, by whoever it was brought him here and staged this scene.

He had a pounding headache, but there was nothing wrong with his memory, at least to the point where that blackguard Duran had landed him a facer. From then until he recovered consciousness was a blank. Fury all but obliterating the pain, he crawled to the bellpull, and a few minutes later, seated in an armchair with an icepack on his head, he was interrogating the two footmen who were supposed to have been protecting him.

They were properly deferential, but their story never wavered. When Lord Duran left the library, they had followed him upstairs, and from there to the courtyard, where he and his peculiar foreign servants departed in the coach. No more than nine or ten minutes passed while all this took place. About twenty minutes after that, a maid had brought a tray of refreshments to the library and found it empty.

More intense questioning added a few minor details, only one of which Aubrey found interesting. Before leaving, Duran had paused by the Lady Jessica's door and slipped something under it.

Worrying at a loosened tooth with his tongue, Aubrey secured a set of keys from the housekeeper and retrieved Duran's note from Jessica's bedchamber. Then he went downstairs and inspected the library. Everything looked to be in order, except that he'd thought a tall, glass-fronted curio cabinet had stood closer to the fireplace. But perhaps not. He rarely spent time in the library, and furniture got moved around now and again.

What to do next?

To follow his own inclinations, which tended toward bloody revenge, was lamentably out of the question. Duran's threat, uttered with gentle intensity, could not be ignored by a man with a wife and four children. Sometimes the cost of pride was too high. And after all, he had proven his valor a half-dozen years ago, risking death for the sake of his family's honor—never mind that his sister had already surrendered hers. If not for his new responsibilities, he would stoically take that risk again.

What to tell his father was another matter. Someone had to rein Jessica in, but since the earl was unlikely to take action, there was little point disturbing his peace.

Well, he would think on it later, when the pain in his head and jaw allowed him to think clearly. He looked down at the folded sheet of paper in his hand, at Duran's seal stamped in blue wax, and resisted the temptation to read the message. Honor forbade it.

And practicality forbade putting it into Jessica's lascivious hands. Striking tinder, he burned the letter in a copper bowl.

It was late afternoon before Jessica arrived back at High Tor. Tired, exhilarated, unable to shed the apprehension that had hovered about her all day, she let herself in through a side door and went directly to her room. Duran could wait. It would do him good. And she wanted to look her best when she gave him her reply.

Spending the afternoon in the company of a woman in love had not changed her mind. Perhaps it made her envious, Mrs. Bellwood's serenity, but Mrs. Bellwood loved a man who had proven his fidelity by cleaving for a quarter century to a woman he feared and loathed. A man as far from Duran in loyalty as the North Pole was from the South. Of course, Lord Sothingdon was also somewhat lacking in beauty and magnetism, but Mrs. Bellwood didn't seem to mind. She valued him for all the things his first wife had carped at—his sweet nature, his regular habits, his attachment to a settled life.

In the early days of her marriage to a soldier, Mrs. Bellwood had followed her husband from one temporary, primitive lodging to the next, washing his clothes and cooking whatever she could scavenge for his meals. When he was killed in a skirmish of no consequence, she returned to her father's property and cared for him during his last illness. After that she lived alone, making friends among the few residents of the area and supplying posthouses and manor houses from her gardens, until she caught the Earl of Sothingdon's eye. They had been lovers for three years, but she refused to accept a penny from him and was careful not to draw attention to their relationship.

"Some people require proof of love," she had said, pouring Jessica a cup of strong tea. "Some demand formalities, legalities, and permanence. I have no quarrel with those things. But I find my true happiness in the life I make for myself, and add to it the love given me freely, sometimes sparingly, by your father. My late husband, chained by his duties, could offer no more than that, and I ask no more from Sothingdon."

"But don't you have a *right* to more?" Jessica had demanded, thinking of herself.

"Perhaps. But one cannot force another to give what he does not have, or is not willing to part with."

Chastened, Jessica turned the conversation to Mariah and her troubles with Gerald. Mrs. Bellwood had noticed, and been alarmed, but felt it was not her place to interfere. Even so, she agreed to provide Mariah a refuge if she required one. "And Sothingdon, while stubborn, can be got around," she added with a fond smile. "While I cannot meddle, I've no objection to a bit of manipulation."

Jessica had started out for home lighter of heart, until she passed by the spot where she and the enigmatic valet had launched their prayer boats. Ever since, subdued and puzzled by the story he had told her, she had been unable to forget the desperate princess and the dying prince and the Lord of Death.

They haunted her still as she lay across her bed, listening to the small sounds coming from the passageway and the adjacent room. The gentlemen had returned from the day's shooting, and the particular gentleman who obsessed her was right next door. It might be Pageter making those sounds, of course. Probably the both of them.

Rousing herself, she rang for a maid and began to

strip off her dusty walking gown. Perhaps she would go to dinner dressed in her finest and let Duran watch her ignore him while he wondered when she would give him her answer and what it would be. He knew her well enough to understand that either way, she'd make a grand production of it.

And he would enjoy the drama. Play along and give her credit for her performance. Would never insist she behave by any standards but her own.

Oh, dear God. How could she tell him *no*?

Such nonsense. Of course she could. Easily. With aplomb. Without regret.

After all, he'd offered only a paltry three weeks of marriage. Why bother? Three weeks was scarcely enough time to require a fresh paring of her toenails. Although, come to think of it, it was precisely the amount of time they'd spent together as lovers.

Well, at least he was consistent.

She was just about to ring for her maid when Mariah arrived at the door, distressed. "Where have you been all day? Aubrey kept asking for you."

"Aubrey!" Jessica stifled an oath that would have shocked her sister. "If he brought along that widowed vicar, the one he keeps foisting on me, I shall throttle them both."

"No vicar. He came alone. Papa wrote, saying we were in residence, and he took the opportunity to see us."

"To read us the ceremonial lecture, you mean. Have you had yours?"

"Some of it. He left out the part about my failure to provide Gerald with heirs, and seemed a trifle distracted. Then, while I was taking a nap, he had an accident."

"Dear me." Jessica sank onto a chair. "What happened?"

"A heavy mirror in his room came loose and fell on his head. He landed on his face, and his jaw is swollen and purple. Rather like a Christmas pudding, actually." Mariah produced an embarrassed grin. "I think the blow addled his brains, because he told Papa that Lord Duran had hit him. Which he could not have done, of course, because by the time Aubrey went upstairs to his room, where he was injured, Lord Duran was well on his way back to London."

"Wh-what?" Jessica felt as if she too had taken a blow. A hard one.

Again. He'd done it *again*! Gone off without a word. Because he'd realized she wasn't going to help him sell that stolen icon, she supposed. And figured she wouldn't marry him, either, meaning he couldn't trade on the good name of his wife.

It shouldn't hurt. She refused to let it hurt.

Mariah was speaking again. ". . . Pageter said a message was delivered this afternoon, summoning him immediately to London. Or to somewhere . . . The destination was unspecified. At first Papa was furious that Lord Duran had not left so much as a note of explanation, but Colonel Pageter calmed him down. He's good at that." Her lips curved into a rare smile. "We should set him to work on Aubrey."

Jessica studied her fingernails. *Don't think. Don't feel. Above all things, do not feel.* "A good idea," she said too cheerfully. "But I don't wish to see him. Aubrey, I mean, even though he's hurt. He grates on my nerves, and I would probably say something awful to him. Besides, I've had a summons of my own, from Helena, and must attend to a matter of business. I shall leave first thing in the morning."

"Oh." Mariah's arms curled around her narrow chest. "For London?"

The gesture, silently plaintive, reminded Jessica how

insignificant, in comparison, were her own troubles. She rose and crossed to where her sister was still standing by the door, as if uncertain of her welcome in Jessica's room. "You are not to worry," she said. "I'm sorry to leave you to cope with Aubrey, but you mustn't let him browbeat you. Think of it as practice for handling Gerald. Although if he is still in London, I intend to deal with him myself."

"But how? You mustn't provoke him. It will make him angry."

"I don't mind. And besides, he requires no provocation to be out of temper. Never mind Gerald. I want you to stay at High Tor, and should he come to fetch you, sneak out of the house and go immediately to Mrs. Bellwood. I visited her today, and she's as worried about you as I am. She will keep you safe until he can be made harmless."

"There is nothing can stop him, Jessica. But I shall do as you say, I promise, if only because I cannot bear any longer to do as Gerald says."

The small light in Mariah's eyes was only that, the barest of glimmers, but it was a beginning. And a challenge.

Precisely what they both needed, Jessica decided when Mariah had gone. A challenge, and in her own case, someone else's problems to solve so that she wouldn't have to confront her own.

After making arrangements for an early-morning departure, she focused all her attention on the problem of extracting Mariah from her husband. Seated at her desk, increasingly discouraged as the night wore on, she jotted down every harebrained scheme that hopped into her head. She even wondered if Shivaji the Assassin could be persuaded to hire himself out, and what would be the price of his services.

At that point she put down her pen and stoppered

the ink bottle. Never mind his arcane tales about the Lord of Death. The man was an inconsequential *valet*. At most, he could give Gerald a shave and iron his cravats.

On the positive side, she had passed several hours without once thinking of Duran.

Oh very well. Not one thought, but a dozen. Per hour. But that was better than she'd expected when first she learned he had done a moonlight flit. She was angry, that was all, and not at him. He wasn't worth that much effort. No, she was furious with herself for letting him slip past her defenses and . . . what?

It didn't matter. He was gone. More distant, more *irrelevant,* than when he'd been in India. The next time he crept into her thoughts, she'd fling him out again.

Chapter 15

Accompanied by her prim and acerbic secretary, Jessica spent two days and evenings paying calls on people at the fringes of respectability, trying to track down her brother-in-law. There were only so many places a gentleman could be found in London at this time of year, and fewer still that would permit the likes of Sir Gerald Talbot to cross the threshold.

It was Helena, using the mysterious network that connects servants throughout the city, who discovered that Gerald had weaseled his way into Beata Neri's circle.

Jessica admired Beata, a woman whose disregard for convention debarred her from the first ranks of society. After seeing three aged and wealthy husbands to their graves, she had set herself up on Paradise Row and opened her doors to people she found interesting.

There were plenty of doors in Beata's immense villa. Decorated in the Italian Renaissance style that suited her own striking looks, it was a rabbit warren of passageways and rooms suitable for private meetings. Now and again she entertained the Chosen with a masquerade ball, a play, or a concert in the large salons, but most of the people who came to Palazzo

Neri came there to gamble, do business, or talk. Mostly talk.

Her hospitality embraced scholars and soldiers, actors and scientists, gamesters and poets. Aristocrats dipping their white-gloved fingers into trade met there with associates more than a little rough around the edges. In back rooms, politicians made deals with the opposition only to undercut them in other back rooms. Everyone of importance came to Beata's, if they were lucky enough to secure her favor.

Which is why Jessica was astonished to learn that Gerald was indeed in the house, last seen entering the gaming room reserved for those who played deep.

"Oh, because he brought along an irresistible passport," Beata said, reading in her eyes the question she had not asked. "Sir Gerald is a toad, of course, but every pond must have one. How else are the others to feel superior? Come. We shall retrieve him."

"I don't want to put his back up," Jessica said. "Not yet."

"Then wait for him in the Sala Dei Medici. He must pass through when he leaves, which will be in a short time. I am told he is losing heavily."

Helena was already there, wearing her smoky glasses and seated on a brocade sofa next to Beata's companion. Jessica thought of joining them, but chose instead an isolated chair in a dim corner where she could think. Having got this far, with Gerald all but wriggling in her net, she still hadn't the least idea what to do with him.

She was no closer to a solution an hour later, when male voices punctuated with laughter signaled that the game had broken up. Men filtered into the parlor, most pausing to speak with Beata, who held court on an ornate chair placed where the light was most flat-tering. Opulent and sensual in scarlet Luccha velvet, she might have emerged from a Caravaggio painting.

Jessica was watching a skinny gallant kiss Beata's hand when Gerald's drawling voice sounded beside her.

"Ah, sister. I had thought you still at High Tor. Isn't that what you told me, Duran?"

Duran!

With Gerald.

Serpent and toad.

Her toes curled in her slippers, as if that could keep her anchored to the floor.

Duran approached her and bowed. "It is the nature of ladies to change their minds," he said, paling slightly when she glared at him. "How fortunate for us that she did."

"Why would you think so?" she inquired, rising. "What have I to do with either of you?"

"Oh, oh, I know her in this mood," Gerald said, wagging his finger. "Even Wellington would call a retreat."

Jessica arched a brow. He was drunk, and displeased, and playacting good humor. It wasn't difficult to guess why. "Lost a great deal, have you? I hope, Duran, that you don't expect him to pay."

"Of course I do." Duran turned his beguiling smile on Gerald. "Gaming debts are the first responsibility of a gentleman. But naturally, he must be given time to secure the funds from his banker."

"Yes, yesh. No hurry, what? Besides, tomorrow night I could win it all back."

"To be sure. The money, after all, is only a means of keeping score. It's the action we crave."

"Children at their games," Jessica said. "If ever you sober up and have a spare moment, Gerald, I have a business proposition for you. Perhaps not exactly what you wish for, but you did express interest in a partner-ship of sorts. If you still wish to discuss it, make an appointment with my secretary."

"P-partners don't make appointments," he said, bristling.

"I beg your pardon." She was trying to reel him in, not drive him away. "It's only that I am scheduled to meet with a number of clients, and Helena keeps my calendar. She's over there, if you care to speak with her."

"I'll give it some thought. Or maybe I'll drop in on you whenever it suits me. Don't forget, Jessica. I'm family. Mariah wouldn't be happy if you put me off."

Before she could parry that open threat, Duran had taken Gerald by the elbow and was steering him across the parlor and out the door. She waited a few moments to be sure they were gone, and then she hurried in the opposite direction, to a quiet ladies' retiring room in a part of the house reserved for secretive meetings. At this time of year, with most important people gone from London, no one was likely to be there.

In the stuffy room she sat on a low ottoman, her face buried in her hands, and fought tears that wanted, of their own volition, to be cried. For her part, she wanted nothing to do with them or the wave of loneliness that had swept over her the moment she saw Duran in company with her greatest enemy.

There was no sense to it. She had lived all but a few weeks of her life without him. And yet, God help her, that brief interval was the only time she had ever felt truly alive. The only time she had not consciously played a role to gain favor.

She wore disguises all the time now, but they never seemed to be the appropriate disguises. Her friends, most of them, would like her a great deal better were

she more conservative, more pliable, more *normal*.
Her family, most of them, would see her properly married and in all things dutiful. Her clients, most of them, wanted her to be, on their behalf, greedy and ruthless.

But Duran—irresponsible, unreliable Duran—accepted all her moods. never sought to change her. Because she was sufficiently useful as she was, she supposed. Why bother to change a woman he didn't mean to keep?

But in his company, she never felt inadequate, or guilty, or lonely. That was something, wasn't it?

No. It was nothing at all, if he didn't want her.

She dampened a cloth, mopped her face with it, and straightened her skirts. He had cut up her peace, but the fault was hers for permitting it. She kept bidding him good-bye—after he'd already gone, of course—and the rascal kept popping up again. The obvious solution was to ignore him altogether.

But when she opened the door, there he was, filling the space with a hand propped against each side of the casing, blocking her way.

Impossible to ignore.

"I wish you would cease accosting me in doorways," she said, giving him her best schoolmistress glower. "If you force me to call for assistance, Beata's large footmen will throw you out on your ear."

"I've called for their assistance myself, as a matter of fact. It required a pair of them to wrestle Talbot into a hackney." He took a step back. "I confess to being astonished that you mean to take him into partnership."

"Take? He is coercing me. If I pretend to go along, I may be able to dictate the terms, or at least keep him under control."

"What do you want to happen, Jessica? You know that I am looking for something to exchange for your assistance. Perhaps I can help."

Her very thought. Or it had been, during the intervals of madness when she'd talked herself into imagining she could trust him. No more. Not again. "Indeed you can," she said. "Go away, far away, and take him with you. That would solve any number of problems."

"Except mine."

"True," she said sweetly. "One cannot have everything."

"No. I have realized that. You intended to decline my proposal, I am sure, but I expected you to do it in person."

"I meant to. But there was the small matter of you not being there."

"That was unfortunate and, I assure you, beyond my control. Still, I left you my direction. You might have got in touch with me. Sent a message."

"You left me nothing. I returned from an errand, and you were gone."

He frowned. Paused. "I slipped a note under your door," he finally said. "And the first time we stopped to change horses, I dispatched a letter from the posthouse."

"Did you? But why do I ask? The Disappearing Note that Would Explain All. The Letter Gone Missing. You have been reading Minerva novels, Duran. And even if I believed you, I wouldn't care. You left, and I want you to stay away. Surely that is clear enough."

"Even if I can render Talbot harmless? In case you failed to notice, I've already made a start."

"By putting him in your debt? You and half of London can claim that achievement. But what's the use of it? He can't be thrown into prison, and his family connections prevent him from being hounded to the Continent by his creditors. Never mind that the family would be pleased to see the last of him."

"*I* could hound him," Duran said. "I can be persuaded. Would you like to try? Not here, of course, if you don't wish to be seen in my company." His gaze became intense. "Remember how I used to come to you, Jessica? Unlatch the window tonight."

Her heart pounded in response, like a hopeful girl's. Like a *stupid* girl's.

"Don't be absurd," she said. "Besides, you told me that you are watched wherever you go. Will your valet permit you to stay out so late?"

"I don't know. But at this point, with nothing going well, he might extend my leash. I'll go ask him, Jessie. You go open your window. And, if you can, your mind."

"Insults are always so effective when trying to win someone over, don't you think?" she said, moving past him and down the passageway.

He soon caught up with her, and when she glanced over, looked entirely unrepentant. "I learned the technique from you," he said. "You insult me constantly, and behold, I am your slave."

Against every instinct of self-preservation, she felt a laugh rise to her throat. *Please, no.* Nothing, not even his skill as a lover, was more dangerous than his gift for making her laugh.

They had come to a crossing of two passageways. Jessica started to turn to the right, wondering if Duran meant to follow her back to the salons, wondering if she wanted him to. But before she could complete the turn, a chubby man with side-whiskers barged out of a room a few yards ahead, staggered a little way in their direction, and halted.

Eyes narrowing, head jutted out like a chicken's, he stared at Duran as if trying to place him. Then his face tightened. "You!" he bawled. "I know you. Know what you did."

Jessica glanced at Duran, but his expression was infuriatingly neutral.

The man jabbed a finger toward him. "Saw you yesterday as well, damned if I didn't, sneaking around Leadenhall, making mischief. Treason, that's what. We—"

She lost what he said next because Duran swung around in front of her, seized her arm, and thrust her to the left. Understanding, she darted into the unlit passageway and pressed herself against the wall.

As always, the stratagems required to preserve her reputation were forcing her to miss out on something she very much wanted to witness. *Treason,* of all things. What had Duran been up to? But she could see nothing, and sounds failed to make the turn without becoming distorted.

The man, whom she hadn't recognized, was still shouting something about theft, treason, and hanging Duran from the highest tree. And for all she knew, Duran had done everything he was being accused of, although the charges stretched from training the enemy and supplying heathens with guns all the way to plucking food from his children's mouths. That last was unlikely, but there was little else she would put past him.

Other voices filtered to her ears. She edged deeper into the shadows, but the shouting had ceased and the more restrained speech of the newcomers was barely audible. What was going on there? Looking around, she saw a door not far from where she was standing and realized where in the villa she had come to. She knew of a perfect vantage point, so long as the gentlemen stayed where they were.

The door opened to a courtyard, one of Beata's Mediterranean fancies, with a fountain at the center and, curled around it, a labyrinth maze marked out with knee-high box hedges and ornamental trees. To-night the fountain was still, and no torches or lanterns had been lit. She slipped outside and paused a moment to get her bearings.

Scents of lemon and orange, lavender and laurel and roses, hovered in the warm air. She looked to her right where a line of windows, some with their top casements lowered to admit the evening air, marked the passageway where the whiskered man had been throwing his tantrum. Holding to the shadows, she stole toward the likeliest of the windows, searching for a good spot to see without being seen. Finally she settled on a fat potted shrub and crouched behind it, peering through the twigs and leaves directly into the brightly lit passageway.

Duran was standing with his back to her, facing an open door through which several gentlemen had emerged. They stood in a semicircle across from him, but with Duran blocking her view, she could identify only one of them.

The Beast. There was no mistaking Jermyn Keynes, Duke of Tallant, with his heavy black hair, harsh face, and the strange, nearly colorless eyes that always reminded her of someone, although she could never think who it was. Like any female of sense, she kept her distance from the Beast, who seemed to relish his nickname and did everything possible to live up to it.

"Is Garvey correct, for perhaps the first time in his life?" the duke was saying. "Ought we to hang you?"

"Leaving aside my personal bias on the subject, I presume?" Duran sounded unperturbed. "In fact, I'm ineligible for the honor, Your Grace. Assuming that a death sentence in England requires me to have broken any laws."

The duke regarded him speculatively. "You know who I am?"

"It was a guess. I am acquainted with someone who looks very much like you."

"Ah. My baby brother, I daresay. How fortunate. I've been trying to locate him these past several years. I don't suppose you know where he is?"

"Oh, still in India, I expect. Our paths rarely crossed. I can, however, tell you this much. He won't be found unless he wishes to be."

"So I have discovered," said the duke with a heavy sigh. "From the reports, he is in the north and the south, the east and the west, all at the same time. But if you think of something useful, let me know. He has been too long from his family, and there is a large reward for anyone who helps me bring him home."

Jessica reckoned that Duran, the master liar, would recognize that for the codswallop it was. Apparently he did, because he responded with a bow half an inch beyond insolence. In response, Tallant's jaw tightened. Like two cocks facing off, she thought, although neither man would issue a challenge without a better excuse than instant and mutual dislike.

From behind the cluster of men, light spilled through the open door into the passageway. Other men—she glimpsed heads and shoulders—were still in the room. It looked as if a meeting had just broken up. She inched closer, trying to identify the gentlemen standing to the right and left of the duke. One had a gloved hand clasped around the forearm of the man named Garvey who had fired the opening salvo.

"Why are you holding *me*?" Garvey demanded, struggling. "*He's* the one bankrupting the lot of us."

"Hardly," came a gentle voice from beside him. "Only the greedy have taken significant losses. When the drink has worn off, you will recall that I have promised to cover the loans you are unable to repay."

Just then Duran shifted his position, and she could

finally see the slender gentleman with the light brown hair and unremarkable face. He might have passed for a bank clerk, save for the exceptional tailoring of his clothes and the sharp intelligence in his kind hazel eyes. Lord Gretton. She knew him slightly. Everyone in society did. An intimate of the king, he was—in spite of his refusal to accept a position of power—among the most influential men in the country. She wondered why he had elected to champion a nobody like Hugo Duran.

"All well and good," Garvey sputtered. "Not that you can afford to let any one of us sink. Investments would dry up altogether. But this fellow has to pay. We'll make an example of him, what?"

"Only if he's implicated," Gretton said in a soothing tone. "And who better to ferret out the malefactors than the very man who has just agreed to make the long journey to India on our behalf. Surely you do not question his integrity and good judgment? No, I shouldn't think so. And having given him our trust, Mr. Garvey, we mustn't anticipate the conclusions he will draw before he has drawn them."

"Your confidence flatters me," came a beautiful voice. "I shall do all in my power to earn it. As for this gentleman, we ought not detain him at present. I'm sure he has other plans for the evening."

Into the light, into Jessica's view, stepped Derek Leighton, Earl of Varden. The Archangel, he was generally called, although unlike the Beast, he loathed the nickname he'd been given by the Prince Regent, now the king. It suited him, though, with his pale gold hair and extraordinary good looks. Like nearly every other unmarried female in the kingdom, she might well have tumbled in love with him, except that by the time they were introduced, she'd already . . . that is, she had resolved never to fall in love.

What an odd assortment of men this was—the king's right hand and the blustering *Mr.* Garvey, the Archangel and the Beast. Why had they been meeting secretly at Beata's house? It had to be important if the Archangel was going out to India to conduct an investigation, but surely treason was not a matter for private inquiries.

Some of her mental questions were answered when the other participants at the meeting began crowding into the passageway. They included three directors of the East India Company, and she recognized several prominent stakeholders and ship owners as well. Commerce, then, not politics. But what had Duran to do with John Company, or with them?

More to the point, what did they think he had done *to* them?

The group dispersed, with a protesting Garvey surrounded and shuffled off, leaving Duran alone in the passageway. He stood for a time, head lowered, before turning to the window and looking into the courtyard, directly at her.

She rose, meaning to approach him, but he lifted a hand.

"Go home and wait for me," he said, so softly that she was reading his lips to make out the words. "I'll come, if it is permitted. Will you admit me?"

She looked at him helplessly. The *no* that should have been on her lips failed to arrive. How could she answer? Of late, she didn't know from one minute to the next what she was likely to do.

With a faint smile, he bowed and left her to make up her mind.

Behind her, from the direction of the roof, a night bird called. Moments later it was answered, perhaps by its mate, and then silence fell again.

On this hot summer night, she felt like a block of

ice. Ice melting at a crossroads, like the one they had been standing in when Duran was accused of treason. She didn't believe that, of course. He was a scoundrel, certainly, but a purely self-indulgent one. Duran would confine himself to lesser crimes—theft, larceny, selling purloined icons, dallying with foolish females. Exploiting them.

So, why shouldn't she exploit him in return? It would be for a good cause, after all, and she needn't feel guilty, because they would be meeting on a level field—her expertise in exchange for his. She would help him dispose of his leopard, and he would rid her of her brother-in-law.

How he would go about that, she had no idea. But he'd think of something. And she was reasonably sure she could find someone to buy the icon. All she had to do was fake its provenance, give her personal assurance of its legitimacy and value, and wave good-bye to her reputation and the business she'd created for herself.

Blow a kiss of farewell to her independence, and to her honor.

Only that.

Dear God.

Chapter 16

They were probably using the roofs, Duran concluded after a while. A handful of times he'd made a sudden turn, lifted his head, and caught out a shadow next to a chimney pot. Or perhaps it was only the chimney pot he'd seen, or for that matter, the shadow of a chimney pot.

He'd been watching the streets as well, as he always did, and with as little success. The Others could not be invisible, but they were certainly undetectable. Although . . . if they were on the roofs, as he suspected, how the devil were they getting across the intersections?

Well, it didn't signify. He had long since stopped questioning their existence, or their perpetual scrutiny. Here in the city he could *feel* their presence as surely as he felt Jessica's longing for him. The Others were there, all right, blocking his escape, and she wanted him. Two dilemmas without resolution, unless he took a hand. A firm hand.

Easy enough to say, for a man being tracked across a slumbering city by invisible assassins. Traveling on foot, naturally, being forbidden to climb aboard anything with four legs or wheels. Oh, yes, indeed. He was very much in control of things.

The detached, bemused way he'd come to look at

life, especially his own life, made it difficult to take his circumstances with the proper degree of seriousness. He'd been nearly killed so often that death seemed unlikely even when it stared him in the face. Nonetheless, he awoke most nights in a cold sweat, his pulse racing as if his body feared what his mind refused to accept. And then he would reflect that no one would miss him, which was not in the least comforting, and feel an aching loss for something that never defined itself. He knew only that it was something he had never possessed.

Nearing the square where Sothingdon House held the prime location, he turned into an alleyway, passed the mews, and arrived at a wall about three feet taller than he. Springing up, he caught the top, pulled himself over, and dropped lightly to the ground.

He was in the herb garden behind the kitchen. Scents hovered on the night air . . . rosemary, marjoram, and lavender. The kitchen windows glowed orange-gold from the light of a banked fire, and on the top floor, a single lamp still burned. In the distance, a dog barked.

He felt, suddenly, as uncertain as a boy with his first woman. She had sealed the entrance against him, he was all but sure, and the pain of her rejection struck him even before he'd put it to the test. Briefly, he considered turning back. But then again, he owed her the satisfaction of turning him away.

He mounted the three steps to a small terrace and crossed to the French window that had been, years earlier, his gate to paradise. Behind it, the curtains were closed. Heart pounding, he reached for the latch and gave it a twist.

With a small click, the door cracked open.

He was so startled that for a moment he stood with his hand still wrapped around the latch, unable to believe his good fortune. Then he pushed the curtain aside and entered the salon.

"In the past hour," Jessica said from the other side of the room, "I have locked and unlocked that window a dozen times."

"How fortunate that I arrived during one of the *unlocked* intervals."

"For you, perhaps."

Her voice was cool and self-possessed. As his eyes adjusted to the darkness, he traced the outlines of furniture and located her seated primly on a straight-backed chair near the door. "I hadn't expected to be admitted," he told her honestly. "Thank you."

"Don't speak too soon. This will be a difficult negotiation."

"I see. Or rather, I can't see. Will you mind if I ignite a lamp or two?"

"Yes. I am susceptible to you, as you know, and prefer not to be distracted. Please be seated. There is a sofa to your right."

As far from her as he could be placed in this room, unless he was dangling from the curtain rods. When he was settled, the crisp, disembodied voice asserted itself once again.

"You have asked for my assistance," it said, "and I require yours. Perhaps we can come to terms. Here is what I propose. My brother-in-law has become a nuisance, and I wish him to be made ineffectual. How you manage that is your concern, but take care your methods do not reflect badly on my family. In return I shall put my experience, reputation, and all the resources at my disposal to help you sell your leopard."

That was plain enough, if misguided. "But I don't

wish to sell the replica," he reminded her. "I am looking for the original."

"If you say so. I don't really care. Simply outline your requirements, and I'll tell you if I can meet them."

The clinical proposition had him somewhat disoriented. Alone with her, his thoughts arrowed to why he'd come here in the past, and what they'd done together. And once honed in on that irresistible target, his mind could accommodate little else.

But it must. Conjuring Shivaji, a squelcher of desire if ever there was one, he spoke by rote. "To begin with, there is information we require from the East India Company, but they will not open their registers to me. If you have connections there, perhaps we can gain access. Also, we wish to learn of anyone who collects artifacts from India, or from any exotic country. Shivaji is convinced that the leopard was shipped from Madras to England. If someone who received a parcel in the relevant time period is also on your list of collectors . . ."

He couldn't go on. It was pointless, Shivaji's quest. Unlikely the leopard ever left India. Impossible that it arrived here in one piece. For him, it existed only as a pretext to lure Jessica to him.

"That is easily arranged," she said when he failed to elaborate. "What else?"

"Calls on potential holders of the icon and collectors who might be acquainted with other collectors. I have to mount an active search, Jessica. Shivaji expects it. Demands it. If you will draw up a list of candidates, we shall map out a route that can be covered within the allotted time."

"That can be done as well. But why would these collectors open their doors to you?"

"Because you will have written to request an appointment and will be standing beside me when I knock for admittance."

"You expect me to *travel* with you?" For the first time, she sounded disconcerted. "The two of us?"

"And Shivaji. Don't forget him." No reason to mention Arjuna and the Others.

"I don't think," she said carefully, "that your valet would be an acceptable chaperon. Not for an extended trip, at any rate. I could bring Helena . . . but no. She's a servant as well. I tend to forget that. Mariah, perhaps, although I doubt she'd agree. Or is it an essential part of your scheme, Duran, that I compromise myself together?"

"I don't want that. You could pass me off as an employee, I suppose, or an expert on artifacts. If you teach me the jargon, and if I wear a disguise and behave eccentrically, we can skate through this with little damage." He took a deep breath. It might be worth a try. "Of course, there would be no question of impropriety if we were married."

The word dropped into the room like a boulder. It seemed to echo from the walls. *Married. Married. Married.*

Silence.

Then—"I thought you'd given up on that benighted notion," she said.

"I had given up on your accepting my proposal, yes. It was, when first I asked you, an impulse. I hadn't thought it out. But when I said the words, they seemed perfectly right, and they still do. To be sure, I have no more to offer you now than I did then. Well, perhaps a little more. I will see that Talbot ceases to trouble you. And there is less time you need to put up with me. Only twenty days remain."

"And then you'll be gone."

"Make no mistake about that. Fair warning this time. I shall leave, and I'll never come back. It's possible, although I don't know how to go about it, to counterfeit evidence sufficient to have me declared legally dead. Failing that, you can devise whatever story you like to account for my absence."

"Such as, 'I'm a fool who married a scoundrel'?"

"I never said you had to tell the truth."

He thought—he was nearly sure—that she laughed. There was a small sound, anyway, and the air in the room did not feel so heavy as before.

"If we married," she said, "who would stand witness for you? Shivaji?"

Was she actually considering it? His heartbeat speeded up. "I doubt he'd be permitted in the church. But you're really asking if he'll interfere, and the answer is, I don't know. He might consent, if your help is conditional on the marriage. Is it?"

"No. You have heard my conditions. A marriage would be solely for my own purposes. If I could think of any."

"Might I suggest . . . nostalgia?"

The sound came again, the one he'd hoped for. The almost-laugh.

It would suffice.

There was a time, he had learned, for diplomacy. For careful maneuvering. On occasion, even a time for retreat. But sometimes, when the blood was up and the foe obdurate, only a direct charge would carry the day.

Instantly he was across the room. Drawing Jessica to her feet, he moved his hands to her waist and paused, testing her response. No struggle. Not the slightest protest. Thank God. He wasn't sure he'd have been able to release her.

Nor was she stiff and resistant, no, she was leaning

into him, head lifted, so he kissed her. And felt her
fingers tangle in his hair, so he deepened the kiss. And
heard her make a purring invitation low in her throat,
so he swept her in his arms and carried her, as he had
done before, silently up the dark stairs and along the
passageway to her bedchamber.

Chapter 17

Duran lounged on a chair at the foot of the bed, gazing at the woman who held his life in her hands. Not his survival—that remained in other hands—but everything he was learning to value.

She was lying across the bed, her disordered hair streaming over the pillows, her legs a little open, one bent at the knee. Above it, a white satin garter winked from the crumpled lace of her petticoats. She lay asleep where he'd left her ten minutes earlier, shortly after she'd ravished him.

His smile—he'd been smiling for ten minutes—widened. Voracious female. She couldn't wait, not for clothing to come off, not for anything. Once the door had closed behind them and he'd set her on her feet, she had pounced on him like a jungle cat. Like a woman who had not been made love to in a long, long time.

Which could not be the case, he was sure. From the beginning, he had admired the way she saw what she wanted, went after it, and secured it for herself. At their first encounter she'd been so bold it had astonished him to discover, at the very moment when it became otherwise, that she had been a virgin. Now he envied the man who had replaced him, and all the men after that.

Perhaps not so many, though. She would be selective. He hoped her discernment had improved since she picked out the likes of him in a crowded ballroom. He'd never told her how he had seen her gaze home in on him and remain there as he moved around the ballroom, and that he'd seen her approach their hostess, gesture in his direction, and sail across the room with the reluctant woman in tow to procure an introduction. In a way he regretted that she had become more careful now, more subtle, more in control of herself.

Until she was alone in a bedchamber with her lover. Then she had no control at all.

He had forgot how she exhausted herself in the first rush of passion, like a bird of prey soaring and wheeling and diving until the climactic blow. Then, breathless and palpitating and triumphant, she dropped immediately into a motionless sleep.

It never lasted long. She would wake soon, he knew, those glorious lashes fluttering, her eyes shining with wonder. Jessica making love was every man's carnal fantasy. Jessica in the aftermath of love made a man think of unfamiliar words like *cherish*. And *forever*.

His smile fading, he rose and went to the bay window beside the bed. Pale light teased at the edges of the curtains. He made an opening with his finger and looked across the walled garden to the slate roofs of the mews, not expecting to see the Others and not seeing them.

A bird announced the dawn. Another acknowledged the message.

And then, a sound from the bed. A yawn, and a small sigh of pleasurable lassitude. Letting go the curtain, he turned to the bed and enjoyed the ballet of Jessica emerging from slumber.

"You'll have to marry me now," he said.

"Why?" She stretched, moving against the counterpane like a swimmer. "I didn't, before."

"I didn't ask you before. And during that time I took care, against your exuberance and every demand of nature, to make sure there would be no unwanted consequences. Tonight I was off guard, and you were unusually—"

"I know." She sat up, pushing her disheveled hair behind her ears. "Exuberant."

"Undeniably. But above all things, utterly splendid."

The shadow that had crept into her eyes vanished. "You always drive me mad," she said. "And you needn't worry, because it isn't the proper time of the month for . . . consequences."

"Well, there's many a man heard that song, followed nine months later by the wail of an infant. I'm sure you think it's true," he added quickly when she frowned. "But contraception by tracing a woman's fertility cycle is notoriously unreliable."

The frown deepened. "You know this from experience?"

"I presume you're asking about little Durans scattered across the subcontinent, and the answer is, there are none I am aware of. I do take care, Jessica. And I'm not nearly so debauched as I should like to be."

"But then, who *could* be that debauched?" The humor returned to her eyes, although her lips were stern. "I'm surprised you are still here. Will someone come storming in to carry you off?"

"I trust not. If the watchers are alert, they will have seen me at the window." He sat on the edge of the bed, not far from that provocative garter. "I didn't want you to wake up and find me gone. My departures seem to nettle you. But remaining may have compromised your reputation, unless there is a secret way out in broad daylight."

"Do you imagine I failed to consider that? When I left for High Tor, my secretary gave most of the servants a holiday, and only two or three have returned. She can call them together for instructions while you slip away."

"Miss Pryce knows? And approves?"

"There's no hiding anything from her, so I don't bother to try. As for what she thinks, she either lets you know or she doesn't. And about you, she didn't. Why did that tiresome Mr. Garvey accuse you of treason?"

The abrupt change of subject caught him off guard. It shouldn't have done, being one of his own favorite tactics, but he might have erred by using it on Jessica. She was a quick study.

And this was a question he preferred not to answer. As a diversion, he began to remove his shoes. "You heard it all," he said, grinning at her over his shoulder. "My guess is frustration over bad investments and too much claret."

Jessica, unsurprised by the evasion, watched him while considering what next to do. Her world and her life teetered on the thin, untrustworthy wire of his disreputable past, the larcenous inclinations of his present, and his mysterious plans for the future. The only sure way to regain her balance was to jump off that wire and walk away.

But she needed the man he was—morally flexible, criminally experienced, smarter and stronger than Gerald. She had overdue debts to pay, to those who had needed her help when she was too selfish to notice.

But did she have the courage?

She wasn't sure. If she took this path, there would be no turning back. Her fledgling business, which had only just tasted success, had been built on her integrity and dedication to her clients. Once she had lied to those who trusted her, set herself to cheat at least one of them, the foundation would crumble.

She didn't want to do this. Perhaps she wouldn't. Probably she wouldn't.

Selfish, selfish, selfish.

It wasn't as if she'd be thrown on the streets to stave. Not an earl's daughter, with a family who loved her in a begrudging way and would love her all the more if she conformed to their notions of propriety. Her father would be pleased to welcome her home, and Aubrey positively delirious at her failure. Jessica back in the fold where she belonged, behaving as she ought, taking orders from the men of the family who fed, clothed, and sheltered her.

Within a year, she would be dead of boredom.

Or perhaps none of it would come about. There was little point striking a deal with Duran if he had offended the powerful East India Company. The supposed threat from his valet was hogwash, she was sure, in spite of her new curiosity about Shivaji. But no one with a grain of sense made an enemy of the Beast. And if that model of chivalrous rectitude, the Archangel, uncovered evidence against Duran, then . . . Oh, nothing at all. By that time, Duran would be long gone.

Now that she thought on it, his entire scheme had begun to unravel the moment Garvey recognized him. He must have hoped to sell the icon without calling attention to himself, which would explain why he refused to advertise it and why he wanted to take to the road, using her as cover and keeping himself out of the way of the authorities.

Yes, a very good thing that Garvey had accosted them at Palazzo Neri. Without this piece of the puzzle, she might have convinced herself that Duran was speaking the truth. For a clear-sighted woman of business, she had a calamitous tendency to cling to illusions.

Returning her attention to the master illusionist, she saw that he had removed his shoes, his jacket, and was about to pull off his shirt. That much temptation was more than she was prepared to resist.

"I'm still waiting," she said, realizing too late that it sounded like an invitation. "I mean, waiting for you to answer my question."

"I was hoping to distract you."

"Well, just stop it. Are you, in fact, a traitor?"

With a grimace, he lowered himself again on the edge of the bed, facing a little away from her. She could see a muscle working at his jaw.

"There was no treason. But I have offended the East India Company, and cost it money, and helped prevent incursions into parts of India that did not want it there. My only regret is failing to do more damage."

Although he had always been careful to reveal nothing of himself, now and again a bit of information had slipped through his screen. One of those bits nibbled at her memory. "Didn't you once tell me your father had worked for the Company?"

He gave a sharp crack of laughter. "Indeed he did. He quite literally gave his life to the job. Do I have to tell you about it?"

"Yes." She thought again. "No. I apologize. It isn't my place to ask about your family."

"Your *place*? Ask what you will, Jessica. I'm perfectly capable of refusing to answer."

When he said nothing more, she presumed a refusal had been issued and immediately began casting about for a question he might attend to. There was so much she wanted to know. What was he hiding? Would she be sorry to learn the truth? Would he ever *tell* her the truth?

"One way or another," he said, startling her, "you always strip me naked."

And what did *that* mean? Another long silence, which she was afraid to break.

"Any other way would be better than this." His voice made her think of ashes falling on snow. "But someone ought to hear the story, I expect. I will soon be gone, and it's certain that no one else remembers. Or cares."

He was on his feet then, in a spurt of the restless energy she understood all too well. In such a mood she never wished to be interrupted, so she banked pillows against the headboard and sat against them, waiting until he was ready to speak. It took less time than she'd expected.

"My father was a younger son of a family with little money, but they saw him decently educated and helped him secure a position with the Company in London. It took a dozen years to save enough to marry his childhood sweetheart, and shortly after their wedding, the Company required him to take a post in Calcutta. My mother miscarried their first child aboard the outbound trader and her second two years later. She was, I am told, never in good health after that. My birth didn't help."

He had been pacing, studying the floor, but at this point he glanced over at her. "The burdens on my father were considerable. Along with an ill and, I have to say, mentally distracted wife, he was cursed with a son bent on a career as a rogue. I appear to have fulfilled all his expectations."

The pacing resumed. "There were plenty of servants, of course, even for Company functionaries, but what my mother needed was a steady routine in familiar surroundings. Instead, by Company directive, the family was moved from post to post, each more primitive and remote than the last, until we found ourselves deep in territory besieged by the Marathas. Soon after, the other employees at the station were recalled, leaving my parents to 'hold the castle for the Company.' Those were the words in the dispatch. I know, because I later tracked down a copy in the Calcutta offices."

She couldn't help herself. "Were you with them? And who precisely are the Marathas?"

"A loose confederacy of ill-tempered tribes who kept themselves busy acquiring territory belonging to others when they weren't fighting among themselves. And no, by then I had been sent off, very much against my will, to acquire polish and self-discipline at a new school established by the Governor-General in Calcutta. Meantime, my father wrote again and again to his superiors, begging to be removed from the station. There was no commerce possible, no profit to be had, nothing for him to do there. But the Company was determined to maintain its foothold—one clerk and his unstable wife—in the area. And father obeyed, because after twenty-seven years, he was so near to qualifying for his pension. With four hundred pounds a year, they could return to England and settle in the Derbyshire cottage my mother had always longed for. He endured until his pension was only a year away, but when nearby villages were being torched and the few detachments of the Company army still in the vicinity gone on the run, he sent an urgent plea for help. It was refused. Not long after, the compound was burned to the ground. Only two bodies were discovered in the rubble. The servants must have fled in time, but my mother was too frail, and my father would not have abandoned her."

"I'm so sorry," she murmured under her breath, imagining more than she wished to know of what had happened.

"The point is, the Honorable East India Company was perfectly content to have them die. It was, I later discovered, an unofficial policy to assign hard duty to employees on the verge of retirement. The fearful ones, at any rate, or those without resources or influence. If they quit, or failed to survive, their pensions need never be paid. And this," he said in a rough voice, "is why I made it my business to play havoc with theirs."

"I have to know," she said after a few moments. "What precisely did you do?"

"First, I prepared. Fifteen and wild as a lynx, I lied about my age and wormed my way into the Company army."

The hard part must have been got through, Jessica thought, because he seemed more relaxed now. He stopped near the window long enough to crack the curtains and look outside, and when he began moving again, his pace was slower. "When I'd learned all I could about fighting in India, I resigned and carried my knowledge and experience elsewhere. The Marathas had long since had their teeth pulled, leaving the Company to devour, one by one, the small independent principalities of India. I hired myself to their rulers, supplying them weapons, training their armies, and if necessary, leading them into battle against Company troops. It rarely came to that. The Company generally preys on the weak and unprepared."

Stopping at the foot of the bed, his hands clasped behind his back, he gazed at her with somber eyes. "I have done a great many things I don't wish ever to speak of, and made enemies among influential people, and have nothing whatever to show for thirty-five years of existence. Even so, the Honorable Directors will do no more than bluster at me. A trial would make public what they are at pains to conceal, and there are others making more mischief with the Company than I ever did. You needn't be concerned."

"Well, you would say that, of course. I am not to worry my little head about matters reserved to men, which includes just about everything of interest or importance."

As she watched, a glint of mischief appeared in his eyes, along with something else she recognized. And wanted.

"What an assertive, audacious, presumptuous creature you have become." His head tilted to one side. "Are you *ever* submissive?"

"Heavens, no. Why should I be?"

"To get me to do what you wish me to do. I should rather like to see you play at being acquiescent. Or perhaps I am mistaken. Perhaps you have been satisfied well enough already."

"I was, before. But this is now, and you are not mistaken. Even so, I do not care to play this sort of game. I have no talent for it."

"Unfortunate. I expect that with a little practice, you'd be quite adept at satisfying all my needs."

"I could . . . try." She was having to force out the words. But resistant as she felt to what he proposed, she was also beginning to find it a little exciting. More than a little. "What shall I do?"

"Can't you guess? Really, these matters are better managed in a harem, where a man chooses from among many women the one to suit his mood." He lowered himself onto the chair at the bottom of the bed, his legs stretched out before him, his long-fingered hands relaxed on the armrests. "Tell me why I should select you."

"Because I'm the only one here?"

The corners of his mouth twitched. "My choices are limited, certainly. In fact, they are two. Shall I take my leave, or shall I have you? Do you want me to have you, Jessica?"

Her attention went to the sweet throbbing between her legs, where he had been. Where she needed to feel him again. "Y-yes."

"Show me how much you want me, then. Persuade me that I want you."

As if he could doubt it. When passion seized her, every speck of restraint flew out the window. In his arms she could withhold nothing of herself and feared what she might reveal to him. Or to herself. This masquerade, she now understood, gave them both a safe place to hide. The games he proposed, the masks they wore, allowed them to indulge their desires without restraint, without deceit, without regret. It was his gift to her.

"I don't know how," she said in a deferential tone that made him smile. "What is it you wish me to do?"

"Well, I should like you a lot better, I believe, if your body was exposed to me. Slowly, a little at a time. And with a bit of style, if you can manage it. I have exotic tastes."

She hesitated. Before, he had always insisted on removing her clothes. It was a ceremony between them. A dance.

"Do you mean to deny me?" He looked arrogant. Surprised at her reluctance.

"I didn't think you favored compliant women."

"I've had the other kind. I had one of them only a few minutes ago. It was satisfactory, yes, but now my palate is for something softer, sweeter, more . . . obedient."

He was so damnably self-assured, a tawny-haired sultan who had only to express a wish to have it granted. Perhaps for him it wasn't a game after all. Or perhaps he simply played it very well. Her mouth felt dry. "I'll require help," she said, remembering the tapes and hooks and ties she could not reach.

"Then you must earn it. Not by talking, though. Not by delaying. Show me what I want to see."

The lazy voice with its undercurrent of command sent tingles of nervous anticipation racing over her skin. She had never before been with him in the daytime. Been naked to him in daylight. What if she didn't please him? Suddenly apprehensive, she reached down, lifted her skirt and petticoats, exposed one silk-stockinged leg.

Remembered that she was no longer wearing her drawers. She glanced over her shoulder, saw them on the carpet beside the bed. He had stripped them off with one hand, using his other to insert himself.

She fumbled with the garter, tugged it over her knee, knew she was the least graceful, least enticing female on the planet. But he didn't complain, so she rolled the stocking down her leg, aware of the moisture pooling between her thighs, wondering if he could see it.

"Come here," he said. "Put your foot—no, the other one—on my knee. I wish a close view of what you have to show me. Yes, there. But your thighs are together, Jessica. They should never be together when you are with me."

With a gesture, he directed her to widen them, and how far. She felt his gaze like a solid object against her opening. "May I see you as well?"

"No. You may only feel me, and only when I decide you are ready. The other stocking now."

When she'd slipped it off, he took it from her and drew her leg up over his so that she had to hop closer to him, between his legs, to regain her balance.

"You may put your hands on my shoulders," he said, "while I untie your laces. If we do this right, I'll be able to suck your nipples at the same time. Would you like that?"

Her expression must have answered the question, because he chuckled softly as he reached under her skirts and detached her petticoats. Then he undid the tapes that held skirt to bodice. Her lower body was tangled in swathes of muslin, lace, and sarcenet.

"What's this? No corset?"

"I don't like them," she said. "I wear one only when I go out in company."

"Good. I don't like them either. Well, your breasts will have to wait, then. Remove everything else you are wearing, please."

He didn't object when she withdrew her leg, and shortly, she stood bare and flushed with excitement before him.

"Come onto my lap now, and put your legs over the chair arm. No, no. They're closed again. Remember what I told you about that. Now settle your back against my arm. Are you comfortable?"

She was, sideways across him, his erection pulsing against her backside. But his shirt and trousers felt abrasive against her oversensitized skin. She knew better than to object, though, so she nodded and was rewarded with a kiss.

"Is there any place on your body I cannot touch?" he said, his tongue moving to her ear and dipping inside. "Tell me I can have all of you, any way I wish, for as long as it pleases me."

"You . . . you can." Her breathing was becoming short and shallow. "Everything. But hurry."

"Oh, no. Hurry is the very last thing I am going to do. Your nipples are already hard, and I haven't gone near them. I wager, Jessica, that I could make you come without touching you at all."

"Yes. Probably. But don't do that."

"Perhaps not today, then. But one day, we shall play that game. Meantime, your breasts need attention. Ask me to lick them."

She did, and fell back against his arm as he caressed them with his tongue, teasing at her nipples, drawing them into his mouth, sucking while she looked down at his head, at his lips and tongue moving on her, feeling the climax building between her legs. She needed pressure there, started to close them, felt him pull away.

"Where is your obedience, Jessica? You are my plaything. Remember?"

"I don't like it that you have so much control over me," she said. "And so much control over yourself when you are with me."

"That astonishes me as well. Do you imagine it is easy? Only a bit of cloth prevents me from sliding up inside you. But when I do, this will be nearly over. And when it is over, I must leave. So relax, Jessie. Close your eyes and feel me. Ten minutes is all I ask. You're not ready yet for longer play. But each time we are together, I shall teach you how to stretch your pleasure, like a single strand of silk, to the breaking point."

She hadn't thought she could, but for what seemed infinitely longer than a few minutes she felt his hands and lips moving on her body, as if he played her like a lyre. It felt so wonderful, and then more wonderful, that she thought a climax would be, at this time, an intrusion on the purest delight.

He withheld it from her carefully, touching every

place but the one place that would shatter her. When he put the first finger inside her, he did so from behind her thighs so that his hand wouldn't set off the fire at her nub. The finger moved deliciously, swirling around, withdrawing, returning. Then it was joined by a second finger, and his mouth was at her mouth, and his tongue moved in rhythm with that invading hand. She writhed against him as one of his hands toyed with her breast, as his tongue plunged in and out of her mouth, as his long fingers reached ever deeper.

Then emptiness for a moment. He sucked on her tongue, adjusting something below. A stretching sensation, not unpleasant, and he wriggled three fingers through her opening. Her head fell back with the excitement of it.

"That's good," he said. "Look down, Jessica. Watch my hand play with you. How many orgasms do you want?"

His dark fingers, slick with her moisture, mesmerized her. She couldn't answer. She could only feel.

"Now, I think," he said. His other hand moved slowly from her breast, down her stomach to the dark curls, combed through them, and with just the right pressure, with her watching his hands make their music, he brought her slowly and then faster and faster to a searing, throbbing climax.

It was so overwhelming that in the aftermath, she felt herself falling into unwanted sleep. Distantly she felt him lift her and cross to the bed. She fought the darkness closing over her. It was unfair to deny him. And however great the pleasure she had just experienced, it was nothing compared to being joined with him in the most intimate embrace of all.

"Please," she whispered when he seemed about to let her go.

"Are you sure?"

"Oh, yes." Raising her hand, she pressed it against the large erection pushing against his trousers. "Give me this. I want this."

"I am your slave, my princess," he said. "I will give you everything I have."

Chapter 18

For Jessica, the next three days passed in a blur. After dispatching Helena to examine records at the offices of the East India Company, she gathered and pawned nearly everything of value she owned, including her jewelry, her small collection of antiquities, and her ermine-lined cloak.

She took the names provided by Helena to every expert she knew who lived within reach of London and culled the list to thirty-four collectors with an interest in exotic and expensive antiquities. Their residences were scattered from Cornwall to Northumberland.

She requested and received favors from a sculptor, a painter, a jeweler, the president of the Board of Control for the Affairs of India, the Duke of Devonshire, and the rector of St. Giles in the Fields.

There had been little opportunity to catch her breath, and none to consider if she was behaving wisely. It no longer seemed to matter. To protect her sister and hamstring her brother-in-law, she had cast her lot with a seductive daemon. There would be ample time for regrets when he was gone.

Meanwhile, with nearly all their plans worked out and most of the arrangements in place, she was waiting in the parlor for him to arrive, passing the time by addressing letters to the last few collectors on her list. It was nearing midnight, and Duran was more than two hours late.

When he finally appeared, arm in arm with Gerald, the reprobates were in high spirits. Disgusted, she watched Duran lurch to the sideboard and pour two hefty glassfuls of cognac. Then, settling side by side on a couch like the best of brothers, they launched into a review of the evening's entertainment at Palazzo Neri. Each had won a decent sum at hazard, but after that, Gerald lost all his winnings to Duran on the single turn of a card. Unaccountably, both men found that hilarious.

Once, when Gerald wasn't looking, Duran winked at her, and she began to suspect he was more in control of the situation than it seemed. But from years of experience, she knew that Gerald managed heavy drinking better than most. He bumbled about, often turned mean, but never lost the cunning that had kept him afloat far longer than others of his kind. She ought to have warned Duran about that.

When the subject eventually staggered around to Jessica's business proposal, she could tell Duran had already laid the groundwork. Before she'd begun to explain her offer, Gerald leaped directly to his catalog of objections.

"For one thing," he said, his drawl less pronounced than it had been, "we haven't discussed advance money, not to mention expenses. And for another, you can't expect me to sell something I haven't even seen."

"Well, keep in mind we're not trying to sell it," Duran said with exquisite patience, "although we shall do so, of course, if all else fails. What we really want is to find the mate."

"So you say. But it sounds havey-cavey to me. And

not quite in your line, Jessica," Gerald added, turning his small-eyed gaze to her. "Do you believe all this business about stolen idols? Especially since he claims to have stolen one of them himself?"

"Now, now," said Duran. "I'll deny that in any court of law. Not that a British court gives a fig what becomes of pagan idols."

"That rather depends on who owned it, and more to the point, who might want to own it. But the lady is our expert. What say you, sister-in-law? Ready to stake your reputation on the word of this paltry fellow?"

"Certainly not. I have had the statue evaluated by several scholars of India antiquities, and they were unable to verify its authenticity. I have demanded provenance of Lord Duran, and he could provide none. What is more, his tale of not one but *two* stolen idols defies credibility. I should think the provincial ruler could manage to hang on to at least one Golden Leopard."

"Y-yes," said Gerald, sounding disappointed. "Exactly the point I was making."

He wanted to believe in this, she thought. A measure of his indebtedness. Of his desperation. "But something about the statue appealed to me," she said reflectively. "I have a sense of quality, you know. A talent for recognizing what is of value, even when it has been scrounged from an attic all covered with dust. So I brought the leopard to a jeweler, who certified the value of the gold and the gems, and to a sculptor, who declared the carving ancient and magnificent. I cannot stand by Lord Duran's story of the statue's origin, or vouch there is another just like it, but without doubt the one we have in hand is worth a tidy sum."

"A small fortune, at the very least," Duran said.

"But the pair, returned to Alanabad, would garner a prince's ransom. I vote we go for the greater prize. Jessica?"

She hesitated. Felt Gerald's avid regard concentrated on her. "I don't know. It would take a long time. And if we find the other leopard, and send you with the both of them to India to claim our reward, what certainty would there be that you'd come back to share it with us? I say a leopard in the hand is worth two elsewhere. Or nowhere."

"Save that I love you," Duran said softly.

She hadn't seen him rise, but suddenly he was there, his hands gripping hers and drawing her to her feet.

"Have you forgot already?" For a moment he gazed directly into her eyes, and in spite of his husky laugh, and the kiss that followed it, there was no mistaking the message in his look. *You've gone too far. Don't fight me now.*

When he'd set her back, squeezing her shoulders as a second reminder, she gave a shaky laugh. "But it was our secret. You said I must tell no one."

"Talbot doesn't count. Among partners, there should be no secrets."

"You have persuaded him to join us?" She glanced over at Gerald, who looked wary. "I'm sorry. I didn't know. And you have come to trust him? I'm not sure that I do."

"Nor do I," Duran conceded. "Not altogether. But he owes me a great sum of money, and the only way to settle his debts and ensure future credit among his peers is to throw in his lot with us." Releasing her, he crossed to Gerald and pumped his hand. "We are to be related," he said jovially. "Each of us wed to a Sothingdon chit. Mind you, Jessie and I are marrying quietly, and by Special License because her father is unlikely to approve. Her brother, when he learns of it, will be apoplectic."

"Aubrey is an ass," Gerald agreed, eyes narrowed.

"We didn't invite you to stand witness," Duran said, "in case you'd rather stay on good terms with your in-laws. But by all means, come make sure of the marriage if you need to. It is on for tomorrow morning. However, you must choose tonight whether to accept our offer or decline it. To be candid, I hope you will decline. I'm not persuaded you are indispensable, nor do I wish to share the profits. It was Jessica talked me into letting you join us."

"Even though she does not trust me?" He cast her a sly grin. "I wonder why she spoke in my favor?"

Without Duran blocking her way, she'd have launched herself at Gerald's throat. But with a large hand solidly on her shoulder, she subsided. Remembered the role she had to play. "Why? Because I cannot do all that must be done. If you are to be a part of this scheme, your assignment is simple enough. I have prepared a list of sixteen collectors, all of them residing within a day's ride of London. You need only call on each one and make the proper inquiries."

Edgy because the moment had come, she went to the corner where a draped canvas was propped on a stylus. Without drama, she withdrew the covering. "This is a painting of what we have to sell."

From the canvas, brilliantly rendered, lavishly opulent, gazed a golden, bejewelled leopard.

To her pleasure, even the calculating Gerald was impressed. But not for long. "This won't do. Who the devil is going to believe a painting?"

"The real question," said Duran, "is whether someone recognizes the image. You're gamester enough to mark the twitch in the hands, the flicker in the eyes.

That's why you are the one to undertake this search. And of course you should make note of anyone interested in buying the icon, should we resort to selling it."

"I have another question," Gerald said, gesturing at the painting. "If I locate someone in possession of one of these, how do you propose getting it away from him?"

"That," Duran responded easily, "would be my concern."

"We'll see. And another thing. You claim to have its twin, but I've no proof of that."

"You astonish me. There is no obligation on your part, sir. If you dislike this enterprise, by all means take your leave. Or is it that you are concerned about the risks? There are some, I promise you, but—"

"I don't object to risks," Gerald snapped. "I enjoy them. But I'll not be exploited. If there's a real icon, I want to see it."

"Certainly," said Duran. "My dear?"

She had concealed the wooden box in the wall safe behind a painting of a Berkshire pig. When she'd removed it to a table, Duran dealt with the locks, unwrapped the statue, and set it on a table for Gerald to examine.

But all the while, it was Duran's eyes she was watching, his reaction she was anticipating. It was all she could have wished.

Gerald whistled between his teeth. "Satan's ballocks! Is that solid gold?"

"Near enough," Duran said, recovering smoothly. "A core of base metal, possibly, for strength, but I'm not poking holes in it to find out. This leopard, like its littermate, must be in pristine condition if we are to sell the pair back to Alanabad. And that's the big game, of course, the gamble of a lifetime. If we succeed, we'll be rich. Second-best is to sell this as a one-of-a-kind artifact. Should all else fail, we render it down for the gems and the gold."

Gerald's eyes, pinpointed on the leopard, were alight with greed. "I begin to like your plot very well. But you can't think to send me out with only the painting. Let Jessica take it. She has experience and reputation to trade on, while I have neither."

"I'm afraid not," Duran said, his voice mild. "I brought this all the way from India, never mind the effort to acquire it in the first place. The leopard stays with me."

Jessica's hands, clamped behind her back, tingled from lack of blood. She could not bear this.

"Jessica?" Gerald slithered in her direction, confident as a man about to toss loaded dice. They both knew the stakes. He didn't trouble to remind her what they were. "Are we partners?"

She hesitated. Loathed him to the killing point. Lifted a helpless gaze to Duran. "Give him what he wants," she said.

After that she scarcely breathed, heard little of what was said, moved like an automaton through the re-packing of the leopard and the placing of the box and, almost as an afterthought, the list of potential customers, in Gerald's blunt-fingered hands. His gleeful acceptance. His triumphant smile. His swaggering exit.

Silence in the room until a short knock on the door by the steward signaled that Gerald had left the house. Then, turning, she threw herself into Duran's arms. "Oh, but it was marvelous! He behaved just as you said. He practically jumped into the trap."

He chuckled, the rumble of it vibrating against her cheek. "You needn't sound so surprised. And I might add, princess, that you have just given me a lesson in chicanery. It was your performance that convinced him. Indeed, you all but convinced *me,* even after I'd seen the painting and been sure the game was over."

Untangling herself, she stepped back and grinned at him, knowing she looked smug and meaning to. "Because it was twin to the real icon. You thought I had overreached myself, until you unpacked the statue and saw that it was identical as well. At the least, it's good enough to pass all but an expert's inspection."

"I should say. But how did you manage it? The Alanabad craftsman required four months to create a reproduction, and you produced a remarkable likeness in three days. How did you procure the gems? The gold? The artist?"

"As for how, Shivaji brought your leopard for the sculptor to copy. The gems are paste, of course, save for the eyes, which were impossible to match. Those are stained glass. The gold is real, although there's not much of it coating the lead, and the sculptor a talented forger. It was Helena who recruited him and procured the materials. I had not known it before, but she numbers a great many felons among her acquaintances. What is more, they will be pleased to testify that Gerald hired them to produce the replica."

"My God," Duran said, astonishment etched on his face. "I handed you the bare outline of an ill-conceived plan, and you transformed it into something that might actually work."

"Do you think so? I've been too busy to consider the possible results, but honestly, I can't conceive how providing Gerald with a model of the leopard will accomplish anything. He'll decide that paying calls on collectors is too exerting, and that he can do better by converting the gems and gold to gaming stakes."

"It's possible, certainly. And if he settles for that,

he'll quickly learn that he's been gulled and we will have failed to entrap him. But he's lazy, greedy, and ambitious for a big score. I think there's a good chance he'll take a shot at the larger prize. Should he find the real leopard, he'll likely try to steal it, in which case we'll take it off his hands and make sure he's blamed for the theft. Or he'll try to sell the copy he just left with, opening himself to charges of extortion. One way or another, he'll not be roaming free and making trouble for very much longer."

"I defer to your expertise," she said, the exhilaration of her success already beginning to dissipate. What did it matter that the latest model of the icon was immeasurably superior to the rough imitation Duran had been expecting, the one she could have better afforded to provide? Really, she ought not to have got carried away when Helena suggested an expensive alternative, but the opportunity to link Gerald directly with thieves and forgers was too good to pass up. Gerald had taken the bait, but if he failed to swallow the hook, she'd put herself back in debt, deeply in debt, for no reason.

Oh, for Mariah, to be sure. But what was the use, if the scheme fell apart?

A finger, callused at the tip, lifted her chin. "Second thoughts are serpents' fangs, Jessie. Don't let them bite you. If we fail to entrap Gerald this way, I'll come up with another. He'll be followed, by the way. We'll know which collectors he visited and at which point he stopped making calls."

"That might be helpful," she said, unable to imagine how. "Who is following him?"

"Shivaji delegated one or two of his squad. He has become singularly cooperative since your secretary began providing information he had not even thought to request. I suspect she even talked him into permitting the marriage. He was certainly opposed to it until she came on the scene."

Jessica kept a polite expression on her face. An odd pairing indeed, Helena and Shivaji. *Is he a thief?* she had asked her secretary. *Could he be an assassin? Or is he merely a valet?* But Helena refused to discuss Shivaji, the way she invariably refused to discuss anything not strictly connected to business.

The mad rush of the past three days suddenly caught up with her. She felt her knees shaking. The light grew dim. Next she knew, Duran was sitting beside her on a sofa, her head against his shoulder, his arm wrapped protectively around her. She looked up at him, at the concerned look on his face, and mustered a smile. "It isn't a headache," she assured him. The arm relaxed a trifle. "I'm only tired. Will you stay the night?"

Color tinged his cheekbones. "Shivaji, I'm sorry to say, has turned out to be something of a prude. The negotiation for a private room together on our journey was successful, which is the important thing. But until we are married, I must retire to my chaste and too-short bed."

"Not to mention that you've an early appointment with Devonshire." Disappointment brought an edge to her voice. "Is there some problem with the legal arrangements?"

"He sent a message to that effect. I don't know what snags are holding things up, but the duke's solicitors expect to have them ironed out before our meeting. And you needn't worry, princess. I'll sign whatever they put in front of me."

"Then you'd better run along, hadn't you? Tomorrow is going to be a busy day."

"Yes." His lips brushed her forehead before he stood. "Our wedding day."

Chapter 19

Not to every man does it fall the honor, on the morning of his wedding day, of receiving a lecture about his marital responsibilities from a duke.

A redundant lecture, Duran was thinking, since he'd heard most of it at their previous meeting two days earlier. But he didn't mind. He quite liked the tall, terribly earnest Duke of Devonshire, if only because the fellow was so intent on protecting Jessica's interests.

This time, however, His Grace's eyes were flashing with restrained anger, and Duran had yet to twig a reason for it. If anything, he had expected to be basking in ducal approval. By Jessica's instructions, the original contract presented to him had contained a provision according him one quarter of the income from his wife's business interests. He still wondered why she had insisted on that. In any case, he had flatly refused to sign a contract that gave him so much as a penny rightfully belonging to her, and had assumed today's meeting to be a formality. He would accept the revised contract prepared by the lawyers, and Jessica would know nothing of the alteration until after the marriage.

But it wasn't a simple matter after all, he had just been informed. Husbands possessed an overabundance of legal rights, and doing away with them required twists and turns only a duke's expensive solicitors could navigate. Moreover, those same solicitors had suddenly paddled into rough water, although what that meant, His Grace had not got around to saying. All would be made clear when they arrived. In the meantime, Duran was being reminded that if ever he did the slightest disservice to his wife, the Duke of Devonshire would twist his guts into guitar strings.

Yes, he very much approved of the duke, and hoped that he would continue to protect Jessie from bounders like her short-term husband.

The stiff-necked butler appeared, the duke followed him out, and Duran was left alone with a cup of cold coffee and his thoughts. Primarily they concerned being late to the church. St. Giles had been selected because getting there would require only a short walk from Little Russell Street, and he hadn't wanted to stand disheveled and sweaty at the altar.

So much for careful planning. Thanks to the mysterious problem uncovered by the lawyers, he'd been compelled to tramp all the way to Piccadilly and Devonshire House, and soon would be required to tramp back again. He hadn't yet figured out how to explain to His Grace, whom Jessica had asked to stand as groomsman, that he was not permitted to accept a lift in the ducal carriage.

A thrum of excitement vibrated under his skin. She was going to have him, in spite of everything. She would wed him, never mind his wilted collar and dusty shoes and the small deception about the settlement provision, which would make her angry when she discovered it. Jessie. His bride. His ferocious, glorious bride. This was by a long shot the best day of his life.

He was drifting into a fantasy about his wedding

night when Devonshire returned, a scowl on his face, his hands full of papers.

Rising, Duran felt the air in the room go cold. This was not going to be good.

"I believe I now understand," said the duke in a stony voice. "It was only because my solicitors are both meticulous and well connected that this situation was discovered in time. Unfortunately, they have not yet succeeded in finding a loophole in the law that prevents you from later claiming what cannot go into effect until a great many contingencies are met. Nor can they, or I, figure how you came to know of it. Unless Sothingdon confided in you. Excepting the solicitor who drew up the will, he was the only one aware of the clause. Come to think of it, Jessica mentioned that you had bribed yourself into his favor with one of Manton's expensive guns."

With some effort, Duran found his voice. "I beg your pardon, Your Grace, but I haven't the least idea what you're talking about."

The troubled brown eyes regarded him sternly. "Must we play out this charade? Very well, then." Riffling through the papers, he selected one and passed it over. "You need only examine the last paragraph."

He did, reading it twice through before turning the paper facedown on the table in front of him, as if that could make it disappear. Every good thing he had been feeling drained out of him, leaving him hopelessly muddled. "I must speak with Jessica," he said after a long time. "May I take this paper with me?"

The duke tossed the sheaf of papers he was still holding onto the table. "This is the unsigned revision of the marriage contract. Take it as well. But know this, sir. Until Jessica assures me she understands and accepts every single word, I shall block this marriage."

*   *   *

The ceremony was scheduled for ten o'clock, and it was well past that. Jessica, fidgeting next to Helena in a front pew, told herself bracingly that it was something about the marriage contract making Duran late. Or traffic between Devonshire House and St. Giles in the Fields. After all, Hart hadn't arrived either, and until he did, she needn't worry she'd been jilted.

The wide grosgrain ribbons of her bonnet scratched at her chin and throat. If ever she had imagined her own wedding day, she would definitely have imagined herself wearing something else. But they were to leave on their journey directly after the wedding, so Helena had selected for her a blue carriage gown with long sleeves and a high neck to protect her against dust from the road, along with kid-leather half boots and a hat that had been chafing at her since first she put it on. Overheated and agitated, she squirmed on the seat until Helena put a restraining hand over hers and gave it a squeeze.

Nothing ever ruffled Helena. Never a hair out of place on Helena, nary a ripple in her calm disposition. Jessica found that exceedingly annoying.

The vicar popped his head out of the vestry, looked around, and disappeared again. He had been doing that regularly, agitated because there was another wedding scheduled for eleven o'clock.

After a few more minutes, someone came into the church. Heart thumping, she turned to see Hart striding alone down the aisle, a severe expression on his face. She waited for him to stop and speak to her, but he only shrugged and folded himself into a pew across the aisle.

She felt suddenly furious. And mortified. She could leave now and never see or hear or think of Duran ever *ever* again. That's what she ought to do. But she continued to sit there, watching dust motes dance in the blades of light slicing across the nave while ice crystalized in her veins.

The vicar's head emerged again, followed by the vicar himself. Pudgy as a cherub, he crossed to the gate in the communion rail, to a certainty on his way to inform her that time was up. She wouldn't argue the point. He had done her a favor by agreeing to conduct the last-minute ceremony, and being a kind man, he would regret having to call it off. She was already stepping out of the pew when he advised her that Lord Duran wished to speak privately with her in the vestry.

He was waiting for her beside a round table, his collar limp, his hair disordered, his black coat askew over a white brocade waistcoat. He looked, inexplicably, as if he'd been running.

"You are late," she said, trying not to sound shrewish.

"And you probably thought I never meant to come," he replied, raising somber eyes to her face. "Little ever goes right for us, does it?"

"Not easily, at any rate. What has gone wrong this time?"

"For you, nothing. You may even find it excellent news." He took the top sheet from a small stack on the table and held it out. "This will explain nearly everything, and I shall tell you the rest. The part, at least, that I am permitted to divulge."

The distance from where she stood to his hand seemed a long way. Before she got there, she could tell by the quality of the paper and the meticulous handwriting that he was giving her a legal document. A glance verified that it was a will, and she recognized the first several lines. She'd heard them eight years earlier, shortly after her mother's death.

The section that related to the second daughter, consisting of two clauses, had been transcribed at the top. She was to receive a few pieces of jewelry—the ones she'd recently pawned—that her grandmother had wished her to have, and fifty pounds to purchase a black gown and gloves in the event she felt inclined to mourn her mother's passing. Everyone had recognized that for the slap in the face it was. There was nothing else for Jessica. The considerable legacy that Lady Sothingdon had inherited from her own mother was distributed among her two obedient children, her demonic companion, and the artisans who had produced the garish monument she'd designed for her tomb.

"Well?" said Duran.

"I'm still reading." The next section, set apart, introduced a codicil that was not to be disclosed, save to Lord Sothingdon, until the occasion of Jessica Carville's marriage or her thirtieth birthday, whichever occurred beforehand.

And then the provision itself, a bequest to Jessica on the condition she was married before her thirtieth year to a man who met with the approval of the deceased's spouse, should he still survive, and his heir, the present Aubrey, Lord Buckfast. Should those requirements go unmet, the bequest would revert to her son, Aubrey. The amount, to be held in trust and invested, was twenty thousand pounds.

Stunned, Jessica continued to stare at the paper, a rush of pleasure sweeping through her. Although she had always pretended otherwise, she'd been heartsick when Lady Sothingdon made a public display of disinheriting her. But at the end, her mother had changed her mind. Or had a change of heart.

Or remained intent on controlling her, even from

beyond the grave. Yes, that was more likely. The pleasure swept out again, leaving her empty.

She turned back to Duran. "I didn't know of this. But I can't see that it creates a problem. And there's another wedding to take place at eleven o'clock, so the vicar is somewhat anxious that we get on with ours."

"No, Jessica. We cannot marry. I should never have suggested it in the first place. But I was concerned for my own interests and persuaded myself that you had a little to gain, perhaps, from the marriage, and nothing whatever to lose. This changes everything."

He meant it. She had never seen such a look of conviction in his eyes. "But how? Papa was annoyed that you failed to take proper leave of the shooting party, and Aubrey will not be impressed by your background and lack of fortune. Nonetheless, they both wish above all things for me to take a husband. They can be brought around."

"Your father, perhaps. Not your brother."

"You don't know that. You don't know him."

"I'm afraid I do. The day I left High Tor, we quarreled. I lost my temper and struck him. He elected not to tell anyone?"

"As a matter of fact, or so I heard from Mariah, he accused you of striking him. But there was some confusion about what actually occurred, and everyone but Aubrey seemed to think you'd departed for London well before the accident." She studied his face. "*Why* did you quarrel?"

"It doesn't matter. The point is, he will never give his approval to this marriage, which means it cannot take place. It was bad enough I hadn't a groat to settle on you. Then I couldn't pay for a Special License, so the duke gave me the money. I had to convince Shivaji to provide a wedding ring. It's as well you won't be wearing it, for the one he produced is no more worthy of you than I am. Under no circumstances, Jessie, will I come between you and financial security for the rest of your life."

"Except that you're not. It has never been my intention to marry, and if we had not entered into this arrangement, I'd have assuredly got to my thirtieth birthday without satisfying the conditions of the will. The money changes nothing."

"It might. It ought to. You are how old, princess? Four-and-twenty. Five?"

"Seven." Said aloud, it made her feel ancient. "What of it?"

"Then you have three years to find a husband who will meet with your family's approval. And if you don't wish to go looking for one, you can't rule out the possibility that you'll one day encounter someone that you'll fancy, or develop a *tendre* for an old acquaintance. You could . . . you *should* . . . fall in love."

"How uncommonly sentimental of you, Duran."

"A misstep. I meant to be entirely practical."

"In that case, allow me to remind you that we have an arrangement. A verbal contract, if you will. I expect you to honor it."

"Then you will be disappointed. The marriage was undertaken to preserve your reputation while we traveled together, but I'm calling that off as well. And as for making yourself a wife, or better, a widow, to more easily carry on your antiquities business, that could easily backfire. Marrying the likes of me won't enhance your reputation, Jessica."

"It's odd, but I recall you arguing the opposite viewpoint just before you proposed. Society would forgive my small lapse of taste, you said."

"I was wrong. I was being selfish. I told you I was

concerned about myself. That alone should send you running for cover. And you can do far better than me. With a trifling effort, you could have potential husbands queuing up to pay court to you."

"But how could I be sure that any one of them would be so obliging as to disappear within a few weeks of the wedding and never return to plague me? And what about the plot to send Gerald into exile or prison? You underestimate the appeal of your offer."

"Now you're just being obstinate. I won't renege on the plot against your brother-in-law, so you lose nothing there. As for the plaguey husband, there isn't a man alive you couldn't twist around your finger if you put your mind to it. And once you claim your mother's legacy, you'll have no need to earn your own living. You can collect antiquities for yourself, as a hobby."

"Ah. How easily you transform my profession into a mere pastime. Apparently I have overlooked the advantages of spending the rest of my life as a wealthy widgeon."

"That's not what I meant." His eyes looked fevered. "Do you imagine this is easy for me? But I have no choice. You are an impulsive creature, Jessica. You cannot deny that. And you're proud as well, perhaps too proud to back away from an agreement that can only hurt you. But it all comes down to one obvious truth—a two-and-a-half-week marriage with me is not worth twenty pounds, let alone the twenty thousand you stand to lose by it."

"And you imagine that I would consider marrying for money?"

"You were prepared to marry me for a good deal less. I understand how you feel at this moment, but you'll soon get over it. And yes, perhaps you'll never marry. But I want you to have the next three years to change your mind, or the chance to seize an opportunity that may arise. I'm only thinking of you."

"No. You are only thinking *for* me. Spare me your high-sounding excuses, Duran. If you are inclined to call off the marriage, there is justification enough to be found in my character. I am, as you say, obstinate and impulsive and proud. But do not take it upon yourself to protect me from the consequences of my decisions or deprive me of the right to make those decisions for myself."

"We all make mistakes, princess. If you saw me about to do something hopelessly foolish, would you not try to stop me?"

"I might. But you wouldn't listen, any more than you are listening to me now. The money does not signify. I will never marry for it, nor will it stop me from marrying. And to prove that, I am going now to stand before the altar in company with the vicar and our witnesses, where I shall wait for five minutes. Unless I leave this church as your wife, I wish never to see you again."

Cheeks burning, she turned on her heel and swept out the door, gathering the bewildered vicar on the way and towing him to the altar like a dinghy. Beckoned, Helena and Hart joined her there, Helena serene and Hart trying without much success to conceal his anger. One look at her face and he closed his mouth.

For several excruciating hours, or so it felt to her, the three of them stood facing the vicar, who clutched his prayer book between trembling hands and, from the movement of his lips, appeared to be praying for a miracle.

No miracle appeared, but the eleven o'clock wedding party did, boisterous and cheerful until, or so Jessica surmised, they became aware of the grim little company frozen in place before the altar. The laughter faded to whispers and shuffling, followed by silence.

Proud, impulsive, obstinate. She'd brought this humiliation on herself, dragging her friends and the hapless vicar into the soup as well. No wonder Duran considered her incapable of making a sane decision. If this was any sample of her judgment, she might as well consign herself to Bedlam and be done with it.

She thought about moving, resolved to do so, but nothing happened. Her feet seemed rooted to the marble floor. She looked down at them, wondering why they refused to obey her. Perhaps they didn't trust her brain to give the proper directions. She could scarcely blame them.

She looked back to the vicar's flushed, unhappy face. His eyes pleaded with her. *Go, you unfortunate, demented creature.* And she would have to walk past the people standing in the back of the church, the happy bride and groom and their friends. What if she was acquainted with someone there? What if one of them recognized her? Dear God. They'd almost certainly recognize Hart. He was the most famous peer in the kingdom. In another five minutes, the story of Lady Jessica's jilting would be all over town.

But so far, they'd only seen her back. The encompassing bonnet with its wide ribbons concealed her face well enough, and while Hart was distinctive from any angle, he would never betray her identity. Duran must be long gone by now. Perhaps she could safely exit through the vestry. If only her feet would do her bidding.

She looked in that direction, at the portal that seemed a hundred miles away, and closed her eyes in a silent prayer for mobility. When she opened them again, Duran was coming through the door.

He was carrying, she saw through tear-blurred eyes,

a small nosegay of flowers, which he put into her frozen hands.

"The stems are wet," he said. "I took them from a vase in the—"

"You robbed a *church*?"

"Borrowed. We'll put them back when we sign the register."

"And the contract."

"Sign that before you're married," said the duke. "I insist, Jessica. There's nothing to compel him to sign it afterward. Miss Pryce and I will stand witness."

So they all swooped into the vestry, inscribed their names on the marriage settlement, and swooped back out again. On the way to the altar, giddy with relief and a swarm of other feelings that had yet to identify themselves, Jessica noticed that about twenty people had ensconced themselves in the back pews, watching like an audience at a comedy.

"What took you so long?" she whispered to Duran as they took their places again.

"I was trying to escape," he said. "But I couldn't find a back way out of the church."

It was the most inconsequential of remarks, designed to tease her past the last of her anger at him. Past the fear that had paralyzed her, although he couldn't have known of that. He would have intended nothing by it. But something had happened to her between his last word and the moment she began to smile. And it was when she realized that she *was* smiling, simply because she was happy, that she understood why she was standing here, prepared to marry him. Against all reason, *determined* to marry him.

Her breath caught. *Dear God, no. Please no.*

Her turn to leave now. Her turn to run away. She could not bear this. Could not.

But again her feet refused to move. And her voice,

detached from the rest of her, spoke vows that had no meaning. They would not be together for better or worse, richer or poorer, sickness or health. They had no intention of being true until death did they part. By agreement, they were to part in three weeks. Not so many. Sixteen days. Fifteen and a half.

It was ridiculous. They were lying to God right here in His house. Lying to each other.

No. This one time, Duran had not deceived her. Not about their counterfeit marriage.

She was the one telling lies. The vows were, by agreement, intended to be smoke. She wasn't supposed to mean what she said.

But she did.

Every rational part of her protested the madness of it. The unsuitability. The absolute futility. By the time his warm hand took her cold one to slide the small circle of gold onto her finger, she had recognized the brief flight of fancy for what it had to be, the product of exhaustion and near disaster. She clung to him only because, through her own fault, she had come so near to social disgrace. She felt relief. She was pleased by their temporary but useful contract. No more than that.

But all the while, as they made a mockery of a kiss, and signed the parish register, thanked the vicar and the clerk, walked with high heads and bright smiles past the curious wedding party soon to replace them at the altar—all that time, she knew.

She *knew*.

Chapter 20

Outside the church, passersby stopped to gawk at the carriage emblazoned with the Sothingdon crest, or rather, at the servants and their decidedly unusual livery. Duran took quick note of the driver and the man seated beside him on the bench, both of them light-skinned, hawk-nosed, turbaned fellows clad in khaki tunics over loose khaki trousers. Each wore a wide leather belt slung with a curved sheath for his kukri, the deadly Gurkha knife.

His first glimpse, Duran suspected, of the Others. Two of them at any rate. Shivaji was nowhere in sight, but he located Arjuna atop the coach next to a considerable pile of luggage. The bride, it seemed, did not travel light.

She did, however, travel without a maid. That surprised him, and he might have inquired about it, except that his bride was not speaking to him. Handed into the coach by yet another silent warrior masquerading as a servant, she slid across the burgundy leather squabs and pressed herself against the paneled enclosure, her face averted, her expression concealed by the brim of her bonnet.

Why the devil was she vexed with him now? She'd got what she wanted, hadn't she? And he had done as well, except that he hadn't wanted her on the terms he'd been forced to accept. Each minute she spent as his wife was costing her money, twenty thousand pounds of it, not to mention the accumulated interest. He ought to have walked away.

But the sight of her standing at the altar, stubborn and defiant and a little forlorn, had been more than he could bear. He could not bring himself, not again, to abandon her.

Was she having second thoughts now? Regretting what she'd done?

Well, he'd let her sulk for a while. Then he'd do his best to coax her into better humor and out of her clothes and into his arms. Meantime, he looked out the window at the city he would probably never see again. Too bad, that. He quite liked London and felt, for no good reason, that he belonged there.

They had left the city proper and driven a considerable way before his bride removed her bonnet and tossed it on the bench across from her. "Well," she said, "I made a proper fool of myself, didn't I?"

He could see where this was heading. "Is that one of those trick questions, princess, where I am wrong no matter how I answer it?"

"It was a rhetorical question. I've no intention of taking out my anger at myself on you."

"Good. It isn't that I'd mind, but there are so many better ways to pass the time. Now, let me see. What could we possibly do, being newly married and lusty creatures into the bargain? Something will come to me. Why don't *you* come to me?"

"Duran!" She'd gone red. "Not in the carriage."

"Why not in the carriage? There's plenty of room, not that we'll require much of it once we're joined. Unless you mean to flap around a good deal. I'd enjoy that, actually."

"I am *not* flapping in this coach, or doing anything

that could be mistaken for flapping. We have no privacy here. There are three men directly overhead, and Shivaji is riding alongside. They'd all . . . *know*."

"Of course they would. They no doubt assume we're already flapping. It's what brides and grooms do, first chance they get. Besides, they can't hear us above the rattle of the wheels and the traffic noises. Unless you think you might scream. They would probably notice that."

"No screaming. No flapping. It would be embarrassing."

"It's true, then," he said mournfully. "Once a female has got a man leg-shackled, she parcels out her favors like a miser. Will you be as reluctant in our bed at night, knowing that Shivaji is somewhere in the same posthouse? He has eight children, you know, and he didn't find them floating on lotus pads."

She turned, brows arched with astonishment. "He does? My heavens. It's a little difficult to imagine that. I mean, he's always so dispassionate. So—"

"Unflappable?"

Laughing, she slid across the bench and settled herself in the curl of his arm. "He told me a story once, about a princess who begs for the life of her prince from the Lord of Death. Her request is denied, she returns to her father's kingdom, and that is that. It disturbed me, because of what you have told me about Shivaji. And, I suppose, because you sometimes call me *princess*."

"Yes, well, I have always done so, since long before I had the misfortune to make his acquaintance. I know the story, though, as it's told in the *Mahabharata,* and you are very like Savitri. She was famous throughout the world for her beauty and intelligence."

"You won't win my favors with flattery, Duran."

"It was worth a try. But there is more to the tale

than you appear to have heard. Savitri persuaded the king to let her choose her own husband, unheard of in those times, and wouldn't you know she lit on Satyavan, who was not a prince at all. Merely a poor but virtuous sod with only a year to live. Which makes one question her intelligence, come to think of it. Anyway, when time was up and Yamaraj took Satyavan away in spite of her pleas, she wouldn't take no for an answer. Instead, she tagged after the Lord of Death, nagging his ears off."

"Shivaji didn't tell me this part."

"He wouldn't, would he? It might inspire you to start tagging and nagging. Anyway, the unfortunate Yama finally granted her one boon, so long as she consented to go away and let him get on with his business. And she must not ask for Prince Satyavan's life, which he was not permitted to give her. That's how she secured long life and prosperity for the king her father."

"It wasn't what she wanted, though."

"No." He ought not have started this. And he'd said too much. His own story was not going to end as Satyavan's had done. "But she got something for her trouble, which is often the best a mere mortal can do. I don't suppose, if I did a bit of nagging, I might get a little something from you?"

She threw him an annoyed glance. "I might have known you would twist the story for your own purposes."

"Everyone does." He pulled down the window shade. "One paltry kiss, then, in exchange for my cleverness? It's not what I want, of course, but surely you can be at least as gracious as the Lord of Death."

"Oh, very well, if it means you will cease badgering me. One kiss."

"Excellent." He pulled down the other shade. "A

boon indeed. It will give me the opportunity to show you, princess, how to make a kiss last for an hour."

Two hours later, as Jessica slept in his arms, Duran saw through the window that they were passing through Colchester and nearing the estate of General Sir Grant Calhoon, retired from the East India Company army several years before Hugo Duran had become its least favorite ex-officer. Although they had never met and there was no reason to anticipate trouble, he was not looking forward to the first call on one of Jessica's collectors.

He hadn't exactly been raised by wolves, but he'd spent precious little time in aristocratic British company and wasn't at all sure what she expected of him. Probably to keep his mouth shut and look wisely ornamental, so that she needn't be ashamed to present him as her husband. Things would be easier, he trusted, once he'd had the opportunity to watch her in action, after which she would no doubt acquaint him with his inadequacies in blistering detail.

In one respect, at least, he'd arranged matters to his liking. Their route, which began with stops in the east and north of England, would place him during the last week of the journey within reach of Liverpool, Bristol, Plymouth, and several other ports.

Jessica's secretary, who had made the arrangements for horses and lodging, had become an unexpected ally. In addition to keeping track of Sir Gerald Talbot, she was to act as intermediary between Duran and John Pageter, still at High Tor, sending coded messages in her letters to Jessica, who knew nothing of their scheming. That made it something of a challenge to get his hands on her letters, but any communication sent him directly would be intercepted by Shivaji.

Miss Pryce had also become quite the expert on shipping schedules, which was going to prove useful to Duran. It had already done so for Shivaji, when she discovered, in the records and registers of the East India Company, an indication that the leopard might indeed have been destined for a trip to London.

The name of the thief, they had always known, was Thomas Bickford, although the other members of the hunting party hosted by the nizam could provide little information about him. A lieutenant in the Company army on leave after taking a wound, he had ingratiated himself with Lord Clery, the nizam's principle guest, and because he was a good sportsman and ostensibly well bred, he had been added to the party without question.

Following the theft, Shivaji tracked him to Madras and located him in a rooming house not far from the docks. He was dead, most likely of a fever infesting the area. About sixty pounds in English banknotes and nearly the same amount in rupees were discovered in his saddle pack, but of the leopard, there was no sign.

During her research, Helena learned that an officer named Thomas Bickford, only just promoted from the ranks, had been killed in a skirmish two years before the theft of the leopard. Surmising that the thief had appropriated his identity, she looked for the name, or one similar to it, on the passenger lists of ships sailing from Madras following the theft. The search proved fruitless. If he'd meant to take ship, he must have secured passage under his true name or some other alias.

So she recorded the names of men who had booked passage and subsequently failed to board ship. There were eleven in all, three scheduled to travel with their

families and several others found to have taken later
sailings. Eventually the search narrowed to four men
whose whereabouts could not be established.

Those names shot immediately to the top of Shivaji's must-find list. Helena was attempting to learn if
any one of them had dispatched luggage or parcels to
the trader before failing to board it, and if so, who
had claimed the shipments when they reached England. The line of investigation seemed promising, but
there was little chance she'd come up with a lead before Duran's scheduled execution.

At least they now had four names to float by the
collectors they were to visit, and during the next few
days, Duran came to admire the way Jessica slipped
them into her inquiries. He had always been impressed
with her wit, her temper and pride, her iron will and
surprising uncertainty. He was especially partial to the
boundless and uninhibited passion with which she
flung herself into their lovemaking.

What he'd not been privileged to see, until now,
were the qualities a wiser man would have intuited
from the first. The social skill of an earl's daughter,
for example, and her impressive knowledge of art and
artifacts. Her talent for steering a conversation the
direction she wanted it to go. She knew all the right
questions to ask, the ones that flattered the collectors
and gave them a chance to show off, and the ones
that led, inexorably, to queries about feline-shaped
icons from the subcontinent. He began to believe that
if the leopard were in the possession of someone on
their list, or if any of them had a notion of where it
might be, Jessica Carville would find a way to elicit
the information.

One evening, while they were undressing in their
room at the posthouse, he had congratulated her on
the aplomb with which she'd handled an especially

cantankerous collector. Her pleasure at the slight compliment had taken him aback. How hungry she was for approval, how uncertain of her own gifts. Her bitch of a mother had a great deal to answer for.

It was the third day of their journey, and as she often did, Jessica had snuggled against him for an afternoon nap. He didn't allow her much sleep at night, nor did she seem to want him to, and she had overcome her resistance to sporting in the carriage. If not for Shivaji's quelling presence, he could almost forget they weren't on their wedding trip.

When the coach turned onto a long drive shaded with tall lime trees, he gently shook her awake. Sleepy-eyed, Jessica straightened her hair and scrubbed her face with a cloth dipped in water from a canteen while he studied the card of information provided by Helena.

"A widow," Jessica said as he handed her from the coach. "It surprised me to see her name on the list. I had not thought her interested in antiquities from India, but perhaps her husband was a collector."

The answer came over a tea tray. "Oh dear," said Lady Glinth, raising apologetic blue eyes to her guests. "It's *Italian* antiquities I collect, as did Lord Glinth. But of course, his handwriting always was indecipherable. For the most part, he limited his interest to Etruscan artifacts."

"Indeed?" Jessica sat forward, her eyes alight. "It happens that I have a client in search of an Etruscan necklace. Have you any you'd be willing to part with?"

Etruscan jewelry? They had wandered rather far afield, Duran was thinking as Lady Glinth escorted them to a room crowded with display cases.

"If only I had brought the drawing he sent me,"

Jessica said, clearly displeased with herself. "But the pattern was distinctive, and I remember it fairly well."

There were six or seven waist-high, glass-topped cases crammed with jewelry, but Jessica found nothing that matched what she was looking for until the widow unlocked a drawer and pulled out a baize-lined box.

"Ethan kept his favorites in here," said Mrs. Glinth. "I never could understand why he hid the pieces he most enjoyed looking at. What good are they in a box?"

"This is very like the drawing," Jessica exclaimed, untangling a heavy gold circlet studded with lapis lazuli. "But I'm ashamed to say I have failed to do the proper research. Do you know its value? And if my client is still interested, would you be willing to sell it?"

"Indeed I would. There's a new roof to be paid for. Besides, collecting was Ethan's passion, not mine. Shortly before his death, he had an appraisal of his finest things done by Malcolm Fife. Will that help?"

"He's exactly the man I'd have consulted," Jessica said. "I'm sure Lord Philpot would accept his evaluation."

"Philpot? You mean the baron, Darius Philpot, from Somersetshire? My Ethan was at Eton with him. More than half a century ago, to be sure. We . . . I . . . have not seen Darius for this last decade or more. What a coincidence, though. Only Monday last I read a notice concerning him in the *Times*. He'd been called to his Somerset estate on account of Lady Philpot's illness. The implication was that she hadn't long to live."

"It *will* work!" Jessica said, jabbing at the map with her pencil. "Lord Philpot's estate is southwest of Bath, near to Glastonbury." Another jab. "We are here, just beyond Cambridge."

"And heading due north," Duran pointed out, not pleased where her schemes were about to take him. "Keep in mind, I'm not the one you have to convince."

"I needn't trouble to convince either of you. If Shivaji refuses to alter the route—"

"Backtrack, you mean. What is it? A hundred miles?"

"Not so far as that."

But it might be even farther, he knew. Since they'd settled again in the coach and she'd pulled out her maps and lists, she had been calculating routes, not distances.

"We'll lose time at the outset," she conceded. "But once I've delivered the necklace, we'll simply reverse the order of the calls on our list. We can do the western locations on our way north and finish up in the southeast. What difference does it make?"

A great deal. Her revised plan would put him a long way from any useful port just when he needed to be near one. "None," he managed to say after too long a silence. "But our schedule is overfull as it is, and changing course will eat up time we cannot spare. Besides, what is the urgency about this necklace? Can't you post it to her, or take it to her later? I don't mean to sound heartless, but if Lady Philpot is ill, she won't be wearing it any time soon. And if she dies, she won't need it at all."

The look she turned on him would have reduced paper to cinders. "I shall pretend I did not hear that. And if you refuse to support me in this, I shall simply leave you to continue the leopard hunt while I secure passage on a mail coach."

Desperate men say stupid things, he was thinking even as he did so. "Need I remind you that four days ago, you vowed to obey me?"

"Poppycock. You must be thinking of some other female. I would never promise obedience to a man who takes orders from his *valet*."

He realized, belatedly, that it was time to do some backtracking of his own. "Look, Jessie, it's obvious this means a great deal to you. If you would explain—"

"If you would trust me, no explanation would be required."

With interest, he watched her blush to the roots of her hair.

"I admit," she said in a subdued tone, "that after my mortifying behavior in the church, it is possible that my credibility is somewhat—"

"Reduced to mincemeat?"

"Open to question! But since you are determined to be provoking and recalcitrant for no plausible reason . . . Or have you one? In fairness, I ought to ask."

Not one he could admit to, although the border separating his promise that Jessica would not help him to escape Shivaji and his wish to inform her of his intention to escape Shivaji was becoming somewhat blurred. *Knowing* was not *helping,* precisely. But it was conducive, he supposed, to eliciting help. Damn and blast. This sort of moral tiptoeing was not within his compass. "I'll not stand in your way," he said at length. "But you must deal with Shivaji on your own."

"Why not?" She took a fresh sheet of paper and began sketching out the proposed change of route. "*I* am not afraid of him."

Half an hour later, munching on a sausage roll at the posthouse where they'd stopped to change horses, he watched Jessica circle the expressionless Shivaji like a whirlpool engorging an island. Now and again she paused to show him something on her map or one of her lists. She'd dropped one, and the breeze had carried it across the courtyard, but she failed to notice. All her attention was on her argument, which beat against Shivaji's silent resistance like a wave against a rock. In time, of course, she could wear him down, but time was the one thing none of them had.

Resignation settling like a boulder in his belly, Duran tossed the remains of his pie to a delighted mongrel and sauntered into the fray. "We really can't do without her, you know," he told the impassive Shivaji, wrapping his arm around Jessica's waist to hold her still. "Half the people we mean to visit won't admit me if I show up alone, and the other half are unlikely to disclose their secrets, if they have any, to me."

"Arrangements have been made," Shivaji said. "Others have been sent ahead to prepare."

Jessica looked a question at him, which Duran pretended not to see. "Then call them back," he said. "Surely you can cope with a simple change of plans?" If he'd not been watching closely, he'd have missed the flash in Shivaji's eyes, the one that acknowledged the implications behind what he'd said. A network of guards that could not respond quickly and flexibly would be ineffectual if confronted with, say, an escape attempt by Duran.

Not at all sure why he was cutting his own throat, Duran followed up on his advantage. "We can't afford to lose our key to the elite society of collectors," he said. "And short of binding and gagging her, we cannot prevent her from leaving us. If it's the delay that troubles you, we can travel at night until we're back on schedule."

Shivaji's response was to put out a hand, and Jessica must have known what he meant because she gave him the map and the new schedule of stops that she proposed. Then she went into the posthouse, and Duran saw her speak to the owner. Arranging alternate transportation, he deduced.

It was the toss of a coin which of them—Jessica or Shivaji—was more obdurate. He climbed into the carriage, propped his feet on the opposite bench, folded his arms, and awaited developments.

"I wrote to Helena," Jessica said brightly as she entered the coach a few minutes later. "She'll have my letter with our new route by the day after tomorrow. And Shivaji says we will be required to sleep in the carriage tonight. The innkeeper is bringing blankets and pillows, and I smuggled a flask of cognac, but don't ask me to remove it from where it's stowed until after dark."

"You are singularly pleased with yourself, princess."

"Yes." She leaned back against the squabs. "But sad as well. I had entirely forgot Lord Philpot's necklace, and we may be too late delivering it because of my neglect. A promise ought to be kept, don't you think?"

"To be sure," he said untruthfully. *Some of them,* he was thinking. *Not all.*

Not, for instance, Shivaji's oath to the liver-spotted little nizam, the one that inscribed his own death in, what? Sixteen days? Fifteen? He'd lost track. While he had been teasing Jessica, laughing with her, making love with her, the rest of the universe had moved on without him. Now he couldn't even remember when he was scheduled to die.

Chapter 21

"You mustn't weep, my dear," Lord Philpot said, patting Jessica's hand. "She likes the necklace very well, I'm sure."

They were standing in the graveyard of St. Mary's church, where the freshly turned earth over Lady Philpot's resting place was mantled with a carpet of grass and strewn with flowers. Five days after her funeral, the blossoms still perfumed the air.

Duran's silent, reassuring presence was a comfort to Jessica. She had never before dealt with unhappy circumstances except alone, even when surrounded by her family. Their disapproval and her own resentment always kept her isolated. But on this warm summer morning, her husband by her side, she needn't guard her feelings or pretend she had none.

She had failed Lady Philpot, who would never see the necklace she had longed for. Lord Philpot's refusal to hold her accountable only heaped coals of fire upon her head. But Duran understood. He had helped convince Shivaji to bring her here, and he stood by her now, and he'd passed her his handkerchief when she required it.

After a last moment of respectful silence, the small procession, flanked at a distance by Shivaji and his cohorts, walked slowly from the churchyard and along a walled path that led to Greenbriar, Lord Philpot's estate. Just as he'd insisted on taking them to visit his wife, he now urged them to take luncheon with him.

"But of course I mean to keep it," he said when they were at table, gesturing with his fork at the necklace spread out on the cloth beside his plate. "Whatever the price. I've a fancy to bring in an artist to paint it around Clarissa's neck on the portrait in my study. It will adorn her beauty, and I shall always be reminded how wasteful it is to let a day go by without giving something special—even if only a smile—to those one loves."

He gave Jessica a look of affection. "But you, of course, know that very well, newly married to a stalwart young man. Will you accept a bit of advice from a silly old one? Do not settle into habits, my dear, as I did, and take for granted what can vanish between one breath and the next."

She glanced at Duran, seated directly across from her, but he was studying the wine swirling around in the glass suspended between his hands. She continued to watch him surreptitiously as Lord Philpot described the visit of his son and daughter and their families, the stately funeral, and how he had arrived home in time to hold Clarissa in his arms while she drew her last breaths.

For all the solemnity of his monologue, the luncheon was surprisingly pleasant. Lord Philpot sometimes got lost in his own reminiscences, but she was fascinated by the picture he sketched of a long and happy marriage. By the time they moved to the drawing room for coffee, she was entirely at ease with him, so much so that she found herself describing the purpose of her unusual wedding journey.

"A native idol, you say?" Lord Philpot rubbed his chin. "I'm a shareholder in the Company, as you are aware, but I've no interest in Indian art. Not to my taste. All arms and legs, those carvings and statues. And that monstrous Pavilion at Brighton! What happens when an Englishman gets caught up in a passing fancy."

"But other than the king," she said carefully, "do you know of anyone with a passing fancy for Indian artifacts?"

While Philpot considered the question, he offered Duran a cigar that, to her disgust, was accepted. "Do you mind, my dear?" Philpot asked belatedly. "Clarissa always left the room when I smoked."

She shook her head, but when neither man ignited his cigar, she knew her true feelings had been obvious. She must learn how to conceal them.

"There's Old Holcombe, of course, up in the Mendips, but I've heard nothing of him for several years. He's the one restored that castle, you know, or worked at it until his money ran out. He had a nephew, his sister's son, taken in as an infant when both parents went down from typhus. Doted on the boy, never mind the hands. Webbed like a duck's paddlers."

From the corners of her eyes, she saw Duran come to attention.

Philpot was absorbed in his story. "The story was he had his forefingers cut free before he went off to school, but it turned into a bloody mess and he wouldn't let a surgeon have at the others. Later, after being sent down from Oxford, he took up with a bad crowd. Flattered they'd have him, I daresay, but the gaming cost him every penny he had. Then they let him sign vouchers, and soon he was nose-high in River Tick. The Beast is no man to be indebted to, I can tell you that. He holds the mortgage on the family estate in Kent. That drove Holcombe north to the castle keep, and he never comes out of it that I know of. Odd bird. Always was."

"I know his reputation," Jessica said. "What became of the nephew?"

"Went out to India five or six years ago, which is why I thought to mention him. Swore he'd pay off the mortgages and restore the family fortune, such as it was, or die trying. I heard he wound up in the Company army."

"His name wasn't Bickford, by any chance?" Duran had put down his wineglass and was leaning forward in his chair. "Is Holcombe the family surname, or a title?"

Philpot's wide forehead wrinkled as he considered. "Never heard of Bickford. The family name is Holcombe, but the old fellow picked up a baronetcy or something of the sort by selling Egyptian gewgaws at a loss to the Regent back in '07. It didn't stick, though. He's always been called Old Holcombe. Never married, either. As for the boy, he is meant to inherit the castle, but the estate is probably willed to the legitimate heir, Holcombe's brother. The Beast will have it in the end, though. He always gets what he sets his sights on."

"A most unpleasant gentleman," Jessica said, looking for a way to bring the subject to more fertile ground. She couldn't imagine why Duran had developed a sudden fascination with Old Holcombe and his relations. "It happens that we are also attempting to trace four men who spent time in India and may have returned to England within the last year. Are you by chance acquainted with Percival Fairleigh? Geoffrey Laxton? Paign Goudhurst, or William Romsey?"

"I'm afraid not. Well, I knew a Fairleigh from Norfolk, but that was at Eton. No contact since." His brow furrowed. "The other . . . How is Goudhurst's first name spelled?"

"P-a-i-g-n. An unusual name."

"For a Christian name, yes. But it was the surname of Old Holcombe's nephew. Richard Paign, or perhaps Robert. I cannot recall, and it probably means nothing. I'm sorry I cannot help you, my dear."

Duran spoke up. "As you say, there is unlikely to be a connection. But if Holcombe's castle is not too great a distance, it might be worth paying him a call."

She could tell he wanted her to agree. "I don't see why not. But if we are to make a stop before Clifton, where lodging has been reserved for tonight, we must be on our way. Would you be so kind, Lord Philpot, to provide us the direction?"

Disappointment in his eyes, Philpot nonetheless smiled and lumbered to his feet. "I'll have John Coachman sketch a map for you to take," he said, tugging the bellpull. "The castle is perched in the Mendips, and the roads in that area are poor. Mind you, Holcombe may not admit you. Reclusive chap, and certain he is about to be robbed at any moment. I'm told he hires bullyboys and keeps dogs."

When Philpot had gone to secure the map and a basket of refreshments for their journey, Duran rose and beckoned Jessica to a display of hunting scenes occupying most of one wall. A younger, more slender Lord Philpot rode to hounds in several of them.

Duran, laughing, pointed to the hind end of a horse jumping a fence, but his eyes were intense. "Listen carefully," he said, "and pretend we're talking about these paintings. Shivaji is to know nothing of what Philpot just told us. Do not under any circumstances mention Paign by name, or refer to a nephew of Holcombe who went to India."

"You think it's significant?"

"I know it is. Shivaji found Bickford's body, I told you that, and described to me what he'd seen. The fingers, some of them, were deformed. He didn't specify how, but I'd wager that Bickford, like Paign Goudhurst, was a name adopted by Holcombe's nephew."

"Goudhurst is a village in Kent," she said. "It makes sense he'd choose something familiar to respond to, such as part of his real name and a place he knew well. But why are we concealing this information from Shivaji? I thought you wanted to go to the castle."

"I do." He directed her attention to a picture of a fox encircled by a pack of long-toothed hounds. "It will be your task to persuade him to make the detour without handing him our trump card."

"I . . . But how? He didn't want to come *here*. I'll never convince him to follow another of my whims."

"On the contrary. You could talk the paint off a wall. But this time, princess, you'll be strictly on your own. If Shivaji thinks I'm in favor of dropping by the castle, he'll whisk us off in the opposite direction."

"He will in any case. Without an incentive, such as the information you intend to withhold, why should he listen to me? And you overestimate my talents, Duran. When we were gulling Gerald, my knees were knocking the entire time. Matched against Shivaji, I haven't a chance."

"Ah," said Lord Philpot from the doorway. "You like my paintings. Well, mine in that I commissioned them. Did you recognize anyone in the pictures?"

"If you are referring to the handsome gentleman on the splendid bay, I did indeed," said Jessica, smiling. What a love he was, and only days after his wife's death, how lonely he seemed to be. She resolved to visit him whenever she could. When Duran was gone, it would probably be often.

The compliment pleased Lord Philpot, who, she was sure, had never much resembled the Adonis in those pictures. "Here it is, then," he said, beaming. "A map to Holcombe's Folly—that's what we call it, but don't tell him—and a letter of introduction in case it proves useful. A gift as well, because he's a greedy chap. And there's a nice basket being put into the carriage, although your valet insisted on inspecting the contents."

That last was a question, Jessica apprehended.

"Old habits die hard," said Duran with a shrug. "Before I employed him, Shivaji was a food taster for a petty tyrant in the Punjab. Poisons ate away half his stomach, which is why he's always got a sour expression on his face."

Lord Philpot's eyebrows shot up. "The devil you say! But they must hire out cheaply, those native chaps. I mean, that is quite an entourage of foreign servants you travel with."

"An affectation, m'wife tells me." Duran lifted his arm, letting his coat sleeve fall back to disclose the jeweled bracelet. "Like this one. The spouse of a successful businesswoman has to keep up appearances."

"Never mind him," Jessica said, crossing to take Lord Philpot's arm. "Sometimes he fancies that he's amusing, but that's only when the malarial fever is on him. Happily, it's not contagious."

As she bade farewell to her host in the courtyard, she saw Duran emerge from the house with a lit cigar between his teeth. He sauntered to the carriage, slouched against the door panel, and said something to Shivaji, who was standing quietly nearby. When the valet glanced in her direction, she assumed the remark had concerned her.

Because she was nervous, or perhaps because she sensed Lord Philpot would be glad of it, she drew closer and brushed a kiss over his flushed cheek. "I shall call on you soon," she promised, "here or in London."

Tears sprang to his eyes, and unable to bear seeing them, she kissed him again and fled in the direction of Shivaji. From deep sorrow to deep trouble, she thought, mentally girding herself for battle.

"*Memsahib,*" he said, bowing, "your errand has been satisfactorily concluded?"

"Oh, yes." She gave him what she hoped would pass for a smile of gratitude. "Lord Philpot said that we arrived at precisely the moment his spirits were plummeting. His family had just gone, leaving him to mourn alone, when the necklace his wife had longed for was given into his hands. It was as if she'd put it there, like a message of enduring love. Is that possible? Might *we* have been sent, as emissaries of a sort, to . . . But no. How absurd. And yet, such a pleasant concurrence, don't you think? My insistence on honoring an obligation, and his need of what I brought to him. So strange. Oh, but you have been waiting, and we must be off. Clifton next, is it? Well, I shall have a nap."

With another smile she turned toward the coach. "You had better finish that quickly, Duran, or throw it away."

Eyes narrowed, he took another draw on the cigar while Arjuna opened the carriage door and lowered the steps.

Philpot's map was scrunched in her hand. One foot on the step, she looked down as if she'd never seen the paper before, removed her foot, and stood for a moment as if undecided. Then, with a small sigh, she went back to Shivaji.

"I suppose I should tell you about this," she said, "although it is no doubt unimportant. When I explained to Lord Philpot why we could not remain longer, which he very much wanted us to do, he became quite enthusiastic about our errand. I think he wished to be of help, to repay us for our trouble, but unhappily, he did not know of any collectors we might have overlooked. Then, just before we were to depart, he recollected that a well-known but somewhat dodgy character connected to the antiquities trade is in residence not far from here."

"Well-known, but not on our list?"

"He dropped from sight a few years ago, and his reputation was none too good in any case. Besides, I've never heard him to have collected imports from India. But Lord Philpot insisted on providing a map to the castle that Mr. Holcombe is restoring, and I am going to present it to you as if we plan to use it. Otherwise he will think me ungrateful."

"If not Indian antiquities, what did Mr. Holcombe procure?" There was no trace of interest in Shivaji's voice, and while he accepted the map, he did not look at it.

"Oh, just about everything, at one time or another. I've never met him, you understand, but his quest to become a member of the Royal Antiquarian Society is something of a legend. He began with the excavation of a Roman villa, but sold more of what he found than he preserved. Then the craze for Egyptiana came in, and he was accused of importing empty sarcophagi and stuffing them with fake mummies. He dabbled in Chinese art when it was the fashion and, claiming to know the location of Confucius's skull, petitioned the Society to finance an expedition to retrieve it. They declined."

"A madman, in your judgment? Or criminal?"

"Perhaps a little of both, at least by repute. Putting together everything I've heard, I would say he is a man of small talent who is obsessed with finding a shortcut to social approbation. His latest project was to restore a twelfth-century castle, but the construction ceased when he ran short of funds. The castle isn't far, and the map shows the route from there on to Clifton. But the roads are bad."

She covered her mouth for a yawn. "Anyway, if you'll be kind enough to nod at me and appear enchanted by the prospect of a detour, Lord Philpot will be pleased. Then we can toddle off to wherever we were headed in the first place."

Shivaji didn't smile—in her experience, he never smiled—but he did nod, and as she ascended the carriage steps, she noted that he was examining the map.

Moments later he approached Duran, who was enjoying the last of his cigar, and spoke in an expressionless voice. "Have you an opinion of this Mr. Holcombe?"

"The old bird in the turret? I wasn't paying much attention." Duran lowered his voice. "Philpot is a friendly chap, but he chattered like a magpie all through lunch. The food was good and the wine exceptional. That's about all I remember."

"You do not think we should call there?"

"I'm thinking about a good inn with a large bed, clean sheets, and sirloin for breakfast. So long as that's where we wind up, stop wherever you like along the way. Not for long," Duran added quickly. "Last night we drove straight through, and you must be tired as well. A direct line to Clifton has my vote."

It was nearly an hour before Jessica could be sure Duran had been outvoted. She had spent it in the circle of his arm, aware of the tension in his body and the surreptitious glances out the window to see if they continued north on the good road or turned west onto a bad one. Now and again she caught a glimpse of Shivaji, straight-backed and at ease in the saddle, showing no sign that he'd gone without sleep for nearly forty-eight hours. Unless he could sleep on horseback with his eyes open, which would not have greatly surprised her.

When the coach took the left fork at a crossroads and begin to climb into the Mendips, she felt Duran release a long breath and sink back against the squabs.

"Clever girl," he said, stroking her cheek with an idle finger. "If ever I underestimated you, be certain I shall never do so again."

"Of course you will." But she was glowing at the praise. "What did you tell him when I was speaking with Lord Philpot?"

"Hmmm?" The finger paused while he considered. "Oh, that. I advised him you'd tippled heavily at luncheon."

She sat up and looked at him. "Why?"

"Because I thought you might elect to cover your story by pretending to be foxed."

"Well, you were wrong. I was pretending to be sleepy. Too exhausted to think or speak clearly."

"I see." He pulled her onto his lap. "How glad I am you were only pretending. Philpot was right. This road is poor and certain to get worse. Remember the last time we traveled a bad road, on the way to Sir Grafton's country house?"

Heat rose from her toes all the way to the ends of her hair. "It was . . . nice," she conceded. "But difficult."

"I know," he said. "You always want to rush, or you want me to rush. Leaving it to the motion of the carriage, to the rocking and the bumps, requires discipline. You haven't much discipline, princess. Not when I am inside you. Would you like to try again? See how long you can endure before demanding the first climax? And the second? And the third?"

Already her breasts ached to feel his mouth. The burning between her legs entreated to be quenched. She swallowed. Gazed at him helplessly.

"No answer? Then we'll do what *I* want. Let me think what that might be." He studied her body. She was sitting sideways on his lap, his right arm wrapped loosely around her back, her legs stretched on the padded leather bench. "Your legs are closed," he said in mild rebuke. With his left hand, he gently lifted her knee.

She felt the touch through her skirts and petticoats and chemise and drawers.

Then he arranged her foot on the bench so that her knee was bent up, and all he had to do was raise her skirts and push aside all the rest and . . . But he didn't. His gaze had moved to her bodice, the russet bombazine covering her to the collarbone and a fringe of lace concealing all but an inch of flesh below her neck.

His forefinger moved to that inch, stroking it before lifting her chin for a light, tantalizing kiss.

"Are you playing sultan again?" she murmured when he went back to looking without touching. "Arrogant man."

"That too. But primarily, I'm teaching you the joys of anticipation. They can be better than—"

"Not *better*. Nothing is better."

"No? We'll see. I shall leave you dressed, because I don't know how far this castle is. And we should get on with things, because I want to be inside you for a long time. Can you feel my cock?"

She could, pulsing against her thigh, strong and importunate. Then his left hand moved to her ankle, slid under her clothing, and glided upward. A low moan escaped her throat. She began to wriggle as his fingers came closer, closer still, and he stilled her with his other hand.

"Soon," he said, dipping his tongue into her ear.

At the moist invasion, she nearly cried out. The silk of her drawers felt rough against her skin as his finger meandered over it and approached the slit, already damp, that would admit him where most she wanted him to be.

He stopped.

"If I touch you there, you'll come," he said. "Won't you?"

"Even if you don't touch me," she said breathlessly.

"Are you swollen, Jessie?"

"Y-yes."

The finger brushed the soft hair near to the proof of it, brushed again, and then his large hand cupped her mound.

She pushed against it. He removed the hand.

"Always so eager," he chided. "You can have everything you want, you know. I'll give it to you. But at the time of my choosing, when it accords me the most satisfaction."

"The coach is jolting about," she said. "What are you waiting for?"

"An excellent question. How good are you with buttons?"

She was very good with them, in spite of trembling hands and a precarious balance. When he sprang free, large and hard and pulsing, she clamped her lower lip between her teeth and wrenched her gaze to his face.

"Now, please. Please, now."

"As you desire, princess." He brought her forward, raised her skirts and placed her knees astride his thighs so that she was open to him. Moving his hands to her waist, he held her above him for so long that she began to struggle.

"Shhh," he said. "Slowly. Come down on me slowly."

The knob of his cock slid against the hot, wet entrance to her body. Held there. The hands at her waist tightened and began to twist her left and right, left and right, so that she felt him there, up and down, forward and back, but never at the nub of her pleasure. Not so far as that.

"Kiss me," he murmured.

Bending forward, only so far as he would allow, she felt his shaft between her legs, clutched in between her thighs, rubbed herself along it as his tongue slipped into her mouth and began to move in rhythm with her.

Not for long. Holding her still, he threw his head back against the cushions. "You make it impossible, wife. I am, as always, your slave."

Raising her carefully, positioning her, he pressed upward even as he drew her down onto him, slowly down so that every inch of his penetration became a symphony of pleasure. More and more he filled her, thick and so deep. So very deep. When she thought he could give her no more, he did, and did again, until he groaned and held her tightly against him.

"Are you comfortable?" he said. "Legs? Arms? No cramps?"

"I am. Yes. Oh my."

"Then don't move. Not deliberately. Feel the vibration of the coach. The straining of the horses. Above all, feel me inside you, as I feel you encompass me. You are so tight, princess. So wet. So warm. Rest your head against my shoulder. Lick my throat, if you will. Yes. That's good. Ahhh. No, don't squeeze. This time we won't make it happen. We'll let it happen. And after, if that was not enough for you, we'll let it happen again. Then, I promise, I'll turn you on your back and give you the drumming you are asking for."

She could not bear it, the waiting, the unexpected motions, the urge to move against him, the need to finish. To experience the hot pleasure that built and built and built for endless minutes. Hours, it seemed. Aeons.

His face was taut with restraint. He wanted it too, that rush, as the coach jiggled and she slipped up and down him, his flesh so deep inside her they might have been one creature with one single goal.

"Soon now," he said in a ragged voice. "We need to do this right so that I can pull out in time. Go first, Jessie." He pulled her so close against him that all her being was centered where she rubbed against him, harder and harder, until his hand pressed over her mouth to cut off her scream and his other hand lifted her off his throbbing shaft. She sagged against him, blood tingling, her skin so sensitive that when he licked a drop of perspiration from her throat, she came again.

"That was good," he said after a long time. "Very good. Shall we do it again?"

"*Can* you?" she asked, sitting back to examine his face. Sitting back farther to look down at the slick, limp penis nestled against his heavy scrotum. At her glance, it seemed to stir.

"I expect I can," he said.

And soon she was riding atop him again, rocking to the motion of the coach, the power of his manhood throbbing inside her.

He always had more endurance the second time, but she never did. The climax swept over her all too soon, while he remained hard as a standing stone inside her. As ever, he was patient when she rushed past him.

After her breathing had steadied and the pulsing at her genitals had ceased, she looked into his appraising eyes and smiled. "I would like that drumming now, if you please."

With a purely male laugh of satisfaction, he laid her out on the lush padded bench, raised her knees and spread them apart, and looked down at where he intended to put himself. "Prepare yourself, Jessica. Stop me if you need me to stop, and I will. But unless you do, I want everything you have to give, and I mean to take it."

He did, plunging inside her and thrusting with a primal force that slid her up and up until her head bumped the panel of the coach. Then he took hold of her, tugged her down until her knees were bent nearly to her breasts, and began again. And again. His hand slid under her buttocks and lifted her to him. She lost count of how many times he brought her to the brink of climax, let her fall back, and drove her there again.

The orgasm burst upon her with the force of an explosion. She was barely aware of his leaving her until the last twinge pushed at her nub and left. Then she opened her eyes and saw him sprawled along the bench across from her, his eyes half open, a smile on his face.

"Come here, princess," he said, opening his arms. "Sleep on top of me until we get wherever we're going."

Her last thought, as she slid into dreams of remembered pleasure, was that she wished he hadn't been so careful. She wished, inexplicably, profoundly, that he had given her his child.

Chapter 22

Jessica adjusted her clothing and pinned up her disordered hair, her body languid as seaweed drifting in a lagoon. The enclosed carriage had become a place of refuge, where for a few hours each day, nothing they said could be heard and nothing they did could be seen. Where for all too short a time, she had Duran all to herself.

But as ever, it ended too soon. Already the outside world had begun to intrude. Her lover, slouched beside her, appeared relaxed, but she sensed the tension growing in him, and the anticipation. She felt it as well.

Of course, with Duran, scarcely a day passed without a crisis of one sort or another. Within hours of meeting him, answering the primal call of a male to his mate, she had joyously surrendered her virginity. And within seconds of his return six years later, she'd swooped into orbit around him like a moon circling a volcanic planet.

She was not sorry for it. She had thought herself incapable of love, and he had proved her wrong. For that lesson, she would willingly pay whatever price the universe exacted from her.

Which wasn't to say that an experienced woman of business could not find ways to cut her losses. If it was her burden to have fallen in love with a deceitful, unreliable scoundrel, it was also her pleasure to outwit him now and then. With Duran, one seized the gratification of the moment, whatever it might be.

"You believe it is there, don't you?" she said, startling him. "At the castle."

"The leopard? No. But there might be a way to use Philpot's information to distract Shivaji. I just haven't figured out how."

He was lying, she was sure. But with him, direct confrontation was generally ineffective. "You're probably right. It does seem that Paign, pretending to be Bickford, stole the idol and got all the way to Madras with it. He might very well have meant to bring it to England, but it's equally possible he sold it, or had it stolen from him. There is no reason to think he shipped it to his uncle."

"Precisely. For all we know, the nizam's rival beat Shivaji to Madras, got his hands on the leopard, and waited for the right moment to launch his coup. He might be sitting on the throne of Alanabad as we speak."

"That would be Malik Rao? The cult leader?"

Duran frowned. "I told you about him?"

"Having trouble keeping track of your stories again?" she inquired kindly. "Don't worry. You may always consult me. I remember every word you ever said."

"Lucky me," he said with a grin meant to disarm her.

It didn't work. "Isn't it strange, though? The same night you appeared at Christie's, I was trying to escape you when Lord Philpot blocked my way, nattering about his urgent need for an Etruscan necklace to give his wife. Then you enticed me. . . . Don't scowl. . . . You *did* entice me to join you on this search for a stolen idol, but along the way, we encountered a woman with an Etruscan necklace who just happened to know of Lady Philpot's illness. At which point I insisted on rushing to deliver the necklace, and that led to the discovery of Bickford's true identity and the first real clue you have to the whereabouts of your leopard. It is . . . Oh, I don't know. Shivaji would have a word for it."

"So do I. The scientific term is *coincidence.*"

"If you say so." Did he really believe that, or merely want to believe it? For that matter, she could ask the same question of herself . . . except that she might not like the answer.

The carriage slowed, made a turn, and picked up speed again. Not much speed—it had been moving cautiously for the past half hour—but enough to make her snap open the window shade and peer outside.

The road, such as it was, had narrowed until it was barely wide enough to accommodate the coach. Shoulder-high hedgerows scratched against the side panels. Beyond the hedgerows, the rolling hills were studded with sheep and an occasional congregation of placid cows. But even as she watched, the terrain grew progressively more rocky and barren. Distorted trees clawed at the sky. It was as if they'd entered a country designed by a sorcerer, a land of uncertain magic and unhappy dreams.

Then they rounded a curve, and she saw, atop a hill higher than all the others around it, the jagged outline of a castle wall.

A chill nosed along her spine.

As the coach clattered across the plank drawbridge, a pair of unfamiliar outriders drew alongside. Like the two who had traveled with them from the first, the newcomers wore crisp tunics and trousers, had knives at their belts, and carried rifles and sabers in scabbards attached to their saddles. There were eight guards now, counting Shivaji, Arjuna, and the men on the driver's bench. Jessica let go her last thread of hope that Shivaji was no more than a swindler masquerading as a valet. Common criminals, she was sure, did not travel with their own private armies.

Once inside the courtyard, she could see what had not been visible from the road. Nearly two-thirds of the castle wall had been reduced to piles of rubble, the best stones quarried by the locals to construct their own houses and barns. Most of the outbuildings were little more than roofless shells. But the tall limestone castle keep, its oriel windows reflecting the late-afternoon sun, had been lovingly restored.

While Duran was handing her from the carriage, they were approached by a barrel-shaped man with a rifle cradled in his thick arms. He was missing one ear.

"The castle ain't open to visitors," he snarled. "Take them foreigners and get out."

"I am Lord Duran," came the smooth response, "and this is my wife, Lady Jessica, daughter of the Earl of Sothingdon. You are not, I take it, Mr. Holcombe."

"He don't see nobody."

"He will see us. We have brought to him a letter from his neighbor, Lord Philpot, along with a gift, and Lady Jessica, a noted antiquarian who has long admired his talents, wishes to propose a profitable business arrangement. Your employer would not be pleased to learn you sent her away."

At "profitable" the man's eyes lit up. "Wait here," he said. "I'll arsk him."

There was another man with a rifle watching from the shadows of a doorway, but otherwise, the bailey appeared to be deserted. Beyond the walls, rooks cawed from the treetops and a few sheep grazed on the browning grass.

Jessica glanced over at Shivaji, silent and impassive on his disciplined chestnut, his hands folded on the pommel. He must be evaluating the likelihood his leopard was denned in that keep. Duran, beneath a veneer of lazy boredom, practically vibrated with impatience. In that mood, she mistrusted him entirely.

Five minutes passed before the surly man returned and led them into the keep. Her first impression was of chaos. The entrance hall resembled an attic, with vases and statues and knickknacks littering every possible surface. All of them needed a good dusting. Her practiced eye spotted a decent Chinese vase next to a fake Japanese screen, a nice Lodovico plate propped against an ugly brass firedog. Holcombe seemed unable to distinguish between quality and junk, and had apparently lost interest in the pieces he had accumulated over the years. If a golden leopard was lurking in this jungle of odds and ends, she would be hard put to find it.

Holcombe himself, a gaunt man with sparse curly hair and a bad cough, received them in a library overflowing with ill-preserved books. The room smelled of damp leather, ink, and moldy paper. His skin, Jessica saw as Duran presented her, had an unhealthy yellow-gray tinge.

Arjuna had accompanied them, carrying a large wooden box. Holcombe eyed him suspiciously.

". . . and Lord Philpot has sent you this letter and his regards," Duran was saying, "along with a selection of wines from his excellent cellar."

Arjuna deposited the gift on a cluttered table and quietly departed.

"Well, well, then," said Holcombe, smiling at the box. "And what am I expected to do in return for this largesse?"

Duran slanted her a look that said she was to take up the baton.

"Why, nothing at all, sir." Her voice, from nerves, had pitched itself too high. Duran looked pained. "Your reputation among collectors of art and antiquities is sterling, and since I entered the profession, I have heard nothing but praise for you and astonishment that your achievements have gone unrecognized by the Royal Society of Antiquarians. Naturally, the incongruity caused me to want to make your acquaintance."

Holcombe's expression of pleasure was quickly replaced by a scowl. "I was told you had a business proposition to offer. You needn't bother. I don't do business with females."

"I am sorry to hear it, sir. But if you have no need of the money, then I hope you will accept my compliments on your fascinating collection. I have seen only the fringes of it as we were escorted here, but there were a number of pieces that would fetch a good price at auction, and others that private collectors would wish to purchase directly."

"And you, of course, would slice off a hefty commission."

"In general the seller allots me ten percent. But for the opportunity to represent the collection of a legendary antiquarian, I would happily reduce that figure."

Holcombe began to cough and seemed unable to control it. He pulled out a handkerchief to cover his mouth, and when he took it away, the linen was flecked with blood.

Jessica felt suddenly guilty. This man was seriously ill, and she had set herself to exploit him.

A moment later Duran was at her side, one arm wrapped around her, his fingers digging into her waist. He must have sensed that she was wavering. She thought, sometimes, that he knew her better than she knew herself.

"Under ordinary circumstances, Lady Jessica would have written for an appointment," he said. "But we chanced to be passing by and decided to ask if you would permit me to examine what you have acquired from the subcontinent, particularly India. My own expertise is from that part of the world, but since I rarely travel with my wife, this might be the only opportunity for you to have, free of charge or obligation, an evaluation of that portion of your collection."

"Hmpf. Well, nothing much here." Holcombe appeared reluctant to turn down anything free. "No profit to be had importing from India. Everyone and his brother has gone out there hoping to make himself a nabob, only to cart home a passel of trinkets. You can buy everything there is to be had at any village market. But I've no objection to you having a look."

Another spate of coughing. Holcombe lurched toward the door. "My niece will show you around. Wait here. You can send word if you find anything of value."

"He's not got long," Duran said when the door had closed. "If he hadn't insulted you, I'd ask Shivaji to see what he could do for that cough."

"Don't let concern for me stop you. I've spent the past six years letting insults wash down my back."

He pressed a kiss on her temple, a silent reassurance that meant more than words. No one in her life had ever known so intuitively what it was she needed. How would she bear it when he was gone?

The door opened, and they turned to see a frail man in a Bath chair being wheeled in by a strikingly beautiful young woman. Her ice-blue eyes were direct and intelligent, and her hair, held back with ebony clasps, was the color of·a full moon on a clear night. When she spoke, her whispery voice floated to them like smoke.

"I am Miranda Holcombe, and this is my father, Edgar Holcombe, Roger Holcombe's younger brother. He is a scholar and a teacher, but a seizure two years ago deprived him of speech and all but a little motion. Nonetheless, his mind is unimpaired, and he sees and hears as well as we do. You are most welcome here."

Duran bowed to the man in the wheeled chair. "I am honored to meet you, sir, as is my wife, Lady Jessica. We are hoping your daughter will be so kind as to show us the portion of your brother's collection that originated in India. He has asked us to evaluate it."

Speaking first to the father, Jessica saw with reluctant admiration, was precisely the way to win the daughter's approval. She saw Miranda's gaze drop to the limp right hand resting on a bony knee. A finger stirred, lifted, made an up-and-down motion, and lowered again.

"I shall be pleased to do so," she acknowledged in the husky voice they had to strain to hear. "Allow me to settle my father in the solar and retrieve the keys."

Jessica noticed, as Miranda left, that she was wearing—in summer—mittens.

"I can't imagine that a solid gold statue would have gone unnoticed by someone," she said to Duran, "even in all this jumble. But Miranda may know where else Paign might have sent it."

"Perhaps. But don't let on what we're looking for, or why we came *here* in particular."

"Thank you for advising me. I had planned to be indiscreet."

He looked chastened, but not very. Like a runner at the starting line, he was keen for the race to begin.

Jessica was examining a tattered First Folio of Shakespeare's plays when Miranda returned twenty minutes later. She was wearing a dust smock and carrying two others. "You'll want to put these on. If there are India artifacts of any value here, they will have been sent by my cousin, addressed to himself in care of my uncle. By Uncle's account, he opened the first two or three, found the contents unimpressive, and later arrivals were sent directly to the dungeon."

After lighting a candle, she led them to the lower reaches of the keep by a circuitous route that included a concealed door and a short zigzag along a hidden passageway. "No one is permitted to come here," she said when they stopped in what must have once been the guard room. Torches were stored in an umbrella stand. She ignited one for each of them and they proceeded past several heavy barred doors to the end of the stone-walled passage, where she applied the key, as large as her hand, to the lock. "Uncle believes the entire world is plotting to steal from him. When you are finished, it will be necessary to smuggle you from the house."

"But everyone knows we're here," Jessica said. "Our carriage and servants are in the courtyard."

"Not any longer. They were ordered to take themselves out of sight and wait for you at the foot of the hill." She glanced at them over her shoulder, smiling. "I'm the one sent them away. Uncle is already well into his first bottle of wine, and I have provided a special treat for the servants to have with their supper. By the time you are ready to go, they will have forgot your existence."

"Allow me," Duran said, taking the key and wrestling with the lock. "Why all the machinations?"

"Family history. It's complicated. I'm not at all sure what to do if you find anything worth a great deal of money. Uncle will want you to sell it so he can continue with the restoration of the castle, but he is too ill for that. And the goods rightly belong to my cousin Robert, except that he is in debt. If his chiefest creditor discovers they exist, he'll lay claim to them."

"But you wish us to evaluate them anyway?" Jessica said. "To what purpose?"

"So I'll know whether or not they are worth hiding. When Uncle dies, a great jackal will leap in to seize whatever he finds. I mean to deny him as much as I can."

The great jackal was, Jessica expected, the Duke of Tallant. Miranda's cousin was probably dead, her uncle nearly so, and her father a prisoner within his immobile body. So very much for this young woman to deal with alone. Jessica longed to help her, but how could she, overwhelmed with problems of her own?

With a screech of metal against metal and a gratifying click, the lock finally gave way.

"It's a duplicate key I made for myself," Miranda said as the door swung open. "I'm not much of a metalworker. And in all my hurry, I failed to bring a crowbar. Is there something else I should fetch while I'm at it?"

"Nails and a hammer," said Duran, examining a stack of large wooden crates. "We'll need to put these back together again."

"Oh, I'll see to that later. And there are a few tools in that box over there. You can start with the smaller parcels while I'm gone."

Duran was all for ripping into them straightaway,

one after the other, but Jessica pointed out that some were too light to contain the leopard, and others too small. Moreover, there were shipping dates inscribed on most of the boxes, and those in the back, covered with more than a year's worth of dust, had been stored here long before the leopard was stolen. With a bit of sorting to start with, they could save themselves a good deal of time and effort.

Restless and disgruntled, Duran was forced to agree, and within a few minutes, about twenty parcels and boxes had been set apart for consideration. Then he was given leave to start ripping.

Not long after, she caught him examining a small case filled with bladed weapons, many of them boasting jewel-studded hilts.

"A khanjar," he said, lifting one for her inspection. "And this is a khanjarli, with a double-edged blade. A jambiya, ceremonial, with rubies."

"Put them back," she said. "All of them."

"You could smuggle one out under your skirts. I need a weapon, Jessica."

"Perhaps. But I won't help you steal one. Not from Miranda. She is helping us."

"She doesn't know they're here, dammit. She won't miss one inconsequential knife."

"She will when I tell her."

"Shit." He returned the daggers, slammed the lid on the box, and kicked it in her direction. "You are the most self-willed, mule-headed female west of Bombay. Don't let me near them again."

Robert Paign must have educated himself since dispatching the items Old Holcombe had found insignificant. The contents of his more recent shipments were impressive enough that Duran paused now and again to show them to her and explain what they were. Particularly taken with a fourth-century stone head of a bodhisattva, he rewrapped it with care and restored it gingerly to its box.

"I lived in India all my life," he said when she expressed her surprise. "I wasn't drinking and wenching the entire time."

"You needn't be insulted. I just had no idea you were interested in such things."

"Great beauty has always interested me. You, of all beautiful creatures, should know that."

"Oh," she said, her cheeks burning. To cover her embarrassment, she turned back to a small box that had defied her efforts to open it and used a spanner to pry loose a strip of wood. The next came more easily, as did the third, and soon she was tugging out a thick padding of buckram stuffed with straw. Beneath it, wrapped in oilcloth and tied up with hemp twine, was a familiar shape. "Dear God," she murmured.

Could it be?

Did she really want to find out?

Of a sudden, the planned journey with Duran became the sum of her ambitions. It guaranteed her nearly two more weeks in his arms. Two more weeks to tease him and be teased by him. A little more time, far too little, to love him.

She could put aside the box and move on to the next. He would never question it.

Her fingertips went on fire. A simple motion, another box placed atop this one . . . Besides, it might not even contain the leopard.

But she knew that it did. Sinking back onto her heels, she closed her eyes and demanded of herself the honesty she had only just demanded of him. "Duran," she said unwillingly, "you had better look at this."

After a glance at her face, he was immediately at her side, wrenching another panel from the box. She removed a torch from the wall sconce and held it closer as he fumbled with the oilcloth. At last he found a loose end and lifted it.

An ear. A sloping forehead. Two orange-gold eyes burning like coals over a feline muzzle.

"I don't bloody believe this," Duran muttered, burying his face in his hands. "I'd begun to imagine we'd find it here, but then I came to my senses. How can this have happened?"

"The scientific term," she said, "is coincidence. So how do we explain to Miss Holcombe that we discovered a statue worth a fortune and intend to make off with it?"

"We'll have to tell her the truth, I expect, or some of it. She doesn't strike me as a gullible female. And besides, we need her help to keep Shivaji in the dark."

"I beg your pardon? The entire point of this journey was to find the leopard and give it him."

"That would be *his* interpretation. My purpose was to assemble some money—except that you wouldn't let me steal anything—and end up at a port about the time a ship was setting out for a country that Shivaji wouldn't follow me to."

"Should I be flattered that you dragged me along for the ride? And what of your promise to take care of Gerald?"

"I'd hoped to do all of it, Jessica. But you have seen the palace guard. I can't take a pi—a moment in private without being followed. The time spent with you has been the only good part of this. It can continue to be. We'll go on with the search as planned, and when the opportunity presents itself, I'll strike a deal with Shivaji." He patted the leopard's head. "This gives me bargaining power."

"I don't see how. It belongs to Old Holcombe now."

"It belongs to a dead man. More properly, to Alanabad." His strong white teeth glinted when he smiled. "But practically speaking, it belongs to me."

"What belongs to you?" said Miranda from the doorway, a torch in one hand and a crowbar in the other.

After a tense silence Duran rose, took the torch, and escorted her to a wooden box. "Please be seated, Miss Holcombe. And if you will, indulge us for a time. I'm afraid we have not been entirely straightforward with you."

"I rather thought you hadn't," she said with perfect equanimity. "Do you mean to be now?"

"To the extent possible. Some of the story is not mine to reveal, and some of it we don't as yet know. I shall tell you what I can. Will that suffice?"

"How can I say?" She smiled at Jessica. "Is he trustworthy?"

"Sometimes." Jessica could not bring herself to deceive her. "But he does not wish you ill."

"Are you forming an alliance?" said Duran, slumped against the stone-block wall with his arms folded. "I am outnumbered and most likely outwitted. Miss Holcombe, we came here in search of a particular artifact, and as you surmised, we have found it. I am sorry to tell you that it was stolen from a small principality in the Deccan, probably by your cousin."

"I am not greatly surprised to hear it. Robert never troubled with niceties of ownership. Is there some doubt?"

"Very little. The thief adopted the name of a dead man to join a hunting party, disappeared at the same time as the icon got pinched, and was subsequently located in Madras. He had, it seemed, succumbed to a fever. He carried no identification. Just recently we connected him with your relation, partly by another name he had adopted—Paign Goudhurst—and also by the webbing of his fingers."

"Yes. It is common in the family." Miranda lifted her mittened hands. "When was he . . . discovered?"

"About fourteen months ago," Duran said. "He would have dispatched the parcel around that time."

"Shipments used to be delivered here every two or three months, but there has been nothing since January. Uncle wanted to open the last parcel, but because it was addressed to Robert, I sent it down here with the others. We have never known, I'm afraid, where he was or how to contact him. Do you mean to return the icon to its owner?"

"Would you permit us to take it?"

"I don't see why not. It doesn't belong to me, nor would my family be permitted to keep it in any case. May I see it?"

Duran gave Jessica the torch, made an opening in the box wide enough to remove the leopard, and brought it to Miranda.

She shook her head when he held it out for her to take. "It is quite beautiful, in a frightening sort of way. Has it religious significance?"

Duran hunkered down in front of her, the leopard balanced on his open palms. "None I know of. It carries with it centuries of tradition, or so I'm told, and is a symbol of continuity and strength. But of late it has become a pawn in a political game, and rivals for the throne are desperate to get their hands on it. Which means," he said, his voice cool and emphatic, "that whoever possesses the leopard is, by that fact, the object of a search by men who will kill to retrieve it."

"Here?" Miranda's cool gaze lifted to his face. "In England? The men who are traveling with you?"

"Those, yes, and perhaps others as well. We have not encountered the enemies of the ruling nizam, but they know we are searching in England for the leopard. It is possible some were dispatched here. And there could be, as well, spies among the servants of the nizam. I don't mean to frighten you, Miss Holcombe. But it's important that no one becomes aware the leopard was ever here."

"Who would I tell?" she replied, smiling. "And who would believe such a story?"

"Do *you* believe it?" Jessica asked, remembering when she'd thought Duran was making it all up. Now she thought he was making up only some of it. She just couldn't distinguish the true bits from the false.

"I suppose so," Miranda said at length. "The world is filled with things that couldn't possibly happen, or shouldn't. It is not for me to say what is real and what is not." She looked back at Duran. "If you take the icon with you now, will you not be in danger?"

"I'm getting used to it," he said with a wry grin. "But I want to protect Jessica, if I can. Here is the difficulty. The leopard must not be left in your custody, nor can we simply walk out of here with it."

"A dilemma, to be sure. Might I suggest a solution? How if I conceal the icon outside the castle, where you can return for it at a better time?"

"I don't see the point," Jessica protested. "If anyone got so far as to think it might be here, you could be compelled to disclose the location. And we are under constant scrutiny. Duran, enough! We shall take the leopard, give it to Shivaji, and let him deal with whatever consequences there might be."

The look he gave her over his shoulder could have fried an egg, but she'd had enough of his connivances and deceits. She stood, went to him, and snatched the leopard away. "I am very sorry, Miss Holcombe, that we involved you in this. Once we are gone, you will no longer have anything to fear."

"But I fear nothing now," Miranda said. "Nothing concerned with your icon, at any rate. My allotment of worry has been commandeered by other, less fantastical troubles, so I have none to spare for yours. To conceal the icon will be no trouble. And because I have been provokingly helpless to deal with my own problems, it would give me pleasure to accomplish something of use for a change."

She had spoken calmly, but there was a plea in her eyes. Jessica recognized it. She, too, felt helpless in the face of the troubles besieging her. At whatever risk, she wanted to overcome at least one of them. How could she deny Miss Holcombe the right to choose for herself?

Duran had withdrawn into the shadows, blessedly leaving the females to sort things out for themselves. "Are you sure?" Jessica asked, the leopard burning in her hands.

"Quite sure." Miranda rose. "There is an abandoned ice house dug into the limestone not far from here. I came across it quite by accident. It lies in a copse of birch about half a mile directly north of the gatehouse, and only the tops of the trees are visible from the castle. You should have no difficulty locating it and recovering the icon without being seen. Was there anything else you wished to secure?"

"No," said Jessica before Duran could mention the knives. "We are most grateful for your assistance."

"Then one day, if all goes well, perhaps you will tell me what occurred. For now, I'm afraid the dogs will already have been let loose in the house, so if you are to leave, I must distract them. Shall we go?"

Not liking to do it, Jessica returned the leopard to the box and by Miranda's direction, placed it in a cubbyhole behind a small grate. Duran relocked the dungeon and they all trooped back the way they'd come, leaving the extinguished torches in the guard room and reentering the hidden passageway.

When they reached the concealed panel, Miranda gave Jessica the candle she was carrying. "I'll leave the panel a little open so that you can hear what is going on upstairs. There will be a great clamor of barking and probably some swearing. When it concludes, count to twenty and then move quickly. Turn right and go to the door at the end of the passageway. It will take you out the back way, avoiding questions about where we have been and what you have been doing. Good-bye for now. I hope we shall meet again."

"But what are you going to do?" Jessica said. "Will the dogs hurt you?"

"They know me. I wish only to distract them while you depart. My cats will take care of that."

"Good heavens," said Jessica with some awe. Since they met, Miranda Holcombe had not ceased to astonish her. "The poor cats."

"Not at all. They are wily and exceedingly fast. The dogs are stupid, not nearly so fast, and they cannot climb curtains."

Then she was gone, leaving Duran and Jessica to look at each other in wonder.

Chapter 23

Shivaji, flanked by Arjuna holding a lantern, was waiting for them just the other side of the drawbridge. It was only when Duran saw the slight narrowing of his eyes that he realized they were still wearing the protective smocks Miranda Holcombe had lent them.

"No luck, I'm afraid," he said, removing the smock and submitting to Shivaji's light-fingered but thorough search. "The man doesn't collect. He accumulates. Amasses. No discrimination whatever. But he gave us carte blanche to search everywhere, including the kitchen cupboards, so we did."

Jessica pulled off her smock as well and shook it out. Dust flew. "All this long detour is my fault, and I am dreadfully sorry it has been such a waste. Except for bringing Lord Philpot the necklace, of course. But I wish I'd never mentioned his suggestion that we come here."

They both sounded a bit chirpy, Duran thought. On edge, as indeed they were. He'd better provide Shivaji a reason for it. "There were dogs," he said. "Old Holcombe's thugs loosed them when it got dark, and we had the devil of a time getting out. I sent the kitchen cat to draw them off while we made tracks to the back door. Everyone in that wretched place is queer in the attic."

"A little mad," Jessica explained when Shivaji glanced over at her. "And they were drinking the wine Lord Philpot sent as a gift, which made them a little madder. Duran wanted to leave earlier, when it became obvious that Mr. Holcombe had collected little of value, but I insisted we keep on with the search." She sighed. "Until we heard the dogs. Then we ran."

"There is no harm done," Shivaji said as he led them down the winding road to the carriage. "Except to the horses, which have stood overlong in harness. We shall not proceed to Clifton. One of my riders has returned with word of a posthouse, but to go there by the shortest way will require travel on a rough and narrow road."

It was a moonless night, and patchy clouds obscured much of the sky. From several directions, Duran saw, the Others were coming in from their positions around the castle, and by some trick of multiplication, there were twelve of them now. Had he entertained the notion of slipping through a fallen-down wall and into the Mendips, he wouldn't have got far. But now he knew where the leopard could be found, and one way or another, by God, he'd shake loose of his captors and come back for it.

Arjuna ignited the carriage lanterns and pulled several torches from the boot while Shivaji gave orders in a dialect unfamiliar to Duran. Four of the men, flaming torches in their hands, moved in front of the coach, and the others stayed to the rear.

Quite a little procession for this backwater road. Since everyone else was busy, Duran lowered the carriage steps and helped Jessica inside. Her arm trembled, and she caught her foot on the top step. He should have taken greater care with her. Despite his exhilaration, he was tired, and she must be as well.

Also nervous and overset because he had not presented the leopard to Shivaji, which she didn't know
was tantamount to offering his throat for the slitting.

He climbed in beside her, brushed back her hair
with his thumbs, and gave her a soft kiss. "You were
splendid tonight," he said. "As always. I don't want
you to worry about what happens next. I have no
more idea about that than you do. But I'll not be
reckless, and I swear I won't put you in danger."

"Do you imagine that is my concern? Don't patron-
ize me, Duran. We are both in this up to our eyebrows. All I ask is that we take no one else with us."

"Agreed," he said, meaning it. His own selfishness
gnawed at his guts like rats at a cheese. If he could
begin again, he'd not draw Jessica into his ordeal, or
perhaps he only wanted to believe that. In most ways
it was the same old game, the one dealt by the nizam
nearly a year ago, but now he had an ace up his sleeve.
And ten days to see how it all played out, and Jessie
with him until he gathered the strength to send her
away.

But who would have thought he'd find the damn
leopard? Who except Shivaji? He didn't like thinking
about that, and was glad when the carriage began to
move.

They had been traveling nearly an hour, Jessica nestled asleep against his chest, when a scream—from an
animal, he thought at first—stampeded the horses.

Jessica sprang awake. He held on to her as the carriage rocked and swerved. Tree branches slapped the
panels and scraped the window glass.

More screams. Shouts. The blast of gunfire.

He pushed her onto the floor and covered her with
his body. A bullet came through the window, sending

shards of glass raining over them. Tossed about like dice in a shaker, they could do nothing but cling to each other as the coach bounced and swayed.

Jessica gasped out a word. "Highwaymen?"

"No." He couldn't lie to her now. He'd recognized the cries of the attackers. *Jai!* It meant "victory!"

The nizam's enemies had caught up with them.

Another burst of gunfire, some of it close to hand. A scream from the driver's bench. The coach veered to the left. He went with it, his head crashing against the door. Jessica was trapped somewhere under his legs. The carriage rocked, teetered, righted itself again. And then, with a jolt that sent them both nearly to the ceiling and back again, it came to a halt.

Eerie silence. Dragging himself to the broken window, he raised his head and looked outside. Fallen torches, still afire, cast shadows over the trees and the ground and the figures struggling there. Men were fighting hand-to-hand, expending no breath on sound. A riderless horse went by.

It wasn't so quiet as he first had thought. Battles raged some distance in front of the coach and behind it. He heard the clang of swords, the stomping of hooves, and rarely, a shriek of pain.

In the coach, they were sitting ducks. He launched himself to the other door, threw it open, and lifted Jessica from the floor. "We have to get out of here. You first. Stay low."

She scrambled to the opening, turned herself to face inside the coach, and held on to the sill as she lowered herself to the ground.

He heard a cry, saw her fingers clawing at the sill. Just as they lost their grip, he caught hold of one slender wrist. Her other hand waved just within his reach and he grabbed hold of that as well. Bracing himself, he pulled her back inside.

She landed on her knees in front of him. "C-cliff."

"Stay here." He wriggled past her and draped himself out the open door, feeling for the ground. About six inches, perhaps eight, separated the coach wheels from the void. "It might be only a gully," he said. "I'm going out."

Her hand took hold of his hair and yanked him back. "No. There are gorges here. Hundreds of feet deep. Take care."

Gorges on one side, rabid snake worshipers on the other. He'd take his chances with the gorge. But first, hedging his bet, he let himself out, his legs dangling into empty air, and swung them up and under until he lay on his back beneath the coach. Then, slithering to the other side, he peered through the spokes of the right front wheel. Directly in front of him, eyes open and a line of blood streaming from his mouth, lay the Gurkha who had ridden beside the driver.

Beyond was a small clearing. He saw a fallen horse and two more men, neither of them moving. One had been holding a torch, and as he watched, it sputtered and went out. Light flickered in the grove where the fighting continued, and from the lanterns on the coach. The gunfire had ceased. No time to reload, he knew from experience. Combat would be with sword and knife, foot and hand.

It didn't matter to him which side won. He was dead in either case. It was Jessica who required protection now. Shivaji would spare her, if he survived. No certainty of that. If only the coach were not illuminated by those bloody lanterns.

Unwilling to risk exposure to the light, he went back to cliff's edge, grappled the spokes of the left front wheel with both hands, and lowered his legs over the side. One foot caught something solid and held. He felt with the booted toe of his other foot. Had to let go one hand from the wheel to settle.

A ledge. It seemed firm enough, but he couldn't be sure until he put his full weight on it. And tested its width. And . . . What the hell. He loosed his other hand from the wheel.

Nothing happened. Safe for now. He'd have to jump to get hold of the wheel again, but he could probably do it. He looked up and saw Jessica looking down at him.

"Wait," he said. "I'm on a ledge of some sort. Let me see how far it goes."

She vanished back into the coach.

After a few steps he'd moved beyond the light from the lanterns and had to feel his way, advancing sideways like a crab, his hands pressed to the cliff wall. Fairly soon the ground under his feet began to slope upward. When he reached out, his hands met the trunks of trees. Cover. From here they could slip into the woods.

He paused. Listened. It was pitch-black here. Muffled sounds came from not too far away, perhaps a hundred yards. Hard to tell.

He made his way back to the coach. The gorge, if that was what it was, must have taken a curve he hadn't noticed while moving upward, as he'd been doing before, into the darkness. This time he detected a glimmer of light that grew brighter and brighter. Then he saw the coach and the open door protruding over cliff's edge. Something appeared at the door, hung there for a moment, then plummeted down. As he watched, horrified, another life-size figure followed the first.

He hadn't made out what they were. Didn't hear

them land. Couldn't bear to imagine what had occurred at the coach while he was gone.

Then Jessica's head poked out. "Duran?"

"What the devil was that?"

"Never mind. Which way are we going?"

"Move aside." He sprang up, grabbed hold of the carriage wheel, and pulled himself over the lip of the gorge. Once inside the coach, he placed Jessica with her back to the open door and flattened himself on the floor. "Give me your wrists. The ledge isn't far down. Let me know when your feet are secure. Are you afraid of heights?"

"Only of falling from them. Hurry. The fighting is coming close again."

On his instruction and without hesitation, she stepped out into open air and dropped from view. He was halfway out the coach himself, clinging to her forearms with all his strength, more afraid, he suspected, than she was. Then the pull on his arms relaxed.

"I'm on ground," she said.

"Move a little to the left. I'm coming down."

When he was beside her on the ledge, he struck out in the opposite direction he'd taken before. Jessica was immediately on his heels. "Not too close," he advised her. "I may have to make a sudden stop."

"Why this way? What did you find before?"

"A short path to the top of the gorge. We'd be expected to take that way out, so I'm gambling this is some sort of animal track that will carry us all the way to the bottom. What was it you threw down there?"

"The smocks, wrapped around the blankets and pillows we acquired before setting out for Lord Philpot's estate. They were stored under the benches. Anyone looking for us might see them and think we'd fallen, as I so nearly did. It rather defeats the purpose, though, if we're heading that direction ourselves."

"Perhaps. It was a clever idea and may divert the searchers, if there are any. I'd as soon they fought one another to mutual extermination. Keep moving at a comfortable speed, Jessica. I'm going ahead to see what's there."

He should have known she'd stick to him like a burr. But the path, about eighteen inches wide for most of the way, was easy to navigate despite the blackness of the night. The stars were completely obscured now, and the coach lanterns long out of view. Only the two of them, balanced against the side of a cliff, descending to the devil knew where.

After a considerable time, Duran heard the sound of moving water and knew they were close to reaching bottom. They must have traveled at least half a mile. On his own, he'd have taken the next part of the journey in the water to throw off pursuers. But if he was to escape, it could not be in Jessica's company. He had given his word. What he was to do with her had not disclosed itself, although he'd thought of little else all the way down the cliff.

The stream, when they reached it, was shallow and not very wide. They stopped long enough to drink and splash water over their faces before continuing on, picking their way along the rocky ground. There was room for them to walk side by side, and after a few minutes, hand in hand.

"I saw him fight," Jessica said, a touch of amazement in her voice. "Shivaji. He came out of the trees and was heading straight for the coach. I nearly went out the other door, gorge or no gorge, but before I could move, I saw two men drop on him from an overhanging branch. Right away, one went sailing through the air. He hit a tree trunk and slid down and didn't move again. By that time the other attacker was on the ground, Shivaji's foot on his forehead, a knife at his throat. Shivaji drew the blade across his neck and jumped away from a rider bearing down on him with a saber. Somehow he got hold of the rider and pulled him off, right onto his knife. He impaled him midair, Duran. And he did all of this so smoothly, without discernible effort. It was like watching a dancer."

He understood her reaction perfectly. He'd experienced much the same when another contingent of Malik Rao's fanatics ambushed them on the road from Alanabad to Madras. Lashed to his saddle, he could do nothing but watch Shivaji and his well-trained escort beat off a company four times their number with only a handful of casualties. And Shivaji had been at the center of the action, with such effortless skill that Duran had never seen its like. Even Michael Keynes, an unholy terror when unleashed, could do no better than fight him to a draw. Probably not even that.

"Shivaji is a professional killer," he said, squeezing her hand. "But not an indiscriminate one. He won't harm you, unless you come between him and his mission."

"To find the leopard."

"Yes." Among other things. "What do you know about this part of the country?"

"Very little. There are gorges, as I told you, and caves. One very large one a little way north of Wells called the Wookey Hole, which I always wanted to explore as a child. Papa agreed to take me there for my birthday when I was ten, but Aubrey talked him out of it. Devils live in caves, he said." She made a little sound in her throat. "I'm chattering, aren't I? It doesn't mean I'm afraid. Not very. But I don't know what we ought to do next, or where we should go."

"Nor do I, princess. But a cave would be useful right about now. I need to stash you someplace while

I go back and discover the outcome of the battle between evil and worse evil."

Jerking her hand from his, she came to an abrupt halt. "Why? What has that to do with us now?"

"Nothing, I hope. But I'm not counting on that. Malik Rao's thugs might not pursue me, but if he has survived, Shivaji surely will."

"Then we run, if that's what you want. And if he catches us, we carry on our visits to the collectors. We're simply trying to elude his enemies. He would expect it."

They rounded a bend where the stream, once more powerful than now, had carved a grotto in the limestone cliff. Not quite a cave, but it would provide shelter for a time. And if he got safely back, he would be able to find it.

Armoring himself against the objections that were sure to be fired at him, he led her through the small entrance and directed her to wait while he checked for animals and other unpleasant surprises. There were none. The water had scoured out a gourd-shaped enclosure and smoothed the spurs of granite that rose like giant's teeth from the ground.

"This will do," he said. "Jessica, I'm going to find out what happened back there."

"But—"

"You needn't worry. I'm a dab hand at reconnaissance . . . so long as I've only myself to watch out for. This isn't negotiable, princess. If you follow me, I swear I'll bind you with your own dress and stow you up a tree. Wait here." He couldn't see her, but he could feel the waves of heat steaming off her body. "Will you?"

"Are you going back the way we came?"

"That's too exposed. It may take awhile to find a good vantage point, so don't imagine the worst if I'm gone for a considerable time. About all, don't come after me."

"I want to know why this is necessary, Duran."

"And I will tell you, once it's done. Promise you'll remain here. Please." If it sounded like he was begging, he was.

After a few moments she murmured an ungracious agreement and stomped past him to sit herself on a flat tooth. "Run along, then. I shall remain here until dawn. After that, I shall use my own judgment."

Chapter 24

Duran had no intention of coming back for her.

Jessica was so certain of it that more than once she considered striking out on her own to find help. But as the hours wore on she continued to huddle in the grotto, arms wrapped around her knees, waiting like Penelope for Odysseus to return. One last act of faith, she supposed, for the sake of a faithless man.

He might, for once, have told her the truth. But no, that wasn't fair. Everything had changed. Much of what she had failed to believe had proven to be true, or partly so. And all that had seemed so outlandish—the stolen icon, assassins, nizams, cults, the fate of a kingdom—had been sealed in blood and death on the edge of a cliff.

Now, pried from her cocoon, she had no choice but to look at Duran with new eyes. And to defer, however galling it might be, to his judgment. He had the experience she lacked, and the detachment. Unburdened by love, he had no fear of loss, no need to cling, no regard for the future of a marriage taken only for convenience. And he had forces to contend with that she had only just come to recognize.

No more skepticism, then. No more pride. No making demands on him simply to assert herself. No more—she had to face this—burdening him with her unwanted self. Whatever he asked, she would do. She was resolved on that.

She paced for a time. Slipped outside for a drink of water and saw that the sky was clearing. Stars winked in and out of the clouds, bathing the high cliffs in the palest of silvery light. The stream curled like a silver ribbon around black lumps of rock and wispy grasses, and somewhere a nightbird was singing.

The knot of fear in her chest began to dissolve. She could be strong. There was, really, no alternative.

She had just returned to the grotto when the ground began to shake. A rumbling sound, like thunder but closer, rolled through the gorge. She pressed her hands against the stone wall and felt it vibrating. Then all went still.

An earthquake? She had never experienced its like. Oddly, she hadn't been afraid. Not after what she'd already seen that night. But it was frightening nonetheless, in a way that had nothing to do with her.

After a while she went outside again. More stars, more silvery glow limning the gorge, but nothing to say what the thunder had been. Only the whisper of the stream, telling secrets to itself.

If only Duran would come.

He did, when she had made herself stop thinking about him. Hearing her name, she rose from where she had been sitting against the curved wall of the grotto and saw a large black figure filling the entranceway. She wanted to throw herself into his arms.

She didn't move.

He came to her instead and laid his hands gently on her shoulders. "I am sorry I was so long. It was . . . difficult. Are you all right?"

"Perfectly. There was something—a noise, and the ground shook."

"Yes. I'll tell you about that. There isn't much time,

princess. Bear with me. And let us sit, if you don't mind. I've been doing rather of lot of climbing."

She'd had plenty of time to explore the grotto and knew of two stones, reasonably flat and side by side. She led him to one of them and took her place on the other, reflecting on the difference in his voice. It was subdued. Resigned, even, with undertones she could not begin to guess at.

"I found another way to where we were attacked," he said, "but there is nothing there now. Some broken tree branches and grasses, perhaps, and some blood, but the first rainstorm will take care of that. It took awhile to discover where they'd gone. Not far, actually, but there is no road to speak of. All the bodies, of men and horses both, had been taken to another gorge not nearly so wide or deep as this one. I got there as they were being lowered over the side."

"By whom?" She resented the suspense he created, however unintentional. "Who won the battle?"

"Oh, Shivaji, of course. I counted nine of his convoy helping dispose of the evidence. It wasn't possible to tell how many of the enemy had been killed, but it's certain that no prisoners would be taken. Some may have escaped. While I was watching, another Gurkha rode in and reported to Shivaji. No doubt some of the men were dispatched to look for stray snake worshipers and, probably, some sent to look for us."

"What was the noise, then?"

"When the bodies were all at the bottom of the gorge, several boulders were sent off the cliff. They started an avalanche, and now everything is buried under a small mountain of rubble. No investigation, no questions asked. As if it had never happened."

"Unless you testified to what you had seen."

"To what purpose? Had Malik Rao's zealots carried

the day, there would be no one to give evidence of *our* deaths." He paused, his breathing unsteady. "Besides, I won't be here. This is my chance to escape, probably the only one I'll get, and I'm taking it."

She let that sink in. It was not unexpected, but she'd thought he would go without telling her. He could be miles away by now. Why had he come back here? "I don't suppose," she ventured, "that you would consider giving Shivaji the leopard? Then you needn't flee to wherever you are going. Unless, of course, you wish to go there."

"No. I haven't even a solid notion where it will be. Look, I haven't wanted to tell you this. Or perhaps I have already done so. I've long since lost track of what you know and don't know."

There was a rustle of clothing as he shifted position. "A year ago, short a few days, I was sentenced to death. The ruling, I am assured, is immutable. While the nizam ostensibly granted me a period of time in which to find the leopard, turns out it was all a political charade. I was supposed to be secretly disposed of when convenient, and under no circumstances permitted to survive beyond the anniversary of my condemnation. Those were Shivaji's orders. Leopard or no leopard, Jessica, he will kill me by Sunday week."

She wished she could see his face. Except for a patch of ghostly light at the entrance, the grotto was sable black. The disembodied conversation shuddered against the curved wall, producing not so much an echo as resonances in a different pitch. She imagined the spirits of the dead men calling out from under the cairn of stones erected by the avalanche. *Come join us.* She wondered if Duran heard them as well. She thought of all these things because she could not bring herself to speak.

"I'm going to take you back to him," he said into the taut silence. "We should go soon, before he moves to some other place. He won't harm you."

"Nor you," she said. "I don't believe he'd arbitrarily execute you, not if you put the leopard in his hands. Perhaps not under any circumstances. Why should he? Who would know, all the way in that little kingdom in the middle of nowhere, what became of you?"

A ragged breath. "It is, for Shivaji, a matter of honor. His family has served the rulers of Alanabad for . . . I don't know. Several hundred years. They take oaths. They follow orders without question. The divine imperative for them is adherence to duty, whatever the cost. That's as much as I understand, anyway. And that Shivaji will never veer from a course he believes to be predestined."

"Or he wants you to believe so. I know his capabilities. I have seen him kill. But I do not believe he has the soul of a murderer. He has tended me, and a number of the servants, when we were ill. He makes prayer boats."

"Yes. I've seen those on the rivers in India. He's an unusual man, to be sure. His philosophy, character, and profession remain an utter mystery to me. But at the end of the day, Shivaji is what he was bred to be. He is the fabled Sakar ki Churi, the Knife of Sugar. It is smooth and sweet, but still a knife."

There was a conviction in his voice that persuaded her more than his words. And she had deciphered one of those resonances. His fear of Shivaji was genuine. She might not believe in the Knife of Sugar, but Duran most assuredly did. In the shadows of the grotto, death had come to call. "Will you take the leopard with you?" she said.

His relief at her acquiescence, although unspoken, made its presence felt. "I'll try for it," he admitted after a hesitation. "It took my former life from me. It's taking the one I have now, here, with you. Why shouldn't it pay for whatever life I find somewhere else?"

She hardly dared. But this would be her only opportunity. "Must that life, somewhere else, exclude me? I would go with you, Duran, if you'd have me."

Silence. A murmur then, perhaps *Dear God*.

"It isn't possible," he said at length. "I don't know where I'm going, or if I'll get anywhere at all. You should never have got caught up in this. I will answer for that, one way or another. But it stops now. From here on out you have to stay clear of me and what I do."

"Because you say so? Or because you want rid of me?"

"Because there is no choice for either of us. Because I have made a covenant with Shivaji. So long as you are not involved with any attempt I make to escape, he will do you no injury. Jessica, we can debate this until we are found here, still jabbering, or I can lead you to safety and take my chances from there."

She heard him stand, and the scrape of his boots on the stony ground as he went to the entrance and stood there, silhouetted against the starlight. "Or if you wish it, we can walk together into Shivaji's grip and let him make the decision for us. I know only this, princess. It's from a poem by a man named Rumi, and it seems to be engraved on every one of my bones. 'Around the lip of this cup we share—My life is not mine.'"

She would have wept then, for the first time since she could remember, except that it would have made everything more difficult for him. And she had resolved—had she not?—to give him whatever he asked.

How easy to make such a vow before she understood it meant she would never see him again. And how hard to keep it, since the vow was made only to herself.

Coming to her feet, she unclenched her hands and wedged a brisk tone into her voice. "Well, if you are going to deposit me on the assassin's doorstep, we'd best be off. Just keep in mind, Duran, that I am not altogether helpless. You needn't take me too close or linger to see if I have been properly received."

"That's my girl," he said, and she heard the relief in his tone. "Come along, then. If we don't get there before Shivaji has moved on, there will be the devil to pay."

More than an hour later, as Duran led her up a steep, grassy incline, the smell of smoke and something oddly sweet enveloped them.

Duran halted. Took her hand. "I know that odor. It comes from a funeral pyre. They are burning their dead."

"But I thought—"

"The stones were for the enemy," he said. "It was a respectful burial. And they could hardly incinerate so many without drawing attention. If you don't wish to see the fires, wait here for a time. They will soon burn out. Then proceed to the end of the promontory. From there you can get Shivaji's attention."

"I don't mind the ritual," she told him. "But I shall wait long enough to give you a head start. Do go off, Duran, before I embarrass us both with needless sentimentality. I shall miss you. I shall try not to think of you, and after a time, I expect I shall succeed. Good-bye, then. I am glad to have known you."

For a long time she felt him there, still behind her, as if uncertain what to do. But the sensation of his presence gradually faded, and when she brought herself to look around, he was gone.

She gave thought to how much time to wait and decided very little was required. This was to be yet another masquerade, like the one she'd played out with Gerald, like the many she'd played with Duran in their sexual games. When she appeared in front of Shivaji, dramatically exhausted and lost, he would not expect the fugitive Duran to be lurking nearby. But neither did she wish to intrude on the funeral taking place below.

Dropping to her belly, she slithered her way to the narrow point of the overlook and saw a circle of men seated cross-legged around two pallets suspended over blazing fires. The pallets, and the figures laid out on them, were all but consumed by the flames. She could detect only the outlines, nearly transparent now, of what they had been.

Lowering her head, she slipped back a little, rolled over, and gazed up at the stars. All those men, the ones in the flames and the ones under the stones, come so far to reclaim a chunk of gold. They had died for a symbol, and for the political ambitions of their leaders. She had regained her lost love, and lost him again. There was no prayer boat in the world large enough to contain all her questions, or all her tears, if ever she permitted herself to weep.

Some time later, sounds from below stirred her from her reverie. She returned to her viewpoint and saw that the ceremony was done and the traces of it all but vanished. It was time. Rising, she stood directly on the edge of the promontory and waited for someone to notice her.

It didn't take long. A finger pointed in her direction. Everyone looked up at her. And after a few minutes, Shivaji came for her. He was alone, on horseback, riding slowly up the grassy slope she had ascended with Duran.

She watched him dismount, approach her, and bow, and remembered how he had killed three men in the time it would take to close a window. "Were your losses great?" she said.

"Two dead," he replied without expression, as if describing the weather. "Three wounded, but they are able to carry on their duties. Where is Duran?"

"I don't know. He said he was going, he didn't say where, and he left."

"How long ago? In which direction."

"He departed soon after we escaped the coach." Which was, so far as it went, perfectly true. "I don't know precisely where we were at the time, but he turned right."

A silence. "Did he ask you to lie on his account, or to mislead me?"

"He asked me not to make a fuss. I wanted to go with him, but he wouldn't let me. It wasn't a lengthy discussion. He was in something of a hurry." She lifted her chin. "He did mention that if he stayed, you would kill him."

"Do you believe that?"

"Is it true?"

He seemed not to want to answer that. But she couldn't really tell. It was dark, and even in daylight, little could be read from his face.

"I was sent for him," he said.

"Like Yamaraj for the prince. I remember the story. The prince dies, the princess cries a waterfall of tears, and the Lord of Death toddles along to his next victim. Are you quite proud of yourself?"

"I must do the work given me to do, *memsahib*. Duran's fate was declared by another. I am not the wielder of death. Only the instrument. Can a sword choose where to strike?"

"A sword," she said, "does not have a mind to think with. A will to make its own decision. A conscience to guide its action. Two legs to walk the hell away."

He made no reply to that. Nor did he speak again until he had brought her to the carriage, she on the horse and Shivaji leading it as if he were the servant he had for so long pretended to be.

After he had helped her down, his strong hands firm on her waist, he regarded her thoughtfully. "I would like you to continue the journey," he said.

The declaration was so outrageous that she could scarcely believe he'd made it. Continue on as if nothing had happened? As if there were any purpose to it? "Why should I?" she said, not troubling to conceal her anger. "Even if I found the leopard and gave it you, Duran would still be marked for death. Can you deny that?"

"His life is not contingent on the leopard, no. But consider. If I am escorting you, I cannot be searching for him."

The breath rushed out of her. He had a point. For a little time, at least, she could keep this relentless monster off Duran's trail. It was a mercy that he wanted the leopard even more than he wanted Duran at the point of his knife. And she had no other place to go, really, nor anywhere she cared to be. Gerald could wait another few days. He would have to, because she was in no state of mind to deal with him now.

"Very well," she said with patent reluctance. "I shall inquire for your statue, until I decide not to. Or am I your prisoner?"

"You may depart at any time, *memsahib*."

At the least, she reflected, entering the carriage, she would have the satisfaction of pretending to seek the leopard when it had already been found. Shivaji would never have it, that was certain. Duran had got away. And the Lord of Death would be returning to his petty little country in disgrace.

Little enough comfort for the long days and nights ahead, but it was all she had.

Chapter 25

Three days had passed with no word of Duran. It occurred to Jessica, belatedly, that if he'd been captured or killed, Shivaji might not give her the news.

The outriders were hard on Duran's trail, she knew. Only the driver, one guard, and Arjuna remained. And Shivaji. Always Shivaji, everywhere she looked, as if trying to read from her expression what she was thinking. But she wore her face like a mask. He would learn nothing from her.

For propriety's sake, and because Shivaji insisted on it, she employed an abigail provided by an agency in Bristol. Prudence had appeared to be a cheerful lass, but that was only until she clapped eyes on the heathens. From that time on she huddled in the carriage, wringing her hands and moaning about the turbaned brutes who were, she was sure, plotting to ravish Lady Jessica and her hapless maid.

Lady Jessica thought it far more likely that she'd slap the sniveling girl and put her out at the next crossroads.

They had made three calls since leaving Clifton. She moved through each encounter with practiced social skill, making polite conversation and dutifully examining the collections, spending enough time to convince Shivaji her inquires had been thorough. She found it

ironic that two of her hosts had promptly commissioned her to sell a number of valuable items, and the
third wished to be contacted if she came across any
fine Sévigné bows, which his mistress liked to collect.
If this journey continued long enough, she could pick
up several new clients.

To no purpose, she had to remind herself. Her business would soon be brought down by her brother-in-
law. Might already have been, for all she knew.

It didn't signify. She had lost Duran, and nothing
else seemed to matter. If only she could be sure he
was safe. But she didn't know, and might never know,
what became of him. Each night she lay dry-eyed on
her bed and fought a silent battle with the pain.

On the fourth evening, under a leaden sky, she
moved on leaden feet around the deepest puddles in
the courtyard of yet another posthouse, a small one
on the road between Much Wenlock and Shrewsbury.
It had been raining on and off all day, and a biting
wind had sprung up late in the afternoon. Her summer
cloak flapped behind her like wings.

She was expected at the White Stallion, thanks to
the efficient Helena, as she had been expected at each
posthouse since the itinerary changed. The innkeeper,
a small man with side-whiskers and a bulbous nose,
was waiting for her just inside.

"Lady Jessica," he said with a gap-toothed smile.
"You are most welcome. There are two letters for
you, which we have placed in your bedchamber, and
the other member of your party, who arrived earlier
this afternoon, is waiting for you in the private
parlor."

"The other—?" Her heart jumped about in her
chest. And then subsided. It had to be Helena, probably with bad news concerning Gerald. Or . . . might
she have heard something of Duran? No. That was

unthinkable. But what else would bring her all the way from London?

Jessica knew she wasn't thinking clearly. The events of the last few weeks had left her sluggish and numb. They had also taught her three lessons she wished she had never learned. Whatever happened was immeasurably worse than what had preceded it. News was always bad. And pain was more tolerable if one walked directly into it.

Today's pain was waiting for her down a short passageway and behind a closed parlor door, so she walked directly to that door and flung it open.

Her gaze shot to a merry fire dancing in the hearth, the first she'd seen for half a year. She blinked. An awareness, like the moment one almost remembered a dream just before it dissolved, tingled from her hair to her toes. She was afraid to look.

"What kept you, princess?" said a slurred voiced to her right. "The landlord cut me off after one bottle of claret. I don't think he believed you would pay for it, let alone another."

"I'm not surprised," she said, struggling to lock her trembling knees into place. "No one with sense believes anything you say."

"And I thought you'd be delighted to see me. It is perfectly safe to glance this direction, by the way. Feel free to do so at any time."

She did, chin lifted in a show of indifference.

Long-limbed and indolent, he reclined with feline grace in a carved-wood captain's chair. His hair was filthy, his shirt and pants in tatters, his face and hands bruised and scabbed. He was grinning.

"You won't want to touch me, princess, until I've had a bath. But you might wish to come over here and pet my cat."

Her gaze followed his gesture to the small table

beside his chair. To the Golden Leopard, more regal than King George IV had ever been, its lucent eyes staring directly into her soul.

"You were supposed to be on a ship by now," she said, turning back to Duran. "I thought that with the head start I gave you, you'd be clever enough to escape."

"I did escape." He looked offended. "So far as I know, Shivaji's spaniels are still chasing their tails fifty miles south of here. I'd have caught up with you last night, but I went to the wrong posthouse. This one, though, I remembered from the list." His teeth flashed. "The Stallion. Reminded me of . . . well, me."

"This isn't funny." Relief, rage, and pure joy at seeing him again tumbled inside her like a team of acrobats. "If you were free and clear, why in heaven's name did you return?"

"You know what they say, my dear. The cat always comes back."

"Only if he's lost his mind. Now that Shivaji has got his leopard, he will—" She could not bear to say it. "You know what he's going to do."

"Of course. He'll march back to India and save Alanabad from the snake chaps. What else?"

"*Kill* you, you dolt. He is sworn to do it. You told me so. Leopard or no leopard, you are the walking dead. Nothing, but *nothing,* will change his mind."

"I told you that?" He considered. "I must have wanted something from you at the time."

"Yes. The chance to retrieve a fortune in gold and gemstones before gallivanting off to a tropical island."

"I hadn't considered a tropical island. Perhaps I ought to start gallivanting now, before Shivaji knows I'm here."

Her alarm faded to uncertainty. He was too pleased with himself, in too ebullient a mood . . . not at all like a man worrying about his imminent demise. Perhaps she could safely be happy he was here.

"Would I be lounging about, waiting to surprise Shivaji, if I expected him to garrote me? Yes, he made plenty of threats and always kept me well guarded. He assumed I would steal the leopard if I found it, which I did. He did not imagine I'd get away with it, but I did. And it seems neither of you expected me to return with the leopard and put it in his hands. For that matter, neither did I. But here I am."

She sank onto a footstool and gazed into his untroubled eyes. "Why, then?

"Why, for you, lady wife. We contracted for three weeks of marriage, and by my calculations, you still owe me seven days and eight hours. I lost track of the minutes last night under a hedgerow."

She gave him the smile he expected, because she could do nothing else. But her pulse was beating erratically.

He still meant to leave her. Before she had even begun to hope he might stay, he made it clear he would not. *Do not importune me,* he was telling her. *My life will not be here, with you.*

And why should it be? He did not, after all, love her.

"You shall have what you are owed," she said. "In truth, I was more than a little piqued when you took French leave in the middle of our wedding trip."

"I can't help but notice that you continued on without me."

"There were reasons, or so I believed at the time. But it appears that while I was busy keeping Shivaji from joining the search, you were even busier catching up with us. Have you eaten?"

At the change of subject, he blinked. "Miss Holcombe left a packet of nuts, dried fruit, and biscuits alongside the box with the leopard. She rightly guessed I'd soon be paying a call at the icehouse. Oh, and she left me a pistol as well. If Shivaji shows signs of doing me in, I shall promptly shoot him."

"That is comforting, to be sure. Not that I think you could hit a hay wagon in your present state." She rose, pleased to find that her legs had stopped shaking. "I'll see to a bath for you, and a hot meal. Do you wish me to fetch Shivaji?"

"By all means. And if you don't mind, leave us in private for a short time. I'm hoping to negotiate a favor or two in exchange for the leopard."

"Indeed? What's to stop him from simply taking it from you?"

"An overwrought sense of duty and a healthy respect for karma. To be mean-spirited when a gift is put in one's hands can never lead to good. It is my karma to take advantage of that."

"What is karma?"

"I've never been altogether sure. Perhaps it's akin to the Pool of Bathsheba, where an angel comes down and stirs the soup. Or something along that line." He poured the last of the claret into his glass and took a deep swallow. "Fortification. Now that is something I *do* understand."

Hugo Duran, drunken, prevaricating, overconfident lunatic. And she, madly in love with him. An angel ought to come down and knock some sense into the both of them.

She went off to find Shivaji.

Duran's grinning pose vanished the moment he heard the door click shut.

He'd given a damn good performance. Just about anyone else would have believed it. In fact, he rather thought Jessica had done, at least for the moment. But in a short time she'd start picking at what he'd said, and comparing that to other things he'd said and done, taking it all apart the way she could fillet him with her tongue. And then she'd realize he'd been lying to her. Again.

What he required was someone to back up his story. The most unlikely of allies. The man who had opened the door so silently and closed it with such stealth that he was in the room before Duran looked over and saw him.

Straight as a lance, his empty hands relaxed at his sides, Shivaji gazed back at him with the same unruffled, mildly disapproving look that never failed to scratch at his nerves.

To demonstrate that he possessed no nerves, Duran drained the wineglass, set it down, and folded his arms across his stomach. Let Shivaji make the first move.

He wished he really did have a gun.

"I am glad of the leopard." As always, Shivaji spoke softly. "But nothing has changed."

"I didn't expect it had. Nevertheless, there is time remaining on my lease, and I must insist on claiming it. You will not begrudge me a few more days."

"For self-indulgence?"

"Some of that. As much as I can squeeze in. But— and you will appreciate this—I have made a promise, and it is my duty to keep it. This matter concerns my wife's brother-in-law, a menace who must be exterminated. I, being for all practical purposes dead, am just the man for the job."

"I am to permit you to live long enough to kill another?"

"Unless you'd like to do it yourself." A pause. "No? I didn't think so."

"I am not called for him."

"But *I* am. You may fancy yourself the Lord of Death, but we mortals have got rather good at slaughtering one another as well. I may fail, of course. Time is limited and my quarry is the devil knows where. But I've earned the chance to try."

"You did only as the gods directed you. The leopard is restored to its rightful place, or soon will be. If you are to be rewarded, the prize is not mine to give."

This wasn't going well. But he hadn't expected it to. Duran felt every cut and scrape on his body, the ache of overstrained muscles, and the beginning of a headache from the bottle of wine he'd guzzled. Somewhere under all that, curled like a serpent, was a fear so acute he couldn't begin to address it.

"Never mind me and my god-directed fate," he said. "I ask nothing for myself. This is for Jessica. And make no mistake about it. If not for her, your precious leopard would be a brick of gold in my satchel and a pouchful of gemstones in my pocket. I had got free of you and your associates, and you were not going to catch me."

"Perhaps. You believe, then, that it is your dharma to kill this brother-in-law?"

"Dharma, karma, angels in the bathtub. If I ever had a philosophy, I've long since forgot what it was. You owe me time, and I want it. I intend to use it to honor a debt. And there's something else I want. Jessica is not to know how this little adventure is to end."

"If that was your wish, you should not have told her that it ends very soon, and how. She is under no misapprehension about your fate."

"I've told her so many contradictory versions of the story that she no longer knows what to believe. Not unreasonably, she has ceased to trust me. But she will credit your word, so I want you to convince her that with the leopard's return, my death sentence has been commuted."

"But that is not the truth."

"Oh, right. I'd forgot. You steer by a skewed compass. Lying is prohibited, but it is acceptable, even commendable, to slit my throat."

The brown eyes clouded. "It need not be that way. There are swift poisons. Philters that will draw you into a peaceful sleep."

"I am to have a choice? How nice. Why don't you draw me up a menu of execution techniques, and I'll let you know which of them I fancy."

Shivaji, not unexpectedly, said nothing.

"You continue to miss the point," Duran said, frustration edging his voice. "Have I asked you to spare me? Pleaded for my life?" He patted the leopard. "Eight days is little enough in exchange for this, don't you think? And because it is Jessica who led me to return it, can you not grant her, for that short time, a little peace of mind? Is there no mercy in your philosophy? No kindness?"

After a lengthy silence, Shivaji inclined his head. "I see no purpose to delaying what must be, nor do I expect you will use the time wisely. But up to the day and hour when your sentence was pronounced, I shall permit you to live. I will not, however, tell a falsehood."

Relief drained the blood from Duran's face. For a while there, he'd been sure he had miscalculated. It wouldn't have been the first time.

"A direct lie is not required," he said. "She is looking for reassurance and will want to believe you. Just serve up one of those delightfully inscrutable pronouncements you're so good at, the ones that sound like they mean one thing and really mean another. Or mean nothing at all."

"I shall consider it. For now, I must secure the leopard. If I may—"

"Oh, permit me," said Duran, rising. "A little ceremony is in order, don't you think?" He picked up the leopard, dusted its muzzle with his sleeve, and held it out. "With my compliments, sir. I confess myself amazed that I did, as you predicted, find the damn thing, and even more amazed that I am giving it to you."

Templing his hands, Shivaji bowed. "It was written, Duran-sahib. You have always questioned that such a thing could be. Refusing to accept your destiny, you have sought to create your own. But this world, says Krishna, has no significance unto itself. It is no more than a play that God acts within himself."

"Is that so? Then God must be partial to farces. Here's your cat. And I hope it's written somewhere that your beastly little nizam chokes on his own tongue."

With a degree of reverence that surprised Duran, Shivaji accepted the leopard and stood for a time, looking down at it like a man who had come to the end of a long journey. Then he turned and started for the door.

He was halfway there when Jessica burst into the room, an open letter in each hand, a worried expression on her face. She stopped just short of colliding with Shivaji, backed up a few steps, and looked a question at Duran.

"You're just in time," he said. "This gentleman and I have come to terms. All is precisely as I told you it would be."

"Oh." She visibly brightened. "What excellent news. Will you be returning then to India, sir?"

"As soon as arrangements can be made," Shivaji replied gently. "My countrymen must first be located, and passage booked."

"Oh," she said again. And appeared to forget him. "Duran, Gerald sold the le—the item we lent him, to the Marquess of Wallingford, who quickly discovered it to be all but worthless. He demanded his money back, but since Gerald already disposed of it, he is laying charges. Fraud, probably, but Helena isn't altogether sure. Wallingford is tenacious. He'll pursue Gerald until he gets him."

It was good news, but her blushed skin and the taut hands clutching the letters carried a different message. "It worked, then," he said, watching her eyes. Why was she overset?

"Yes, except that Gerald went to the town house, looking for us. When Helena refused to tell him where we were, he struck her. She is bruised, but otherwise intact. Those are her words, but from the shaky handwriting, I suspect he hurt her rather badly."

Anger tightened his voice. "And the other letter?"

"From Colonel Pageter. Gerald showed up at High Tor, but the messenger Helena dispatched got there before him and Mariah was safely smuggled off to Mrs. Bellwood's cottage. It was, from the colonel's account, something of a scene when Gerald arrived. Papa is frantic, Mariah terrified, and Colonel Pageter uncertain what to do. I must return home, Duran."

"We were going there in any case." He glanced down at his filthy clothes and the filthier skin showing through the holes in them. "You wish to leave immediately, I suppose."

"Yes. But we no longer have a driver. Unless you can manage a team, we'll need to hire someone."

Shivaji moved forward a step. "Ghiya will remain in service until you are delivered to your home," he said. "And if it pleases you, I shall provide escort."

"There's no need for—"

"A capital idea," said Duran, acknowledging the inevitable. Wherever he went, Shivaji was sure to follow. "While you are waiting for your compatriots and arranging transportation to Alanabad, you can earn your room and board as my valet. Don't count on a salary, though."

"I will not. You have never paid me."

"And you were worth every penny. What say you, Jessica? For old time's sake, shall we take him in?"

She looked back and forth between them. "I don't think that would be a very good idea."

Duran heard the uncertainty beneath her words. She did not altogether believe the execution had been called off. "In the normal run of things," he said, "I'd be glad to see the last of him. But I cannot deny that he is remarkably efficient, gives a decent shave, and has certain other skills that might prove useful." He crossed to her and placed his hands on her taut, resistant shoulders. "Gerald will come for us now, you know. And he will punish Mariah as well, or try to. He won't succeed. I mean to draw his fire. But he is a treacherous son of a bitch, and I wouldn't mind having Shivaji at my back."

Silence. "I suppose so," she conceded at length, but the doubt was back in her eyes. And the fear.

"If you will pardon me," Shivaji said, "I shall arrange a change of horses and the restoration of your luggage to the coach."

She withdrew from Duran's light grasp and crossed to the assassin, who waited for her calmly, the leopard cradled in his hands. "We can see to all of that," she said. "You should go."

"As I will, when I can no longer be of service." Raising the leopard like a votive offering, he regarded her solemnly. "I now have what I sought. Be at peace, *memsahib*. In the time of miracles, even a sword can find itself with legs."

Jessica's face lit up with a dazzling smile, and when

Shivaji had left the room, she turned it on her husband.

He marveled. What Shivaji said had clearly turned the trick. But—*swords with legs*?

That was, he thought, welcoming Jessica into his arms, as inscrutable as it got.

Chapter 26

They traveled straight through, stopping only to change horses and return the unhappy abigail to Bristol. For most of the journey Duran slept, his head on Jessica's lap, and pretended he was asleep whenever he wasn't. He didn't feel up to a private inquisition by his wife, and by this time he was so deep in lies that he was having difficulty keeping his own stories sorted out.

She seemed equally reluctant to begin a conversation, as if worried what she might hear. So he kept his silence as she kept hers, and listened for the sound of her breathing over the rattle of the coach, and was soothed by the play of her hands in his hair.

Too soon for him, the carriage pulled up at High Tor, where Jessica stole him into the house, installed him in her bedchamber, and left him to bathe.

He had just finished dressing, with Shivaji's deft assistance, when she returned, brimming over with news. "Gerald left this morning. John Pageter told him a lie, can you imagine it? He said that Mariah had received a letter instructing her to return to Dorset, and that when the shooting party ended, she immediately left for home. So Gerald has gone after her, but when that fails, there's no telling what he'll do."

"We'd better hope he comes back here. I've had enough of tracking down stray animals."

"I have already dispatched a message to Helena. If he shows up in London, he'll be redirected here. Meantime, because one cannot rely on Gerald to hold to a plan, Mariah is keeping at Mrs. Bellwood's cottage. And in case you were wondering, Aubrey returned to his own home as soon as his jaw returned to a normal size and color."

"Now *there's* a blessing," he said with sincerity. "And the earl?"

"Well . . ." She appeared to be looking for the right words. "He thinks I am mad, but is pleased that I am finally married. He regrets my choice of bridegrooms, but reckons that a female in trade could probably do no better. He wrote the news to Aubrey and received a reply that is unsuitable for me to read. And he wishes to see you."

"I expected that he would."

"You are to join him in the study. I shall wait here with wine and bandages."

All things considered, the meeting with his father-in-law did not go badly. After a stiff greeting, a brief scolding, and a sorrowful lament about being denied the privilege of seeing his daughter wed, Sothingdon poured out two glasses of brandy and turned the conversation to guns and shooting.

By the time Duran, pleasantly foxed, made his way upstairs again, Jessica was stretched out atop the counterpane, still dressed and sound asleep. He peeled off his clothes and joined her there, his fingers busy at her bodice.

Two days, perhaps three, before his quarry returned to High Tor. Six days before Shivaji's quite literal deadline. "Gather ye rosebuds," he murmured, his lips trailing down a smooth white throat and over a creamy breast to the sunrise pink of her nipple, already puckering as she awakened to his touch. His lips closed over the tip and his hand began its slow voyage up her thighs, already falling open to welcome him, to the soft curls and slick dampness that marked his goal.

With time's winged chariot at his back, he rode her harder and faster than death could chase him, all his world concentrated between her legs and in the twining dance of their tongues. He let her feel him everywhere he could reach.

"More," she said when he was finished.

"Soon," he said when he could catch his breath.

Very soon he gave her more. And after a longer time, even more.

That evening, leaving Jessica to finish her interrupted nap, Duran joined the leftover shooting-party guests, the ones who would stay as long as they could because they had nowhere else so pleasant to be. Most had toddled off to bed before Duran and Pageter settled at a small corner table in the drawing room for a game of piquet.

"I have secured passage for you on three ships," Pageter said, shuffling the cards and setting the pack on the table. "The first departs on Thursday from Bristol to Newfoundland, the second on Friday from Plymouth to Jamaica, and the third, leaving Saturday, is a coaster from Dartmouth to Southampton, where you will transfer to a ship bound for Caracas."

"You have been remarkably efficient," said Duran, cutting the deck.

"Not at all. Helena Pryce took care of everything but the payment, which was covered by your winnings. There is plenty left over for expenses and a good start wherever you choose to go."

Duran watched Pageter deal. The blunt fingers were uncommonly agile, and to his surprise, three ship-boarding vouchers appeared among the cards dealt to him. He gathered up his hand and sorted it, squirreling the vouchers under the table. "An admirable fabrication, although I doubt there was a sou left over. I probably owe you for the tickets as well."

"But you cannot prove it," said Pageter with a smile. "You haven't been keeping track. And besides, you'll be cashing them in now that you mean to stay in England. The ring arrived, by the way. I did not expect you to return it."

"Another of my unfortunate impulses. I don't suppose I could have it back?" Duran played a card. "Thursday is too soon, I think. Talbot is unlikely to return before tomorrow or the day after, and when I've done with him, there's the small matter of getting to the ship. On the other hand, Saturday is a trifle too late, at least for my comfort. Shivaji is always on guard, but the closer we come to Sunday's deadline, the more cautious he will be."

"You still mean to go? But Lady Jessica told me he'd got his leopard back."

"Nevertheless," said Duran.

"I see." After a long hesitation, Pageter made his play. "I am sorry to hear it. Keep all the tickets then. But I will continue to hope they will not be needed. Circumstances may change."

"They generally do, just when you wish they wouldn't I want you to make preparations as well, John."

At the use of his Christian name, a sand-colored eyebrow lifted. "To do what?"

"To transport your lady love to the port of your choice and from there, far as you can from Talbot's reach. We haven't the luxury, either of us, to put off hard decisions. Talbot will come first for me, and if he doesn't get here in time, I shall do my best to go after him. But Shivaji may prevent me. And in that case, Jessica will be the next target. I am making provision for her."

"And the third target will be his wife."

"Without question. He'll not rest until someone pays for his inadequacies. What I'm telling you, John, is that you are Mariah's last, best hope. It's obvious you are mad for her, since before you went out to Africa, I expect. But as she was already married, you gave up hope of ever having her."

"I have attempted to conceal my feelings," Pageter said stiffly. "I thought I had succeeded. She has no idea of this, I am sure."

"Probably not. But as an unwitting expert on doomed love, I could not mistake the symptoms when I saw them in you. The thing is, you *can* have Mariah. If fortune allows, I shall serve her up to you on a platter. Never mind that it is properly your task to dispose of Talbot. I know you will not."

Pageter's face was as red as the ten of diamonds he'd just played. "To kill a man in order to possess his wife would be dishonorable."

"That's the trouble, isn't it? You confuse protecting her, which you ought to do at whatever cost, with *having* her, which raises all those bothersome ethical dilemmas about honor and decency and guilt. Lucky for you, I have nothing to lose that is not already lost. But if I fail to dispose of Talbot, you'd bloody well better be ready to let go your stiff-lipped British sensibilities, gather up your lady, and take a runner."

"Even if I did as you say, Lady Mariah would never countenance it. And I could not in conscience go against her wishes. Her regard for high principles is among the reasons I have always admired her. We share a common fealty to honor and duty."

"Honor is well and good in its place, I suppose, but it makes a damn cold bedfellow. And duty, I have learned, is a matter of interpretation. Shivaji's duty is to kill me. Mine is to kill Talbot. As a solider, you have no doubt killed in the line of duty. The men you killed thought it their duty to kill you. Where is the moral imperative? In the commandment, *Thou shalt not kill?* Is it permitted to kill in order to save your life, or someone else's life?"

Pageter, looking troubled, gathered up his cards. "We do as we are taught, I expect."

"Generally speaking. Then comes along a circumstance that our lessons failed to cover, and we are required to make an independent decision. Often a quick decision, and always a hard one." Duran sorted his hand. "I know you would give your life to protect your lady. Can you not relinquish your honor to keep her safe?"

"As you are doing?"

"It's simple for me. I have no honor to surrender. I shall dispose of Talbot because I like to stay busy."

In silence they played out the hand, Pageter inscribing a false score because neither of them had been paying attention. "What should I do, then?"

"Decide where you wish to go and let me know your decision. Make arrangements with your banker. Take Mariah to the ship and wait there. If I arrive before you sail, it will mean I've eluded Shivaji and Talbot is no longer a threat. Then I'll be off to stir up trouble in a new country while you get leg-shackled in England. But I should advise you the odds on that scenario playing out are not good."

"I will ask her," Pageter said, transparently averse to doing so.

"That's not good enough. *Convince* her. There isn't time for moral hemming and hawing." Duran shuffled with practiced fingers and dealt the next hand. "I need another favor, if you will. Have an apothecary prepare a sleeping powder or draught, something that will be undetectable in wine, and make sure it's effective but harmless. I'll need instructions for its use. And no one is to know of this."

"You wish me to procure narcotics?" Pageter produced a grim chuckle. "Good God. Before I have the opportunity to sacrifice my honor for Lady Mariah, you will have filched it all away."

Leaving Pageter to wrestle with his exacting conscience, Duran devoted his next days and nights to pleasure. To Jessica's pleasure as well as his own, to be sure, but in bed, they became one and the same thing. He held nothing back from her, nor she from him . . . except the truth.

He had never mistaken her for a fool. He believed, but could not be certain, that she still thought Shivaji no longer meant to harm him. But she had become increasingly chary of revealing her thoughts. She never spoke of his declared intention to leave her when the terms of their arrangement were fulfilled, nor did he. It sat in the corner, their awareness of his going, like a corpse at the marriage feast.

With so little time remaining, he refused to squander a moment of it in sleep. While Jessica dozed late into the morning, he joined the earl's guests, all of them thirty years older than he would ever be, in the breakfast room for sirloin, eggs, and strong coffee. He went fishing with his father-in-law, found a book in the library that he liked and wanted to finish, thought up ways to make Jessica laugh.

He tried not to think of all the time he'd wasted,

the friends he'd lost touch with, the love that had curled around a heart that would soon cease to beat.

Most difficult of all, he resisted Jessica's silent efforts to hold him inside her at the climax of their lovemaking. To deny her grieved him; but if he gave her a child she might not marry again, as she ought to do, and secure her mother's legacy.

Now and again he considered the problem of escaping High Tor. Arjuna, dispatched to inform the Others their search was over, had returned, and whenever Duran stepped outside the house, he felt again the sensation of being watched. His hope of escaping, he was forced to acknowledge, was little more than a mirage.

But the hidden passage at Holcombe's Folly had given him an idea, and some of the information he'd elicited from his father-in-law looked promising. Although the manor house at High Tor dated to the early sixteenth century, much of it had been torn down and rebuilt over the years, and other parts added on. There was no telling what might lie within its moorstone walls.

Family history was encouraging as well. The Carvilles had remained staunchly Catholic long after it became dangerous, and High Tor had been a small center of rebellion until the eleventh Earl of Sothingdon elected to play safe. This was a family that might have found it necessary to conceal a priest or make a quick and secretive departure.

At an opportune moment, Duran confessed an interest in historic houses with hidden passageways and asked the earl if any were to be found at High Tor.

Sothingdon, engaged in pulling in the plump salmon he'd just snagged from the Dart, gave the question little thought. "None I know of," he said. "Never been interested in such things."

Disappointed, Duran held out the netted pole and complimented him on the fish. A secret exit would have been too easy. And for as long as he could remember, nothing had come easily.

"Mind you," said the earl, "Jessica used to slip the net. For some offense or another, Lady Sothingdon would order her confined to the house, but she'd invariably go missing. We never knew how. Allies among the servants, I always figured. They liked her. Probably took her down the back stairs and out through the kitchen."

Probably. But Duran was reminded of the night he'd spent in her room when she suffered the headache, of the lone candle on the mantelpiece, of his curiosity when it flickered in the hot, motionless air.

On Wednesday morning, while Jessica and Pageter paid a call on Mariah, he had an opportunity to investigate. To throw Shivaji off the scent, he went to breakfast as usual, yawned over his plate, pleaded exhaustion, and returned to the bedchamber for a lie down. The servants were to inform him if Sir Gerald arrived, but otherwise, he did not wish to be disturbed.

Alone in the unlocked bedchamber, left that way to avoid suspicion, he began by methodically sealing the windows, closing the curtains, and stuffing a blanket up the chimney. Then he lit several candles, lined them up along the mantelpiece, and watched the flames.

Nothing. He moved them to other positions, and others. Each flame remained as unbending as a Calvinist spinster. The candles went to the flagstone hearth then, with equally disheartening results.

He pulled up a chair and sat, rubbing his chin and considering what he knew. He hadn't imagined the flickering candle that night, but it might have been caused by a trick of the air coming through the chimney. Rising, he withdrew the now-sooty blanket, rolled it up, and for lack of anything better to do with it, kicked it under the bed. The candles he realigned along the mantelpiece. Then, stepping back, he studied the flames.

There! The one to his left, near the edge of the mantelpiece, swayed like a belly dancer. But what of it? If the flame was stirred by air from the chimney, he'd learned nothing of use. He could scarcely get out that way.

Back to the chair for more contemplation. Jessica's childhood escapes belonged in the mix, but confiding in her was out of the question. He had sworn that she would have no part in his escape, and for her safety, she had to be kept clear of it.

Odd that only the one candle was affected. Rising, he moved it an inch to the right, another inch, and a little more. The flame steadied. Might there be a crosscurrent? After returning the candle to its original position, where the dance resumed, he retrieved another blanket from the chest, unfolded it, and stretching his arms as wide as they would go, held the blanket against the wall. His motion sent the candle into a frenzy, but when he held still, the candle flame did so as well.

That was it, then. Somewhere behind the blanket, there was another source of air. Elated, he tossed the covering aside and examined the wall. Pale green damask met the paneled cherry-wood wainscoting, ornately carved, at about the level of his waist. There was an opening concealed by the wood carving, he was sure of it. And amid the whorls of flowers, birds, faeries, and fanciful animals, there must be a trigger to release the latch.

But an hour later, after poking and prodding every inch of eligible territory, he was still confronted with a closed wall.

From sheer frustration he gave thought to kicking it in. Then, starting this time from the bottom, he knelt and worked his way from left to right, feeling for a bit of wood that yielded to pressure. Some time later, only three inches from the floor, a thumb-sized unicorn shifted when he touched its rump. Barely shifted, though, and nothing else happened. He played with it every which way, but the slight motion had no effect on anything but his patience.

Sitting back on his heels, he put himself in the place of the craftsman who had fashioned the panels and the means of opening them. It would have been serious business, with lives at the hazard should enemies figure how to break through. He'd have devised something clever and obscure to fool a pursuer, but easy to locate by a harried fugitive who knew the secret.

Perhaps not one trigger, but two or three, pressed in sequence or simultaneously? It made sense, and besides, he was running out of time and options. Several other unicorns pranced around the wainscoting, so he tried them all in various combinations, but without success. There was nothing for it but to push his original unicorn at the same time as every other figure on— No, wait.

What does the unicorn seek, and what is it seeks the unicorn?

A virgin.

That ruled out the flowers and probably the birds as well, leaving the faeries. Who might or might not be virgins, to be sure, but he was going to give them all the benefit of the doubt.

He didn't have to. The third faerie, when mated with the unicorn by dint of his fingers pressing them both at once, turned the trick. He heard a scraping sound, a click, and then a groan of unoiled hinges as a small section of wood swung inward.

Hallelujah.

The opening, perhaps eighteen inches high, was about the width of his shoulders and lay precisely against the floor. He'd have to wriggle like a snake to pass through.

His first instinct, to go exploring straightaway, ran up against a soldier's common sense. He began by stretching out on his belly and thrusting a candle through the opening, illuminating a crawlway thick with cobwebs and dust. He could not tell what lay beyond the reach of the light.

Well, he couldn't go in there wearing clothes. Shivaji, who tended to his small wardrobe, would draw bothersome conclusions from dirty or missing items. Peeling down to his drawers, he decided to play it absolutely safe and removed those as well, leaving him clad only in the golden bracelet.

He looked down at his naked body. Already scratched, scabbed, and bruised from his cross-country adventure, it could take on a few more abrasions without attracting notice. But not too many. He required a bit of covering, and Shivaji did not tend to Jessica's wardrobe. Rifling through her clothing chest, he located a cotton petticoat, tore it into long strips, and wrapped them around his knees, elbows, and palms. The last segment was used to pad the deadly bracelet.

All fine as far as it went, but he was going to be moving low to the ground. Certain vulnerable bits of his anatomy remained unprotected and would be, well, *dangling*. Back to Jessica's stock of underclothing.

Shortly after, wearing his bandage-guards, the bracelet, and a pair of knee-length female muslin drawers edged with lace, he slid two lit candles in brass holders through the opening and slithered in after them.

The narrow crawlway extended only a few feet before connecting with a stone staircase, equally narrow but with more headroom. Not enough of it, though. Even doubled over, he could not descend the stairs on his feet. After maneuvering to a sitting position on the top step, he went down on his haunches, holding out the candles like a figure of Shiva carrying tokens of Agni, the fire spirit.

Next came a landing, followed by another flight of stairs. The wall to his left felt warm, and soon he heard the muffled sounds of voices and the clanking of metal. He must be passing alongside the kitchen. Then a second landing, a third staircase.

At what he guessed to be cellar level, the stairs ended in what might have been, a century or two earlier, a small storage room. The remnants of worm-eaten shelves were attached to the cinder block walls, and he saw on the floor the remains of hemp sacking, insects, and mouse droppings.

All this way for nothing. Discouragement lodged in his throat like a rock.

But he'd come too far to give up yet. There was a door-shaped outline to his left, probably leading to the cellar proper, but it had been bricked over. Lifting the candle, he examined the mortar. It appeared crumbly and far older than Jessica. If she had used the tunnel to escape the house, she'd have found another way out of this room.

He studied the floor. The layers of detritus. The slightly clearer area near the far corner to his right. He'd learned one lesson from the entrance in Jessica's room—when in doubt, look low. Sure enough, a push at a cinder stone smaller than the others dislodged it straightaway, and its companions on either side could be pulled out and set aside with ease.

The next stage of the journey was through a tunnel

so small he could navigate it only on elbows and knees. When it became too difficult to proceed with a candleholder in each hand, he left one behind him.

The passage curved. Curved again. And then his arms and head came into a tunnel that was nearly as tall as he was. Scrabbling through the opening, he stood and stretched his cramped muscles.

The air was fresher here. There must be an opening to the outside not too far away. He let out a vigorous sigh of relief and, to his horror, saw the candle flame go out.

Careless! But not disastrous. Not yet. A warning, though. He'd found his way to the exit, or near to, but next would come Talbot. And always, always, Shivaji. In future there would be no margin for error, no recovery from a mistake.

In inky darkness, he felt his way along the tunnel. Originally dug out by tin miners, he reckoned, and linked to the house by an especially enterprising Carville. Trailing his fingers along the way to orient himself, he guessed he must have come a quarter of a mile or more from where he'd begun.

Just when he was congratulating himself, he ran smack into a pile of rocks.

But the news wasn't all bad. From overhead came a few slivers of light, pronging down like dagger blades, and with imagination filling in the black spots he could trace the outline of a trap door that must be partly covered with debris.

He was nearly afraid to give it a try. Should a boulder have been pushed atop the exit, not unlikely if someone had discovered the trap door and decided to seal it off, he would have to try and find where it was from the outside. And that he could not do without Shivaji or one of his minions taking note. Either the trap door opened now, or it was useless to him. Heart pounding, he raised a hand and pushed.

Resistance. Another push.

The trap door went up an inch. Two inches. Three. Hosanna!

He let it drop again. When the time came, it would readily open and he could hoist himself up and out. That was all he needed to know.

Amazed at his good fortune, he made his way swiftly back the way he'd come. Now he had a sterling chance of escaping, a God-given, Jessica-inspired exit from the house that Shivaji didn't know about.

The notion of departing early, perhaps even that night, slid into his mind. And slid quickly out again. Old territory. He had already fought this battle with himself. When he might have ducked off with the leopard, he had instead put himself back in the assassin's grasp. And the reasons for it had not altered. They would hold him here until he'd accomplished what he meant to do.

In the bedchamber he stripped off the wrappings from his knees and elbows, removed the lacy drawers, and stashed the lot in the crawlway. Remembering the blanket under the bed, he tossed that in as well. He used the pitcher of water in the dressing room and the water from a pair of flower vases to wash himself down. The dirty towel joined the pile of linens behind the wainscoting, along with two fresh candles. Later, he'd filch a tinderbox.

With the panel closed and the room in order, he speedily dressed, settled on a wingback chair with his ankles crossed on an ottoman, and was immersed in *Pride and Prejudice* when Shivaji came to tell him that Sir Gerald had arrived.

His heart jolted up to double time. It would be tonight after all. Just as well. No one would be expecting him to act so soon.

"Colonel Pageter and Lady Jessica must be notified before they return to the house," he told Shivaji on his way to the writing table. "Will you see a message delivered?"

"I will send Arjuna."

Marveling at the unquestioning agreement, Duran scribbled two notes. The first required Pageter to keep watch over Mariah at the cottage while Mrs. Bellwood, if she would be so kind, removed to High Tor. In the next few days, the earl would need her steadying presence. Jessica was directed, on her return, to enter the house without being seen and take herself to the one room no one would think to search.

"And what will you do, Duran-sahib?"

"I am going out. Come watch me. Then, if you are asked, you can truthfully reply that you saw me leave and had no idea where I was going."

"Where are you going?"

"Dear me. If I tell you, you'll have to lie. Or betray my location, which would be inconvenient. Besides, it's not as if I can go anywhere unobserved by your watch dogs." He raised an eyebrow. "Or can I?"

"No."

"Well, then, what are you worried about? I'm only trying to disengage you from any illegalities I may be required to undertake. If you could bring yourself to tell a corker, these precautions would be unnecessary."

"When Sir Gerald inquired for Lady Mariah," said Shivaji, ignoring Duran as if he hadn't spoken, "he was disturbed to be told she was not in residence. There were threats, I believe. He departed soon after."

In some regards, Duran was compelled to admit, Shivaji was a better game player than he. "I'm almost afraid to ask. Where was he going?"

"To locate a constable. He believes the family to be guilty of withholding a wife from her husband. This is illegal in England?"

"How would I know? I grew up in India, where law

is a matter of whim. Take, for instance, a certain nizam—but I digress." Sealing the notes, he passed them to his nemesis. "Is there anything else I ought to know?"

"When Sir Gerald demanded to see you, Lord Sothingdon said you were not to be disturbed. He also said that if Sir Gerald was unable to behave with civility, he should take himself . . . elsewhere."

"Will wonders never cease? Papa-in-law has located his backbone." Duran glanced at the letters in Shivaji's slender hand. "Well, be off with you."

The brown eyes fixed on him. "I suspect you intend to fight Sir Gerald, but it will not be permitted. I cannot allow you a weapon."

"Would you accept a battle of wits, then? Insults at dawn? Sarcasm at twenty paces?"

"You can do nothing, Duran. He is for his family to deal with."

"But I *am* his family. And until Sunday, my life is my own."

"I was mistaken to grant the time," said Shivaji, regarding him thoughtfully. "I have had a dream. The pathway to death is under the ground and in the country of stones. You will be lost in white darkness. Thunder will bring you down."

"Ah. A poetic demise. Entirely wasted on a plebeian like me, I'm afraid, but at least you will be denied the pleasure of doing me in." Duran chuckled. "All assuming, of course, that dreams really do come true."

Chapter 27

"I won't have it, Duran. When you deal with Gerald, it is my right as much as yours to be there."

"Point taken." He watched her stride back and forth in front of him, eyes flashing, skirts swishing, hair springing loose from its pins. Jessica in a temper drove through the room like a Ship of the Line under full sail. "But it will go better if I handle him alone. Might you, this once, do as you are bid, if only for the novelty of it?"

"I am here, am I not? As I was *bid*. That is sufficient novelty for one day."

They were in Lady Sothingdon's bedchamber, the late-afternoon sun spiking through the windows, Jessica keeping her distance from the portrait and the painted woman that appeared to scrutinize the both of them simultaneously.

For all the energy with which Jessica defied him, shadowed eyes marked her weariness after the long journey to and from Mrs. Bellwood's cottage. He had resolved to make her even wearier before the afternoon was over.

"Why are we skulking here?" she demanded. "Do not tell me you are afraid of him? He can do us no harm under my father's roof."

"But if he returns with a constable, you will be

questioned about your sister's location, and the false-hood you will undoubtedly tell might later come back to haunt you. It's as well to avoid vexation whenever possible, don't you think?"

"How could I, when you insist on doing all my thinking for me? What is more, I take exception to the reasonable-male-condescending-to-irrational-female tone in your voice."

"My apologies," he said equably. "I shall make every attempt to sound less reasonable. So long as you understand that I am *being* reasonable. We elected to deal with Gerald using less than legal methods, and the—"

"See!" She jabbed a finger in his direction. "You said it. *We* elected. I concede your point about staying clear of the authorities, but I am as much a part of this scheme as you. I helped plan it, arrange it, and carry it out, and I intend to be present at the conclusion."

"What you really want, princess, is to gloat."

"Precisely."

"But you are losing sight of the objective. We wish him to go away and stay away, quietly and without making more trouble for anyone. Yes?"

"Of course. But why can I not watch him squirm?"

"Because—" He swiped his fingers through his hair. "Jessie, this is one of those things that has to be dealt with man-to-man."

She whirled on him, fur all puffed out and claws unsheathed. "Toad-to-snake, you mean."

He guessed she had cast him in the role of snake. But maybe not. "Try to put yourself in Talbot's place. You have taken his measure. He is an arrogant man with aspirations beyond his capacities who frequently meets with disappointment. He also has an entirely misguided contempt for females."

"In that," she said acidly, "he is not alone."

"I'm sure your experience in business has led you to believe so. But Talbot is not merely unenlightened. He loathes you. And because you are stronger, more intelligent, and far more accomplished than he will ever be, he fears you as well. You demonstrate that he cannot claim even the superiority he feels entitled to for having been born a male."

"Born? He was spawned. In a pond."

Ah, good. Talbot had been appointed toad. And what had he come to, Duran wondered, to be pleased at his own elevation to snake? "Then consider how he will react when I point out to him, in quelling detail, his exact circumstances. It is bad enough you were the architect of his downfall. He will not stand for you to witness his humiliation."

She dropped onto a chair. "How does that signify? His sensibilities are of no concern to me."

"Nor to me. But a man trapped in a corner can either yield or fight back. Add a woman to the mix and the man will nearly always choose to fight. If the woman is you, even a toad will fight to the death."

"I see. How provoking. But is he truly cornered?"

"Near enough. My fear is that given a short list of bad choices, he may select one that will do damage to your family. Your presence would all but certainly goad him to retribution."

"He's not overly fond of you, either."

"No. But since I am of his kind, a wastrel and a gamester, I do not threaten his *amour propre*. Let this be, Jessica. I'll tell you all about it afterward."

"The censored version, I have no doubt." Her eyes narrowed. "What are you going to say to him that you don't want me to hear?"

That was too near the mark. He contrived a look of surprise, as if the thought of deceiving her was the

furthest thing from his mind. "Why, nothing I can recall at the moment. You know the arrangements we've
made and what we hope will come of them. I simply
intend to point out that his situation is irreparable, his
options few, and that a quiet departure is in his best
interest. Have you anything to add?"

"A great deal. But never mind. I accept that you
will do as you like, and that I ought to be grateful for
your assistance." A brief smile took the sting from her
words. "I truly am, you know. It is unfair that by
wedding me, you have become enmeshed in the Carville family squabbles."

"My pleasure," he said, smiling back. "Especially
when it means drawing Aubrey's cork."

That earned the laugh he was aiming for, but the
worry in her eyes returned all too quickly. "What if
it doesn't work, Duran? What if he refuses to leave
the country? There is little we can do, really, to compel him. And if he does go, what's to stop him from
taking Mariah along?"

"Colonel Pageter. That's who I'm counting on, at
any rate. But we'll have to see if he can ungird his
honorable loins long enough to do what is required."

"John?" she said in a strangled voice. "I *knew* there
was something you weren't telling me. What has he
to do with this?"

"You noticed nothing today at the cottage?"

Her brow furrowed. "Only that Mariah is looking
well. Mrs. Bellwood insists that she eat regularly, and
she has been helping in the garden. But she remains
terrified that Gerald will find her."

"I meant, princess, between your sister and
Pageter."

"*Between* them? Well, nothing, of course. They
scarcely spoke. Mariah pottered around setting the
table, chopping vegetables, brewing tea, while John

sat still as a washboard and stared at the wall. It was kind of him to escort me there. I thought at the time he was finding it an uncomfortable experience, but gentlemen often feel that way when surrounded by females."

"I don't." He stretched out his legs and crossed them at the ankles. "But I can quite imagine the scene. What you witnessed, my dear, was a case of mutually unrequited love."

Her mouth opened, closed, and dropped open again. "Oh, no." She shook her head. "Mariah has been married since long before they met, and John would never dangle after a married woman."

"Quite right. And he hasn't. But that does not preclude falling in love, which he has. Mariah as well, I expect, although she has not confirmed it to me."

"John *told* you he . . . Oh, my. That would explain why he kept coming around after I made it clear we would not suit."

"I expect so. Courting you gave him an excuse to spend a little time in her company, until it became too difficult for them both. So he requested a posting to a faraway place. But instead of being a good lad and taking his lady with him, he left her to Gerald's fists."

"He couldn't have known. None of us did, back then."

Duran relented, to a degree. "If you say so. But he knows now. I think we can rely on him to keep Mariah safe, although it may require them to go into hiding for a time."

"Together? My heavens. I find that difficult to imagine."

"Oh, they'll probably take up residence in separate pastures and gaze at each other over the fence of their rectitude like a pair of lovelorn sheep. I much prefer your direct approach, Jessie. Come to think of it, you never asked if I was married before hauling me to your bed."

"Who else would have you?" she retorted, color flooding her cheeks. "Besides, I asked Lady Fielding. We were at her ball, remember?"

"I remember only you, princess. Only you."

Her gaze caught his and held it for a long moment before her lashes fluttered down. He thought, then, that she would ask why he still intended to leave her, and had long since prepared a glib response for just this occasion.

But when she spoke again, it was to turn the subject. "When will you meet with him?"

"That depends, of course, on when he returns. Your father has agreed to invite him to stay the night, and I am hoping to snag him after supper. Which means," he added, glancing at the mantelpiece clock, and from there to the canopied bed, "that we have several hours to ourselves. Any suggestions how to fill them?"

Her gaze followed his and speedily returned to his face. "Not in here, Duran. Not on that bed. Not with my mother watching."

"Well," he said, uncoiling from the chair, "we have to remain here, at least until the constable has come and gone. But I'm fairly sure I can make you forget where you are. And we don't require the bed. There is plenty of furniture, or the carpet. Although . . . now that I think on it, I don't believe I have ever taken you against a wall. Shall we begin with that?"

Her eyes, round as a kitten's, fixed on him. She looked down to where his erection had begun to strain against his trousers. She shivered.

"As for Mama," he said, "voyeur that she is, I shall direct her attention where it belongs." With some effort, he wrestled the portrait from its hangings and dragged it to the farthest end of the room, where he stood it—Lady Sothingdon's face to the wall—in the corner. "And now, princess, where would *you* like to be?"

She had risen, arms clutched around her waist, and was examining a stretch of bare wall near the fireplace. "It doesn't look very comfortable."

He approached her with deliberate intent, unbuttoning his trousers with one hand and his waistcoat with the other. "It's not supposed to be comfortable. It's supposed to be rock hard, like this"—he freed himself—"and urgent, also like this. It's supposed to be me plundering you, with this. Are you ready?"

She was breathing heavily. She nodded.

"Then what are we waiting for?" He was directly in front of her now, his cock several inches closer than the rest of him, nearly touching her skirts. He placed his hands on her shoulders and began backing her up until she was pressed to the wall. Then he lifted her skirts, slipped his fingers through the slit in her drawers to make sure she was ready to receive him, and moved his hands to her waist.

"When I am inside you, wrap your legs around me and hang on. This is going to be a wild ride."

"Hurry," she begged.

"Always so impatient. Very well, then. Here we go."

He raised her up, put one arm behind her back to secure her, and with his other, inserted himself just a little inside her. She moaned, gripped his shoulders, tried to wriggle down on him.

"You'll get your turn later," he advised, holding her still. "As many turns as we can survive. But this time is for me."

With that, he brought her down until there was no part of his cock that wasn't engulfed in tight, slick, glorious female flesh.

Her legs came up to enclose his hips. He let her back go against the wall, held her by the waist, and moved her up and down on him, up and down, feeling her squeezing him as she built to her first climax. He helped her, moving her faster and faster, making sure he pressed against her swelling nub. Then she began to come, and he cut off her cry of pleasure with a kiss.

Until she ceased rippling around him, he held her close, letting her enjoy every pulsing moment. Her head slid to his shoulder and rested there.

"Oh," she murmured. "That was lovely. But you said it was to be for you."

"Did you imagine I was finished?" He adjusted his position, bending his knees slightly and placing his hands firmly on her hips. "A different motion this time, I think. I will go up and down, while you go around and around. Will you like that?"

"I always like what you do to me. . . . Yesssss. Oh, oh, oh. Yes. I do like that."

He had started, and it was a longer time than he'd expected before his own urgency brought an end to the ride.

When he released her, she nearly fell asleep right there, slumped against the wall. Holding her upright with one arm, he found his own careful completion. Then he carried her to a chair and settled there until her body caught up with the passionate spirit that inhabited it.

He tried to empty his mind, but the voice in his head would not be stilled. This was the last day he would spend with Jessie. These were the last times he would make love with her. Perhaps tonight as well, but he couldn't be sure. And then she would sleep, and he would leave, and they would never meet again.

Chapter 28

At supper that evening, Duran felt Sir Gerald Talbot's glare against his skin like a flatiron. They were seated some distance from each other and on opposite sides of the table, Duran placed with honor at Lord Sothingdon's left and Talbot isolated between the half-deaf Mr. Fenwick and an empty chair.

No one spoke to Talbot during the meal. He had, from all accounts, made a considerable fuss that afternoon, returning as promised with a constable and demanding that all the house guests and servants submit themselves for questioning. When the earl refused to cooperate, Talbot towed his befuddled constable from room to room, shooting off questions like Congreve rockets. *Where is Lady Mariah? When did you see her last? Whom was she with?* And eventually, *Where are Lady Jessica and her scurrilous dog of a husband?*

The scurrilous dog, reluctantly taking leave of his dozing wife, had arrived late to supper. He wasn't the least bit hungry. From this point on, things would proceed rapidly, and even as he made polite conversation with his neighbors, he was running through a mental checklist of the arrangements he had made.

Jessica was to remain in Lady Sothingdon's chamber until Talbot had retired, after which she would be escorted to her own room. Duran had ordered a meal to be prepared for her and delivered when he rang for it. With care, he would slip into her food and drink the powder obtained for him by Pageter, who reported that it was undetectable, worked imperceptibly at first, and then sent the subject into a deep sleep that lasted for several hours. Being the sort of chap he was, Pageter had tested it on himself before delivering the powder to Duran.

The tinderbox liberated from a rarely used parlor was stashed in the crawlway, along with a small wallet containing several hundred pounds in banknotes, again courtesy of Pageter. There were two ship vouchers in his pocket, for Bristol and Dartmouth. Pageter had come around. If it became necessary to flee the country with Mariah, he would try for Plymouth and had kept that voucher for himself. When Talbot was no longer a threat, Duran would bring the news and take their place aboard the ship.

He did not think it a likely outcome. Nothing short of a bullet in the head would free the Carvilles of Talbot, and he was starting to doubt his ability to fire the shot.

He had killed in battle, of course. He'd cut down dacoits who attacked him on the road. He had even fought a pair of duels, although neither ended fatally. Death was no stranger to anyone who had spent time in India.

But cold-blooded, premeditated murder? That was Shivaji's province, the proper business of an assassin with ice water for blood and a stone where his heart ought to be.

Which left Gerald Talbot, a blight on the earth who ought to be planted under it. Duran, no candidate for a heavenly reward in any case, hadn't the slightest moral qualm about killing him. He just didn't think he could come to scratch unless there was at least the semblance of a fair fight. It surprised him, that tattered remnant of long-abandoned chivalric idealism, but there it was.

Perhaps Talbot would be rash enough to call him out. That would solve everything.

When supper was finally done, Duran nodded in Talbot's direction and proceeded to the library, certain his unspoken message had been received. This confrontation was inevitable, and Talbot wanted it even more than he did.

Slopping over with wine and indignation, Talbot stumbled into the room and poked his brother-in-law on the chest with a forefinger. "About time," he said, his breath stinking of onions and claret. "Where's the slut?"

Duran clasped his hands behind his back to keep them from targeting Talbot's jaw. "Which slut would you be referring to?"

"M'wife. Or Jessica. Either one. Both."

It was going to be a difficult conversation. "What say we leave the ladies out of this? Because if you don't, I shall stuff an inkpot down your gullet."

"They don't much matter anyway, females," Talbot said, dropping onto a chair.

"No."

"But that is the last time we will agree. You think me drunk, and in part I am, but the details are stored in m'brain box. You will pay for what you did."

Duran had seen men feign drunkenness to throw others off their guard. Hell, he'd done it himself. He ought to be able to tell how far gone Talbot was now, but he couldn't be sure. Jessica had warned him Talbot was more clever and resilient than he appeared to be. Centered in the bloodshot whites of his eyes were two cold, pale blue pebbles, and what lay behind them at any given moment was impossible to know.

"What exactly was it I did?" Duran rested his hips against the desk and folded his arms. "I've scarcely been out of bed since my wedding night."

"You've heard nothing?" Talbot regarded him doubtfully. "Wallingford bought the leopard, discovered it to be worthless, and is bringing charges. I'm thinking he won't prosecute, though, if he gets his money back. It's up to you to repay him."

"Why would I do that? Never met the fellow. Nor am I acquainted with any leopards, worthless or otherwise. You must have me confused with some other chap."

"Cut line, Duran. It was your leopard, your scheme, and I sold the thing believing it was worth more than the price Wallingford paid. I was your dupe."

"Is that to be your story when you stand trial? I am all astonishment. Now I shall tell you *my* story. It is what you might expect. I mean to deny all knowledge of leopards, schemes, and arrangements with Sir Gerald Talbot, whose sole connection to me is that we both married into the Carville family. Oh, and that he owes me two thousand pounds. I can only think he is attempting to escape both the consequences of his crime and his debt of honor by casting blame on me."

By this time, Talbot's hands were clenching and unclenching. "That cock won't fight. I had to have been misled. No one would knowingly sell a counterfeit to a downy old bird like Wallingford."

"Except, perhaps, a desperate man. Or a fool. And you are widely known to be both. Furthermore, there is nothing to connect me to the leopard."

"Jessica will. She was there when you perpetrated your fraud. And she knows what will happen if I am displeased with her. She'll testify against you."

"She might," Duran said reflectively. "If she is permitted. These fuzzy points of law are so confusing. Can a wife testify against her husband? Indeed, I'm rather sure her legal status has been absorbed into mine, meaning that I would be speaking for her in court. Odd way to do things, but so convenient for me."

Talbot, perspiring, had pulled out his handkerchief. "Why should anyone believe you? I've heard rumors. You were a traitor and a gunrunner in India, and now you are a forger here. There's your reputation against you, and my word against yours."

"Not precisely." Duran rolled his shoulders and stretched his arms, signaling boredom. "Much as I'm enjoying this exchange of pleasantries, I think it may be time to put all my cards on the table. It turns out, my good fellow, that you purchased a quantity of gold and paste gemstones, which you then provided to a craftsman with instructions to sculpt a leopard from base metal and coat it with the gold and paste." Gasping sounds were coming from Talbot's throat. "That surprises you, I know. But those involved in the transactions will bear witness that Sir Gerald Talbot, and only Sir Gerald Talbot, caused the counterfeit icon to be made. Oh, and you still owe the sculptor half the agreed price. He's a trifle put out about that."

"But no such thing ever happened!"

"No? Well, it doesn't matter. That's what you get for doing business, or not doing business, with disreputable fellows who are perfectly willing to lie to the authorities. In fact, they delight in it. And then there's the matter of your gaming debts. Since I dislike exerting myself to collect what's owed me, I sold your signed notes to a man with the influence to squeeze you like a lemon. The Duke of Devonshire is fond of Jessica and does not like to see her distressed. You have distressed her. He will make you sorry for it."

Duran came up from the desk, dominating the room by the simple act of standing. "Here is what is going to happen, Talbot. Devonshire will see you driven from society. Wallingford will see you in prison or transported. And I have already seen to it you will never again lay eyes or hands or fists on your wife. Do you, at last, understand your position?"

Talbot half rose from his chair. "By God, I ought to call you out!"

"Oh, would you? I should like that above all things."

"I daresay." Talbot sank back again. "You'd choose pistols. And you're a crack shot. Do you ever play fair, Duran?"

"Would you know fair if it bit you on the arse? I do what I must. Which is why, against every instinct, I am going to do you a favor. This"—he tossed a square of paper onto Talbot's lap—"represents passage on a ship departing Bristol tomorrow midnight. I'm not altogether sure where Newfoundland is, which makes it the ideal place for you to hide from creditors and the law. No one will bother to chase after you. If you are capable of making a fresh start, this is your chance. I strongly advise you to take it."

With shaking fingers, Talbot picked up the voucher and studied it, as if something more than price paid, ship name, origin, destination, and other pertinent information were inscribed there. For a time, Duran fancied he meant to take the offer and found himself sorry for it.

The voucher fluttered to the carpet. "If you want me to do this, stands to reason it's a bad idea. I think you want rid of me for fear what I can do—*will* do— if I remain. You tricked me, and you will pay for it. Before I am done, everyone will have paid. The scandal will ruin you all. Your wife's business, Aubrey's pride, the earl's reputation, all of them in the sewer."

"How so? Most families boast a black sheep or two. The Carvilles won't be blamed for your crimes."

"We'll see. It's not as if I'm the only black sheep in the paddock." Talbot came up from the chair like a toad springing off a lily pad. "Consider your wife. Will spread her legs for any man, will Jessica. Gets half her clients that way. Insatiable, too, but I expect you know that. Near to wore me out every time, and then she'd want another go, and another. Likes to give orders, the bitch, but I know how to stop up her mouth."

Duran stopped Talbot's mouth with a backhand across the face. "That's quite enough. I don't believe a word of it, but damned if I'll let you sprew that poison beyond this room."

"You're calling me out?" Talbot looked as if he hadn't expected it. "Dueling is illegal. If you kill me, you'll have to leave the country."

"That's my problem. Yours is being dead."

"Don't be so sure of it. Your challenge, my choice of weapons. And I don't expect the son of a John Company writer had the education and training of a gentleman. It will be swords, and my fencing master was Antonio. But you won't have heard of him."

"No. Nor do I have a sword. You will have to provide me one. When and where?"

Talbot thought it over. "No point waiting. Devil's Tor at dawn tomorrow. Near the top is a ring of standing stones around a patch of flat ground."

"I know the place." It was a risk, but Duran thought it necessary to ask the question. "What about seconds? I'm not sure I can scratch one up before morning, and most of the gentlemen in residence could not climb so far."

"Shall we agree to dispense with seconds?" Talbot seemed both nervous and elated, an incendiary combination. "Let's keep this to ourselves. There are places below the escarpment to dispose of the evidence. The winner tosses the loser into a bog and walks away whistling."

He sounded like a man with an ace up his sleeve, or one who had no intention of keeping the appointment. Perhaps he thought his opponent would not. Duran wanted him there and ready to fight, but unable to read his intentions, he was uncertain how to play the final card. Goad him? Show fear? Disclose weakness?

Ah, well. It was all a gamble, wasn't it? And with Shivaji circling overhead like a great vulture, his choices were decidedly limited. "By God, you're a cold-hearted bastard," he said in an admiring tone. "Not so much as a corpse for m'wife to weep over? I wonder if she would. No question about your wife, though. She'll be dancing a jig."

"When my sword is stuck in your belly," said Talbot between his teeth, "you will tell me where she is. Then we'll see who dances."

It would have been a grand exit, Duran thought, watching him with wry amusement, if Talbot hadn't run into trouble with the door latch. When it finally came free, he flung open the door and stomped out without a backward look.

Duran remained in the library for several minutes, allowing sufficient time for Talbot to get out of the way before he went to fetch Jessica. In the quiet room, his heart thumped like a drum. The air he breathed hissed in his throat. His body, tuned to the rhythm of the ticking clock on the mantelpiece, counted down the last hours and minutes of his life.

He would probably survive the duel, if there was

one. Talbot had been right about the fencing master he'd never had, but he had been a cavalry officer. How much difference could there be, swordplay and fighting with a saber?

He had no objection to throwing Talbot into a bog. And he might even get all the way to the ship and be on his way to Jamaica without Shivaji and the Others catching him. It was a long shot, but he was getting used to betting against the odds.

What he lacked, what there could never be, was time enough to steel himself for what was to happen next.

With no reason to put it off any longer, he went to where his impatient wife was waiting, led her to the room where virgin and unicorn were poised for the touch of his fingers, and set himself to disarm her.

Not unexpectedly, she demanded to hear every word of his conversation with Talbot. He gave her what he could, embellishing some parts, omitting entirely those relating to the duel. Talk ceased when the servants arrived with Jessica's supper and resumed again the moment they had gone.

"You never told me you'd sold Gerald's gaming vouchers to Devonshire," she said irritably.

He helped her settle at the small round table by the window, elicited a smile when he draped a napkin over his arm, and went to the sideboard to pour her a glass of wine. "*Sold* is rather an overstatement. I gave them to him, more or less, during the legal arrangements for the marriage. You know, the ones where I so confused his solicitors that they inadvertently granted me full rights to everything you own, right down to your underdrawers."

"You will look splendid wearing them. But I dislike inconveniencing the duke. He has been a good friend

and does not merit being punished by having to deal
with my brother-in-law. You should have asked me
before taking such high-handed action."

He gave her, with a flourishing bow, the glass of
drug-laced wine. "My humble apologies. Of course
you must have your say. In future, I shall ask your
permission before so much as breaking wind."

"I'd rather you leave the room, thank you very
much." She was, greatly to his relief, trying not to
smile. "What will Gerald do, then?"

"Sleep late, I expect. He was fairly well gone before
he got to supper, and he emptied his glass several
times that I saw. When he sobers up and remembers
what I said, he'll go abroad. It's that or prison."

"And what if he forgets?"

"Then I'll remind him. And put him aboard a ship
with my own two hands if it comes to that." He stirred
a little of the sleeping powder into the lobster bisque,
carried the bowl to the table, and set it in front of her.

His hands were shaking. Quickly returning to the
sideboard, he planted them on the wood and pressed
down hard as he drew in a series of deep breaths.
This was even more difficult than he had imagined.
Could have imagined. Lie after lie. Betrayal upon
betrayal.

And yet, he was pleased when she spooned the soup
into her mouth, raised the glass to her lips. He re-
joiced when time came to refill it. Jessica smiling her
thanks, swallowing the wine, sliding into his trap.

What separated him from Gerald Talbot, he wondered, except the different ways they found to hurt
the women they were supposed to protect?

Jessica ate a little of the cold roasted chicken and
a bite or two of cheese before covering a yawn with
her hand. "I think the journey to Mrs. Bellwood's
must have done me in," she admitted with obvious

reluctance. "And I do want to be bright in the morning to see Gerald slinking away." Another yawn.

He assisted her to her feet, and when she asked, helped her undress. And when she was in bed, he thought that it was over. But she lifted her arms and smiled at him.

"Will you not make love to me? Perhaps not with so much energy as this afternoon, though. I feel a bit cotton headed. But I should like to go to sleep in your arms."

He hadn't anticipated this. He didn't think he could bear it.

But . . . one more chance to hold her. Bury himself inside her. Give her what little of himself remained to be given.

Leaving his clothes in a heap beside the bed, he slipped in beside her and began gently to caress her. Dreamy and languid, she unfolded under his hands like a waterflower, and when he slid into her moist center, her low sigh of pleasure whispered against his cheek. He loved her slowly then, and tenderly, fulfilling his wedding vow, the only one of them he was permitted to keep. *With my body, I thee worship.*

He was still inside her when she quieted. Lifting himself on his elbows, he looked down at her face, and was surprised when her eyes opened again. Gazing up at him, she raised a hand and brushed the damp hair from his forehead.

"I am so very glad you came back from India," she said, her voice husky with sleep. "And came back again, when you might have escaped with the leopard. I didn't expect it, and yet I did. It is so very strange." Her hand moved to his cheek and rested against it. "I have never trusted you, Duran. But somehow, I cannot say why, I have always believed in you."

At the declaration of faith he had never expected or

deserved, his eyes went on fire. She seemed to dissolve beneath him. He felt her hand leave his face, and when he was able to see again, her eyes had closed.

He remained there, enclosed in her body, for a long time, painting into his memory the wing of mahogany hair against her fine-grained skin, the curve of her chin, the heavy lashes fanned against her cheeks, the impertinent nose. Jessie. His wife. His beloved.

Sometime later, careful not to disturb her, he removed himself from her flesh and her bed, took up his clothes, and went to the dressing room to put them on. Leaving a single candle burning there and taking another with him, he closed the door, extinguished all lights in the room but the one he carried, and crouched in front of the carved wainscoting. At his touch the panel opened.

This was it, then. He should have ducked through and kept on going. That had been his intention. But he rose again, returned to the bed, and lifted the candle for one last, lingering moment. Golden light danced with the shadows on her face.

"I'm sorry, princess," he told her soundlessly. "But think of it this way. I will never again lie to you. And this is the last time, my word on it, that I will ever leave you."

Shortly after, he pulled the panel closed behind him and began his journey under the earth.

Chapter 29

Duran had left early for the rendezvous on Devil's Tor, intending to arrive at the stone circle well before sunrise, find a concealed spot with a good view of the footpath, and keep watch for his adversary.

Talbot might actually keep the appointment, although the odds were against it. In the sober light of morning, he'd more likely roll over and go back to sleep. Or perhaps he would come to his senses, decide to flee the country after all, and go looking in the library for the bill of passage he'd dropped.

Duran had left it there in the event Talbot changed his mind. Or it might be discovered by Shivaji, who would realize fairly early in the day that his sacrificial goat had slipped the noose. With any luck, he'd hare out to Bristol while the goat loped on down to Plymouth.

More than likely, though, a servant would find the damn thing. Making plans, Duran had learned, had a good deal in common with spitting into the wind.

The trip through the narrow crawlway was as unpleasant as it had been the first time. When he was finally able to stand, he took a few moments to stretch his aching limbs and look around. The air in the mine shaft felt thick and damp. Beads of moisture had condensed on the chiseled stone, glittering in the candlelight like yellow diamonds. It was like walking through a tunnel of stars.

Distracted, he forgot to watch where he was going and ran for the second time directly into the pile of fallen rocks that marked the end of the passageway. The candle fell, sputtered, and went out.

At this point, it didn't matter. He felt overhead for the trap door, found it, and pushed upward. As before, it lifted without difficulty, sending a scatter of dirt and pebbles and wet leaves over his face and shoulders. Rising to tiptoe for more leverage, he kept pushing until the heavy board toppled over. Then, gripping the frame with both hands, he pulled himself up and out.

The air felt thick as water. It was like that night off the coast of Madagascar . . . no moon, no stars, no visibility whatever.

The Dartmoor fog. He'd heard about it. Sothingdon had described being trapped for hours on the moorlands, unable see so far as his nose and afraid to move for fear of tumbling into a bog. His best hound had led him to safety.

And what was it Shivaji had said? Something about the pathway to death lying under the ground. Then . . . *You will be lost in white darkness.*

Just what the world needed. A prescient assassin.

After some fumbling he replaced the trap door, kicked leaves and dirt on top of it, and with arms elevated like a sleepwalker's, picked his way out of a shallow crater onto level ground. Shortly after, when his fingers brushed the rough bark of a tree, he decided this was as good a place to wait as any.

Settling down with his back against the tree trunk, he laced his fingers behind his neck and lifted his gaze in the direction of the obscured sky. Within the hour, the first light of dawn would creep up from the east, giving him a compass point to steer by. Assuming he was able to see it at all.

He spent what felt to him a great deal longer than an hour mapping in his mind what he knew of the estate. Always aware he might need to make a run for it, he'd paid close attention during the shooting expeditions to the landscape and its landmarks. He was fairly sure he could find his way to his destination.

Unless the Others stopped him. He'd planned to travel under protection of night. Now he hoped the fog would persist long enough to conceal him, at least until he arrived at Devil's Tor. He didn't have a good feeling about what was likely to happen after that.

He could go the opposite direction, of course. Board the coaster at Dartmouth, carry on to South America and more soldiering. There was always a battle going on somewhere, as Michael Keynes used to say. You need only get to it in time.

But none of those battles were meant for him. The only one that counted would take place a mile or so from where he was sitting. He had a promise to keep.

I have always believed in you.

The last words he would ever hear from Jessica's lips. Nothing in his life had ever meant so much. More than escape, above all things else, he wanted to give her a reason for that unreasoning faith. But the only service he could provide her was to save the family from Talbot, so whatever the consequences, he would try. Pray God the son of a bitch showed up with his swords, ready to fight.

Like a ghostly apparition, not necessarily real or to be trusted, a glimmer of light teased him from his left. Not a glimmer, really. A sensation more felt than seen, but it beckoned him like a Siren's song.

Rising, turning to face it, he still could not be sure.

The impenetrable fog admitted no certain light and only a begrudging trace of air. But he did the mental calculations, formed a notion of where the high, misshapen hill with its outcroppings of granite, its escarpments and cul de sacs and stone ring might be found. Then, moving slowly and feeling his way through the trees, he proceeded in a direction that might or might not be the right one.

Jessica sat up with a start, her heart pounding, sweat streaming down her forehead and between her breasts. She felt weak. Groggy, as if her brain were wrapped in wool. Her eyes must have been sealed with glue. She had to force them open, and immediately they wanted to close again.

The room was dark. And Duran was gone. She knew it even before her hands reached for the empty space next to her, before she dragged herself from the bed and stumbled over to the dressing room. A slice of light showed at the bottom of the door. She entered, not expecting to find him, and used the candle burning there to ignite a lamp in her bedchamber.

The clothes he had been wearing, the ones he'd left beside the bed, were gone. Nothing else seemed out of place. She had noticed his comb and brush alongside his shaving gear in the dressing room. For something to do while her head cleared, she looked in the armoire and checked the drawers where his things were kept. It didn't appear that anything was missing.

Nothing except Duran.

Perhaps he couldn't sleep. He might have gone downstairs to read, or smoke a cigar, or locate a bottle of cognac. But it was nothing so simple as that. Her heart burned with the truth. Sure as he'd left her before, he'd left her again.

And with only three more days remaining. Could he

not endure staying with her to the end of the contract? Perhaps he'd feared an awkward scene, her begging him to stay the way she had once begged him for a child. That had been an impulse. A mistake. She had no right to ask, or to assume he would think nothing of giving her his seed in the way a man thought nothing of offering a woman his handkerchief.

But he needn't have worried. She had firmly resolved to make all she could of their time together, and then smile and wish him well as he walked away. She might even have succeeded in doing that. But as always, he'd forestalled her plan. He had done the thing she least expected, the thing she ought to have known he would do. Possibly he'd decided it would be kinder this way. That she would not be hurt this time by his vanishing trick.

If so, he had been wrong.

She kept worrying at the problem while she dressed. Their private contract was all but finished. Why shouldn't he leave if he wished to? Gerald, if she was to believe Duran, would make no more trouble for the family. There was nothing else to hold her husband here.

She pulled on her half boots, shook down the skirts of her plainest dress, and tied back her hair with a length of ribbon. If asked, she couldn't have said why she had clothed herself for walking. Her eyes kept drifting shut. She felt weak and her mouth tasted of ashes. She wanted to curl up in bed and sleep. Or cry. She wanted very much to cry.

But a voice was stirring inside her, cutting through the porridge in her head, telling her something was dreadfully wrong. Worse even than . . . Well, she mustn't think on it.

The clock showed a little after six. Near to sunrise now. The servants would be at their breakfasts. She didn't wish to disturb them, but if she went to the kitchen, someone would give her toast and tea. Perhaps some news.

With so few guests in residence, few of the wall sconces that lined the passageway were kept lit. She was just coming on the servants' staircase when a figure seated cross-legged beside the door uncoiled itself and rose up.

Arjuna. She hadn't seen him until he moved. But why in blazes was he here, on watch, when there was no longer—

And then she knew.

She smiled. He bowed. She moved on by him to the main staircase, descended a little way, and then stole back up to see what he was doing. Sure enough, he had gone to her bedchamber door and was standing in front of it, probably as undecided as she was feeling at the moment. But no. He raised the latch and stepped inside.

Oh, God. Why couldn't she *think*? Just when she started to figure something out, a curtain would drop over her mind.

Keep moving. Keep moving. But where? Soon they would know Duran had gone. What would they do then?

Instinct was driving her now. She rushed down the stairs to the ground floor and her father's study. Most of his guns were stored in locked cases, but in a small cupboard he always kept a rifle and at least one pistol primed and ready to hand. She slipped the pistol, a small one, into her pocket. Fairly sure she'd not escape the house carrying the rifle, she raised the window casement and lowered it to the ground. She was about to follow it there when the slightest of sounds from just outside the door caused her to lower the window and speed across the room to the desk. She had just got there when the door swung open.

"*Memsahib*," said Shivaji, bowing.

Arjuna must have just roused him. He wore white muslin trousers under a knee-length, unbelted tunic, and his thick black hair, streaked with gray, hung straight and loose to his shoulders.

"Good morning," she said cheerfully. And waited. This was his nightmarish game, and she didn't know the rules.

He came straight to the point. "How, excepting the door, might one leave your bedchamber?"

She considered. Frowned. Brightened. "Through a window? But it would be a long way to the ground."

"The windows are watched. How else?"

"There is no *else*. Why would there be?" She thought she sounded fairly convincing. And even if he knew she was lying, he couldn't prove it. Not in time. She couldn't imagine how Duran had worked out there was a concealed passageway, let alone the combination to open it. "Are you by chance looking for my husband? So was I, as a matter of fact."

"You do not know where he is, or where he means to go?"

"Truly, I have no idea. But do you believe me?" She slouched against the desk, the fog in her head even thicker than the fog she'd seen outside the house. "We've done this before, haven't we? Conversed in questions, I mean. That was the day you told me the story about the princess and the Lord of Death."

Death. Her heart skipped a beat. But when there is pain, she reminded herself, it is better to walk directly into it. "Shall we cease the dancing about? At the posthouse, when Duran brought you back the leopard, you lied to me. You mean to kill him after all."

A long pause. "I am sorry, *memsahib*," he said. "There is nothing you can do for him now. You will remain here, please."

The door had scarcely closed behind him before she was out the window.

Grabbing the rifle, she took off through the fog, surefooted as a Dartmoor pony. She had navigated this territory since childhood, eluding the servants dispatched to track her down, vibrating to the rhythms of the land and the weather. All her fear was for Duran. She knew the place where he'd have exited the tunnel, but he would not remain there. Where would he have gone?

There was no answer to that. But the fog would slow him down. He'd surely avoid the road, which was the first place Shivaji would go looking for him. And she hoped he had better sense than to strike out across the moors. If he'd done that, he could be up to his neck in a bog by now. Or under it altogether.

No. He had figured out the virgin and the unicorn. He'd escaped Shivaji once before. She must not underestimate him.

He would do the unexpected, she decided. Go the direction he was least likely to go. Or not go very far at all.

It was only a hunch, but once it came into her head, it felt exactly right. On Devil's Tor were any number of places to hide. When the fog cleared he would have a good view of the landscape for miles around, and best of all, no one could sneak up on him because there was only one way to the top.

Unless you knew the other one.

Leaving behind the rifle, which was too cumbersome for the voyage she was to take, she crossed the moorland between the house and the Tor, found her way to the narrow break between a stand of tall rocks, and stopped there long enough to knot her skirts between her legs. The last time she'd ascended the Tor from this direction, she had been considerably younger and smaller. Now the concealing fog became her ally, forcing her to climb by feel, guided by instincts that came back to her like old friends. She wriggled through tight spaces and scrambled over boulders, her hands and knees scraped raw on the rough moorstone.

Something was going to happen. Was already happening. She felt it, like electricity in the air, and drove herself harder. She must not be too late.

A clap of thunder. She paused. Listened. Then another, just like the first. Then silence.

Feverishly she scaled a steep incline, skirted a clump of nettles, and came up behind one of the Druid stones. Sunlight dazzled through the mist, which was beginning to clear, and a small breeze stirred her hair. She pressed her cheek against the stone and gazed one-eyed into the circle.

Across the way, about ten yards from where she stood, Shivaji was crouched beside a figure lying prone on the ground. The milky fog swirled around them like silk scarves. For the barest moment, light flashed off a circlet of gold and jewels on the fallen man's wrist.

Her heart gave a lurch.

Oh, God. Oh, God. It was over.

Shivaji lifted his head like an animal scenting danger. He rose. Turned. Blotches of red stained his tunic and smeared the blade of the large curved knife he was holding. Blood dripped from its point.

Her hand dove for the pistol in her pocket, got it free, pointed it at his chest. She moved toward him. "Drop the knife," she said. The fog blurred her target, but at this range, she could not miss. "If he is dead, I will kill you."

Shivaji held out his arms. "I will not prevent you. But he is badly hurt. If you wish him to live, you must go for help."

"And leave you here to finish what you started?" Was Duran still alive? She couldn't tell, dared not shift her gaze from the assassin. Her pulse beat in her head. What choice had she now?

She steadied her hand, sighted down the barrel, saw his eyes look past her.

An arm lashed around her from behind. She cried out as the gun was wrenched from her fingers. Then, at a nod from Shivaji, she was released.

Helpless, numb with despair, she watched him kneel beside Duran and place a finger on his throat.

"What I say is true, *memsahib*. He lives, but there is great loss of blood. The bullets must be removed, and it cannot be done here." With his knife, he began slicing strips of fabric from the hem of his tunic. "My servants may not be heeded if I send them to the house. You must go yourself. Have a litter brought here and make the necessary arrangements."

He glanced over his shoulder at the man standing at her side. "Return the gun. The decision must be hers alone."

She looked at the brown hand holding the barrel of the pistol, at the curve of the grip offered to her, and shook her head. "I'll go," she said from a burning throat.

And then she began to run.

Chapter 30

He was underwater. A horse was sitting on his back.

No. It was standing on his back, one hoof just below his left shoulder blade, the other to the right and lower, near his waist. Damn fool place for a horse to be.

He could breathe, though. Strange that he could, given where he was. But it hurt a great deal, so he tried not to do it often. A little air, a little more. God he wished that horse would go away.

Another breath. And with it, something hot and sulfurous burning his nostrils. And a voice, distant, as if it originated in the depths of a cave.

"Duran-Sahib."

So. He was in hell, then. No surprise there. Stood to reason he would be.

Acrid fumes swirled around him like the fog that . . . Ah. He remembered the fog. And the thunder. And the horse kicking him in the back. After a struggle, he opened his eyes.

The demon's face, golden-lit by the candle he was holding, swam into view.

"I didn't know," said Duran in a husk of a voice, "that Hindus went to hell."

"We go where God wills," Shivaji said. In his other hand was a small copper beaker emitting curls of astringent smoke. "You must pardon this. It is harmless, but necessary to bring you awake."

Awake. That sounded . . . well, unexpected. "Is water permitted?"

It was given him soon after, a glass held to his lips, cool water in his mouth and dribbling down his chin. Only a little, but he was allowed to drink at intervals, and between times, feeling marginally better, he took stock of his surroundings.

A small parlor, he decided. A dark one with two or three pools of light from candles or lamps. With the curtains closed, he could not tell the time of day. He saw a table strewn with basins, folded towels and bandages, small bottles and jars, ominous-looking metal implements, and a mortar and pestle. Another table held Shivaji's wooden Cabinet of Horrors, as he had come to think of it.

And the horse was not, after all, on his back. Turned out he was sitting nearly upright on a bed, held in that position by pillows at his lower back and behind his neck, but more amazingly, by a contraption slung around his shoulders and attached to some sort of pulley device. He could reason it all out within a week, he was thinking when the water glass was offered him again.

"The sling holds your back clear," Shivaji said, "permitting the wounds to receive air and be tended. I rigged it because when you were lying on your stomach, your breathing became labored. Do you remember what occurred?"

The fog in his head was more dense than the fog that had swaddled Devil's Tor. He cast back, snagging bits and pieces of that morning. He'd got all the way to the stone circle. Lost a boot in a patch of bog on the way. He remembered that much. And the silence. Like cotton balls were stuffed in his ears. He'd come to level ground, found by feel one of the standing stones, and was just turning when the thunder . . . No. It was a blast of noise, muffled a little by the fog, echoing a little from the rocks, not like any sound he'd ever heard before. And at almost the same time, the horse kicked him.

Not a horse. That was when he'd been so sure the assassin would kill him with a knife. That's what he was thinking when he grabbed hold of the granite spire with both hands, felt them slip, felt himself slipping, knew he'd been shot.

Thunder will bring you down. Well, he couldn't say he hadn't been warned.

Then more thunder, a blow to his side, and the fog took him altogether.

Again, water to his lips. He kept forgetting what he'd known just a moment earlier. His body, hurting like the devil was sticking pitchforks in it, now suspended in space. Not quite. His bottom and legs solid on the bed. Bits of him against pillows. Other bits wrapped up and strung out with ropes. Where was Jessie? She wasn't here, which told him quite a lot.

He wanted to have this conversation with his killer some other time, when he was more than a mole in a black tunnel. But he'd been brought awake for a purpose. He honed his brain, flint against mush, to a semblance of awareness.

"You knew of the stone circle because we met there," he said to the assassin, standing loose haired and solemn at the foot of the bed. "I take it you knew of the tunnel that got me away from the house. You made the thunder yourself, damn you. What I can't figure is how you predicted the fog. And why, after your sworn declaration to carry out my execution, you appear to have been keeping me alive."

"A puzzle," Shivaji said from the table, where he

was emptying a packet of something green into the mortar. "I will tell you what I can. But of the tunnel and the fog, I knew nothing save for my dream. I claim no gift for interpretation. The confluence of what I dreamed and what transpired surprises me as much as it does you."

"You seemed to believe it when you told me about it."

"Yes. It was . . . startling. So vivid that I understood it clearly, until I awoke. After that, I remembered only the images. As for the thunder, it was not I who shot you. Two bullets hit you in the back. I arrived shortly after."

"Talbot, then." Duran dropped the words like two lead balls. In the great scheme of things, he no doubt deserved what he had got. Unpardonably arrogant, he had been so sure he'd outwitted Talbot. And he had kept assuming, against all evidence to the contrary, that his opponent was a gentleman, a principled man who would fight with swords if he declared swords. Who would not, after agreeing to an honorable duel, shoot a man in the back.

Anyone else would have expected treachery. Come prepared for it. But Hugo Duran, longtime cynic, had wandered onto the killing field like a woolly lamb, betrayed by his own unsuspected idealism.

"Sir Gerald was observed leaving the house and approaching the Tor," Shivaji said, "but that did not appear significant until we learned of your departure. At that time I followed. When I arrived, he had reloaded his pistols and was moving toward you. My knife cut him down."

"Why not let him complete the job? Save you the trouble?"

"He was not, it appeared, called for you."

"That, or he was a shockingly bad shot. So, I was down and you were there, blade in hand. Why didn't you finish me yourself?"

Shivaji shook the powder he'd ground into a cup, added what looked like oil, and followed it with a brownish liquid. "It seemed the killing of you had been taken from my hands," he said quietly, "and the healing of you put there instead. To know one's duty is not, perhaps, so simple as tradition and experience would have it. But I cannot say what I would have chosen to do, had not the Lady Jessica at that moment come into the stone circle. When she stood before me and demanded your life, I was unable to refuse her."

At the sound of her name, Duran's heart had jumped. The room was so absent of her. So empty without her. But she had wanted him to live. Might she, then, one day forgive him? Well, too soon to start hoping for another miracle. "Did she trick you," he asked, "like the princess tricked the Lord of Death in the story? The real story, not the self-justifying version you told her."

"Lady Jessica was not so devious as the princess. She brought a gun."

Duran started to laugh and instantly regretted it. The horse stampeded across his back, leaving him a puddle of sweat and pain.

"I advise you to be cautious," Shivaji said, blotting his face with a damp towel. "You have been so near to death that more than once I believed you to have stepped upon the moon. Indeed, perhaps you did. For you have died to your former life, I think, and rekindled a new one. Now you must take care to preserve it, and to live more virtuously than you did before."

"I could h-hardly live worse," Duran managed to choke out. Shivaji was leaning over his back now, doing something that hurt even worse than laughing. "Did you burn that concoction under my nose so that I'd be awake while you tortured me?"

"An interesting idea, but no. When asleep, you cannot control your movements, and you must keep perfectly still when I remove the bracelet. Tell me when you feel ready for me to attempt it."

Attempt? That sounded ominous. And just thinking of those poisoned needles gave him a case of the shivers. His arm, a little elevated by the sling, rested on a pillow at his side. He looked down at it, at the bracelet, and released the breath he'd been holding. "Whenever you like," he said. "The nizam wants it back?"

"It is marked as proof I have carried out your death sentence. I am ordered to return it, still wrapped around your wrist."

"You were supposed to lug my body all the way back to Alanabad?" He had a mental image of Admiral Lord Nelson preserved in a brandy barrel after Trafalgar.

"Only your arm, Duran-Sahib." Shivaji had returned to the bedside table and was removing something from his cabinet of drawers. "But if you have no objection, I shall use Sir Gerald's instead. The Star of the Firmament will not know the difference, and it will spare me a good deal of trouble. Amputations on the living are usually bloody affairs."

All of a sudden, Shivaji had decided to play comedy. "You *have* Talbot's arm?"

"He was found in a bog, his right arm chewed off below the elbow. It appeared that an animal had got to him before he sank, but of course, he was dead well before that." Shivaji brought a small table to the bedside and arranged several lamps where they would cast light over Duran's wrist. "It was regrettable, but necessary."

"Let me get this straight. You excised Talbot's arm. And you mean to use it to deceive the nizam. You intend to *lie* to him?"

"Certainly not." Shivaji cast him a look of reproach. "I shall employ one of those—how did you put it?— delightfully inscrutable pronouncements. But since I also bring him the leopard that will secure him on the throne, along with sufficient proof of Malik Rao's treason to justify both his execution and the suppression of his cult, the nizam will not question me too closely."

Duran regarded him with astonishment. "I am devastated to hear it. The incorruptible has been corrupted."

"I fear so. You have been a bad influence, Duran-Sahib. It is fitting we shall not meet again. You understand that you must never return to India?"

"Wild horses couldn't drag me there. But really, you should drop off the leopard in Alanabad and keep right on moving. That nizam doesn't merit the devotion you waste on him."

"I serve him because it is my dharma. It does not fall to me to question his merit, any more than the Lady Jessica questions yours."

Point scored. "You think I am *her* dharma?"

"Or her curse." Shivaji crouched beside him, a small silver implement in his hand. He set another on the bed. "Now you must lift your arm and hold it steady. You are aware, I believe, of the consequences if the procedure does not go well."

Duran planted his elbow on the pillow and gingerly raised his forearm. "Comforting a patient is not your forte, is it?"

"I beg your pardon." Shivaji, bending forward, held the bracelet between thumb and forefinger and explored its underside with the metal probe. "I ought not criticize you when I cannot prevent my own hands from trembling."

Snatching his arm away, Duran sagged in the sling and gave in to the laughter he could no longer control. It hurt—God how it hurt—but it was like the pain of cauterizing a wound. And when he was done, and could breathe again, Shivaji plumped the pillow under his elbow and set to work again, this time in earnest.

"It is salutary, Duran. You are not now so tense. Keep patient for a little time longer."

It was a long time longer. Duran felt as if he were sliding into another place, where the air was so thick he couldn't move. But only because he chose not to move. For the first time since the shackles were clamped about his wrists and ankles in Alanabad, the apprehension of what might happen in the next moment, the sensation of everything spinning out of his control, was gone. He was far past worrying about the deadly needles and what would happen if they sprang into his flesh. Karma, Dharma Angels in the Pool.

But he would like to see Jessica again. He had something to tell her.

A click. A nearly imperceptible sigh from Shivaji. A warm hand lowering his forearm to the pillow again. Duran opened his eyes and saw the bracelet, carved gold nubbed with ruby and emerald cabochons, gleaming in the lamplight. Shivaji slipped it into a velvet pouch and pulled the drawstring.

So it was over. The life or death question, at any rate. Only after he'd spoken with Jessica would he know if there was any point to his survival. He glanced over at Shivaji, again busy with his powders and potions like a warlock bending over a cauldron. Hair of dog. Eye of newt.

"You told me it was written," Duran said. "My destiny. Mapped out. Unalterable. But it wasn't, after all."

"Your destiny has been written." Shivaji came to the bed with a cup in his hand. "Not because it is designed, but because it is known."

"Not by you."

"Not by me," Shivaji agreed. "When I said your death at my hands was written, I had simply not read far enough. You will drink this now. It will ease your pain and help you to sleep for a time."

Duran already felt limp as overcooked cabbage, but he obediently swallowed the bitter drink. He had just passed the cup back to Shivaji when there came a knock at the door. Moments later, though, his hopes were dashed.

It was only Arjuna, carrying a familiar box. At Shivaji's direction, he placed it on the table beside the bed.

"This is the replica of the leopard," Shivaji said. "I give it you as your dowry. You will understand that it cannot be kept whole."

Astounded, Duran could only stare at him. Already the drug had thickened his tongue and dimmed his vision.

In company with his son, Shivaji went to the door, where they both turned, put their hands together beneath their chins, and bowed. Arjuna left then, but Shivaji lingered for a moment.

Serene as a temple carving, he gazed across the room at Duran. *"Shanti,"* he said. "Peace. In another lifetime, if it is so written, perhaps we shall meet as friends. May God shower blessings upon you and your lady."

And then he was gone, disappearing in the narcotic fog that clouded Duran's eyes and all too quickly, his mind.

Chapter 31

At midmorning, after the breakfast Mrs. Bellwood had insisted she eat, Jessica resumed her vigil in the small ground-floor parlor where Duran had been carried eight days earlier.

He would recover, Shivaji had assured her before departing with his men for the ship. Lined up on the bedside table were the medicines and ointments and bandages he had prepared, and she had memorized his instructions. A doctor would come in from time to time—Aubrey had insisted on that—but after a week at Shivaji's side, and with the confidence he had engendered in her, she felt capable of tending her husband without supervision.

It had been quite different in the beginning, when she was all but paralyzed with fear. He had come so near to dying. Every hour brought a new crisis, a fever, more bleeding, and through it all, Shivaji worked calmly to restore him while she stood by, holding a jar, cutting a thread, doing what little she could.

The nights were the worst. Sometimes Duran would appear to waken. His eyes would open, and when she bent over him, he looked at her. But there was nothing there, no recognition, no awareness.

"His strength is turned inward," Shivaji had told

her. "His body devotes itself to healing. He will return to us in time."

He hadn't done, not while she'd been there. In retrospect, she felt certain that when Shivaji exiled her to her room last night for some uninterrupted sleep, he believed that Duran was close to waking. And so he had, in the small hours of the morning, and she had missed it. She was still angry about that. But relieved as well, because Shivaji had spoken with him, found him lucid, and judged him well enough to do without his own attentions.

Now she was charged with his care, and the long sleep had done her good. It was time to dispel some of this gloom, she decided. Let in some light and air. When she drew the curtains she saw Aubrey's two older children on the lawn directly outside, playing with the new puppies. Their mother, Harriet, an infant at her breast and another in her swollen belly, sat with Mariah on a blanket nearby.

They might have been on their way to South America, Mariah and the gentleman who had loved her for so long, except that John Pageter, always pragmatic, had confided their intentions to Mrs. Bellwood. Thanks to her and the speed of Sothingdon's messenger, they were plucked from the ship just in time.

Mariah looked up, gave a tentative wave. She felt responsible for what Gerald had done to Duran, which made no sense whatever. Aubrey felt responsible as well, and that made perfect sense. While overlooking the sister who needed his protection, he'd been ruthlessly tending to Jessica's business, dispatching her lover back to India and later banishing him from High Tor.

She thought she might forgive him one day. His abashed confession had helped, as had his signature beside her father's on a document that would release

Lady Sothingdon's legacy to her. She now had the family's approval of her marriage. All she lacked was a husband willing to stay in it.

She waved back at Mariah, added a smile for good measure, and turned to the bed.

Duran's eyes were open. She drew a little closer, evaluating him as Shivaji had taught her. The eyes followed her motion. They were clear and alert. He looked a bit piratical with a week's growth of beard, but his skin had good color. His breathing was steady. A little raspy, but she'd been told to expect that. Her heart began to race. For the first time, she sensed that he was fully here in the room.

"Hullo, princess," he said, his voice husky and not very strong. "Have I been a great deal of trouble?"

"When are you not?" She came to the pillows, felt his cool—blessedly cool—forehead, and examined the bandages wrapped around his shoulder and back. No stains. "How do you feel?"

"Like a Christmas goose strung up for the plucking. How long am I to remain suspended by ropes and pulleys?"

"Until you can be trusted to behave rationally. It is for your own good, as you are so fond of telling me."

"I detect that you are a trifle put out with me."

"Indeed I am." Of a sudden, unexpected and unwelcome, all the tension and fear she'd contained inside herself these agonizing days and nights broke loose. A great wave of anger rushed over her. She was shaking with it. Unable to bear looking at him, she took herself to the other end of the room and began to pace it off. "Oh, I can understand a little why you thought it necessary to drug me. I was not to know of your escape, or to help you achieve it. But you didn't escape, did you? You got away through the tunnel, but instead of taking ship like a sane man with an assassin on his heels, you went for a stroll on Devil's Tor. In the *fog*. What in God's name possessed you to do something so . . . so *bacon-brained*?"

"Is that a rhetorical question?" he ventured after a moment.

"No. It's one of those questions that no matter how you answer it, you'll be wrong. But I want an answer anyway."

"If you insist. But you won't like it. Gerald insulted you. I called him out. We were going to fight a duel."

"Yes. Well, you see how *that* turned out. But I think the truth is somewhat other. He wasn't going to give up, was he? In spite of what you told me, he had set himself to punish the family. You needn't go on pretending otherwise, because John Pageter and I have spoken at length. You stayed to fight Gerald because that was the only way to get rid of him. You must have known he wouldn't fight fair, and you didn't even have a *weapon*. There was no gun from Miranda Holcombe. That was another lie."

"I'd have had a knife," he reminded her a little plaintively, "but you wouldn't let me take one."

"You cannot be trusted with sharp objects." She came to a halt by the window, aware that the wave of fury had begun to recede. She couldn't have said why she blamed him for stepping up to protect her family, taking Aubrey's place, her father's place, all their places, standing alone for them. He had been heroic, in a ham-handed sort of way, and it made her so proud. And so afraid, so terribly afraid, that she was about to lose him now. She was, she supposed, doing everything possible to *drive* him away because she could not face him wanting to leave her. "What will you do now?" she asked, turning to the window, her hands clutching at her skirts.

"Not much," he said, "until you cut me down from here. Why, princess? What do you wish me to do?"

She took a deep breath. She took another deep breath. She had imagined herself saying this, not sure she would be able to do it. *Walk into the pain,* she reminded herself. *Nothing can be so bad as what has been, or what you fear.*

"Shivaji told me how the story really ended," she said. "The part neither of you saw fit to mention. Princess Savitri kept on following the Lord of Death after he granted her the first boon, nagging him until he granted her another. And that time, she tricked him. She asked for a hundred children, and when he agreed, she pounced. 'But I can have no children,' she said, 'none at all, if you take my husband. For I will never love another, or have another to my bed. So how will you keep your promise, Yamaraj?' And he had no choice but to let her beloved Satyavan live after all, because above all things else, he must honor his given word."

With all the courage she possessed, Jessica went to the foot of the bed and looked into his eyes. "I, too, want children. But I can have none, none at all, without my husband. Because I can never love another, nor take another to my bed. Not since the first time with you, not any time after. Only you, Duran." Tears were streaming down her face. Like the waterfall.

Her hands dropped loosely to her sides. She had not thought she could weep, or beg, or lay out her heart upon the anvil for him to strike. But it was so easy. What would she not surrender to him? Nothing.

A great heaviness lifted from her. It was her pride, she thought. And her fear. She was filled with love, airborne with it, light-headed and happy.

"If you will have me," she said simply.

Forever, it seemed, he looked at her. And then she realized he was leaning forward, straining against his harnesses, trying to hold out his hands. She came around the bed and dropped to her knees at his side, resting her head on the pillow near his arm. After a moment, she felt him stroking her hair.

"I must have you," he said. "Like Yamaraj, I have given my word, and I shall honor it."

"The wedding vows?" she murmured.

"Not those. I made no true promises then, because I thought I could not keep them. But the night I left you, I vowed that I would never again lie to you, nor would I leave you."

"I don't remember you saying those things."

"You were asleep at the time. But I think they still count."

She raised her head, looked over at him. "They needn't. I'll not hold you to any promise you regret making."

He brushed a finger down her wet cheek. "I have many regrets. But falling in love with you has never been, will never be, among them."

In wonder, she gazed through the mist in her eyes to the softness in his. "I had no idea you loved me. I didn't expect you could."

"How could I not? You really don't know, do you, how splendid you are. The truth is, I was never good enough for you. A jumped-up aristocrat without money, land, reputation, or character. When you came to me in that ballroom and looked me straight in the eye and told me without words that you wanted me, I thought surely I must be dreaming. I think so now." His smile warmed the space around them. "If you are really here, princess, and really telling me you want me to stay with you, I think you had better kiss me straightaway. Unless I am likely to wake up and find you gone."

She rose and with care, because he was very much an invalid and would be for a considerable time, sat next to him and leaned forward and kissed him.

"You're still there," he said when she leaned back again. "Well, then. I am alive, and forever in love, and not without a dowry and, it seems, not without a wife. There is only one problem."

No jolt of apprehension. She gazed at him with perfect trust. "I'm afraid to ask."

"It's about the children," he said. "Mind you, I'm willing to try. Eager to try. But I rather doubt I can manage to give you a hundred of them."

"I see. Disappointing, to be sure, but I think I shall keep you anyway." He was fighting it, she could tell, but the weariness and pain were unmistakable. "And now, as your physician, I must advise you to rest. Shivaji left something for the pain, if you would like it."

"No. I have never felt better, in every way that matters. And I want to keep my mind clear, or as clear as it ever gets, so that I can think on what has just happened and think on it again." His good intentions were overtaken by a yawn.

"Sleep is good for you," she said. "And I'll be here when you wake up, with a delicious meal of thin broth and gruel."

"Evil woman. Oh. There is one more thing we should get straight," he said through another yawn. "For when we set up house and start making all those children. I'm speaking of pets."

"You don't want any?"

"That's not it. Dogs are fine. Rabbits and ducks and hedgehogs acceptable. Parrots will do and even, if you must, a monkey. But soon as I've melted down the one in that box, Jessie, I don't care to be in company, not ever again, with a cat."

Read on for an excerpt
from the next book
in Lynn Kerstan's trilogy.

Coming in 2003

London, 1823

Mira glanced back. Michael Keynes was still there, shoulders propped against the wall, unshaven, unkempt, looking directly at her. A dangerous presence blocking the way out.

But she had no excuse to linger, and besides, he would surely outwait her. He had come for her. What did he want?

"Ah. There's Michael," David said, clearly delighted. "I know he looks awful, but really, he's not so bad as he would have you think."

How could he be? she wondered as David took her arm.

Keynes's disturbing eyes glittered as she approached. He seemed to drag himself away from the wall, lurched, produced an awkward bow. The smell of brandy made her wrinkle her nose.

"Miss Holcombe," he said, ignoring David. "You are radiant. You outshine the sun."

"Simple enough," she replied, disgusted. "It's nighttime. And you are drunk."

"That's the consensus."

He was repellently cheerful. Except for his eyes, which were . . . oh, she could not say. Intense. Urging her to pay attention.

He turned to David. "Come take supper with me."

His voice was slurred. "You'll have to bring the supper. Will you? I'm hungry enough for two or three people. You can stay the night if you like. Hari's gone somewhere. It's raining. Did you know it was raining?"

And just when she had decided he was altogether cat-shot, he said with perfect clarity under his breath, "Miss Holcombe, go to the Limonaia. I'll follow you. David, say something idiotic."

David, trying to think of something idiotic to say, could only manage to look idiotic. Finally he produced, in a cracking tone, a question about what Michael Keynes wanted for supper.

"Bread. Meat. Cheese." Keynes poked David on the chest. "Hot tea." And softly, almost without moving his lips, "Arrange it, and then come to the Limonaia. Miss Holcombe, why are you still here?"

She might not comprehend the purpose of it, but she recognized a staged scene when she saw it. And felt, for no accountable reason, a wish to impress this man she feared. "Sir, you are no fit company for a lady," she declared with an excess of dramatic fervor. And then she flounced through the door and into the passageway, a little embarrassed but greatly curious.

If he was planning to seduce her, which had been her initial thought, he'd not have invited David to join them. And there was something new in him, a sense of purpose she had not seen in him before. Until tonight he had seemed to be marking time, waiting for something over which he had no control. And for him, she expected that was neither a comfortable nor a natural state of mind.

She, on the other hand, had become an artist of waiting, an expert at marking time. But like him, she sensed that events were about to converge with her at the center of them. And this time, she would not be found wanting. This time, she would control the outcome.

The Limonaia, another of Beata's Tuscan fancies, had been constructed in the western wing of the villa, with a glass wall to admit afternoon sunlight. Tiles of glass were set in the ceiling as well, and large windows opened onto corridors connecting the Limonaia to the section of the building set apart for meeting rooms. All were empty at this time of year.

She slipped through the door, cedarwood studded with medallions of stained glass, and breathed in the fragrance of citron trees and smoke from the braziers that kept them warm. The Limonaia, octagonal with walls of stone tracery and glass, had floors of enameled tile, marble benches, and two score small trees—lemon and Spanish orange—set in ceramic pots. A few, cultivated in a greenhouse on the edge of the property, were heavy with fruit. The others, defying the change of seasons, flaunted lush leaves. They were dusted weekly, she knew, by the servants.

Rain streaked the glass wall and beat on the ceiling. It was well after midnight, and an orange glow from the braziers and the wall sconces in the corridors provided the only light. She felt nervous, like a maiden in the Colosseum waiting for the great-toothed cats to be let in. And because she must reveal nothing of her anticipation or her fear, she went to a shadowed bench near the center of the Limonaia, sat neatly on it with her hands folded on her lap, and waited for the electric hum in the air that always signaled the presence of Michael Keynes.

It came to her shortly after, the sound that wasn't quite a sound. She rose, arms at her sides, and turned.

In the dim light, he was a tall, wide-shouldered shadow with ghostly eyes. *"I was followed,"* he said in a tone that could not be heard beyond the small room where they stood facing each other. "You didn't have to run from me." This time his voice, a little too loud, startled her.

She moved away from the bench. "I didn't run. I never run. But I prefer to be alone."

"And so you are. Alone with me." Then, quietly, *"There is a woman in my casina—"*

"I've no doubt of it." Her voice, always a husky whisper, required no disguise. "And I am not adept at games, sir. What do you want of me?"

A long silence. Things unspoken. She felt them, like the vibration of his presence. Like the mysterious summons in his eyes.

"What do I want?" he echoed with a laugh. "Can't you guess?" Then, *"It's the Duchess of Tallant. My brother's wife. She requires help."*

"She came to *you?*"

"A measure of her desperation." Loudly, "Why don't you like me, butterfly?"

She lifted her hands in a gesture that held him away. "What should I do, then?"

"Let me close enough to speak without being heard. But make it seem you fear me."

Oh, I do, she thought, wondering at it. At that moment she was absolutely sure he wouldn't hurt her, and even more certain he could easily destroy her.

"Stay away!" she said when he took a lurching step forward. He was pushing her toward the marble bench, using the motion to cover his speech. She resisted to give him time, surprised that she was enjoying this dance they did, this game they played. How long since she had enjoyed anything at all?

"She has come a long way through the rain. She needs something warm to wear and advice I am unable to give her. One kiss," he demanded. "Just one."

When she felt the bench against the backs of her legs, she sank onto it. "Why this charade?"

"Dear God but you are lovely. *To keep her safe. To keep you safe.* Let me, Miss Holcombe. Miranda. 'Oh brave new world, that. . . .' That does something. I can't recall what."

" 'That has such creatures in it,' " she said, sounding like a schoolmistress, rather impressed that he'd guessed the origin of her name. *The Tempest* was her father's favorite play.

His teeth, when he grinned, were tinged with red-orange light. "*I need you to come to my rooms without being seen.* I'm fond of the theatre. Fond of you."

"Who is watching us? And why?"

"*I don't know for certain. But anyone associated with me is at risk. If you agree to help, you must take great care.* One kiss, Miranda. One little kiss. Then I'll go away."

"You can't mean that."

"*I do. All of it. Let me kiss you, or nearly. I'll make it appear you are forced. Then slap me and go.*" He stumbled forward until he was bent over her, caught himself by putting his hands on her shoulders. "*Unless you want out of this entirely.*"

She ducked beneath his arms and escaped the bench. There was the sound of his palms hitting the marble, an oath, and the shuffle of his feet moving closer. She spun around to face him. "No," she said, hands raised to ward him off. "You are foxed."

"Come on, butterfly. *Settle your father and come to my casina. Don't be seen.* I wager you'll like it."

He took hold of her wrists and drew her inexorably closer. His eyes glowed red, as if a fire raged behind them. One hand, large and firm, burned at her waist.

The breath caught in her throat. Frozen, she gazed

helplessly at the lines of his face, the black hair limned with firelight, his mouth a little open as he brought his lips nearer hers. Fingers slipped into her hair, cradled her nape.

Her heart thumped wildly. His breath tingled at her cheek. Heat came off him like a brazier, heat and strength and purpose.

He would choke her now.

And then . . . and then . . .

"I can't believe I'm saying this, but now would be a good time for you to slap me."

The spell broke.

She wrenched loose, brought back her arm. A loud crack as her gloved hand caught him on the face. A louder oath.

She rushed to the door and fled down the passageway.